BORROWED TIME

Books by Tracy Clark

BROKEN PLACES

BORROWED TIME

Published by Kensington Publishing Corporation

BORROWED TIME

TRACY CLARK

KENSINGTON BOOKS
www.kensingtonbooks.com

KENSINGTON BOOKS are published by

Kensington Publishing Corp.
119 West 40th Street
New York, NY 10018

Library of Congress Card Catalogue Number: 2018912558

Kensington and the K logo Reg. U.S. Pat. & TM Off.

ISBN-13: 978-1-4967-1490-9
ISBN-10: 1-4967-1490-3
First Kensington Hardcover Edition: June 2019

ISBN-13: 978-1-4967-1492-3 (ebook)
ISBN-10: 1-4967-1492-X (ebook)

10 9 8 7 6 5 4 3 2 1

Printed in the United States of America

For the Little Dudes: Jonathan, Christopher, David, and Luc

Acknowledgments

Thanks to my editor, John Scognamiglio; my agent, Evan Marshall; and the entire staff at Kensington Publishing. You guys are awesome. I want to thank also Detective Gregory Auguste, Detective Tracey Mathis, and Detective Laura Skrip of the Chicago Police Department for giving me an insight into how cops do their jobs. I give a special nod to Laura and Tracey for breaking it down from a female's perspective. Though they do the same work as the guys, they approach the challenges of the job a bit differently. It was truly enlightening finding out how. Thank you both for sharing your stories. To Jennifer Auguste, *gracias,* for the eagle-eyed story adjustments. Thanks also to family and friends for the enthusiastic cheerleading, and to Mary Carter, author extraordinaire, for giving this book the once-over and pointing out the clunkers. And, of course, thanks to Mom for everything else . . . and more.

BORROWED TIME

Chapter 1

A PI's life isn't glamorous, not by a long shot. I spend half my time sitting in a cold car, watching people do the dumbest things, and the other half typing up reports about it. But that's when business *isn't* slow. When it is, like now, I, Cass Raines, PI, contract myself out for steady pay. Today, I was riding out the latest dry spell working for the law firm of Golden, Sprague, and Bendelson, trying to hand off a summons to a Chicago blues man named Big Percy Prescott, who'd somehow forgotten on his rise to the middle that he'd left behind a long-suffering ex-wife and two little Prescotts in desperate need of child support. Big Percy, apparently not just any man's fool, knew the suits were after him and was making himself not only scarce, but downright invisible.

Others before me had tried to ruin Prescott's lucky streak; none had succeeded. Now it was my turn. The work didn't exactly thrill me, but it kept my office lights on. It was Tuesday, just after eight, my first night looking for Big Percy. I started my car and let it run a bit while I thought things through. I'd dressed for business in jeans, a light sweater, and Nikes, and in anticipation of a long night, I'd brought along snacks: a banana, granola, and a chocolate doughnut for dessert. All set, I pulled away from the curb in front of my apartment and got to it. *Now, if I were a kid-dumping bluesman, where would I be?*

I didn't know jack about blues guitarists. I didn't get blues. Real life was hard enough. I wasn't about to pay good money to listen to somebody sing about his runaway dog or faithless girlfriend. But if Big Percy was like any other musician, he was likely ramping up for a late-night set somewhere. I had a list of clubs to check, but before I did that, it wouldn't hurt to take a pass at his last known address. Big Percy's ex-wife reported that she hadn't been able to get a nickel out of him in over a year, and now couldn't find him at the place he'd been staying. I flipped his file open on the passenger seat, committed the address to memory, then headed there—on the move and on the case for Golden, Sprague, and Bendelson.

I woke up Big Percy's landlady, Mrs. Ocela Pinkney, by leaning on the bell. The old lady groused some at first at the lateness of the hour, but then calmed down enough to tell me Big Percy had moved out more than a month ago. I got her to show me his apartment and, sure enough, the place was empty, not a stick of furniture in it. Prescott left her high and dry, Pinkney said, without so much as a "lah-dee-dah," and she passed along a few choice words she wanted me to convey to him when I finally tracked him down.

Back in the car, I hit every legit blues club and hole-in-the-wall masquerading as a legit blues club. Chicago had to have a million of them. Nobody I asked would admit to having seen Big Percy. Half of them were likely lying, but there wasn't a thing I could do about it. I'd have to keep looking and hope for a break.

It was well after midnight when I pulled up in front of the Purple Tip on North Halsted, the eighth club on my long list to check. I'd eaten the chocolate doughnut, leaving the banana and granola for later. I was just about to get out of the car and go inside, when I saw a freshly washed turquoise Caddy matching the description of Prescott's car ease up the street. I caught the plate and matched it to the info in the law firm's file. It was Prescott's, all right. Though, frankly, how many folks would choose to roll around town in a gaudy turquoise Cadillac with whitewall tires, unless, of course, they were an old-school pimp caught in a Huggy Bear time loop?

I slid down in the driver's seat as the car moved past me and parked at the curb across the street. I watched, my head barely above the steering wheel, as a big, dumb-looking bruiser got out from behind the wheel of Big Percy's pimp ride and adjusted himself. He had to be Prescott's muscle, hired to discourage the unwelcome. The bruiser wore a red velour warm-up suit with white stripes down the outside of the pants underneath a fur coat made from what looked like synthetic muskrat. He reached into the backseat and came out with a beat-up guitar case. That's when Big Percy got out on the passenger side and scanned the street. He wasn't a complete idiot. He knew he was dodging the court.

Big Percy, 250 pounds of unadulterated ugly, was decked out in a knee-length snakeskin coat worn over a tangerine suit, the coat shimmering like wet sealskin when it caught the streetlights. Sticking close to muskrat, he headed for the door to the Purple Tip, as if he hadn't one single care in the whole wide world.

Folks were milling around in the street, even at this hour, coming out of bars, going in. I had my car window open a crack so I could hear the street noise, but the crack also let in barbecue smoke, the sour scent of rancid fry grease, and the musky stench of everyday street grime. I knew these streets; I patrolled them for more than three years as a cop in uniform. They could be both mean and good, but rarely good this late at night. Anyone out at this hour was likely not in the running for sainthood. I got an idea. I felt for the gun in my ankle holster, just for reassurance, and then stuffed the summons in my back pocket, bounded out of the car, and rushed across the street, dodging potholes nearly big enough to drop a casket in. "Big Percy?"

Prescott froze midstride, reeled, his eyes wild, wary, a cornered rat caught flat-footed mere inches from his hidey-hole.

I clasped my hands together gleefully. "Big Percy Prescott? I can't believe it."

The bodyguard, deciding now would be a good time to earn his keep, moved to act as buffer between Big Percy and me. I sidestepped him, gave him a flirtatious wink.

"I *love* your music." I fluttered my eyelids a little. I really was shameless. "You have the fingers of an angel. I'm such a big fan."

To all outward appearances, I was a groupie in the presence of true musical greatness unable to control my sublime rapture at my "up close and personal" moment with musical royalty. Truth be told, I'd never heard of the man until yesterday when I got the job. The photo of him clipped to the law firm's paperwork did him more justice than he deserved.

Big Percy brushed the muskrat aside, sidled in closer to me, and shot me a megawatt smile that revealed a shiny gold tooth right up front. "Is that so, pretty lady?"

I smiled. "Oh, yes indeedy. Would you mind?" I slid the summons out of my pocket and thrust it forward, seal side down. "I would just *love* your autograph." I eyed the muscle. "You wouldn't happen to have a pen on you, would you, handsome?" Best to keep him busy. He smiled back, patting at his breast pockets as though trying to put out a small fire.

Big Percy checked for a pen, too, feeling around in his trouser pockets, coming up with one in record time, which surprised the heck out of me. How many autograph requests did he get?

Big Percy leered at me. "Now, where'd you get that sexy smile from?"

I grinned foolishly. Really, I should take to the stage. I was a natural. "It came with the ears."

Prescott's eyes clouded over, confusion wrinkling his puggish face. He was back quickly, though. "Everybody knows I got a soft spot for the ladies." He took a long survey of me. It started high, lingered a bit in the middle, and stopped at my shoe tops. "And I like 'em lean, leggy, and caramel colored, just like you."

He plastered the summons to the bodyguard's back and prepared to scribble his John Hancock on it. Technically, the minute he took the summons from me, my job was done, but I was having way too much fun.

Big Percy gave me that look. You know the one. "You married?" he asked.

I nodded. "With triplets." The lie tripped off my tongue as easy as anything. It amazes even me how I can lie with a straight face and not feel the least bit funny about it, at least while working a low-down, dirty blues hack who skipped out on his kids.

"Well, you'd never know it. Your shape held up real good." He shook his head. "Triplets? Huh. And you looking like *that*? God almighty. That's some good genes working there."

I giggled. Also a lie. I never giggled. Giggling was something twelve-year-old girls did at slumber parties. Thirty-four-year-old women with brains in their heads did not giggle. *Ever.* "You really think so?"

He nodded. "I know so. Who do I make this out to, sugar cheeks?" He licked the point of the pen, then poised it over the paper, not bothering to look at it, the lascivious grin widening on his child-support-dodging face.

"Ruth, Antoine, and Dawn," I snapped. The smile was gone, the giggle, too.

Big Percy blinked; the pen shook a little. I'd given him the names of his ex-wife and children, and it took him no time to realize it. He turned to his bodyguard, looking for a little of that buffer action he was likely paying good money for. Too late. The man's hands were occupied holding Big Percy's guitar case. Looks like a certain somebody in muskrat failed "Bodyguard 101."

"You've been served, Mr. Prescott. Oh, and your landlady

told me to tell you she thinks you're a scumbag. She had a few other choice words, but I'm too much of a lady to repeat them. Have a nice night."

I strolled back to my car, leaving Big Percy and his porter standing on the sidewalk, their mouths agape, sucking in air like grounded river pike. I punched the button on my radio and caught the tail end of "Papa Was a Rolling Stone." It could have been Big Percy's theme song. I couldn't have planned it better if I'd planned it.

Chapter 2

Deek's Diner was nearly deserted when I cruised in at eight for breakfast. I'd managed to get a good solid six hours' sleep, riding on my Big Percy win, and I was feeling refreshed, triumphant, and hungry. It was not an unusual thing to find Deek's at far less than capacity. That's why I liked the place. You could always find a seat. People flocked to other diners, but they didn't flock here and wouldn't, even if Deek were giving away free bacon. That's because Willis Deacon, Vietnam vet turned surly fry cook and unrepentant social pariah, would go down in the annals of history as the grumpiest black man this side of Hades.

Deek had to be in his early seventies, dark, barrel-chested, with tatted forearms that looked strong enough to wrestle cattle without benefit of a lasso. He always wore a plain black baseball hat, more grease than cap at this point, and I'd never seen him smile, not once. Deek didn't make small talk. He could not care less how your day was going. In here, you got it the way he fixed it, or you didn't get it, and service with a smile was only a silly fool's Christmas wish. The quicker you got in, ordered something, ate it, and got the hell out, the better Deek seemed to like it. Look at him wrong or do something stupid, like ask for a salt-shaker or an extra napkin, and you were likely to get your feelings hurt. Deek slung plates and tossed silverware. He snagged picky diners by the seat of their pants and threw them out onto the sidewalk. Willis Deacon didn't know the meaning of the word "decorum."

He did, however, know his way around a buttermilk pancake. His food was hot and made to order and really cheap, once you factored in the floor show. The indigestion brought on by his rampaging performances? Well, Deek threw that in, gratis. The fact that I could practically spit on the diner from the swivel chair in my office a few doors down wasn't a bad deal, either. Did I mention Deek delivered? So, for convenience sake, I could deal with surly, especially since, for some inexplicable reason, he left me alone.

I don't know what made me special. I've never asked the question and Deek, in all the years he's growled over his greasy griddle, has never volunteered the information to me or anyone else. He scowls at me plenty, sure, but a scowl beats a pants toss any day of the week. You can rise above a scowl. It was nearly impossible to shrug off another man's grip on the seat of your pants.

I snaked through the maze of wooden tables, past the few diners spread out around the place, breathing in bacon and coffee fumes. I made a beeline for the back booth, the one I preferred and considered mine, the morning paper tucked under my arm. I'd come to eat. I didn't need to do it in the middle of Deek's gladiator pit.

Sliding onto the cracked vinyl, my back to the mustard yellow wall, my view of the front door unobstructed, I tossed the paper on the table, picked up the laminated menu, and watched as Muna, one of Deek's battle-tested waitresses, ambled over to take my order.

I eyed the room. "You alone, Muna?"

"Wasn't. Am now. Adele walked off twenty minutes ago."

Adele and Muna made an efficient team of opposites, or did,

until twenty minutes ago. Adele was small, thin, quick moving, and overly skittish; Muna was big, broad, and loudly indelicate at the best and worst of times. Adele was also easily offended and quit at least twice a month. I often wondered why she'd chosen to work here in the first place. I mean, it's not like she didn't know what she was letting herself in for; Deek was Deek 24/7.

I grimaced. "Deek?"

"Well, it sure wasn't me." Muna licked the tip of her short pencil and poised it over her order pad. I smiled thinking of Big Percy. This was the second time in the span of eight hours that I'd watched people wet their writing utensils with spit. "I've been polite as pie all mornin', and if I were you, I wouldn't be ordering nothin' from that man's griddle. He's been revving up back there since Adele walked off, and it's only a matter of time before he clears the place out."

I snapped the menu closed, defiant. I wasn't about to let Deek ruin my vibe. "I'll risk it. Blueberry pancakes, skim milk, bacon, extra crispy. And you really ought to put a sign on the door when Deek's in a snit. Warn a person."

"Tried that," Muna said without missing a beat. "Griddle Man ate it."

She moved off toward the kitchen, the rubber soles of her wide, comfy shoes squeaking across the sticky linoleum.

"Way too early for funny, Muna," I called after her.

"Never too early, you ask me," she shot back over her shoulder.

The front page of the paper offered nothing new. There was city corruption, tax hikes, Washington chaos, dozens felled by city violence. Every day it was the same old thing, and it just made you tired. I'd made it to page four when a familiar voice roused me from my melancholy.

"You're here. I have to talk to you."

My eyes drifted off the paper to the patch of floor to my right, where I found a pair of scuffed combat boots with thin hairy legs standing in them. I scanned up past knobby knees, cargo shorts, and a wrinkled T-shirt into the flushed face of Jung Byson, Deek's indolent delivery boy. He was new to the place, just a month or so since he'd been hired. I didn't know too much about him, but what I did know seemed weird.

Jung strolled Deek's food up to my office at least twice a week, and I do mean "strolled." He never rushed. A University of Chicago student on the lifetime plan, Jung, now in his early twenties, was slowly working his way through every academic concentration they had over there. At last report, he had chucked archaeology for philosophy, and worked for Deek whenever he remembered to show up for his shift. I had no idea what he did the rest of the time, or why Deek hadn't yet chopped him into a stew.

"What's up, Jung?"

He slid in across from me, a shell-shocked expression on his equine face, offset by blond peach fuzz under his nose and a scraggly soul patch. I looked toward the door to make sure he wasn't fleeing someone from outside, then watched uneasily as he squeezed his eyes shut and took a deep, cleansing breath before opening them again. "Transcendental breathing," he said as way of explanation. "Swami Rain recommends it in times of flux."

I blinked, but said nothing.

"He's my yogi," Jung added. "My spiritual adviser? He's the real deal, too. His teachings got me centered. I consider his place my true spiritual home."

Jung was average in build and height, and his short blond hair, today, was moussed to death and sticking up like railroad spikes. I stared at him, bewildered by his fashion choices, stuck on Swami Rain, the yogi. Jung wasn't bleeding; it didn't look as though he'd been attacked, so I spread my napkin over my lap.

His clear blue eyes held mine. "I have a problem. A big one."

Muna popped up with my breakfast, shot Jung a withering glance, her arms akimbo, big hands on full hips. Jung stared back, clueless. I ignored them both. My breakfast was getting cold and I wanted to eat and get out of here before Deek went apeshit.

"I'm not on the schedule today," Jung said. "Personal time. Deek knows."

Muna sniffed. "Wondered why you were sitting there like real people instead of carting Deek's food to folks on that slow boat to China you're captain of."

Jung held his ground. "Everything in its own time."

Muna folded her arms across her triple-E bosom. "Eggs and bacon got six minutes before they go stone cold, Speedy Man. Any time after that is the wrong time." She walked away, having said all she felt she needed to. Muna Steele, mistress of the exit line.

I smeared butter over my flapjacks. "What kind of problem?"

Jung swallowed hard. "I went by your office. You weren't there."

"No, I'm here waiting for Deek to give me indigestion. What'd you need?"

He glanced nervously at the swinging kitchen doors. He knew the drill. He leaned in, lowered his voice conspiratorially. "I want to hire you. I mean, I *need* to hire you."

I poured maple syrup from the sticky dispenser, my thumb pressed down on the lever controlling the spout. "To do what?"

Jung leaned farther in, his chest practically touching the table-top. "Find a murderer."

I put the dispenser down, looked at him. "Say what now?"

It wasn't what I expected. I mean, this was quirky, "not in the world the rest of us live in" Jung Byson. What could he possibly have to do with a murderer? I studied him for a time, convinced he was putting me on. But I noticed that his eyes weren't as spacey as they normally were. He seemed dialed in. He was serious.

Jung started again, louder. "I said I need—"

I waved him quiet. "I'm not deaf. I heard you. Explain yourself."

He raked his fingers through his hair. "It just happened . . . well, a couple days ago . . . whatever went down. He's dead, I know that."

"Who's dead?"

Jung took another deep breath, and let it out slow. "My friend drowned, and it wasn't an accident. I don't care what the cops say. I need you to prove it." Jung reached into his pocket and pulled out a wad of bills, tens and twenties mostly, a few fifties, but oddly folded, like he'd gotten them dancing for tips in a strip joint. "I've never hired a PI before. I can get more if this isn't enough."

I stared at the money, then at the confused look on Jung's face as he shoved the bills into the center of the table next to Deek's cheap salt and pepper shakers. "He was killed, and no one believes me. You know the spot I'm in. The priest?"

He caught me off guard and I drew back. The priest. He meant Pop. The image of his dead body flashed in my head, and my breath caught. I'd noticed his shoe first, sticking out of the confessional. I pushed back against the memory now, against the familiar ache of loss. . . . I could tell Jung hadn't meant to plunge me back into the depths of grief, but the closer I looked, the more I could see a familiar pain crushing down on him like pressing stones. Yes, I knew how that felt. I leaned back and shoved my plate aside, breakfast now the furthest thing from my mind. "Go on. I'm listening."

Chapter 3

The priest was Father Ray Heaton, *Pop*—the nearest thing I'd had to a father. When I found him, a bullet in his head, I knew it wasn't suicide, because I knew him. The battle with the police had been a hard slog, one I didn't want to repeat, at least not so soon. It'd only been two months. I still found myself picking up the phone to call him, only to realize too late that he'd never be on the other end. That's why, for now, I was sticking to work I didn't have to think too much about, giving myself time to get used to a new normal. Jung's problem didn't sound like it'd offer me either time or space, and my first impulse, my prevailing impulse, was to push it and him away as surely as I'd pushed away Deek's pancakes.

Jung folded his arms across his chest, as though giving himself a much-needed hug, as though he were cold right down to the bone and couldn't get warm. "My friend. His name is . . . was . . . Tim Ayers."

I recognized the name from the papers. Ayers, the scion of a notable family, had been found floating in Lake Michigan, his yacht adrift. Though his death had quickly been ruled "accidental," as I read the news reports, there was some speculation that Ayers may have deliberately caused his own death. "DuSable

Marina," I said, recalling the details. "He took his boat out in a storm."

Jung shook his head. "The papers got it all wrong, the cops, too. He never would have done it."

I cocked my head, more than a little skeptical. Ayers's death had gotten a good deal of coverage due to his family's prominence, but not much had come of it. Money has a way of insulating those who have it from prying eyes and intrusive questioning. Ayers drowned, the victim of a tragic accident, case closed. As such, the media spotlight quickly turned elsewhere, leaving the Ayers family to deal with the death on their own.

"There was no evidence of foul play," I said gently. "He was drunk. There was nothing missing from the boat."

Jung read my look and shot me a wan smile. "And now you're thinking what the cops are, but I'm telling you all that's wrong. I mean, those are the facts, but they don't mean what everybody thinks they mean. Tim was solid. He was a painter, a good one, I guess. I don't know much about it. He wasn't a Warhol, or anything, but he was good." Jung smoothed down the hair he'd disrupted moments ago. He rolled his eyes. "He wasn't careless and he wasn't depressed, and I know for sure somebody did this to him."

I watched as a family with two toddlers bustled into the diner, dragging along massive strollers and booster seats, one of the kids wailing for his "baa-baa." Arms shot up at the few occupied tables, diners calling for their checks. Deek had no patience for tiny humans. I had to speed this up.

"You sound sure."

Jung bit into his lower lip, eyed a spot on the wall above my head. "I am. I talked to him that morning. In fact, I'm probably one of the last people on earth to talk to him. He was his same old self—talking shit, full of plans, ready for the next big thing, maybe a little distracted, but nothing major. He had something for me, he said, and he wanted me to stop by and get it. He seemed serious about it. I told him, 'Dude, no way, there's like a monsoon breathing down our necks.' I told him I'd catch him mañana, but when I showed up—" Jung stopped, gulped. "If I'd gone over there, maybe . . ." His chin fell to his chest. This was the thing that propelled him, the missed chance, the guilt that grew out of it. "I saw them tow his boat in, then his body." Jung looked up, despair all over a face that wasn't used to handling it. "Somebody killed him, I know it."

"Who would want to do that?"

Jung shook his head. "I don't know. Maybe a lot of people? Tim was an 'in your face' kind of guy, but he wasn't a prick . . . well, not a big one. He was just living his life, you know? I've been wracking my brain, trying to think who'd take things this far. I know those stuffed shirts at the marina didn't like him. They're old-timers, real set in their ways, and Tim liked to have a good time. He could sometimes get a little out-there. The guy in the office, the one who got the complaints, ragged on him all the time. Maybe him?"

"Family? Girlfriend? Wife?"

"There's only his mother and brother. His dad died years ago. Tim was gay. He wasn't married, or anything. Maybe somebody he met? He liked the bar scene. I don't think it was Stephen. They weren't close, but you don't drown your own brother.

"Tim wasn't some stoner. He dabbled, okay—who doesn't?—but he wasn't stupid about it. And he'd never get shit-faced on the boat. Another reason I know for sure? He wasn't wearing a life jacket or slicker when they found him. It's raining buckets, wind's whipping around mad crazy, and he goes up on deck, out-of-his-head drunk, with nothing on? No way. Not Tim."

"Unless he wasn't concerned about his safety."

"Like he wanted to kill himself? No way. And stop thinking like a cop, will you?" Jung's voice rose. "I knew the guy. He used to be a certified boating instructor, an absolute lunatic for water safety. No one could get anywhere near that bucket without him shoving a life jacket at them. You need to look at the guy here, not the facts. He was pushed, I know it. You have to trust me on this."

He was hurting and I certainly didn't want to add to it, but I didn't think Tim not wearing a life jacket proved anything. Suicides were often happy, elated even, before the act. They gave cherished things away to those closest to them and didn't always leave parting words or long letters of explanation. Sometimes they just did it, leaving unanswered questions and a lot of regret behind. Or, maybe, it was simpler than that. Maybe it was just as the cops pegged it. Tim got drunk, unwisely took his boat out in inhospitable weather, and fell overboard. I wasn't exactly sure what I should say to Jung, so I sat there for a moment not saying anything.

"You've spoken with the police?"

Jung frowned. "They've closed the case already. Just like that. Accidental drowning. I'll bet the family just wanted the whole thing to go away. 'Out of sight, out of mind.'" Jung placed his hand on the money pile. "I know you can figure this whole thing out. Can I count on you?"

I hesitated. Tim had been drunk. There were no signs of foul play reported. But Jung was too shaken to let any of that get through. He looked haggard, spent. "When's the last time you slept?" I asked.

He rubbed his eyes. "I don't need sleep. I need to know what happened to Tim. Now, are you going to help me, or not?"

When I took too long to answer, Jung leaned back against the booth. "Why don't you just come out and say it? You think I'm full of shit, a flake, some idiot who just delivers sandwiches, right?"

"Of course not . . . but I think you're looking for answers when there might not be any. If you'd stop and give yourself time to really think—"

Jung interrupted me, bristling at my efforts to settle him. "You can manipulate facts."

"In this case, who would do that?" Jung didn't appear to have an answer to that. "If you know something the police don't, share it with them. Otherwise, I don't see any daylight here." I slid the pile of money back toward him. "And I won't take your money, if I don't think I can help you."

Jung turned away from me. He shook his head.

"Go home, Jung. Get some rest. Let things settle."

He turned back, his eyes full of fire, resolve in them. He angrily gathered up the money, stuffing it back into his pockets, rising. "Tim didn't want to die, not like that. The cops don't know anything. You want to side with them? Fine. But I know what I know, and I'm going to prove it. Sorry I wasted your time."

Jung stormed off, and I shot up from the booth, following after him. "Jung, wait." But he was through the dining room and out the door before I could catch up. I burst out onto the sidewalk, scanning right, left. He was gone.

"The skinny guy jumped on a beat-up–looking ten-speed and booked it. Want me to give chase?"

I turned to see Detective Eli Weber leaning his long body against an unmarked cop car. He smiled, nodded. "Which way did he go?" I asked.

"West, then north. Seriously, do I need to send a flash?"

I looked west, sighed. Setting the cops on Jung wouldn't do any good in the long run. "No. Hopefully, he'll just go on home."

Weber unstuck himself from the car and walked over, his intense brown eyes lasering in. He wasn't hard to look at, I had to admit. He was midforties, six two to my five seven, dark, clean-shaven. His angular face, I'd come to realize, was capable of revealing absolutely nothing, unless he wanted it to. I suspected there was a lot going on behind his probing eyes, and that intrigued me, but that's as far as I'd taken it. We'd met on Pop's case, and hadn't gotten off to a good start, though I slowly found out that he was a stand-up guy, real police. Weber was also married, which right off the bat made his business none of mine.

"Somebody call for a detective?" I asked.

"Personal call. Thought I'd stop by and see how you were getting along." He glanced at my leg. "Last time I saw you, you could barely stand on that knee."

"How'd you know to check here?"

He smiled. "Your place, isn't it?"

The hospital. Late April. That's the last time I'd seen him. I bent my left knee, a quick demonstration of how good the knee had mended. A murdering bastard had stomped on it in a church, right before I'd threatened to blow his head off. The knee was still a little wonky, not yet a hundred percent, but it'd be okay. "No permanent damage. I meant to call and thank you for sitting with me in the ER. That was nice. I guess I got busy."

He nodded, the eyes never once wavering. "Mickerson said you've been busy."

My eyes narrowed. Since when did Weber and my ex-partner start hanging out together? And why was I the topic of conversation when they did? Weber chuckled, but the eyes, more chestnut than true brown, clamped on and wouldn't let up. What was he trying to do, take an X-ray? I checked my watch, feeling my face flush.

He grinned. "Relax. I asked him how you were. He told me to ask for myself. So this is me asking."

I was relaxed. Didn't I look relaxed? I shot Weber a look. Who'd he think he was impressing? "Yeah, okay. Well, it's been a slice . . ." I turned to break it off. I had stuff to do.

"What's going on with the bike kid? Don't tell me you're working for him."

"He's the delivery guy here, and I'm not." I glanced surreptitiously at his ring finger. When I found nothing on it, I took a second to let that register. The last time I'd seen Weber, he said he was separated, and I'd given him the widest berth a human person could give another. Now the ring was gone. There was only a faint band of lighter skin where it used to be.

"Do you know anything about the drowning at DuSable Marina a couple days ago?" I asked. "Timothy Ayers?"

Weber folded his arms across his chest. "Rich kid. Too much alcohol, not enough common sense. Accidental. What about it?"

"He was a friend of the bike kid's. He thinks someone may have killed him. He wants me to find out who."

Weber laughed, then figured out I was serious and stopped. "And you turned him down. That's why he lit out?"

"I don't think I'd be any use to him."

"You're right. You'd be spinning your wheels. The kid was tanked. He either slipped or jumped, either way nothing says he had help doing it."

"Who was lead on it?" That information hadn't been in the papers.

Weber's eyes narrowed. "I thought you said you couldn't help?"

"I'm just curious."

The slight grin he gave me told me he didn't believe me. He slid his hands into his pockets, cocked his head. "Marta Pena."

I knew Marta. She was good. "Thanks."

"No problem."

We stood there and watched the street traffic whiz by.

"Where's your wedding ring?"

Weber's brows lifted. "Just like that?"

I didn't answer.

"I told you I was separated."

"Men say that all the time."

"In my case, it was true. Divorce came through six weeks ago. The ring's in a box in my sock drawer, if you want to see it."

I said nothing, but I was thinking a whole lot of things.

"My ring didn't stop anybody but you. You took one look at it and not only closed the door, you dead-bolted it and walked away like you never even met me."

Dead bolt? What was he talking about? "I have a rule about getting in the middle of marriages." He looked at me expectantly, waiting for more. "I don't do it."

He nodded. "I can respect that. But now the ring's gone. What do you say to a second date?"

"*Second?*"

"The hospital was the first date, so when we go out again, hopefully, someplace nice with white tablecloths and overpriced valet parking, that'll be our second."

"You're counting the ER as a date?"

"I had a good time, didn't you?"

"My knee was wrecked. I was half out of my head on pain meds."

"We can skip all that next time."

I searched his face. I didn't know him well. Maybe he was playing around. He had to be. "I don't date cops." It was my fallback response. Eli Weber looked complicated and I wasn't up for it.

"You went out with *Detective* Marcus Jones."

I balked. "How do *you* know?"

"I know how to run a decent investigation, but I only got the high points. I figured I'd wait and get the rest from you." He backed up, headed for the car as smooth as anything, irritatingly unruffled, like he owned the street and every brick on it. "I'll call. We'll set something up for when you're not so *busy.*"

"I didn't say *yes*. Did you hear me say 'yes'?"

He opened the driver's door, held it. "You're still standing there. That's my 'yes.'"

Chapter 4

Earlene Skipper owned Speedy Cleaners. She was also being sued for damages to Loretta Kenton's five-thousand-dollar mink coat, which Speedy had not only failed to service correctly, but had, in fact, ruined, separating a good portion of the expensive fur from its pelt. I was the lucky so-and-so chosen to give Skipper the sorry news in the form of legal paper.

On my way over there the next morning, I stopped at a card and novelty shop for six helium balloons tied together with colorful ribbon, which I stuffed, with great difficulty, into the backseat of my compact Nissan. Pulling up in front of Skipper's business on the Far South Side, I took the summons and wrapped the tail end of the balloon streamers around it, like a present, then walked inside, an official-looking clipboard under my arm.

There was a short black girl behind the counter, who couldn't have been older than twenty. She eyed the balloons, though it didn't appear they impressed her much. The cleaners was hot, oppressively so, and smelled of spray starch and toxic chemicals. I could almost feel my lungs fold in on themselves in an act of self-preservation. I smiled politely. "Hello, is Earlene Skipper here?"

The girl, popping gum, eyed the balloons again, sighed, and

then turned and bellowed toward the back. "Miz Skipper? Something for you up here."

I held my fake smile and waited, trying not to breathe too deeply. The girl watched me wait. As I waited, the balloons hovering over my head, I thought of ways to increase my client base so that I wouldn't have to do things like this anymore. *Maybe an open house? Get some potential clients through the door. Come in, grab a fresh-baked cookie, watch me frisk a guy. I need to work on it.*

About a minute later, a rotund black woman, wearing a shirtdress bulging at the seams, padded up to the counter. She was middle-aged, very settled in, and by the disagreeable scowl on her face, it didn't appear that the balloons were doing anything for her, either.

Faded tats ran along the side of her wide neck and down both arms—fire-breathing dragons, elaborate lotus flowers in bloom, and on her right wrist, for some inexplicable reason, a rendering of Yosemite Sam. I could only imagine what kind of life she'd led up to this point.

"Earlene Skipper?"

"So?"

Skipper was a rough one. I handed her the balloons, took a step back, and pointed at the summons dangling at the end of the streamers. "There's a note attached."

Skipper yanked the summons free, and then thrust the balloons at her startled counter girl. Just like with Big Percy, my job was done, but this time, I had no desire to stick around hoping for a good time. This was an easy job, in and out, and that's how I was going to play it.

"Have a good one," I said, making for the door.

Halfway there, the cussing started, followed by the scrape of fast-moving feet across the dirty floor. I turned to confirm my suspicions, and saw Earlene Skipper, half-crazed, coming after me at full throttle. I flew through the door, ran for my car, slid

over the top of the hood, Starsky and Hutch style, and then jumped in and peeled away from the curb. No shame in that. Live to fight another day, yada yada yada. I glanced in my rearview to see Earlene charging up the sidewalk after me, brandishing a handful of wire hangers, as though she had a chance of catching me. I rounded the corner and left her to it. "Yep. That's some-body I'd trust with a mink."

"Balloons?"

I turned to Ben. "It worked, didn't it?"

We were in the second-floor apartment of my building, empty since the Kallishes, my previous tenants, moved away. The place needed painting, and I was here to get it done. I'd have to rent the place soon. After the drive-by, it was obvious that Stuart, Marie, and little Nate weren't coming back. Besides, I needed the income the apartment would bring in.

Ben picked his way gingerly around the splotchy drop cloths. "Only because she didn't catch you."

I slid him a sideways glance. "She had *zero* chance of that."

Ben looked around. He was off duty, dressed in fancy duds, freshly shaven, smelling of cologne. That meant he had a date, one of many. He'd divorced while we were still working to-gether, and ever since then, he kept it light, casual, and frequent. He was not one to hide his burly cop light under a bushel.

"Never been down here before." He rapped beefy knuckles against one of the walls I hadn't gotten to yet. "High ceilings, crown molding, solid wood floors, good light—mirror image of your place upstairs. You lined up new tenants yet?"

I went back to the wall, running the roller over the latest coat, eggshell, matte finish. The painting was going slowly, mainly be-cause I didn't want to do it, didn't want to turn the apartment over, didn't want to have someone new living under my roof. "Getting around to it."

Ben walked around, tapping walls, side-kicking baseboards,

stalling. I'd ridden with him in a squad car for five years. I knew when he had something to say. "Spill it, or pick up a brush and hit a wall."

He looked down at his clothes, sharp, neat, well fitted to his linebacker frame. He'd even gone in for a haircut, his sandy hair shorn close, parted on the side. "Eli Weber. What's up with you two? There, I said it."

I stopped the roller, peered down at him from the top of the ladder. "What?"

His steady blue eyes met mine. "Don't cop stare me. You? Weber? You interested? Because he sure is. Know how I know? He's hitting me up for information on you almost every second. What's she like to eat? Who's she hang out with? My lips are sealed, of course. I've got my loyalties, but, just letting you know, he's got a thing, and I want to know if you got a thing, too . . . I think you do. You two have been flitting around each other for months. So what gives?" He slid his hands into his front pockets, his eyes glued to the roller brush in my hand as though it might jump down and roll all over him. He cleared his throat nervously. "That's right. I said it. We're family. Family can ask."

I dropped the brush into a paint tray, climbed down off the ladder, my sweatshirt, jeans, and hands smudged with damp paint. As though I had the plague, Ben backed away from me, his hands outstretched, as if to ward off an attack. "Watch that paint, will ya? These are new shoes."

I fisted my hands on my hips. "Since when are you and Weber bosom buddies?"

He shrugged, paused. "He's around. I'm around. Cops talk. He says you took a pass on that drowning case. Ayers? Good. Clear case of rich-kid suicide."

"You all came to that conclusion awful quick. Was it really that easy?"

Ben rolled his eyes. "Stepped right into that one. Go back to your wall. The burning issue here is how you want me to handle Weber."

"I know we're close, but I don't need you *this* close. My bedroom's my business, yours is yours. Got it?"

"So you *are* interested," Ben said.

I picked up the roller and brandished it in his direction, which sent him backpedaling. "One more word about Weber and I go full-on Jackson Pollock."

He flicked his eyebrows like Groucho Marx. "I could pass him a note in study hall."

"And I could paint your new shoes."

"Gotta go." He hightailed it out, slamming the door behind him. *What I like to eat?*

Chapter 5

Friday morning, I stared at the ad I'd just written for the apartment I needed to rent. It was propped up on my office desk, leaning against an old pencil box that only held ballpoint pens. It read simply: *Two bedrooms/full bath/hardwood floors/full kitchen/close to U of C campus and public transportation/no pets.* It was all I had so far. I flashed on little Nate's face as he cowered in a niche clinging to his mother, and then drew a pen out of the box and scribbled an addition: *no children.* I held the ad in my hand, read it over, then balled it up and threw it in the wastebasket at my feet.

I rose from my squeaky chair, restless. I'd tried sleeping on Jung's problem, but hadn't been able to. My thoughts kept coming back to the wounded look on his face. Why did I feel so guilty? I hardly knew him. We weren't friends. I ordered the sandwich; he delivered the sandwich. It was a fair exchange, and I always tipped well. What did I have to prove?

I stared out the window at the apartment building across the street. Sometimes a few of the blinds were open and I got a show—today no dice. Deek's was three doors down at the corner. If I craned my neck just so, I could barely make out the front door. My building, the one I owned and lived in, was four blocks farther south, two blocks north. Living so close was one of the benefits of renting space here. The four-story building wasn't much otherwise. It was old, temperamental, and the plumbing iffy, but I could walk or ride my bike to work. Plus, from this exact spot, I could smell hot food sizzling on Deek's griddle.

There was a dentist across the hall from me—Dr. Gupta—whose drill often set my teeth on edge, but even that wasn't enough to get me looking for better digs. I was a nester, and once I found a nest I liked, I tended to stay put. I had no idea who owned the building now, ownership turned over on the regular. I sent my rent check to a faceless management company somewhere I didn't care about. As long as they didn't bother me, I had no reason to bother them.

There was a mess on my desk: newspapers, contracts I needed to file, bills I needed to pay, and invoices I had to send out so that I would have something to pay the bills with. It was a soul-sucking, never-ending cycle. And then there was Weber looming. I had backed away, sure, but dead-bolted the door? Maybe. I made it a point to keep out of people's marriages, both personally and professionally. I didn't take domestic cases and I didn't waste time with men who were separated from their wives. But now the ring was in a sock drawer and Weber was counting every encounter we had as a bona fide date. And Ben for some strange reason figured he had a stake in how it all turned out. What was that about?

I sat down again, drumming fidgety fingers on my desk blotter, then reached down and plucked the ad out of the trash and called it into the newspaper. It took all of five minutes, and I breathed a sigh of relief when it was done. I held the receiver in my hand. Maybe I could make one call about the Ayers case. What could it hurt? If I had more information, I reasoned, I might convince Jung to let things drop. Detective Marta Pena knew her stuff and she also knew I could be a pain in the ass, so I wouldn't even have to make nice and pretend I didn't have it in me. I eyed the invoices. I eyed the phone. I thought of Jung racing off, Lord knows where, half-cocked and stupid, and dialed Marta's cell phone.

She answered on the second ring. "Cass Raines, PI," she chuckled. "Where've *you* been hiding yourself?"

I slid back in my swivel chair, all easy, propped my legs up on the desk. "I've been around."

"Last I heard, you were wearing a pair of Farraday's cuffs and headed for the women's lockup. I knew he'd never get you there, though. You're like a feral alley cat, wily, slippery."

I frowned, not sure if I should feel insulted or not. Who wanted to be likened to a feral alley cat? "Yeah, okay. Look, Marta, I need a favor. The drowning at the lake? Tim Ayers? Can you tell me anything about that?" I listened hard, squinting, as if that would help me pick up stray sounds from her end. "You still there?"

"I closed that case." Marta's voice was tight, all the friendliness sucked out of it. "Go sniff around someone else's alley."

Again with the cat thing? I frowned, braced myself for more heat. "You're sure it was accidental, that it couldn't have been anything else?"

"Like what?"

"Like a push instead of a slip? A shove instead of a jump?"

She let a beat pass. "The only push is the one Ayers gave himself. He either jumped or slipped, either way he was the only one there. Now it's done. We released the body to the family. You're too late to try and poach."

I dropped my legs, leaned forward. "I do *not* poach."

"You poached Farraday. He's a prick, but you poached the hell out of him."

"That was personal, and you know it . . . and I was right. Don't leave that part out."

"Right, wrong, I don't give a shit. A poach is a poach."

"You're sure nothing smelled a little off, a little weird? You're certain he either jumped or fell?"

"Everything smelled just fine to me," Marta said. "But what's any of this got to do with you?"

"I'm asking for a friend of Ayers's."

"A friend? What friend? . . . Oh, no. It's that spacey guy—the dopey one with the kooky name. Something dumb . . . Byson . . . *Jung* Byson. That's him, isn't it?"

"He's taking his friend's death hard. Toss him a bone."

"I see him again I'll toss him into a cell. How's that?" I could hear Marta breathing heavily on her end. She didn't like to share. She also didn't like to be questioned or second-guessed. I knew all this going in, which made dealing with her, especially on something like this, not a lot of fun.

"Marta, I can almost hear the steam flooding out of your ears. I'm not checking over your shoulder. I just want to know what you think happened. For old times' sake, just a little info, and I'm out of your rapidly graying hair."

"You're a pain in my ass, you know that?"

"Yes."

"You're working for Mr. Dippy Boots?"

"Marta, please, give me some credit. I told him straight out that if you were on the case, then you ran it like it should be run. But if Mr. Dippy . . . ugh . . . Jung can get a grip on what happened, he can start to put this whole thing behind him. Five minutes. Just the highlights, and I'm a ghost."

"Until next time you want a favor," Marta groused.

"Just remember, that door swings both ways," I said.

She let out the mother of all exasperated sighs, followed by the sounds of muffled footsteps and a door opening and closing. "You get this on one condition. You keep whatsahoozits away from me. Deal?" Marta's voice carried with it an echo, like she was standing in a wind tunnel. I figured she'd gone looking for a private spot, and had ended up in a stairwell or the women's bathroom.

"Easiest one I'll make all day."

"Listen good, because you're only getting one pass, and I'm not diving deep. You're also not getting a look at any departmental files. Understood?"

I rolled my eyes. So much drama. "Got it."

"First off, Ayers was wasted. His blood alcohol was off the charts, and if that weren't enough, he had enough prescription meds in him to kill a moose. All kinds—I won't bore you with the Latin. We bagged a ton of med bottles for the ME, most of them almost empty. Ayers really went to town. We left almost as many duplicate bottles as we took away, which shows the volume we were dealing with. ME puts time of death between nine PM Sunday and midnight."

"No signs of force?"

"Contusion on the right side of his head, likely banged himself going over, unsteady on his feet. No evidence of trespass, nothing stolen. Nobody saw him take the boat out and nobody saw anybody come anywhere near it the night he died.

"We got nothing from the marina's security cameras. The storm obscured everything for the time window we looked at. We couldn't have made out Jack the Ripper in that downpour. The cabin was clean. Immaculate, in fact, every surface polished, the carpet freshly vacuumed. It was like Ayers cleaned up for company, and then decided not to wait for it. The marine unit found the boat drifting ten miles out, like a ghost ship. Bottom line, one minute Ayers is on it, the next he's off it, and the boat floats away like it had a mind of its own. We didn't find a single print."

"How'd you get tox screens back so fast? It's only been a couple days."

Marta didn't say anything for a bit. "He's an Ayers. They rub elbows with the mayor. You know what that means, you don't depress me by making me say it."

"And you don't find the lack of prints or any of that other stuff a little odd? How do you not leave a single print behind on your own boat?"

All I heard was quiet from Marta's end.

"Marta, I'm good for it," I said, jumping in. "You know whatever you tell me stays with me, but give me something that wasn't already in the papers, will you?"

"We weren't dealing with some ordinary guy, apparently," she said, her voice lower than before. "According to the victim's brother, Ayers was seriously OCD. He went bonkers over the slightest mess."

"But you can't determine his intent," I said. It was not a question.

"My feeling is this is a self-termination, but for the family's sake . . ." Her words trailed away. "Word came down from the top to pretty this up and do it fast. Since we couldn't conclusively say he meant to kill himself, we didn't. There's still a stigma to suicide. Besides, the family's apparently been dealing with some rocky shit for a long time with this kid, and wanted it all put to bed."

"What kind of 'rocky shit'?"

Marta chortled. "Byson didn't give you the backstory?"

I sighed. "Apparently not."

"The victim had a few minor scrapes, mostly in high school—possession of marijuana, underage drinking, speeding tickets, trespass. Then there's his history of depression and anxiety, strike two. Maybe he was bipolar, the brother suspects as much, but Tim was never officially diagnosed. Guess the family didn't want that hanging over their heads either. Strike three? Tim Ayers was dying of some god-awful kind of cancer, and didn't have much time anyway. He was still up and on his feet, by all accounts, but his better days were behind him. That's got to be tough for a guy still in his twenties., which possibly contributed to his state of mind at the time he died."

I hung on the line, shocked into silence. Jung hadn't mentioned that Tim was dying or that he had had a history of depression and anxiety. My grip tightened on the receiver. Here I was feeling guilty for turning him away when it now appeared that that's exactly what I should have done. I narrowed my eyes. He knew what he was doing, too, didn't he? I thought. If he'd told me all of this up front, that would have put quite a different spin on Tim's "accidental" death.

"I deduce from your uncharacteristic silence that this is your first time hearing any of this?" I could almost see the self-satisfied grin on Marta's face. I'd seen it before. I knew it well. "My informed opinion, which none of the evidence proves wrong, is that Tim Ayers simply got tired of fighting a losing battle and checked himself out. We didn't find a note, but that's inconclusive. Bottom line, there's no smoking gun. I know because I looked for it, and didn't find it. Now everybody's okay with moving on, except for your pal Byson. When he kept harping on about murder and killers, I even asked him, why anyone would go to the trouble of killing a dying man?"

"What'd he say?"

Marta chuckled. "He didn't have an answer for that one, and neither do I."

"You trust the brother? He could have been playing you. He and Tim weren't close."

"I don't get along with my brother, Manuel, either," Marta said, "but I wouldn't kill him, at least not intentionally. The brother, Stephen, seemed okay enough, a little stiff in the neck for my taste, but I got the impression all this came as sort of a relief."

"Where was he the night Tim died, do you know?" I asked.

I heard a door open and male voices speaking loudly. Marta said nothing. Then the voices trailed away.

"You're in the stairwell?"

"It's what you've reduced me to," she shot back. "You've worked suicides." There was a note of challenge in her tone. "How many suspects did *you* question?"

I massaged my forehead, just above the eyebrows, where a headache was starting to form. "Is the boat still at the marina?"

"Far as I know. We had no cause to haul it away. Satisfied now? Or would you like to poach another of my cases? I've got a desk full. You can take your pick."

"Again, I do *not* poach."

"Yeah, you do. Now tell Byson to get lost."

The line went dead. Glowering, feeling put upon, lamenting the time I'd wasted wallowing in guilt and worry for someone I barely knew, I grabbed my jacket and headed to Deek's to speak to Jung about the virtues of forthrightness. God help the man.

Chapter 6

I flew through the door, scanned the place, and found Muna holding up Deek's counter, sipping coffee out of a mug, the aroma of fried eggs, bacon, and hash browns floating over the tables. The few diners present looked like they'd been sufficiently attended to, at least for the moment, so Muna was taking a break. No sign of Adele. Looked like this time her huffy resignation might stick.

"Where's Jung?"

Muna's brows lifted. "And hello to you, too, Miss I Was Raised By Wolves."

"Good morning, Muna. And how are you this fine, wonderful morning?"

"Oh, can't complain." She spoke as if she had all day to talk about it. "All you can do is hang in and hope it gets better, right?"

"Right." I let a beat pass. "Where's Jung?"

"Don't know. But when he didn't show up this morning, Deek fired him. He left you something, though. I've been calling you all morning, kept getting your voice mail." She pointed behind me, toward a booth. I turned to find a scruffy-looking twentysomething coloring the paper menu reserved for toddlers, a chocolate shake next to him. I turned back to Muna. "He left me a person?"

"Says his name is Bucky T. Something. I'm sure he said more than that, but he tickled me so, I missed the rest of it. He's been here a couple hours. That's his third shake and his second kiddie menu. I think the word game stumped him, so he moved on to the coloring portion about a half hour ago. What's going on?"

I turned back to the scruffy boy, who appeared consumed by his coloring project. "No idea, but I'm going to need Jung's phone number and address."

"Mr. Byson doesn't have a phone, but I think I've got his address here somewhere. You see to him, and I'll get it for you. And if Mr. Crayons knows what's good for him, he better have money for those shakes. Deek ain't a freebies kind of person."

Bucky was short and squat with a prominent widow's peak and heavily hooded eyelids, which gave him the look of a sloth-like basset hound. I stood at the booth, towering over him, watching as he colored an apple in orange crayon.

"Bucky T.?"

He looked up. "Yeah?"

"I'm Cass Raines. You're here to see me?"

His face brightened, his eyes danced. "Oh, yeah, sure am." He got to his feet, smoothing out his faded Grateful Dead T-shirt and grungy jeans. "Hi. Name's Bucky T., but my friends just call me Buck." He reached into his front pocket, pulled out a folded piece of paper. "Special delivery from one Mr. Jung Byson, one of my main bros." He handed it to me, then sat back down and took a long swig of shake. I slid in across from him, watching him work the thick liquid through the red-and-white-striped straw.

"Go on. Open it," he said when he came up for air. "Dude was totally jazzed about your getting it ASAP." He folded his chunky fingers over a paunchy middle, relaxing as though he had all day to wait. He reminded me a lot of Jung.

"When did he give you this?"

Bucky snorted. "Whoa. That was like a million years ago. I'd have to think long and hard to remember the deets."

I folded my hands on the table, the note in front of me. "Whenever you're ready." But instead of starting in on the "long and hard," Bucky T. just sat there staring at me, a blank look on his face. He frowned. "What's today again?"

"Friday," I said.

He smiled, nodded. "Right. I knew that. Then yesterday. That'd be Thursday, right?"

"Jung gave you the note *yesterday*." I wanted to be sure.

Bucky pressed his eyes closed, thought about it. "Yep. Late. He came by, tossed the stones at my window, and I . . ."

I held up a hand to stop him. " 'Stones'?"

Bucky blinked, smiled. "The bell's out at my place. Stones work just as good if you hit the right spot and you're tuned in to the message."

"*What?* Never mind." I waved for him to continue. "Go on."

"Dude tosses the stones, I heard them, seeing as I was tuned in." He winked as though sharing a secret. "I opened the door. There dude is. Says he's got something he wants delivered to you. He hands it over. Says if you weren't at your office, I was to come here and wait because you'd eventually stop in. Oh, then he said he didn't want me dicking around with it, pardon my parlance, which I kinda took offense to. I'm all about the follow-through."

"I was *in* my office," I said. "In fact, I just came from there."

Bucky blinked again, nothing seemed to be going on behind his glassy eyes. He shrugged. "I was starved. I figured I'd flip it and wait for you here."

Jung Byson was weird enough. Now there was Bucky T. to contend with. Where did they grow these kids? "Do you know where Jung is now?"

"Nah. He dropped the note, turned down some brews and some primo . . . never mind . . . which is so not like the dude, then he booked it. He said he had to get back out there."

"Out where?"

Bucky took another long draw from his straw. He had to really work at it. "Didn't say, and I didn't ask. I took it in general terms, you know, out there . . . in the world . . . mingling with humanity. Dude seemed committed to it." Bucky scanned the diner. "This looks like a cool place."

"It isn't." I unfolded the paper, read it: *I thought at least you'd believe me, but it doesn't matter. I'll prove I'm right, then you'll see. If you've changed your mind, though, tell Buck. He knows how to get in touch.* I groaned. Who knew flaky Jung could plunge the knife so deep?

"Something heavy?" Bucky asked. "You look a little weirded out."

I held up the note, waved it. "Jung says you know how to get in touch?"

Bucky nodded. "Dude's renting my cell. I guess I could maybe call it."

I took a moment, studied Bucky. "Do you also know where he lives?"

"Sure."

I pointed to the crayons and paper on the table. "Write his address down." I reached into my pocket and dug out my cell. "What's your number?" I dialed while Bucky recited it, and then waited while the phone rang. Folded notes, disappearing delivery boys, spacey messengers, there wasn't this much intrigue in a le Carré novel.

"Yeah?" It was Jung.

"Jung, what are you doing? Forget it. Whatever it is, stop doing it."

"Did you change your mind? Will you take my case?"

"Jung, you have no case. Look, I asked around as a favor to

you. Your friend's death was a tragic accident, and you're just going to have to accept it. But since we're on it, you conveniently left out a few things about Tim, like the fact that he was dying of cancer."

There was a long pause before Jung spoke again. "If I'd told you that, you never would have listened in the first place."

I looked over the table at Bucky. He was back to the shake, his cheeks sunken in midway through a long draw, but seemingly mesmerized by the call. "Jung, there is no murderer out there."

"You're wrong. The police are wrong. I told you—"

I cut him off. "Jung, you are going to get yourself in trouble. Where are you?"

"No way. If you're not in, then you're out, and don't need to know. I've got this."

"You've got nothing," I shot back, my voice rising. "Your friend had a history of depression and anxiety, not to mention the fact that he was OCD. Stop and think—"

Jung interrupted me. " 'OCD'? Who told you that?"

"It came from someone who ought to know, his own brother."

Bucky had almost finished his shake and was sweeping the straw along the bottom of the cup to pick up any last remnants. I glared at him. He stopped. "This is news to you?"

"I gotta go," Jung snapped.

"What? No."

The line went dead.

"Jung!" I dialed right back, but the call went to voice mail and I got Bucky's dopey message asking me to "leave my digits."

"That was some major intensity," Bucky said. "Mind if I borrow some of that?"

I glared at him. "What?"

"I'm an actor. Third year. I positively breathe character." He eased into his pocket and pulled out a blue flyer. "See? 'Bucky T. Scanlon, MacGuffins Theatre Troupe, U of C.' I'm playing the hostess with the mostess in our latest revue. I nail it, by the by."

I held my hand out for Jung's address. Bucky had written it

down in purple crayon. Jung didn't live far, but it was still farther than I wanted to go. I didn't want to do this. I was tired. I
needed to work for real pay, not trail around after Jung. I also
had another summons sitting on my desk that I needed to hand
off. That was money in the bank. Jung's little game was a dis-
tracting time-suck I literally could not afford.

Who died and made me his babysitter, anyway? Nobody,
that's who. I scribbled a note on the back of Bucky's menu in
black crayon—a color that matched my current mood. I looked
up to catch Bucky grinning like an idiot. "Does Jung have any
family in town?"

"Dude doesn't have family anywhere. Lost his folks in a car
crash some years back and he's an only kid. I think he mentioned
an old uncle once, but don't hold me to that. Jung's made his
own family. Me too. My folks aren't dead, but they might as well be.
We hang together, along with a few other misfits." He shrugged.
"It's what we call ourselves. It's almost as good."

I felt like whimpering, not for Jung, for me. Jung was getting
under my skin, and I didn't want him there. That his family history closely resembled mine didn't help one bit. Little by little, I
could feel Jung reeling me into his nonsense, and I was fighting it
hard, like a ten-pound catfish caught on a fifty-pound fishing line.

I handed Bucky my note. "When you see him, give him this.
If he calls you, read it to him." I handed him one of my cards.
"All the numbers work. Tell him to use one of them."

Bucky read the note aloud. " 'Knock it off. Call me. I friggin'
mean it. Cass.' " He gave me an off-kilter salute. "Roger that."

After slurping up the last of his shake, he stood. Sheepishly he
patted his pockets, posturing as though he'd misplaced his wallet. It was a timeworn ruse, but Bucky T. had misjudged his en-
vironment. Deek wouldn't just make him wash dishes to pay the
shakes off, he'd likely feed his compact body into the massive
meat grinder he had in the back room, then make hamburger
patties out of what came out of the business end.

"I'm, like, way short here," Bucky offered apologetically.

"Go," I said. "Go quickly, or your friends will never see you again."

Bucky double-timed it to the door. Muna walked up with Jung's address on an index card, though I no longer needed it.

She eyed the table, and then shot me a look that would have melted Bucky T. down to a puddle of human fluid. "Why am I not seeing any money on that table?"

I dug a twenty out of my bag and handed it to her.

She eyed the twenty, eyed me. "No tip? I walked three shakes over here."

I added another ten.

Muna shook her head, tsked, glanced at the door Bucky T. just exited by. "That fool has no idea how close he came to dying today."

I sighed. "Not a clue."

Chapter 7

I headed to Jung's apartment, which was just south of Midway Plaisance, an expansive stretch of dipped lawn running four or five blocks through the U of C campus. You'd have thought with the school being so close to his front door that Jung would have managed to complete his studies in a timely manner and get up and out into the world, yet he seemed hell-bent on matriculating forever. I wondered who was footing the bill.

No one answered when I rang the bell. None of Jung's neighbors answered their bells, either. That made it official. Time-suck. And that was it. I was done. Jung was chronologically an adult. If he wanted to do something stupid, I couldn't stop him. He was just going to have to cinch up his big-boy pants and work it out for himself. I had real work to do.

Just after five that evening, I managed to track down the last target on my list for the law firm. This time I didn't have to buy balloons, giggle, or run for my life. I just walked up to the guy, tapped him on the shoulder, handed it over, said my bit, and walked away; sometimes simple works. To celebrate a job well done, I took my bike out and did a twenty-mile loop of the Lake-front path at a fiendish clip, hoping the speed and the sweat washed thoughts of Jung and Bucky T. out of my head, then I stopped by my office to work up my final bill for Golden, Sprague, and Bendelson. The sooner they got my invoice, the sooner I'd get paid. I added in the charge for Earlene Skipper's helium balloons, too. I wasn't in the charity business.

It was close to seven when I bounded up the stairs to my apartment. No fear of incurring the landlord's wrath for running in the halls, as I was both landlord and owner of the neat little three-flat, bequeathed to me by my grandparents. It'd been a long day and I needed food, a shower, and sleep, in that order. The first two I could guarantee, the third not so much. I'd been working nonstop for weeks, trying to keep busy, distracted, hoping the more I worked, the less time I'd have to focus on Pop being gone, and on Ted Raines, the runaway father he'd had to step in for.

You'd think a guy who walked out on a kid of twelve wouldn't have the nerve to come back half a lifetime later with hat in hand wanting to pick up where he left off, but that's how it happened. Ted Raines, the stranger who shared my DNA, had stood in my front yard days after I'd lost Pop in the most horrendous way wanting to get to know me, wanting to make amends. It didn't end well for either of us. How do you make amends for dumping a 12-year-old off on her grandparents a day after her mother's funeral?

In the months since, he'd taken to writing me letters, none of which I'd opened. If Pop were here, we'd talk everything through over a game of chess. I'd rail and beat back against the man, his nerve, his encroachment, and Pop would gently guide me into meeting him halfway, moving past the anger, embracing forgiveness. But Pop wasn't here. Someone evil yanked him from me. I was going to have to punch my way through on my own, like I did with most things, two steps forward, one back, longing for Pop's calm, quiet counsel.

I sped past the second floor, avoiding the Kallishes' door. It was still difficult seeing their apartment empty. That drive-by had been meant to send a message, to warn me off. It failed, but the nightmares it spawned still startled me awake at night drenched in fear and sweat, my mind reeling with what-ifs. The building was different now, quieter with only me and Mrs. Vincent rattling around in it, and I know she hated the feeling of emptiness just as much as I did.

The phone woke me with a start from a fitful sleep, my head popping up from the pillow, my body on full alert. I squinted at the clock on the bedside table, its glowing numerals cutting through the dark: 3:18. Phone calls at that early hour were rarely good news. Somebody was dead. I grabbed for the receiver, answered.

"Hello?"

"Cass? It's Jung."

I sat up on the side of the bed, panic replaced by a smoldering urge to reach through the phone and pull Jung back through it by his combat boots. "Oh, no, it had better not be. Not the same Jung I've been looking for?"

"No kidding?"

"Where are you?"

"Jail?"

I switched on the bedside lamp. "What?"

"I was sort of arrested."

"What do you mean 'sort of'?"

"Well, like, see . . . I'm not really . . . sure?"

"Are you allowed to leave the building?" I asked.

Jung was quiet for a moment. What was he doing, checking? "Yeah, I'm sure that's a negative."

"Then you're not *sort of* arrested, you've been *arrested*. What'd you do? Never mind, don't tell me. Call a lawyer."

"I'd rather not. I don't think he gets me."

I flopped back on the bed, my head landing on the pillow. "And I do?"

"Well, yeah. I know you. You know me. You know the cops. I figured you could vouch for me."

I stared up at my ceiling, shook my head. "What did you do?"

"Sort of trespassing."

"Stop using the words 'sort of'! What kind of ninny gets arrested for trespassing?"

"Trespassing with a crowbar and a glass cutter?"

I waited. There was more. There was always more with Jung. I also knew that whatever the *more* was, I wasn't going to like it. I closed my eyes, breathed in, preparing myself.

"At the police station," he added.

I bolted up. Crowbar. Glass cutter. Police station? "Jung, why on earth would you try to break into a police station?"

"They wouldn't let me see Tim's file. I thought I might be able to find something they missed, and figured if I could sort of sneak in and . . ."

"Where are you?"

He paused. "The sign says 'Area Four Headquarters'? It's . . ."

I slammed the receiver down with Jung still talking, then sat there for a time, waffling. *Not my problem,* I thought. *Not my deal.* I turned the lamp off, determined to go back to bed, then quickly turned it back on again and began rummaging for my clothes, some on the chair across the room, some on the floor.

"Damn."

I shimmied quickly into a pair of jeans. I didn't know anyone at Area Four anymore. I found my phone and sent Ben a text asking him if he had a contact. I was snaking into a T-shirt and looking around for my shoes when my phone pinged back. He knew a guy. Detective Sammy Hicks. I sent back a hasty thank-you, and then went back to looking for my shoes. I found one and stomped my right foot into it, not bothering with the laces; the other I had to get on my hands and knees to find. A crowbar? Really?

My phone rang. I answered. It was Ben.

"What do you need Hicks for?"

"He pinched an acquaintance of mine for trying to break into Area Four using a crowbar and a glass cutter."

A beat passed. "Are you high?"

I found my other shoe. "He just called. He wants me to vouch for him."

"Seriously, what are you on?"

"It's Jung from the diner."

"That weirdo kid in the clown clothes?"

"That's him." I grabbed my bag from the dresser, headed for the door. "He won't last five minutes in lockup."

Ben sputtered. "No shit. So what are you going down there to do?"

"I'm going down there to wring his neck."

Chapter 8

Area 4 Headquarters was at Harrison and Kedzie and I pulled up to it and sat staring at the front door for a few minutes, composing myself, dreading going inside. The building was all red-brick and reinforced glass. The only way to break into the place would have been to liquefy yourself and ooze through a freaking air vent. Jung was a putz.

The front desk was packed with cops, unusual for four in the morning. A blue wall of uniforms turned to watch me make the long, lonely trip from the front door to the counter. It was obvious from the smirks on their faces that Ben had made a call and everyone knew who I was and why I was there.

"You Raines?" the stocky detective standing front and center asked, jaded eyes holding me to the spot. I nodded. "Then you're here for the criminal mastermind." The cops behind him chuckled. This was the most fun they'd have all tour.

Hicks was an old-timer, a sturdy black man with years of filthy street ground into every pore on his face. The look he gave me told me he'd seen it all a million times over and knew how it all worked. Jung's crowbar assault probably wasn't even enough to raise his heart rate, but formalities still had to be satisfied.

I winced. "How bad is it?"

"On a scale of one to ten? Minus three. For all the elbow grease, he barely scratched the paint."

"Has he been processed and charged?"

"To do all that, the uniforms upstairs would have to stop laughing and talking shit, and that hasn't happened as of yet."

I sighed. "Then he's free to go?"

Hicks scowled, and then shook his head ever so slightly. "Cop a squat. I'll have somebody bring him down." Hicks strolled over to the phone and called upstairs. "We'll be keeping the crowbar and glass cutter," he said when he hung up. "He can come back for the bike he rode to get here."

C'mon, a getaway bike, really? I cleared my throat. "Sounds fair."

Hicks looked at me hard. "You know next time nobody'll be laughing. And you can tell Mickerson this makes us even."

I smiled politely at Hicks, then at the other cops. "I'll relay the message."

Hicks walked away without another word; the cops wandered away, too, getting back to real business. Ben had called ahead, cashing in a favor, and he hadn't done it for Jung, he'd done it for me. Cop favors were precious commodities. A cop never knew when he or she would need an assist from another cop, personal or professional. You didn't squander favors on foolishness. Jung had reeled me into using up one of Ben's, and I was seething by the time he was walked down to me ninety minutes later, dressed in a black T-shirt, black cargo pants, and neon lime running shoes with bright yellow laces. A favor had been done, but that didn't mean the cops had to make it all sunshine and lollipops. There had to be at least a little suffering. I was so angry I didn't trust myself to speak to him, and so we walked in silence out to my car.

"Let me explain," he said as he slid onto the passenger seat.

"Not one word," I hissed, my jaw tightly clenched. "Not a single syllable."

And that's all either of us said the entire way to Jung's place. Pushing the speed limit, I got there in record time. When Jung got out, I barely looked at him as he lingered at the door, as though he wanted to say something but didn't know where to start.

"I know you're mad, but listen," he said. "You're right. I kept some major things back when I talked to you at first. I knew how it looked, and I didn't want you jumping to the wrong conclusion, and you would have, because the police did, and sorry to say it, you think like they do."

I slid him a sideways look, but kept my mouth shut.

"But I don't care what Stephen said. Tim wasn't some basket case that you had to keep eyes on. I wanted a look at the cops' report, is that so bad? I don't have your connections. Sneaking in was the only way I was going to get it. That's all."

I listened as his voice cracked with emotion, and some of my mad melted away. My hand still gripped the steering wheel, though. I wasn't completely sure I wouldn't still throttle him.

"We were planning Tim's memorial, *with him.* We had musicians, poets, dancers, the whole nine, lined up for one awesome send-off. Why would he go through the trouble of all that, if he planned on killing himself? And why put together a final trip to St. Maarten? He was shoving off next week. I know because I was going with him, along with a couple of other buds. My stuff's packed and ready to go. That's why he was giving stuff away. He was clearing things out, lightening his load. Maybe I should have told you, but I really didn't think I had to. I thought you'd believe me and trust that I knew him better than the cops did, but you didn't. You don't."

Jung looked like a lost puppy left out in the rain. Obviously, he hadn't thought the break-in through. He had no clue what he was doing. There was nobody on the street but the two of us. I turned and stared at him as he stood there on the curb. *This is it,* I thought. *This is the moment.* Either I'd drive away and leave him and Tim Ayers behind, or I wouldn't. Everything about the case seemed locked up tight. Marta was a good detective, solid. Not much got by her, but a planned memorial, a trip to the Caribbean, and what about the lack of fingerprints? That still bothered me. I wondered why it didn't bother Marta. Every inch of Ayers's boat would have been checked. How'd he get over the side without touching anything? I idled for a time, my eyes peering through the windshield, aware that Jung was watching me sit there, waiting for me to decide.

Dying didn't mean despondent, but that's exactly how Tim's brother described him to Marta. Something was off, but Marta had a point. Who'd go to the trouble of killing a dying man? She'd been adamant that the logic in the statement validated her theory of either accidental drowning or suicide, which she did not press, out of respect for Tim's family and pressure from her bosses. Could Tim's death have been murder?

I turned to Jung. "Who'd want to kill a dying man?" It was the question Marta had posed to me. I didn't have an answer then, or now.

His eager eyes widened, appearing as though I'd startled him by speaking. "Somebody who didn't know he was dying. That lets out everybody who knew him, though, right? This could have been, like, a kidnapping gone bad. Somebody out for money, but Tim gets away somehow? Only he didn't."

I thought for a moment. A kidnapping? I hadn't thought of that angle. It was a possibility, though. The Ayerses had tons of money. It wouldn't be a stretch to believe somebody out there might have wanted a piece of it. I let out a deep sigh, a mournful exhale. I'd wanted easy work I could do without thinking too much about it. This wasn't it, not by a long shot. I'd have to go up against the police department again, up against Marta specifically, and no way was she going to make that easy. I had a very bad habit of tilting at windmills, poking the bear. *Why? What the hell is wrong with me?* Why couldn't I let a loose thread be, why'd I always have to be the one to worry it? Jung Byson, sandwich guy. Nobody wipes their prints before downing a lethal dose of pills, hurling themselves off a bridge, or drinking themselves blind and jumping into a cold, dark lake. So, in Tim's case, if he didn't do it, who did? Who didn't want to leave any trace of themselves behind?

"My office. Monday morning. Ten," I said resignedly. "We're going to have a long talk."

Jung nodded, then closed the door and stepped back, watching as I sped away.

Chapter 9

Jung stepped into my office on Monday as though he hadn't woken me up at 3 a.m. the previous Saturday and forced me down to Area 4 to get laughed at by battle-worn cops. I'd spent all day Sunday getting my mind right for this meeting. I was still a little put out, but at least now I was ready to hear his side of things. I shut down my computer and gestured toward the client chair facing my desk, watching as he folded his skinny body into the seat.

He stared at me sheepishly. "So, about what happened?"

"First, explain the shoes."

Jung glanced down at his feet. He was wearing flip-flops.

"Not those," I said. "At Area 4. You dressed all in black, you brought along a crowbar. Your shoes were neon green with yellow laces."

He blinked. Lost.

"Conspicuous," I said. "Rookie move."

"I didn't think of that." It'd been a while since I'd seen a face as blank as Jung's was now. Even Bucky T.'s hadn't come this close. "The shoes are new. I needed to break them in."

I shook my head. It was sad, really. Jung Byson, clueless, out in the world, a babe in the woods. "Tell me what you think you know."

Jung's eyes met mine. "You're still mad."

"I've passed mad. Don't make me go back for it. Go."

"Okay. I *know* Tim didn't just drown. I *know* whoever did this to him he had to, at least, know them a little. He didn't let just anyone on his boat. The *Safe Passage,* he said, was a no-asshole zone. When you blew me off, I went by there, tried talking to his neighbors. I thought maybe they saw something without realizing they saw it, you know? That happens all the time." Jung paused, maybe to make sure I was listening. I was. Intently.

"And?" I prompted.

"Like I said, most of them are real old, at least sixty. None of them had good things to say. They didn't like Tim keeping up all the party noise. He left behind some hard feelings. They didn't like me asking questions, either. One guy even threatened to call the police. But it got me thinking, if Tim got plastered, like they say, what happened to all the bottles? At the marina, the one cop who'd actually talked to me like a person said they didn't find anything like that. So how'd he get shit-faced? That's something, right?"

I leaned forward in my chair, folded my hands on the desk. "Maybe he threw them over the side when he finished them and they sank to the bottom of the lake. Maybe he got shit-faced someplace else and weaved his way home."

Jung shot me an incredulous look. "In a thunderstorm? Shit-faced? On all the meds he was taking to keep himself going?"

"If he were in an altered state . . ." I left the sentence unfinished. Jung knew where I was going with it.

"Okay, I know. Or maybe the killer took them so no one would know he was there, because maybe they had his prints on them somewhere?"

"Saturday you mentioned a possible kidnapping. Did Tim worry about that? Take precautions? Had he encountered any such attempts before?"

Jung shook his head. "It was just an idea. I don't think Tim ever worried about that or bothered too much with security. He kept things low-key. But I guess it could have happened."

"Was he OCD, or not?"

Jung snorted derisively, then dug into his pockets and came up with a stack of photographs, fanning them out on my desk. "That's Stephen's lie and I can prove it. These are photos of our first dorm room, undergrad, and a few of a recent party at Tim's. Does that look like the room or the boat of a guy with OCD?"

I leaned over to get a closer look. The dorm room looked like a bomb exploded in the center of it: beds unmade, clothes discarded everywhere, stacks of dirty dishes. The party pictures looked almost as bad.

"And that's before the party even got going." Jung sat back and watched for my reaction. "People with OCD go bananas if a paper clip's out of place. They scrub their hands a hundred times a day, repeat the same action over and over in exactly the same sequence. Tim didn't have any of that, and I've known him for practically forever. I don't think he even knew how to make his own bed. Lucky for him, the boat was easy to keep straight, when he thought to do it. Stephen sold the police a line and they bought it."

I pushed the photos back toward him. "Why would his brother do that?"

"Resentment. Stephen wanted everything to himself, the money, his father's love and attention, all of it. Tim couldn't keep up—he never fit in. Eventually he gave up trying."

"What do you mean 'fit in'?"

Jung shrugged. "Wealthy family, influential circles, there are . . . expectations. Stephen toed the party line, followed in his father's footsteps, never made waves. Tim tried, but couldn't hack it in the end. He was an artist. He was gay. They didn't approve of either. Add to that, Tim didn't give a shit about his family's legacy. When his father died, he had a choice, go with the flow or get the hell out. He got the hell out. That's when his mother froze him out. Stephen too. Then he got cut off from the money, and he had to go it alone. His father left him the boat outright, though, so Tim decided to live on it."

"How'd he get by?"

"He worked odd jobs, a year here, a year there. He sometimes would sell a painting or two. Mostly, I think, he lived off his insurance. He called it a vertical settlement? Sounded strange to me, but he seemed stoked about it. He said it gave him his insurance money upfront, enough to get by on, instead of it coming in after he died when he couldn't use it? It's legal. He was doing okay out there on the lake." He shook his head, grit his teeth. "Man, Stephen's a real tool. I wish I could punch his face right now."

So much for Swami Rain and Jung's yogi business, I thought, smiling. I scribbled *viatical settlement* on a notepad so I could check it out later. "What did Tim have that somebody might want?"

Jung leaned forward, his head in his hands, out of his element, in way over his head. "The only important thing he had was time, and what kind of creep would take that from him?" He looked up, searched my face. "So? What do you think? I convinced you, right? Please, you have to help me here."

"There are some inconsistencies. Maybe they mean something, maybe they don't."

Jung slid onto the edge of his seat. "So you're definitely in, right? Like *in* 'in'?"

I thought it over. "I'll take a look. No promises. If I come up with nothing, I'm out, but, more important, *you're* out. Got it?"

Jung grinned, pumped his fists, and then reached into his pack and pulled out a checkbook with the symbol for yin and yang on the cover. Leave it to Jung to flake up a check. "You wouldn't take my cash before, so I brought a check this time. It's more professional, anyway. I know I'm right about this. I can feel it. How much?"

I charged up to two hundred dollars an hour, depending on the complexity of the case, but I didn't think asking around about Tim Ayers rose to the level of *complex*; besides Jung slung sandwiches for a living. How much could he afford to pay? I calculated the discount in my head. "Let's round it off to an even hundred." I was taking a bath on the deal.

He wrote out the check and handed it to me, beaming like a four-year-old buying cotton candy at the circus. "We're going to catch a freaking murderer."

"No *we*. *Me*. And that's *maybe*," I clarified emphatically. "Condition two. You stay out of my way."

His face fell. "What? But . . ."

"Out of my way, or I drop this right now."

He began to fidget in the chair, his eyes quickly scanning the office. I could almost see him trying to think up a way to circumvent my conditions.

"I want to hear you say the words, Jung."

"Fine. Out of your way."

I slid a piece of paper over to him and a pen, then reached into my drawer and pulled out a standard contract. Business was business.

"Good, now give me Stephen Ayers's information and the names of anyone Tim might have had a beef with—friends, partners, all of it. Then read and sign the contract."

"Stephen won't see you. He's way too important for that." He looked the contract over. "And is this really necessary? It looks, like, official."

I slid Jung's New Age check into my top drawer. "Just write. Let me worry about getting to Ayers. And, yes, it's necessary, and it *is* official. Read it. Sign it. Then go about your business. If I need you, I'll call Bucky's phone or buy a bag of rocks."

Jung and I shook on the deal. We were now, for better or for worse, client and operative.

And I already regretted it.

Chapter 10

Even though it was just the first week in June and summer was officially weeks off, Chicago was in high gear, anticipating the calendar's formal pronouncement. The Loop, the city's very public face, was already dolled up for the spate of fests, concerts, tourists, construction, and traffic snarls to come. All of it was as much a part of a Chicago summer as the ivy on the walls at Wrigley, fried ice cream at the Taste, or the one-note saxophonist who played "Harlem Nocturne" on the Michigan Avenue Bridge for dull nickels. Welcome to the glittering Land of Oz.

I eased into DuSable Marina's lot and pulled up to the yacht club, following the sign to the office around the side. It was one of those sunny, breezy, lazy days that compelled people to call in sick or dead at their jobs. However, it didn't appear that a lot of boats were taking advantage of the calm waters. Most of the slips were full, and the parking lot hadn't a single car in it.

Steady traffic whizzed by on Lake Shore Drive, and the pedestrian paths circling the marina were jammed with joggers, bikers, and striders, none of them giving a fig about Tim Ayers. I pushed open the office door, triggering a tiny bell above it, me burning through Jung's hundred bucks. "Yeah, hold on. Be right there." A man's voice came from the back room. I waited at a counter cluttered by boating paraphernalia: pamphlets on water safety, info on slip fees, and big, thick rope that looked strong enough to wrangle in a T. rex. A small fan farther down blew a mean wedge of hot air around, fluttering the metal window blinds and spreading the smells of algae, seaweed, and diesel oil. I eased my sunglasses off, tucked them into a pocket, and kept my breathing light.

After a time, a tugboat of a man, with a scruffy gray beard, walked out of the back. He was dressed in rumpled jeans and a faded polo shirt, the name of the yacht club stitched across the right breast pocket. On top of his ball-shaped head sat a battered captain's hat, and his tight, round stomach hung well over a wide leather belt that must have been working overtime to hold up its end of things. The man took one look at me, registered surprise, and then followed it up with a flicker of caution. I watched as he slipped a key out of his pants pocket and locked the door behind him before slipping the key back.

"I thought you tecs were done. What's the problem now?"

He padded over to the counter, stood facing me. His suncracked skin looked like he'd been left out in the elements fifty years too long, the wrinkles as deep as river channels. I thought the hat was taking the nautical theme a bit too far, but maybe it came with the job, like blue shirts at the Apple Store. In a far corner, an old office phone sat on a desk piled high with newspapers, boating mags, and more thick rope tied in odd knots. After a full sweep, my eyes settled on a large glass container down the counter a ways. The sign on it read TIPS. I wondered what the man possibly did to warrant a gratuity.

I handed him my card and waited while he read it. He looked from it to me, then blinked, trying to work it through. Maybe he'd never encountered a working PI before, or was it that I was a female PI? Or perhaps he just didn't get a lot of black chicks down here in the old marina office.

"I'd like to ask you a few questions," I said, "about Tim Ayers."

He flicked a look at the card again. "Huh, I wouldn't have pegged you for a private peeper. You got *cop* written all over you. My Spidey senses must be off." He held out his free hand for a shake. I took it.

"Quint Anderson. Cap, if you want to get familiar." He pointed to the captain's hat, then took a full, and very obvious, sweep of me. "Nope, you don't look like a peeper at all."

I met his eyes again when they made their way back up to my face. I'd already taken my sweep when he ambled over. Only fair.

"Tim Ayers," I repeated.

"Heard you."

Cap looked like he drank a lot. His nose was splotchy, bulbous, and spider veins crisscrossed flushed cheeks. I got a faint whiff of hard liquor, masked some by bath soap and aftershave. Watery dark eyes met mine and held. Sneaky. That's how I'd describe the look. Like he was a banker of secrets, but dealt only in deposits, not withdrawals. That didn't bode well for my getting anything useful, but I wasn't about to let things go without at least giving it a shot.

His chin flicked upward; he cocked his big head. "You working for somebody, or just nosing around freelance?"

I smiled. "I'm not at liberty to say. What can you tell me about Ayers? Who'd he hang out with around here? Did he have any run-ins?"

Cap ran a beefy hand along his chin scruff, the bristling sound of it loudly audible on my side of the messy counter. His hands were deeply calloused and they looked like they'd been that way for half his life. "You don't look like a peeper, but you sure talk like one. Trolling for dirt right under the cops' noses, huh?"

I took a moment. "Trolling for dirt" kind of chafed, but I'd get nowhere antagonizing the man. "You knew Mr. Ayers. You know this place. You must know something the cops don't."

Cap rolled his eyes. "*Mr.* Ayers? Well, fa-la-la. All I know is Mr. High and Mighty Ayers was a real piece of work."

I ignored the mocking tone. It was obvious there was no love lost between the two men. Jung had said as much; something to do with Tim's partying causing a problem for his neighbors. Cap didn't look too broken up over Tim's passing. In fact, the contrary appeared to be true. He seemed almost giddy that Tim was gone and out of his hair. I'd never understand why some people could get turned on by violent death, and approach it in a party mood, as though it were a sideshow attraction they'd paid good money to see. Maybe it was just that they hadn't seen enough of it, or seen it at its worst. I had. I'd seen more than enough.

"I heard he wasn't very popular."

Cap stared, nodded slightly. "Oh? Who'd you get that from?"

I didn't answer.

"Right, you're not at liberty to say. Got it."

I studied him for a time, hoping to find a glimmer of feeling, but found nothing remotely like it. The eyes, the color of cold black coffee, stared back at me, without a single spark of empathy in them, as if we were discussing something trivial and not the tragic death of a young man.

"Ayers is dead," I said. "I'd think you'd be interested in knowing how and why."

"Know how. Cops say he got hammered and slipped clear off his own deck. Why?" He shrugged. "Makes no difference. Dead's dead."

"Were you here the night he died? Maybe you saw something odd, something that stands out?"

Cap watched me with keen interest, his eyes all but dancing. He was enjoying himself quite a lot. "Look, I told the cops all that already. Telling you, well, that's something different."

He rocked back on his heels, his grin mischievous, roguish. He then quietly moved down the counter to grab the tip jar and walk it back. He placed it between us, turning the jar so I could read the sign on it, nudging it closer to me. I didn't have to be a genius to see how this was going to go.

"I could talk or not, up to you," he said. He placed a proprietary hand on the jar and waited while I thought it over. Maybe he knew something, maybe he didn't. I wouldn't know unless he talked, and he wasn't going to unless I fed the jar.

"Or you could decide to be a decent human being and answer my questions . . . in the interest of getting to the truth."

Cap scoffed, his thin lips twisting into a distasteful sneer. He tapped the jar.

I sighed. "Yeah, that's what I thought." I slid my wallet out of my bag and tossed a twenty inside. Cap showed his appreciation for the forced donation with a little head nod, but his hand stayed where it was. I'd have to feed the jar again.

"Wasn't here," he said. "Like I told the cops, I locked up early. I didn't hear about Ayers or his boat till the next morning when I found cops clomping all over the place. In fact, I hadn't seen the guy in almost a week before he went over, which was fine by me."

"Security cameras didn't pick up anyone boarding Ayers's boat because of the storm. Maybe they picked up something before the storm got going? A strange car in the lot? Someone unfamiliar walking near the slips? Or maybe the cameras weren't working at all?"

"Don't fiddle with the cameras. They're run by an outside outfit. Tech, something. If the cameras petered out, that's on them, not me. Besides, they wouldn't have done any good. They're pointed the opposite direction to cover the paths and the lot, hoping to cut down on property theft and the like. Folks who tie up here don't want cameras pointed right at their top decks. A lot goes on out there they don't want their wives or their husbands knowing about, if you get my drift."

"There's a lot of that going around?"

"Lady, there's a lot of *everything* going around. Only this set doesn't get rousted by the cops."

"How'd you and Ayers get along?"

"Couldn't stand him. I don't like any of them out there, quiet as it's kept. I hate how they prance around here on those prissy boats, making all kinds of demands. They love being catered to. Ayers? In his twenties and he's lounging around on a seventy-footer, as sleek as anything."

Seventy feet sounded big, though I had absolutely no frame of reference. Cap caught my confused look.

"I'd call that a 'yacht,'" he said, disdain dripping from every word. "Half a mil, easy, and that's before you put your personal stink on it with your customizing. They all do that. It's ego, pure and simple. Anyway, I steer clear. I do what they pay me for and leave them to it."

"Why didn't Ayers fit in?" I asked. "This seems like it'd be his kind of crowd. Well-heeled."

"'Square peg, round hole' situation. The old-schoolers out there like it slow and quiet. Ayers burned his candle like it had three ends instead of two." He cocked a thumb behind him. "I got a stack of noise complaints over there halfway to the ceiling with his name on 'em. Parties went on down there on the regular, grungy visitors popping in and out at all hours. Typical rich kid, always out for a good time."

"He was ill," I said. "Dying." Cap's face registered slight surprise, but little else. "You didn't know?"

"No reason I would. Like I said, I steer clear. Explains a lot, though. Guess he was trying to cram it all in before he kicked it. That wouldn't have mattered to these marshmallows, though. They want what they want and they wanted him gone by hook or by crook, and with what they pay to anchor up here, they figure that gives them the right to say what goes."

"So why didn't they kick him out?"

Cap sniffed. "Because his last name was Ayers, that's why."

I thought for a moment, looking for an angle. "Anyone want him gone so badly they'd do something besides gripe about it?"

Cap's eyebrows flicked up. "*That's* what you think happened? That one of those Cartier cream puffs offed him?" He let out a gurgled roar of a laugh as dry as leaves. It sounded like it started way down at the balls of his feet and bubbled up through a constricted esophagus caked by years of nicotine and whiskey gunk. The raspy report crawled under my skin and burrowed deep.

When he was done, he said, "Look, PI, believe me, nobody out there's got the stones to kill a guy, even if it was Ayers."

I eyed the Navy tats peeking out from under the sleeves of his shirt. He worked at a marina. He served on the water. "You could easily have taken his boat out."

"*Me?*" The laughing started up again. I waited for him to stop, though patience wasn't my strong suit. "You come right out and accuse me of tossing him over? You got some balls." He shook his head. "Look, maybe you could've gotten me to go along with the crazy idea somebody killed him, if I didn't know for a fact that Ayers was off his rocker. You trying to prove different, well, that's just a waste of your time and somebody else's money. End of story."

"'Off his rocker'?"

"And *that's* from a reliable source."

I had a good idea, but asked, anyway. "What reliable source?"

Cap shook his head, tapped the jar. "Typical peeper. You don't want to give any information, but you sure want to get it."

"Your source wouldn't by any chance be his brother, Stephen, would it?"

Cap's face fell. I'd guessed right. Then suddenly he brightened again. He'd obviously thought of a different angle. "All right, but you got no idea what he wanted, or what he said. Only I got that. So? What's it gonna be?"

Another twenty left my reluctant hand.

Cap grinned. "He called himself doing a wellness check, and I got a real earful, let me tell you. Yakked his head off. Tells me Tim suffered from real bad depression and got into drugs big-time before he supposedly straightened himself out. Sounded like looking after him was a full-time job for the family, what with them bailing him out of one thing after the next. This Stephen says he even spent time in a mental institution. And, well, considering what he did to himself . . ."

"Why'd he stop in here? Why not go straight to Tim's boat?"

Cap shrugged. "You'll have to ask him. Never saw him before, or since. The family couldn't even be bothered to talk to the cops when they found the body and boat drifting. They sent their lawyer. Guess that's how those people handle things. This Stephen talked a blue streak, though, like I said. Left his card and asked me to call if I saw anything strange. Guess it looks like he nailed that on the head."

This time, it was my turn to eye the jar, as I wondered how much Cap had gotten from Stephen Ayers in return for promising to make that call.

"I could show you the card," Cap said, "but it's gonna cost ya." His eyes danced. He wanted another twenty. Fat chance. I had Jung. He knew Stephen and how to get in touch with him.

I smiled. "I don't need to see it. Anyone else come in here asking about Tim, besides Stephen?"

Cap clamped his lips shut. So far there was forty dollars in the jar and a question hanging. Cap stood there, hand on the jar, mouth closed, waiting me out. I'd stiffed him on the last exchange. The set of his jaw told me he wasn't about to let that happen again. The seconds ticked by. Only a wide streak of stubbornness kept me from dropping more money in the jar, and the money wasn't even mine. I was spending Jung's retainer, but still it galled me to give it up. My eyes narrowed. Cap didn't look at all worried that I might not play along.

"Okay, let's try this one," I said. "You mentioned visitors?"

"One particularly interesting one," Cap said. And that's all he said.

I glowered, slowly peeled off another twenty, watching as his glacial expression warmed. He was a greedy old goat.

"A woman. I don't remember the face, just the wiggle. Wore a suit and carried a briefcase, looking like business. Redhead. Real nice caboose."

Cap's eyes began to wander again from my face downward. I cleared my throat and they jumped back up again. "When was this?"

"The same day the brother stopped by, only a little later. She headed straight for his slip. I tracked her through the window, enjoyed the view."

I blew out a breath. Universally hated, a resentful brother conducting a wellness check, a mysterious redhead with a nice wiggle, a history of depression and drug abuse—what was Jung trying to get me into? I checked my watch. There was still way too much time on Jung's meter.

"Did you notice anyone strange hanging around Tim's boat?" Cap shook his head, smiled.

"How about Ayers's paperwork. Do you still have it?" I wanted to see if Tim had named anyone else besides his family as emergency contacts, someone who might have had reason to kill him. "It should have his emergency contacts on it, a permanent address?" Cap shot me an empty stare. He was likely still on the redhead's caboose.

"Yep."

He didn't move. I didn't, either. Ditto the jar with Jung's sixty in its belly. My eyes hardened. No smile. "I'd like to take a look at it."

Cap stood his ground; my wallet stayed closed. If I had to stand here all day, I would. It was the principle of the thing. Nothing moved except the undulating fan down the counter and the flutter of the blinds. Cap blinked first. Frowning, he slowly pulled back the jar.

"I guess it's no good to me. This one's on the house." He padded back to the cluttered table, opened a bottom drawer and rifled around some, finally pulling out a couple sheets stapled at the top left corner. "This is it."

"It doesn't look like much," I said.

"Yeah, well, renting a slip's not like buying a house." He walked the papers back and watched as I read through them. It didn't take long. I didn't think I'd need Tim's Social Security number or his bank account info, but I made note of them, anyway. Tim hadn't listed a permanent address, apparently the boat was his one and only. I groaned when I got to the line for emergency contact. Tim had chosen Jung. Dejection gave way to lighter spirits, however, when the back of the sheet held the phone number and address of an Elizabeth Ayers, identified as Tim's mother. That would save me some time.

I handed the sheets back. "Would you mind making a copy?"

Cap flicked a look at the jar. I reached over and shoved the jar down the counter, sending it flying like a slippery mug of sarsaparilla across the bar of an Old West saloon. "We're done with the jar. A copy, please. Let's, at least, try to pretend you give a damn a man died on your patch."

Whatever Cap saw in my face, he didn't challenge. Instead, he shuffled over to the ancient copier and began feeding the pages in as the machine groaned and wheezed in protest. It had to be twenty years old by the look of it. He walked back and handed the sheets to me. I folded them, slid them into my bag.

"You sure about that card? For another twenty, it's all yours. Like I said, the brother was really looking out. 'Course, Tim didn't see it that way." He was trying to goad me into feeding the jar again. No deal. I'd ask Stephen about his brother myself.

"What's in the back room?" I asked.

Cap stopped smiling. "What?" His eyes held steady, almost too steady, as though he were trying to win a "who'll blink first" contest. "The back room?"

Liars always did that; they answered a question with a question. Buying time. I pointed at the door. "Yeah, *that* back room. The one you locked. You slid the key into your front right pocket." He didn't blink. I could tell he wanted to, but he didn't.

"Something important? Extra keys to the boats? Lockers, maybe, for stowing emergency equipment?"

Cap recovered, smiled wide. "Boy, you have a rich imagination, don't you? That's the storage room. Nothing back there but paper for that crap copier, some old buoys, a radio for the Cubs games." He slid his hand into his pocket. Was he feeling for the key, reassuring himself it was still there? He winked, tried for charming. "Good spot for a nap, too, but don't tell anybody."

I stared at him, really looked, waiting for it to get uncomfortable for him. When it did, I gave him another moment to sit with it, and then I broke the connection.

"Thanks for your time. Where would I find Tim's boat? The *Safe Passage*?"

I could actually see relief sweep over Cap's face. He padded over, grabbed the jar, and plucked out the money. "Slip eleven. Follow the numbers."

I eased on my sunglasses, headed out. Paper for the copier, old buoys. *Right.*

Chapter 11

I found the boat right where Cap said it was, and she was something to look at, too: white fiberglass, teak decks, silver rails shining like diamonds in the sun. Half a mil, Cap said. It looked it. The *Aubrey Rose* and the *Miraculous* were the two boats on either side of Ayers's ship of dreams. Neither was anywhere near as big or as jaw dropping. That alone could have bred a certain amount of resentment. Was "boat envy" a thing? Wrought-iron gates closed off the narrow walkways between each vessel. Through the gate, I checked out the other boats, but there didn't appear to be anyone on board either one. The gate blocked off the narrow paths between slips, barring trespass; only when I tried the gate, it was unlocked. I didn't question the breech. I wasn't one to look a "gift lock" in the mouth.

I walked along the side of the *Safe Passage,* looking for a ramp, a rope, a conveyor belt. I didn't exactly know how people got on boats this big. Maybe smiling cherubs lifted you up on a big heavenly cloud. I finally found a ladder, grabbed it, and tested it for sturdiness. After a quick check for busybodies or marina security, I slung my bag cross-body over my chest, and then put hands and feet to ladder rungs and started up. Some would call it "trespassing"; I called it "taking advantage of a golden opportunity."

It was all in the perspective. Besides, my intentions were noble. The only thing I hoped to come away with was information. I wasn't interested in Tim's valuables.

Up and in, I dusted my hands off and leaned over the side, gauging the distance back down. It was manageable. If I had to jump, I wouldn't die. Another short ladder led up to the part of the boat where all the steering happened. There was probably a name for it, but I wasn't nautical, so the term was not at my immediate disposal. I tested that ladder, too, then started up, passing the time by reciting all the seafaring expressions I knew: "shiver me timbers," "batten down the hatches," "raise the yardarm," "man overboard," "blow me down." That last one sounded a little kinky.

There wasn't much walking-around room up top. The big steering wheel was worth the trip, though. Two green leather chairs behind it matched the hunter green of the canopy. It's the little touches that make a yacht a home. Climbing down to the deck again, I eased around the back. The police tape at the cabin door sent a clear message, and I stood for a moment, debating whether to heed it or not. Marta was sure Tim had killed himself, though she'd seen fit to do his family a solid by smoothing it all over. The lack of prints still bothered me, though. I stared at the tape. At this point, it was merely there to discourage looters and looky-loos. I was neither, so I could reason that the tape wasn't meant for me. It was PI logic, different from cop logic, but legit nonetheless. I turned the knob. The door was locked. And *that* was the universe's big smackdown.

I checked around to see if anyone was looking, then eased my picklocks out of my bag. I slid in the pick, felt around for the tumblers, and gently jockeyed it up and down, feeling for the give, until I heard the simple lock pop free. It took less than a minute. I pushed the door open, ducked under the tape, and slipped inside, pulling out a compact flashlight and easing my way down the short, narrow steps.

It was musty and overly warm down below, as if the boat had

been closed up tight for weeks, and I immediately felt pinned in, detecting a subtle whiff of seaweed and something else . . . turpentine? I crept up to the kitchen, which was almost as big as the one in my apartment, marveling at the creative use of space. Every pot and pan, knife and fork, had a nook, cranny, or slot, and each cabinet was firmly secured. I didn't see any hatches needing battening. Padding off toward the boat's pointy end, I swept my beam along, keeping it well below window level. I felt immediately claustrophobic, though I could tell efforts had been made to make the space down below feel and look far more spacious than it was; even on a yacht this size, economy had to be considered. I reached the master suite, done up in chocolate brown and rich tan, brass lamps and tables accenting it all. This was where opulence went to die, I thought, mesmerized by the king-size bed and ritzy harem pillows.

I made a beeline for Ayers's small desk, but after a time came up with nothing more interesting than an old laundry ticket being used as a bookmark in a Grisham novel. Apparently, somebody at Randolph St. Cleaners had a funny bone a mile wide; they'd charged Ayers twelve dollars and fifty cents to clean one pair of chinos. I thought of Earlene Skipper and wondered how much she charged to ruin a man's pants.

Oil paintings leaned against a wall, unsigned. I counted seven. I assumed Tim had painted them. Jung said he was an artist. I pulled each canvas out for a closer look. Lighthouses. Lighthouses on craggy hills, lighthouses on wave-swept outcroppings, big lighthouses, little lighthouses. They were evocative, haunting, mildly entrancing. I didn't know much about art, but they didn't look half-bad.

I went back the way I came, but before I hit the steps again, I checked out the gleaming bathroom, letting out an appreciative whistle. Tim had obviously spent some money here. The compact shower stall was fronted by glass with the image of a preening peacock etched into it. Every fixture was stainless steel. Even the little soaps sitting in the dishes pulled their weight, taking on the shape of dainty fish and clamshells; they smelled delicious, like peaches and cream and gold bullion. Pulling my eyes away from all the glitter and snap, I eased open the medicine cabinet and found at least a dozen medicine bottles inside, a sobering reminder of Tim's dire prognosis. This was the overflow Marta had mentioned. The cops had taken the duplicate bottles. He wouldn't have had to go far to find the means to his eventual end. Had the meds dulled his senses just enough to give him the courage to jump, or had they impaired him just enough so that he lost his footing and slipped?

Had it all just gotten too much for him—the waiting to die, the regimen, the winding down of the clock? Going out his way would have been a last grab at control. I thought of Tim's neighbors. Cap was likely right, as much as it burned me to admit it. They'd probably have papered Tim head to toe in injunctions and lawsuits and petitions, but would any of them have risked everything by resorting to murder? If they had, would any one of them have had the wherewithal and presence of mind to remove every single sign that he or she had been on board the *Safe Passage*? I didn't think so. Leaving a crime scene that squeaky clean took experience; it screamed *pro*.

I snapped photos of all the medicine labels. I wanted to know what the meds were for. Maybe that would tell me something. Back on deck, I breathed in fresh air and carefully replaced the tape. I stood for a moment under the boat's overhang and e-mailed the photos to Dr. Sue Jankovic, a physician I'd worked with several cases back. She'd be able to identify the medication and tell me what it was for. Maybe something Tim was taking contributed to his state of mind at the time of his death. The e-mail sent, I slipped the phone into my pocket and headed back to the ladder.

"Hey, what's going on over there?"

I turned to find a white guy with a receding hairline and horn-rimmed glasses standing on the deck of the *Miraculous*. He was middle-aged, dressed in thigh-length swim shorts and a tank shirt, revealing the palest arms I'd ever seen on a living person. He didn't look friendly. The scowl tipped me off. He did, however, look very observant. Needless to say, I'd have preferred it the other way around.

"Now what?" he yelled, his voice more than carrying over the short distance between his boat and the one I was standing on. There couldn't have been more than eight, nine feet separating us. "We finally get rid of one problem and *you* guys bring another."

I peered over at him, my hand shielding my eyes from the sun. "Excuse me?"

"More cops," he called out. "You guys have to get through over there so they can move that boat out. It's a prime slip and I know somebody who wants it. What's your endgame?"

"We're waiting for a respectable amount of time to pass, in deference to Tim Ayers's memory."

I didn't know this to be true. I had no idea what Tim's family planned to do with the boat, or when they'd move it, but I was fed up with all the pettiness—Cap's, this guy's. The man gripped the rail on his boat, his knuckles stone white, testifying to the ferocity of the hold. "Are you kidding me? Do you have any idea how glad I am that guy's gone? The ruckus from over there you wouldn't believe, and him thumbing his nose at all the complaints. Good riddance, you ask me. And exactly how long's all that *respect* going to take?"

I shrugged. "Open ended. You have to feel when the time's right."

The man's face flushed with anger, and he started in on a little tantrum dance. I considered taking my phone out and taping him, no one would believe it otherwise. Instead, I turned and headed for the ladder again. He thought I was a cop, but I wasn't.

I was on a boat I had no business being on. It was best not to push my luck.

"I want to talk to your superior," Dancing Man barked. "That boat needs to move. Hey, do you hear me?"

I kept walking. The ladder was close.

"Hello? I'm talking to you." He leaned forward, staring. He was a persistent little bugger. "What's your badge number and name?"

I turned to face him, stern of face. "We call it a star, not a badge, for future reference. And what's *your* name?" I pulled out my best cop voice. My icy stare took a moment to travel across the expanse, but when it did, the man took a step back.

"Eldon Reese . . . and as a taxpayer, I'm entitled to some answers. I pay your salary, after all."

I glared at him. I hated when people said that. *Entitled? Yep.* "Were you here the night of the accident?"

"So what? Doesn't mean I saw anything. The idiot. He was probably drunk or high, or both. He stayed that way. You people already have my statement. Try reading it. Don't you talk to each other?"

I smiled, but it wasn't at all sincere. Eldon Reese was a piece of work. The two boats were close. He must have made Tim's life a living hell. "You're being uncooperative, and that usually means a person's got something to hide."

"Well, I don't. My story's the same as it's always been. He woke me around midnight with all that loud bumping, nothing new for him. I added it all to my complaints log, and that's all I'm saying without a lawyer. I know my rights." His eyes narrowed. "And you still haven't given me your name."

"What kind of bumps?" I couldn't help myself. I needed to know. "Describe them."

"*Bumps.* Who describes a bump? It sounded like a buoy banging against the hull. I've been asking Cap for months to get a handle on that Ayers, but I guess when your family's loaded, you get all the breaks."

I cut him off. "Get back to the bumps. Did you get up to see what was actually causing the noise?"

"Didn't you hear me? I said it sounded like a buoy. Then when I almost manage to get back to sleep, he starts the engine up and takes her out. Like I said, good riddance. It was always something with that guy—orgies, hookers, loud Devil music. I was building a case to get him thrown out of here on his ear . . . almost had him, too. Now I've got cops crawling around everywhere and guys sneaking around with binoculars." He eyed me suspiciously. "Your name."

"Hookers? How'd you know?"

His eyebrows raised. "What?"

"I said how'd you know they were hookers?"

"I think I know a hooker when I see one, okay? Flashy clothes, big boobs, enough makeup to choke a man."

I thought for a second. Jung told me Tim was gay. That didn't mean he couldn't have hired a hooker, but it was highly unlikely he would have hired one with boobs. So who was the woman in the flashy clothes? Lost in thought, I realized too late that Reese was still yammering away.

"*Hello?*" His strident voice finally got through. "Are you deaf?"

"Did one of these hookers have red hair?"

Reese's face contorted. "Of course. Don't they all?"

I sighed. I could have identified myself at any time, produced a copy of my PI's license. I had business cards in an inside pocket. Nothing but the Devil kept me from stating my business. He rummaged in his pocket and came up with a small notepad and pencil. "Give me your name. I'm writing it down."

I gripped the rails with both hands and leaned over so Deputy Dawg could hear me better. "Mary Meachum." Take that. She was an abolitionist on the Underground Railroad, but no way in hell Reese knew that. My mother had been a teacher, and I flirted with the idea of becoming one myself, so history was my jam. Reese didn't know who he was tangling with.

"Spell it."

"Which name are you having a problem with?"

"I know how to spell Mary. Don't be insolent."

Insolent? That was it. I hit the ladder and headed down.

"Did you say Meechan?"

"MEACHUM. *M-E-A-C-H-U-M.*"

"What division?"

"Transportation. Railroads."

He frowned. "Railroads?"

"Precisely."

"I'm turning you in, Meachum."

I scoffed. "You wouldn't be the first one."

"You wait right there."

Yeah, right. I continued down the rungs at a confident pace.

"Meachum? I've got your name. You haven't heard the last of this."

"Oooh, stop." I shivered facetiously. "You're scaring me."

Chapter 12

I walked the entire marina, looking for someone who liked Tim, but he hadn't a single friend anywhere. Still, no one appeared so bent out of shape about his freewheeling behavior that they'd climb aboard his boat in the middle of the night and toss him over the side, if that's what even happened. And, like Marta, I'd found nothing on the boat that raised any red flags. I assumed the meds I'd found were for Tim's cancer, but if they were for some kind of mental disorder, that might lend credence to his brother's rundown of Tim's history of depression. I'd have to wait for Sue to get back to me.

In the meantime, I'd move on. Maybe I could get Tim's family to speak to me. I slid into my car, my mind on my next move. Reaching to start it, I glanced at my rearview mirror, catching sight of a shock of spiky blond hair ducking down inside a battered orange Chevette parked across the way.

"Oh, no, no, no."

I got out of the car, stormed across the lot, and banged on the driver's window. Jung was slumped over, his head plastered to the passenger seat. I could see him lying there clear as day.

"I can see you, Jung."

He slowly rolled upright, eased the window down just a smidge.

The expression on his face was reminiscent of a toddler's caught with his hand in the cookie jar. There was a pair of giant binoculars hanging from a strap around his neck. Jung was Eldon Reese's skulker.

"We had a deal," I said.

"I wasn't interfering, just observing. I swear. What'd that guy say? Why was he dancing?"

The doors on the Chevette were nearly rusted through. Through the car's front floorboard, I could see the ground beneath. The car was unsafe to drive. It didn't even look safe to sit in.

"There's no backseat," I said. The hollowed-out space behind Jung's head clearly exposed the tail end of the vehicle's bent metal frame. I pulled a face. "Whose car is this? And I'm using the term 'car' loosely."

"Squish's. Ten bucks a day, plus two tickets to Blue Man Group. So what'd the boat guy say? The case is hinky, right? Like I told you?"

Jung stared up at me expectantly. He was my client, technically, at least for a few more hours, so I owed him a report. Still, something didn't seem right about the whole thing. Two days ago, he was just the weird guy on the bag end of my tuna melt. Now I worked for him, and I didn't particularly care for the shift in dynamic. I didn't ask who Squish was. I didn't want to know.

"Never mind the boat guy," I said. "I'm going to ask you three questions, and then you're going to start this . . . this . . . thing and drive off. Got it?"

Jung opened his mouth to protest, but I waved him quiet. "Three questions, then you're out."

I could tell Jung didn't like it, but, resigned, he nodded once. "Fine. Go ahead."

"Cap in the marina office saw an attractive redhead visit Tim the same day his brother came by to check on him. Do you know who she is?"

Jung's brows knit together, his thin lips twisted. "No idea."

"She carried a briefcase, wore a suit."

Jung shrugged. "Maybe she works for Felton? Tim's lawyer. Well, he's actually the Ayers family lawyer, but he handled Tim's stuff, too. Tim had a lot of papers to sign off on, end-of-life stuff. Maybe she was delivering them, or something? You were on the boat. What'd you find?"

"I found where a lot of money went to die. Exactly how rich are the Ayerses?"

Jung gripped the steering wheel, looked away. "Why's that important?"

"Because maybe somebody killed Tim thinking they'd get some of it."

"Money's a dumb reason to kill a person."

I let it go. Even Jung couldn't be that naïve. "How'd you fall in with his crowd, anyway?"

He didn't answer.

"Jung?"

He fiddled with the binoculars. "Prep school."

"*You* went to *prep* school . . . with Tim Ayers."

He cleared his throat. "Our families are similar. Mine's in textiles. But that doesn't mean I'm an asshole. I mean, look at me. Do I look like an asshole to you?"

I stared at him, my mouth hanging open, really taking him in. Jung looked like he'd dressed from a Salvation Army bin. "If you come from money, why the hell are you delivering sandwiches?"

"Because that's the way I like it, okay? Now that's all you're going to think about when you see me . . . the money. That's all people ever see. You know what they don't see? They don't see the hundred little strings that come along with it, all the 'dos and don'ts' and 'better nots.' I gave it up, so did Tim. He was an artist in a family of pinch-faced tight asses. I'm not an artist, but

I'm free to be whatever. My folks are gone, but they left the money behind. Still, I make my own way. I'm proud of that."

Jung Byson is wealthy. Huh? He was right. From here on out, that would be the first thing I thought when I saw him. I shook my head. What a waste of good money. I thought about Reese. "Would Tim have hired a hooker?"

"A *woman*?"

I nodded. "Redhead."

"Not in a million. Not in *two* million. I told you he was gay."

Redhead. Big boobs. A briefcase and suit. *Not* a hooker. I looked over the lot, the traffic and skyline beyond it. "There are oil paintings on board. I assume they're Tim's?"

"Lighthouses?"

"Yeah."

"Sure. He had a thing for them. Something about desolation and resilience, he said once. They're kind of cool, I guess. He left me one, something to remember him by. I told you he'd started to give things away. Now I don't know if I want it. Too sad, you know? Besides, I don't know much about art. Teo knows more."

"Teo?"

"Teo Cantu. He and Tim were together for a while. He's an artist, too, but not lighthouses, more experimental. Teo's too far out there for me."

My eyes narrowed. How "far out there" did you have to be to be "too far-out" for Jung?

"How recently were they together?"

Jung shrugged, thought about it. "I think they broke up right about the time Tim found out he was sick. Some people can't deal, you know?"

I flicked a glance toward the office. "What did Tim ever say about Cap, the guy in the office?"

"That he was a drunken bully who was always ragging on him. Tim thought he was a creep, too. He said he'd see him walking around the marina at all hours like he was looking for somebody. My theory? He was stealing stuff from the boats, but I don't think anybody ever reported anything missing. At least Tim didn't mention it. He's just a creepy old guy."

"Did Tim mention Cap's back room?"

Jung's brows knit together. "What back room?"

I frowned. "Never mind. Tim's brother, Stephen, was here a few days before he died. He told Cap the same thing he told the police about Tim suffering from depression and having a rough past."

Jung thrust himself out of the car, eyes blazing. "That son of a bitch."

I stepped backward to avoid getting swiped by rust.

Jung pulled at his spiky hair, grabbing tufts of it in clenched fists. "What's he think he's playing at? First he tells the police that crap, now he tells the same to this guy? That backstabbing little . . . I'm going to . . ." Jung reached for the door handle, and I blocked him.

"Stop right there. You're going to do absolutely nothing."

Jung tried going around me, but I blocked him again, gently holding him back. "Let me go," he said. "He's making Tim sound crazy. He wasn't."

"Why would he want to do that?" Pena had said the family pressed to have Tim's death ruled accidental. That they suspected he'd killed himself and didn't want the stigma of suicide associated with the Ayers name. So why would Stephen draw attention to his brother's instability? Why make sure Marta Pena knew he'd had a rocky past? What did Stephen hope to gain? "It just doesn't make sense."

Jung stomped around, pulling at his hair, tearing at his clothes. "It does if he hated Tim. That lying, pompous, small little man . . ." He turned to face me, his eyes pleading. "Why would he do it? What possible reason? Jealousy! Tim had friends. He had his art.

He had a life. He got out of that smothering family and didn't look back. Stephen got stuck. He got the power, the status, but he also got all the responsibility, all the burdens. Tim was everything he hated, so whatever he could do to bring him down, he'd do it." Jung's eyes widened. "Maybe he wanted *all* the money, not just his part? Do you think that's it? He cut Tim off from the money, but it was still Tim's. As long as Tim was alive, he had a shot at getting it back. Dead, it all goes to Stephen. That's it. It's the money, isn't it? Why is it always the money?"

Jung, deflated, leaned hard against the rusted car, his head in his hands. The car groaned as if someone had harpooned it and it was dying a slow and agonizing death. I was going to have to talk to Stephen Ayers. Jung had just given me a solid motive for why he might have wanted to kill his brother. Could I be looking at a clear-cut case of fratricide? Was it jealousy and greed that led to Tim Ayers's death?

I stood and watched Jung as he slowly settled. When he did, he said, "I hate this. I hate Stephen." He lifted from the car. "We'll go talk to Tim's mother. She's the only one who can get Stephen to tell the truth."

"Again, no *we*," I said. "Get back in the car."

Jung's eyes fired. "No way. I'm doing this."

"Jung, get back in the car."

"But she won't see just anybody, and she doesn't know you. Without me, she's a wall too high for you to get over. You *need* me."

"I do *not* need you," I said, opening the Chevette's door, unsettling the rust again. "Go home. Go now before you do something you shouldn't."

I stood there with the door open, but Jung wasn't moving. He was deciding. I let him.

"You can't stop me," he said.

I could stop him. "I'm hoping you'll stop yourself."

He quietly slid into the car. "You're making a mistake."

"Not my first or my last. Go home." I slammed the door shut.

I stood and watched as Jung started the iffy Chevette, which, once the engine caught hold, shook like a janky washing machine. This was the vehicle he chose to go stealth in? Slowly the car sputtered away on a cloud of mean-smelling exhaust. I watched it belly crawl out of the lot and make the turn down the Drive before I turned away.

Chapter 13

Later that afternoon, I swiveled in my office chair, staring at my computer at all the write-ups on the Ayers family. They, apparently, were quite the society swells. One particular photo, taken in Stephen Ayers's massive office, his seat of power, showed the pompous-looking man sitting in his chair, legs crossed, languid hands resting on armrests that looked like lion heads, every bit the regal king. I'd just hung up from talking to his snooty-sounding receptionist who'd told me quite coldly that Mr. Ayers was in a meeting, which everybody knew was code for "go take a flying leap."

I left my name and number and a brief message, omitting the words "murder" and "lying bastard." I wanted to know why he sent Felton, the family lawyer, to claim Tim's body instead of coming himself, after making such a show of concern for his brother's welfare. And why had he made such a point about telling Cap about Tim's past troubles? Of course, he'd never call me back, but that didn't worry me. I knew where to find him. In the meantime, I'd start with Tim's ex-partner, Teo. He knew Tim intimately. If there had been something going on with him, Teo would know about it, so I headed out to see him.

Cantu lived in a studio loft in River North, a gentrified enclave of fussy millennials filled with bohemian nightspots and quaint bistros that thrived, despite hawking six-dollar pastries and high-hat coffee blends nobody normal had a taste for. Parking anywhere up north was always a crapshoot, and I had to circle the block five times before I found a spot I wouldn't get towed from. I gave the city meter the stink eye, though. It was going to cost me one quarter for every nine-minute interval, and I resented it. It was highway robbery, pure and simple, and as I slipped my credit card into the meter's voracious maw, I couldn't help but feel as though someone had just picked my pocket.

Cantu's name was on the bell in the lobby, but no one answered when I rang it. It took three rings and a long press before the lobby door finally buzzed open. I made my way up to find the door to 400A standing ajar, the strong odor of fresh paint wafting out into the hall, which I would have expected for an artist. I hadn't expected the sweet stink of marijuana that wafted out with it. I knocked, and then peeked tentatively through the crack in the doorway.

"Enter," a man bellowed from inside. "Watch where you step."

I eased inside to find a tall, rail-thin man, dressed in a black Lycra bodysuit, standing on a painter's tarp spread over the hardwood floor, giving the wall an appraising look. He was covered in splotches of red and brown paint, and there were Slinkys attached to the bottoms of his black ballet slippers. The loud, jangled music piped in from somewhere was about as appealing as the sound of a ham-fisted toddler pounding wooden spatulas against upturned pots. While I watched, the man stepped each Slinky into a flat pan of paint, took a running start, and kicked his feet out—Slinky first—against a huge black canvas anchored to the wall. Bouncing back, he tumbled to the tarp. The canvas hung there assaulted by at least a hundred Slinky circles. He'd apparently been at it for a while. I eased the front door open a little wider for an easier exit.

"Teo Cantu?"

Sitting cross-legged on the tarp, he swiveled to face me, and shot me a bemused look as his breathing slowed. He clapped his hands twice and the music stopped. "You're not my pad Thai. I ordered pad Thai."

"No. I'm a private investigator. Cass Raines. I'd like to ask you a few questions about Timothy Ayers."

I stepped over carefully, handed him one of my cards, which he got paint all over. He looked disappointed. "But I'm hungry."

I stepped back, eyed the wall, the tarp, the slippers, the body-suit. "I can see why. So about Tim Ayers?"

Cantu rolled his eyes. "Nothing to talk about. He's dead. At least that's what the news feed said."

Four floor-to-ceiling windows at the opposite end of the loft were all opened halfway, as a floor fan whizzed back and forth spreading paint fumes around. Cantu unstrapped the Slinky toys and stood, his slender hands on narrow hips. I eyed the Slinky canvas again. Teo caught me looking.

"You want to strap on a pair of springs?"

I smiled politely. "No thanks. I'm good."

I walked farther in, skirting the tarp, looking for a clean place to light. Except for the tarp, Cantu's futon, partly hidden behind a Japanese screen, and four beanbag chairs clustered around a ratty tatami mat, the place was empty. I eyed one of the beanbag chairs, but quickly ruled it out. Only a preschooler could rock a beanbag chair with any finesse. I decided to stand.

"You and Tim Ayers were together," I said. "I was hoping you'd be able to give me some background, some insight into his state of mind."

"Sorry. Can't. I don't rehash."

"Excuse me?"

"Once I close the door on something, it stays closed. I never go back. It's like it never happened. It's my personal philoso-phy." He paused, took a beat. "I don't dwell," he added as if that clarified things.

I stood and watched him, eyeing the forlorn Slinkys on the tarp. "And your philosophy also applies to people?"

"*Especially* people."

"So you're saying you've closed the door on Tim Ayers and won't discuss him now."

"Closed it. Locked it. And, no, *sorry*, I won't." The smug look on his face belied his profession of sorrow. He wasn't at all sorry. He was far too glib for that.

He tried handing the card back, but I wouldn't take it. I'd have a time getting the paint off my fingers. "Okay, then. I'll pass your name along to the detectives in charge of Tim's case. Maybe you'll talk to them." I took a sniff, drawing in the scent I'd recognized out in the hall. Even the strong smell of fresh paint couldn't mask it. "But before they show up, I'd flush the weed and whatever else you've got stashed around here, or get yourself a good lawyer." I smiled, headed for the door. "Have a good day, Mr. Cantu."

I started counting Mississippis, but had a feeling I wouldn't have to go too far with it. I didn't. Cantu bounded off the tarp like a gazelle and slid in front of me to block my exit.

"Whoa. Hey. Slow down there."

The smugness was gone, replaced by panic. Cantu's face paled. He began to sweat. He obviously had something else besides the weed hidden. Cantu ran the back of a paint-splotched hand across his forehead. "Tim drowned, right? I had nothing to do with that. We broke up a year ago at least. Ancient history."

"By mutual decision?"

"Why's that *your* business?" He'd forgotten just that quickly the position he was in.

I reached for the doorknob, but Cantu stopped me. "Okay. Okay. My bad. He broke up with me, okay? One minute, I'm thinking we've got a thing, and the next, he's packing up and heading out the door. That's how it happened."

"No explanation?"

"Oh, he gave plenty. He said he'd gotten some bad news that put his life in perspective, and that he wasn't wasting another second being unhappy. How'd you like to be on the tail end of that, huh?"

"You knew about his cancer?"

"Found out about it then, didn't I? Me, like a fool, told him I'd hang in, help him through. I'm a nurturer. I can't help myself. That's when he tells me that won't be necessary. Just like that. 'That won't be necessary.' He had plans, he said, to travel the world, alone, on his yacht while he still had the time. *Alone.* His *yacht.* Here I'm thinking he's a starving artist like me, and he's got a *yacht*? He worked part-time at the arts center down the street, for Pete's sake, and all the while he's some rich kid from the North Shore? And he's painting lighthouses? *And* he swept out of here owing me six hundred bucks? I'm bouncing off canvases, hoping to make some sales so I can quit my day job, and he's sitting on all that?" Cantu tossed his head back, grimaced. "It got real fast after that."

I looked a question.

"I *may* have tossed some of his clothes down the garbage chute. And I *may* have threatened to strangle him, though, obviously, I didn't. And, once he was gone, I *may* have told everyone we know that he was high-class trash." Cantu folded his arms across his chest, pouted a little. "He deserved it. I've no regrets."

"So he told you he was dying and then walked out on you."

"Calm as anything. Only the more I thought about it, the angrier I got, and then all the second-guessing started. You know how it goes. I convinced myself that maybe he didn't really have cancer and that the whole story was a big lie to cover up the fact that he was sleeping around. He'd cleared most of his things out by then, but the stuff I tossed was still in the Dumpster.

"I found a book of matches in a pocket. It was so 1950s, it was almost a joke. They were to a bar I never heard of, Sophie's Place." Cantu rolled his eyes, smirked, as though the name of the bar just happened to be another indignity heaped upon Tim's brush-off. "At that point, I was just pissed off enough, and wasted enough, to storm over there. Let's just say, it wasn't my kind of place. I showed Tim's photo around and a couple of people recognized him. He'd come in to see a guy named C.D. Ganz, they said." He threw up his hands. "I got control of myself before I made a scene, thank the gods, but frankly what would have been the point? He was on his way to Tahiti, or some-damn-where." Cantu let out a breezy sigh. "It took me some time getting over what might have been. All that money. The yacht."

"Did he tell you he was estranged from his family?"

Cantu pulled a face. "I didn't even know he had a family until the big reveal."

"And the day he walked out on you is the last time you saw him?"

"No such luck. I saw him a couple months ago at a bash. We didn't speak, at least I didn't. He may have mouthed a hello or something from across the dance floor, but I didn't pick it up. Like I said, I don't rehash."

"Sounds like you're still angry enough to want to strangle him."

"Wouldn't you be? I always imagined I was destined for wealth, and here I was cohabitating with it and didn't know it. He robbed me of my dream, that's all I can say. Then he up and falls off the yacht and drowns. God, that's such a rich-kid way to go." He shot me a sly smile. "Isn't karma a bitch? What's all this about, anyway, now that you've gotten all my secrets?"

"Do you know anyone who'd have wanted to hurt Tim?"

"Not off hand, but keep at it, I'm sure you'll find somebody. All *I* know is that I never laid a hand on him. It was a clean break. *Fini.* I've got a new guy now, and I was at his place the night Tim drowned, so don't bother asking. I believe that's an alibi. If I were you, I'd tag Ganz. He's the last one Tim was into. Maybe Tim dumped him, too."

I opened the door. "Thanks."

"You're satisfied, right? We're cool? No cops?"

I took a good look at him. He was half-buzzed now, but I didn't think he had what it took to sell or distribute the stuff on any major level, but I could be wrong. Bottom line, I didn't have the authority to roust him on it. That was someone else's job. "Yeah, sure," I said. "Cool."

I was barely out the door before Cantu slammed it shut and locked it. He was probably busy moving his stash. The last thing I heard before I stepped into the elevator was the sound of Slinkys hitting the wall.

I had three minutes left on my meter, but River North was not an area where you could kick back in your car and eat up the time. The second I slid my key into the lock, there was a Bimmer at my rear bumper waiting to snag the spot. I started up, but apparently took too long with it because the Bimmer driver honked impatiently. I sighed, checked the dashboard clock, and then pulled out. Just past four PM. I'd been working for Jung for only six hours. Felt like longer.

Since I was up north, anyway, I decided to take Teo's advice and see if I could tag Ganz. After a quick search on my phone, I headed for crowded, bar-heavy Clark Street. I found Sophie's in the middle of the lively block, parked, and stepped inside a dim, deep room that felt dense, skittish, close, as though the place hadn't had a door open or fresh air circulating since the Capone era. I stood at the door and waited for my eyes to adjust, breathing in the left-behind trace of old Cosmos and Manhattans. There was no music playing, and strangely no talking, but when the room came into focus, I understood why. There were men dressed in women's clothing sitting at a few of the cocktail tables set up in the middle of the room, and all eyes were on me. For a moment, I stood in the doorway and watched them as they watched me back; then I walked over to the long bar.

The bartender grinned. "Can I get you something?" He was a middle-aged white guy with pink hair pulled back in a man bun. When he spoke, I could see that his tongue was pierced, as were both ears and his right nipple, which peeked out from underneath a woolly bearskin vest, the kind Sonny Bono used to wear before he went political. I flicked a look over the bar to see what his bottom half was wearing, but found nothing more interesting than a beat-up pair of jeans and running shoes.

I took a seat on a well-worn barstool. "Diet Coke, please."

"That it?" he asked, looking a bit disappointed, like he'd been prepared to whip up something frothy in a cold glass and I'd denied him the pleasure.

"Ice in the glass?"

I watched as he sauntered down the bar to the soft-drink spigots before I turned my attention to the clientele. The bar wasn't that busy, but it was early yet. Besides me, there were maybe five or six men at the small, intimate tables. The crescent-shaped booths along the wall were empty. Toward the rear, a large platform of parquet flooring marked off an empty dance area. I glanced up, looking for the disco ball, but Sophie's had gone against convention and had installed instead a series of gel lights, now dormant. There were large boxes stacked toward the back. Looked like Sophie's had gotten some new equipment or furniture or something. One of the boxes had a picture of an electronic amp on it. I felt eyes at my back and swiveled around to see that I was still all the rage, despite being woefully underdressed. I swiveled back around to the bar, watching as Pink Hair strolled back with my pop.

"Diet Coke." He dropped a cocktail napkin on the bar and placed my glass on it. "Ice in the glass."

I grinned. "See? Easy."

He turned to leave. I stopped him. "I'm looking for C.D. Ganz. Does he work here?"

"You could say that. He owns the place. You're here for C.D.?"

I waited a beat. "If he's available."

"Shoulda said. I figured you for a walk-in." He read the confusion on my face and explained. "Off-the-streeters coming in because the name sounds cute. They don't stay long. We mostly get the regulars."

"That would be the well-dressed gentlemen staring at me right now?"

He chuckled. "That's them. Trying to figure you out is all. You're underdressed."

I looked down at myself, taking the survey. I looked fine to me, dressed in my usual knockabout PI uniform: jeans, shirt, Nikes, disarming smile. "But still as cute as a bug's ear."

"You also look like heat."

I shook my head. "Not heat, and even if I were, I don't see anything illegal going on in here."

Pink Hair made an axing motion across his neck with his right hand for the benefit of the gawkers. In an instant, I felt all the eyes that had been boring holes in my back turn away en masse, as quickly as if someone had turned off a light switch. I swiveled around again in time to witness the tail end of the exodus. Absolutely everyone had lost interest. I turned back to the bar.

"That was cold."

He slowly polished the bar top with a damp rag taken from his waist. "They're used to being hassled. It doesn't look like that's what you're here for, so they're leaving you alone, and hoping you do the same. And, believe me, I've seen colder."

"Still . . ." I checked behind me again, nada. I went back to my drink. "So. Ganz?"

"Oh, yeah, I'll get him for you. Name's Mutt, by the way." He flicked his chin up, grinned.

"Your mother named you Mutt?"

He laughed. "It's short for Mutter. First name's Henry. But around here? It's Mutt."

I raised my glass to him. "Nice to meet you, Mutt."

He headed off toward a back room. While I waited, curiosity got the better of me and I glanced at the tables again to see if I was still persona non grata. I was. Big-time. I felt as popular as a vegan at a Texas barbecue. I went back to my glass and tried not to take it personally. When my phone dinged, I dug it out of my pocket and read the e-mail. It was from Dr. Sue. She'd had a chance to look over the photos I'd taken of Tim's med bottles. The prescriptions, she said, were for pain, nausea, and iron deficiency, nothing a doctor would prescribe for cancer, OCD, or bipolar disorder. Sue concluded that Tim was likely no longer being treated, but merely made comfortable, which made perfect sense when you thought about it. The man was dying with no hope of recovery. What more could the doctors do for him? I e-mailed a thank-you to Sue and put the phone away. Maybe Jung was right. Maybe Stephen Ayers was a lying bastard. Or maybe he wasn't and Tim had mental issues, which, given his dire prognosis, he'd chosen not to treat. The meds I'd found, taken in large quantities and paired with alcohol, would have been enough to put Tim in an altered state. Who's to say he didn't plan it that way? But now, I had to deal with Jung and his puppy dog eyes, Jung who couldn't accept what looked to be the truth of the thing. Tim could have wiped his boat clean and done away with the rag he'd used. All he had to do was toss the thing into the lake and jump in after it. But he'd have had to touch the boat's railing to get over the side, wouldn't he? Or could he have rolled himself over? Maybe Marta was right. Gloves? Also a possibility. Same deal. Hoist yourself over the side, ditch the gloves in the water. But all of that took a certain presence of mind, which the drugs and alcohol would have altered. Tim wouldn't have been thinking clearly, if at all. And what about the storm? The pounding rain? The rocking boat? That would have been an awful lot for a dying man, half out of his head, to navigate. And why go to all that trouble in the end? Weren't there easier ways to kill yourself, if you had a mind to do it? Something wasn't right.

When Mutt came back out, he was trailed by a whippet-thin man of medium height dressed in tan trousers and an oversize shirt with pineapples on the breast pockets. I assumed the second man was Ganz. They stopped toward the rear of the bar, and Mutt gestured for me to join them, so I picked up my glass and napkin and headed back.

"This is C.D.," Mutt said when I reached them.

I held out a hand for a shake, which Ganz accepted with a smile. "Mr. Ganz, I'm Cass Raines. I'm a private investigator looking into the death of Tim Ayers. I'd like to ask you a few questions."

Ganz gave me a peculiar look, the kind you might give an IRS agent right after he or she uttered the word "audit"—part shock, part *oh, shit.* Ganz tried holding on to his smile, but it disappeared quickly as he drew his hand away.

Mutt folded his arms across his chest and eyed me appraisingly. "Huh. I did not see *that* coming."

I took a quick sip of Coke, watching them both over the rim of my glass. Just then, the front door opened and the three of us turned to look. Two young women who appeared to have started a night of barhopping way too early swayed in and slid themselves onto stools at the bar. Their backs arched, they lasered in on the room, looking for prospective dates for the evening. Mutt turned and headed back to the bar. "Gotta go."

Ganz pointed at the stack of boxes I'd noticed earlier. "Mind if I break these down while we talk?"

I didn't mind and told him so. I watched as he pulled a box cutter out of his back pocket and started in on the first box. "Get you another drink?"

I held up my Coke, the glass half-full. "Still working on this one. But thanks."

He pulled a martini glass out of the box, checked it for cracks, and then set it on an empty table behind him. "Questions about Tim Ayers, you said?"

"You knew him. He'd been here a few times. What can you tell me about him?"

Ganz plucked out another glass, checked it, moved it to the table. "Not much. We were acquaintances, not friends. He'd come in for a drink now and then. It's sad what happened to him, but—and don't get the wrong idea—it was kind of a blessing, considering what he had to look forward to. Cancer's a slow and miserable way to go."

I rattled the melting ice in my glass, our eyes holding. "What'd you two talk about . . . when he came in now and then?"

I heard giddy shrieks coming from the bar and turned, just as the two women leapt up and hit the door running. Ganz tracked their exit, shaking his head. "They assume all cross-dressers are gay, they're not."

"I've heard that," I said. "Still, a sign might help."

Ganz smiled, went back to the glasses. "And ruin Mutt's fun?"

I eyed the boxes. There were six of them stacked up. At the speed Ganz was going, he'd be here till midnight. "I met Tim in a cancer support group. Sometimes he just needed to talk, and I had no problem listening." My eyes wandered over Ganz's thin frame; he caught the tail end of my survey. "Remission," he offered, in answer to my unasked question. "Nothing I can take credit for. I just got lucky. Tim didn't. Why're you asking about him?"

"I'm looking into his accident," I said. "Making sure nothing got missed."

Ganz's eyes narrowed. "For his family?"

"You knew about his family?"

Ganz nodded. "It just goes to prove the rich are just as messed up as the rest of us. It makes me feel at least a little better about my own crappy upbringing. But you still haven't said what Tim's death has to do with me or Sophie's."

"I didn't know Tim. I'm just trying to get a feel. When was the last time you saw him? How'd he seem?"

"Not for a while. He seemed okay, but I'm no shrink. Honestly, when I heard he'd died, I thought for sure he'd killed himself. Easy way out. Cut your losses. It sounded plausible to me. It's what I would have done."

I sighed. It sounded plausible to me, too. The alcohol, the meds, the death sentence—who says it didn't all pile up on him? So he was planning his own funeral with friends, that didn't mean that in the dark of night, at a low point, he hadn't suddenly said the hell with it. Maybe he reasoned his friends, Jung particularly, would understand and forgive? He'd have been wrong in Jung's case.

The first box emptied, Ganz broke it down, tossed it aside, and started on the box beneath it. A swipe of the box cutter shredded the packing tape into ribbons. Ganz pulled the flaps back. More glasses—this time, wine, not martini. "But they're done investigating it, aren't they? It's a done deal." He slid me a sideways glance. "What's there to look into?"

My eyebrows flicked upward. "Who told you it was a 'done deal'?" That hadn't been announced in the news. In fact, I hadn't found that out for sure until I'd spoken to Marta. So how did Ganz know?

He stared down at the box, the box cutter idle in his hand. "I thought I heard it somewhere. Or maybe it was something I read."

He was lying. The proof was in the way he wouldn't look at me for long, in the way he kept his hands busy and his tone light, but guarded. I set my glass down on the table next to the ones he'd unpacked. "Here's my problem, C.D. I can tell you're lying." He opened his mouth to speak, but I stopped him. "It's in your eyes and in the way you're keeping yourself busy with those glasses." I held my hand out, palm down. "See? Steady as a rock. Let's see yours." Ganz palmed the cutter, and then slid his hands into his front pockets. "So now, I have to figure out what you're lying about. Maybe you and Tim were more than acquaintances. Maybe there was some bad blood between you."

"I told you," he muttered. "I hardly knew him."

"Yep, okay, that's even less convincing than it was the first time you said it. Want to try again?" He said nothing. "Where were you the night Tim died?"

His head popped up, shock blanketing his worried face. "Me? If you're thinking I had anything to do with that, you're barking up the wrong tree."

I folded my arms across my chest. "Convince me."

"I don't have to. This is my place. I can ask you to leave."

I dropped my arms, stared at him. I'd heard the quaver in his voice. He heard it, too. "You could do that, sure."

"But you'd be back," he said, "and you'd hassle everybody here till you got what you wanted. It doesn't matter to you that I'm trying to create a safe place here. You'd make it unsafe."

His words rankled, but I tried not to show it. He had a legit fear. Cops didn't often tiptoe into a place on little cat paws. Instead, they made noise. They blew in like a gale wind. And even though I was no longer a cop, I often covered the same ground, knocked on the same doors. But Ganz didn't know me.

"I'll just tell you straight up," I said, "I don't operate that way." I pulled my phone out of my pocket. "If you don't believe me, if you need to check, call the police and have them verify who I am." I held the phone out for him to take. "You want to dial, or do you want me to do it?"

Slowly Ganz's face fell and his whole body soon followed suit; it was like someone had slowly let the air out of a life-size helium balloon. "I just want him behind me."

I pulled the phone back and held it, just in case I needed it again. "Then start with the truth."

Ganz's eyes scanned the bar as though taking a last look, as though it might all disappear in a puff of genie smoke. Then he blew out a breath and faced me, his eyes meeting mine. "We did meet in the group, that wasn't a lie, and we weren't friends. It was business, settled business. I was angry enough to want to kill him, but I didn't." He let a moment slide by, then squeezed his eyes shut. "Don't look at me like I'm a murderer. Would I admit to that, if I'd killed him?"

If you are a psychopath, sure, I thought. "What kind of settled business? Bar business?"

He frowned. "It's the only business I've got. Tim was my investor, or at least I thought he was . . . I found out too late that he liked to dangle his money like a carrot on a stick." Ganz's eyes settled on something behind my left shoulder. I turned to see he'd been watching Mutt at the bar. "And I didn't ask for the money, not once. He offered it."

"When?"

"Months ago. This place used to be called Lou's. I was working a dead-end job, dreading every minute of it, and happened to see an ad in the paper from the owner who was looking to unload it. I came to look. It was a real dive bar, not much to it, but I saw some potential. I wanted to create a safe, no-judgment zone for people who are different. I gutted my savings, but it still wasn't enough." His eyes settled on the tops of his shoes. "I guess I talked about owning the bar too much, Tim must have been listening. One day, he offers to back me. He pledged enough to close the deal, promising more to get things up and running. It was to be business, not a handout, not a gift. I made sure he knew that."

"And he never made good?"

Ganz picked up the cutter, fiddled with it, retracting the blade, displaying it. "We shook on it, set it all up, how much, when, how I'd pay him back, but Tim's check was always in the mail. I eventually found the money I needed on my own . . . I'd prefer not to tell you how . . . but I'm dancing on a tightrope. Of course, that didn't stop Tim from 'throwing business my way.' That's how he put it. Sophie's provided bartending and entertainment for a few of his parties, no fee, of course, the whole time the money's supposedly on its way. He played me."

I watched as he got hold of his anger, or tried to. Apparently, there was still quite a lot of emotion tied up in Ganz's so-called business arrangement with Tim Ayers. Where *had* he been the night Tim died? "Entertainment?" I asked.

"Dancers, lip-syncers." He shrugged. "It's a niche. The bar's limping along, just making it. Some weeks, I can't even pay Mutt. Last time I saw Tim was at one of his parties. I went to plead my case *again,* but he wasn't in any shape to hear me."

"Why not?"

"He'd been drinking—a lot, it appeared. Add to that someone crashed the party, and it was clear from the way he was acting, he didn't want the guy there. I heard them arguing below deck."

I moved around the boxes so I was closer to Ganz. "What'd they argue about?"

"I only heard bits and pieces. Tim accused the guy of crowding him, not letting him die in peace. He warned the guy to leave him alone, or else he'd be sorry."

"He actually said *or else the guy would be sorry*?"

Ganz nodded. "The guy told Tim he was missing the big picture. Their voices stayed low after that. Besides, I didn't really want to hear any more. I had my own problems, so I left them to it. I figured whatever it was, Tim had it coming."

An argument? A crasher who hadn't allowed Tim to die in peace? What "big picture"? And had Tim's failure to grasp the big picture been enough to drive him to suicide, or, worse, propel this mystery crasher to help him along? Either way, it was a lead, a thread.

"Any idea who the crasher was?"

Ganz shook his head, and there was an air of finality in it. "I've said more than I should have already. And I don't need you or the cops hovering around with more questions. The long and short of it is, I wasn't there when he died and I've got witnesses who can back me up."

From where I stood, Ganz had a good reason for wanting to get back at Tim. He'd nearly cost him his dream of owning Sophie's and making it a success, leading him to fantasize about killing him. But the argument added a wrinkle. It meant there was someone else out there who might also have had a good reason for wanting Tim dead. The big picture?

"Can you at least describe the crasher? Height? Build? White? Black?"

"I said I'm out of it. Whatever Tim got into was his bad luck."

"So your stonewalling me is payback for getting stiffed on a business investment?"

C.D.'s look soured. "I'd like to think I'm not that petty."

"So would I."

"White, average, good looking, but a little rough, unpolished. And I wasn't the only one there. Maybe somebody else saw more than I did. Why don't you go hound some of them? Try that weird guy—midtwenties, blond hair spiked all over, a real character. It looked like he and Tim were kind of chummy. Ask him what he saw."

Blond, twenties, a real character? That sounded a lot like Jung. But it couldn't be Jung, could it? Wouldn't Jung have thought it important to mention that he'd attended a party on Tim's boat days before Tim ended up dead? Why hadn't I heard about the crasher or the argument from him? Wasn't he my client? Hadn't he paid for my valuable time with a yin and yang check? I swept my hands through my hair, my frustration level rising. Hadn't I pointedly asked Jung in my office if he'd given me all the information he had? And hadn't he answered yes? "I'll do that," I said, glowering, "but in the meantime, the crasher?"

"You just will not let this go, will you?"

I didn't answer. I assumed the question was rhetorical.

He reached into his back pocket, drew out his wallet, and

opened it. "Here. You want the crasher?" He pulled out a business card, thrust it at me. "He handed these out like favors. Tim didn't look too happy about that, either."

I read the card: VINCENT DARBY. STERLING ASSOCIATES. INSURERS. "You ever see him before?"

"Not before or since, but check the marina. When I left, I stood outside getting some air, kicking myself for letting it go with Tim. This guy breezes out a few minutes after me, walks right past, and climbs aboard a boat a few slips down."

I turned the card over in my hand. "Which one?"

"They all look the same to me."

"Left or right of Tim's?"

"Left. Blue canopy. That's all I got. Satisfied *now*?"

I tried handing the card back to Ganz, but he waved it away. "I don't need it. It's not like I can afford insurance anymore."

I slid the card into my pocket. "One more question. How *did* you hear Tim's case was closed?"

His expression hardened and he turned and walked away. "Mutt'll see you out."

Chapter 14

Vincent Darby was an insurance man. Tim Ayers was living off an insurance policy, after being disinherited by his brother. That had to be more than a coincidence. Had Darby been the one to arrange the whole thing? Was that the deal they argued about? Why, when the whole purpose of the settlement was to give those who took advantage of it a financial cushion so that they could literally die in peace?

And Jung? I was tired of him dropping bits of information like bread crumbs through a fairy-tale forest, giving me only one tiny piece at a time, holding back the rest. He hadn't said anything about being at a party at Tim's or an argument between Tim and Darby. When I asked him if Tim had any possible enemies, he steered me toward Teo Cantu, making no mention of Darby at all. Jung and I needed to talk.

I started the car, ready to pull away from the curb, but stopped when my cell phone rang. I didn't recognize the number, but answered it, anyway.

"Cassandra Raines?"

The voice was male, tight, snappish, and immediately put me on the defensive. I cut the ignition, upsetting the driver behind me who'd been waiting for the spot. The driver honked to get me moving. I rolled my window up instead, to block out the distraction. "This is Cassandra Raines."

"Robert V. Felton, Esquire. Stephen Ayers's legal representation."

I rolled my eyes, sighed. I hated lawyers. Not like I hated broccoli or cod liver oil, not like an aversion, but like how I hated sand in my bikini bottoms or a fly in my kitchen. Like an irritant. Like a rash. And why did lawyers always use five-dollar words when a two-dollar one worked just as well? *Legal representation. Please.*

"How may I help you, Mr. Felton?"

"You've made several attempts to contact Mr. Stephen Ayers. Might I ask why?"

There was a haughty arrogance in his tone that set me on edge. I took a moment to let that settle, peering out of my windshield at the busy street. *"Might I ask why?"* I shrugged. *Sure. People can ask anything they want. That doesn't obligate me to give an answer.* My questions were for Ayers, not his "legal representation," but I could play nice. It was a tactic that didn't come naturally to me for some reason, but I was no quitter.

"I've been hired to look into his brother's death. I was hoping Mr. Ayers could answer a few questions."

"Questions? And hired *by whom?"*

"Can't say 'by whom,' but the questions are general ones about his brother's personality, habits, acquaintances, enemies—if Mr. Ayers knew of any—also his mental state, which Mr. Ayers seems to know quite a bit about."

Felton heaved out an aggrieved breath. The kind those who thought themselves above it all gave to those they'd placed several rungs below them on the ladder for mere mortals. "Mr. Ayers does not wish to speak about his brother, certainly not to a private detective who has no business asking questions in the first place. I insist on knowing who hired you."

I shrugged again. *People can also insist on knowing all kinds of things. That doesn't compel me to supply the information.* "I understand Mr. Ayers was estranged from his brother. Yet, he conducted a wellness check at the marina a few days before Tim died. He left his card in the office. He must have had some concerns about his brother to make the effort?"

Felton didn't answer. He was probably leaning back in a leather chair that cost more than the car I was sitting in, staring at the head of an ambushed moose hanging on his wall. "Why is this information of interest to you? Timothy Ayers's death was an accident. The family is in mourning. What they do not need is to be badgered by a one-woman investigations agency out to make a name for itself."

I pulled the phone away from my ear, looked at it. *Mr. Robert V. Felton, Esquire, knows how to Google, too? Go on with your bad self, Felton.* I pulled the phone back and narrowed my eyes, though he couldn't see that. The driver behind me honked again, more insistent this time. "There are inconsistencies that should be explored," I said. "I think the reason the family is so anxious to put this to bed is because they fear Tim may have killed himself, but there's another possibility." I listened, but Felton said nothing. "That possibility being that Tim Ayers got on someone's bad side and they decided to do something about it."

My words landed like an A-bomb, with Felton's silence hanging in the air like a mushroom cloud. "If you dare to repeat such a scurrilous claim anywhere, believe me, you'll regret it. You are not to contact Mr. Ayers again regarding this matter . . . or any other. Your 'investigation,' if that is what you're calling it, stops now."

I stuck my tongue out at the phone, but Felton couldn't see that, either. "As Mr. Ayers's legal representation, you, no doubt, know that no one in the Ayers family hired me." I listened to Felton wheeze in and out on the other end of the line. "And, therefore, you cannot fire me."

"Listen, here, whoever you are. You are to stop what you're doing. Immediately." His words came out in a low, snakelike hiss. Felton, apparently, was unaccustomed to having to threaten peons twice. "Am I understood?"

"You're lawyer to the Ayers family," I said. "Did you also handle things for Tim, even after he was cut off from the family money?"

I could have sworn the phone in my hand was heating up from all the fuming Felton was doing on his end. "Drop this. Drop it today, or I will bury you."

"I'll drop it," I said, trying and failing to take his threat seriously. "When I find out what happened to Tim. If Mr. Ayers agrees to talk, I can certainly meet him in his office and make myself available at whatever time is convenient."

Felton chortled derisively. "His office? You'd never make it past security. In fact, I'll see to it."

"I accept that challenge."

"I'll have your license."

"You know what? When I make it past security, I'll give you a copy."

He hung up without another word. I grinned, tossed the phone on the passenger seat, started the car, and gave the driver behind me the spot. I had ruffled enough feathers for one day. I was going home.

Chapter 15

"What you *don't* want is a lawyer on your ass," Whip said. We were at Creole's, a small restaurant on the West Side, where Whip was the cook. The place was packed, lively, and surprisingly loud for noon on a Tuesday. It was nothing like Deek's place. Whip had set me up at a special table near the kitchen and I was midway through my second bowl of seafood gumbo.

"Tell me something I *don't* know."

"My bet's on the brother," Whip said, his massive forearms resting on the checked tablecloth. The table wobbled a bit. "It's the money. There's always a fight over the money. The older one figures out a way so he doesn't have to share it. That's how the rich operate." He drummed his fingers on the table, shook his head. "Greed's a dangerous affliction, especially in a family. See? I made you lunch *and* solved your case for you. You're welcome."

"Then what about the argument on the boat?" I asked.

Whip waved a dismissive hand. "C'mon, when is there ever *not* a drunken argument at a party?"

"There's that weird insurance thing, the settlement. I looked it up. Jung's right, it's legal. But whenever money's in play . . ."

Whip's mouth twisted. "Don't see much of a score, though.

Insurance practices are locked down tight, regulated to the hilt. And complicated. That's why I stayed away from white-collar crime. Too much homework."

"Okay, then what about the investment Tim backed out of? Ganz seems really committed to that bar."

Whip shook his head. "Nope. It's the family. No one loves you like family, and nobody hates you like family. Trust me."

I eyed him quizzically. "What evidence are you basing your conclusion on?"

Whip patted his paunchy middle. "Gut instinct, Bean. It never misses."

I chuckled at his use of my childhood nickname, short for String Bean. When we were growing up, everybody had a nickname, some that honored a skill, a talent, like Hoops or Three-Point, some that described them physically, like Bean or Whip. His real name, the one his mama gave him, was Charles Mayo Jr., but no one close to him ever called him that. I smiled at the delight he exhibited in solving my problem so quickly and, in his mind, so definitively. I slowly drew in the aroma of spicy andouille sausage and warm corn bread. "Yeah, well, as much as I respect your gut, I'm going to need a little bit more than that."

He eyed my bowl, the remnants of his culinary efforts smeared over his white apron. "It's good, right? You like it?"

"It's delicious. You definitely know what you're doing."

He beamed, his wide mouth stretching out into a grin that went from ear to ear. "Told you. It took you long enough to get your skinny tail over here."

"Been busy." There'd been Pop, and other things.

"I know what it was," Whip said, almost as though he'd heard me. He reached across the table to pat my free hand, his dark eyes tracking my progress as I finished my gumbo, pride on his face. "Want pie? I got sweet potato, pecan, apple."

I looked up from the bowl, impressed. "Shut up. You can make pie?"

He let out the warmest belly laugh, like Santa high on sugar cookies. It was almost as comforting as the gumbo. Whip. Here. This was my family. "Bean, I can make whatever you got a taste for."

He'd spent nearly half his life in prison, I thought as I watched him, but he'd finally found something he was good at, besides stealing cars and sticking people up. We'd lost touch for a while, but we were back, and he was doing okay. I was glad. He hadn't had the easiest start: a father who was a mean drunk, a mother who died around the same time mine had. Luckily, at twelve, we'd had Pop to guide us through. It still hurt that Whip somehow got lost halfway there. "I'm proud of you. You know that?"

His face lit up. "Took me long enough, didn't it?"

This time, I placed my hand on his, and squeezed all my love into it. "It took as long as it was meant to."

He nodded, grinning. "Guess you're right about that. It's just too bad he's not here to see it."

It was too bad Pop was missing this, and it always would be. I finished the bowl, pushed it away. I had a redhead and a hooker, or a redheaded hooker, who liked to play office, to track down. Plus, I still hadn't spoken to Stephen Ayers or the insurance guy, Vincent Darby. Yet, friendship and gumbo kept me anchored to the spot. I angled my head, smiled devilishly. "Sweet potato, you said?"

Whip shot up from the table. "Yes, ma'am, coming right up. I got to get you fueled up to catch that murdering brother."

I'd eaten enough to fortify me for a month and decided to work it off back at the marina. I turned left at the *Safe Passage*, looking for a boat with a blue canopy, and found at least half a dozen of them all in the same area. I scanned them all from the walkway, but didn't see anyone sitting on them. I had no way of knowing if anyone was camped out below, of course. It was almost six PM when I trudged up to the marina office, tried the door, and found it locked, the blinds drawn. No Cap, either. I spotted the security cameras that had captured little to nothing the night Tim had died. It'd do no good trying to see the tapes myself. Marta had already examined them and found nothing of value. Dead end there. Besides, even asking to see them at this point would seriously damage our friendship and likely land me in a holding cell.

I went back to my car and made a call to a source I had at the phone company. After a simple lookup and a fair exchange, I had the number and address for a Vincent R. Darby. What had Darby been doing to harass Tim in his last days? It had to be harassment, or Tim wouldn't have had to ask to be left alone. What had been going on between the two? It was also possible that Ganz had lied to me about the argument to get me looking in another direction. He was angry with Tim about the money that never materialized. If that turned out to be the case, he wouldn't find me so amiable when we met again. Meanwhile, I'd keep going, check out Darby, and see what I could learn from him.

He lived off Wabash in the South Loop in a two-story Painted Lady with flower boxes at the windows. I rang the bell and the bright red door opened seconds later, revealing a chiseled Adonis with dark, curly hair and sleepy eyes the color of Chinese jade. There was a deep, healed-over scar on his dimpled chin, but that only made him look all the more rugged and capable, like he could start a fire without matches or wrestle an alligator with his bare hands. His eyes quickly scanned over me, and his easy smile revealed a legion of pearly white teeth, perfectly aligned.

"My day's looking up," he said, his gorgeous eyes latching onto mine and lingering there.

Friendly, I thought, *standing there all tall and athletic too.* For a half second, I forgot why I was there. "Vincent Darby?"

He was dressed in workout clothes, his hair damp with sweat, the ends of it curling up at the nape of his neck in cute, little angel ringlets. He dried long, tapered fingers on a small terry towel, eyed me quizzically, his smile positively lethal. "That's me."

I held up his business card, the one Ganz had given me. "Sterling Associates?"

I could see the wheels turning. He was likely wondering how I got to his front door from the information on the card, which offered nothing more than his name, place of business, and work number. "That's right."

I smiled broadly, knowing that *his* smile was not going to be long-lived. I took one final appreciative look, then waded in. "You handed these cards out at Tim Ayers's party." I put the card away, but plucked one of mine out of a pocket and handed it to him. "Cass Raines," I said. "I'd like to ask you a few questions about Tim, if you have the time?"

Like the sky after a storm cloud passes in front of the sun, Darby's Hollywood smile dimmed, then died. For a nanosecond, something else flickered across his flawless face, something I couldn't immediately put a finger on. Ganz mentioned that something about the man appeared rough and unpolished. For a split second, I could almost see it, but then whatever it was blew away.

"Private detective?" He ran the towel along the back of his neck to dry the sweat, and then ran it across his face and arms. "Sorry. You caught me at the end of a workout. What's this about?"

I stepped up to the top step, so we could be, more or less, eye to eye. "You were at a party Tim threw. You handed out your card. How were you two connected?" He read my card again, but didn't answer. "You two argued. Mind if I ask what about?"

Darby slid the towel under the waistband of his knee-length shorts, fisted his hands on his narrow hips. "I think you've gotten your wires crossed somewhere. I didn't argue with him."

"But you did crash?"

His eyebrows lifted, but he didn't answer.

The smile was back, though, but this time it didn't quite make it to those gorgeous eyes. He chuckled slightly. "I had no beef with Tim, and I certainly didn't crash any party. I stopped by to take a look at his paintings, maybe buy a piece. I thought it might cheer him up."

"Did he need cheering up?"

Darby, again, let a moment pass before he answered. Did he measure every move, every response, before he made it? Why? "He was a little down, but you'd expect that. I can't go into specifics about a client. It wouldn't be ethical."

"He was dying," I said, watching for a reaction. "And he was estranged from his family." Darby drew back ever so slightly.

"He had a lot to deal with," he said.

"But you *were* on the boat?"

"I stopped by, but like I said, it was about the paintings. When I saw he wasn't in a good place, I left. There were a lot of people there. He seemed to be into some things, recreational things. I'm not into that, so I took off. I couldn't have been there more than ten, fifteen minutes."

"Long enough to pass out your business card," I said.

Darby shrugged, grinned. "Hey, they might have all been stoned, but business is business. It's a shame what happened to him." He flashed the smile again. "But when I left, he was literally feeling no pain, definitely not in the mood to get into an argument with me about anything. Whoever you're getting this other stuff from is pulling your leg."

"It sure looks that way, doesn't it? Still, I had to ask." I moved to leave, Darby reached for the door to step inside. "Sorry. Almost forgot. After you left, because Tim wasn't in a good place, and stoned, do you remember what time you boarded your own boat? The one with the blue canopy? And were you in for the rest of the night, or did you go back out later, say around midnight? I ask only because, if you did go back out, you might have seen something or someone out of the ordinary hanging around Tim's boat."

I would swear Darby twitched, just a little, just enough to

catch my eye, but he ramped the smile back up big-time all the same. Darby and I watched each other for a moment or two. I couldn't tell what was going through his head, but it looked like he was cycling through something. He rubbed his hands on the towel at his waist, slowly, as though giving himself time to collect his thoughts. The smile flashed back, and the dimples, too. Seriously, it was like he turned it off and on at the drop of a hat. He let out a slow whistle. "Someone sure has sold you a bill of goods, haven't they? I don't own a boat, never have. Wish I did, though."

I eyed the house, the neat little window boxes. "Then you were home here the night Tim died?"

"I was out with friends and got home late. I heard about Tim on the news the next morning."

"You were out with friends in the middle of a thunderstorm?"

The gorgeous eyes bore into mine. "Most people own an umbrella. Now, if you'll excuse me."

He stepped back to close the door in my face, marking the end of our conversation, but stopped. "How'd you know where I lived?" There it was. I'd been waiting for him to ask the question, and I wondered now what had taken him so long. That didn't mean I'd answer it, though. Had I made him uneasy, nervous? "I'm not at liberty to say," I said.

"Who hired you then?"

I shrugged. "Back to the liberty thing."

His face held no expression. "Cass Raines," he said, seemingly committing my name to memory. "Word of advice?"

I took a step back. "Go for it."

"Don't believe everything some schmuck tells you. Next time, don't go off half-cocked."

He was cute and condescending, what a combination. The door began to close. "Uh, last one. Promise."

Darby glared at me, but held the door ajar. "You didn't buy a painting the night of the party, but did you go back later to buy one?"

For a moment, I thought I'd get a slammed door in the face, instead of an answer, but then he spoke. "No, never got the chance."

The door closed, and I heard Darby lock it tight from the inside. I stood on the stoop, trying to process what I'd just heard. He'd admitted to being on Tim's boat, but to buy art, which he didn't end up buying. He'd found Tim feeling a little down, not himself. That didn't jibe with what Jung had told me about Tim, but it did match what Stephen Ayers told Marta and Cap. According to C.D. Ganz, the night of Tim's party, he was not only down but drunk, which was the same state he was in the night he died. Darby had upped that by saying that Tim appeared stoned. Which one was lying, or was it both?

I could see why Darby might not want to admit to arguing with Tim, in light of what happened. If it turned out Tim killed himself, Darby admitting to arguing with him could lead some to think the confrontation they'd had could have pushed Tim toward suicide. But what reason would Ganz have for making the entire thing up?

Darby didn't have much of an alibi for the night Tim died. Dinner with friends? But if he'd killed him, he'd have had plenty of time to come up with a much better one. Or did he figure not having much of an alibi made him look all the more innocent? If he had reason to kill Tim, didn't it stand to reason it might be related somehow to Sterling? The two didn't appear to be connected any other way. I'd need to keep digging.

I started to walk away, but stopped when I heard Darby's muffled voice coming from inside the house. He was talking to someone, but I could only hear his end of the conversation. He was on the phone and he sounded agitated. Who was he calling so soon after talking to me? I strained to make out what was being said, but couldn't catch any of it.

I made a big show of walking back to my car and unlocking the door, getting in, and driving away, but I didn't go far. I drove up the block, turned around in an alley, and headed back, pulling into a spot across the street and down a bit from Darby's place where I had an unobstructed view of his front door. It was the phone call so soon after he closed the door on me that made me suspicious. Who was Darby checking in with? What had gotten him so upset?

The boat with the blue canopy—it would have been a strange detail for Ganz to offer up if it wasn't true, and an even stranger detail to get wrong if it was. Why deny owning a boat in the first place? Owning a boat wasn't a crime. Mooring a boat at the same marina as someone you knew wasn't, either. Darby hadn't mentioned anything about Tim having OCD or being bipolar. Maybe he didn't know? He wasn't his doctor; he only set him up with an insurance payout. And feeling a little down didn't automatically make you a prime candidate for suicide. If so, half the world's population would be at the bottom of a lake.

I eyed the house, the red door, the windows. Maybe Darby was calling someone to ask them what he should do about the nosy PI at the door. If so, that meant three things: One, Vince Darby, as good looking as any one man had any right to be, knew more than he was letting on about Tim's last days. Two, whatever was going on, he wasn't in it by himself. Three, Darby and his phone mate, whoever he or she turned out to be, were going to have one heck of a time shaking me loose.

I popped a Roberta Flack CD into the slot, but only got two tracks in before Darby rushed out of the house, scanned the street, and jumped into a clean white Mercedes parked at the curb. He started his engine; I started mine. When he pulled off, I waited until a couple of cars got ahead of me and then eased out after him, following at a "tailable" distance.

A rusty Toyota Celica and a fresh Chrysler sedan separated his back bumper from my front fender. None of us seemed to be in any particular hurry as the tiny caravan pulled up to a stoplight at Wabash and Roosevelt, the wide, congested street clogged with cars, trucks, and death-defying Divvy bike riders weaving through the bottleneck. On the sidewalk, texting pedestrians took their lives in their hands as they crossed the street distractedly, a bleating car horn their only salvation.

When the light turned green, Darby turned right, heading toward the Drive. I followed. Halfway through the intersection, though, Darby abruptly stopped with a screech of his wheels. The drivers of the Celica and the sedan honked at the show of bad form, but didn't linger to make a federal case out of it. They swerved around the impediment and took off, which left me with no buffer and a growing unease, my efforts at covert surveillance shot to hell.

"This can't be good," I muttered, my foot still firmly on the brake.

Darby got out of his car, his cell phone up to his ear, glaring in my direction. He could clearly see me; I could clearly see him. I was busted. I waved. There was no reason not to be cordial. He scowled, snapped my picture, and then mouthed something that didn't look at all like a Christian blessing, then jumped into his car and sped away. Vince Darby, one; foiled PI, zip. It took me less than a second to rise above the insult, but now I was well and truly over my crush.

Chapter 16

Wednesday morning was a perfect day for either a bike ride or to sleep in with all the windows open to let a light breeze in, but Darby's slip the day before still stung. I was bound and determined to find out what he was up to, but first, I wanted to take a shot at talking to Tim's mother. Stephen had gone out of his way to cast Tim as unstable, and I wanted to know why. So far he'd done a good job of avoiding me, going so far as to point his lawyer in my direction. If I wanted to get anything from him, I was going to have to try to force his hand by going over his head.

I slipped out my back door just after ten and raced down the back stairs. There were no strange cars idling in the alley, nor did I see anyone loitering anywhere. Good. I breathed a sigh of relief. Since the assault on my home months earlier, I saw shadows and threats looming around every corner. I couldn't convince myself, no matter how hard I tried, that all I was seeing were ghosts of past tragedies. My home was safe. My family was safe. Yet, the ghosts remained. I ran down the wooden steps, past the second-floor landing, headed for the first floor. I was hoping to breeze right past Mrs. Vincent's back door without rousing her, only to round the corner and come face-to-face with her. I stopped, dead in my tracks.

"Looks like you're in a hurry." She rocked slowly in her patio rocker, as though time meant nothing, as though she were looking out onto some scenic vista, instead of out over the alley and the city's battered garbage carts. "Haven't seen you much lately."

She was dressed in a pink housecoat and matching slippers, her gray hair pulled back from her round, dark face and held in a neat twist. She was sitting at her white café table, a teapot and a dainty plate of tea cakes on top, hanging pots of fragrant hydrangea swaying gently in a light breeze. She stared up at me, and I stared back.

"Work," I said.

The rocking was steady, slow, a little creepy. Like that rocking-chair scene at the end of *Psycho*. A slow, steady, dead-body rock. "Uh-huh."

"Everything okay with you?" I asked.

She smiled, picked up her teacup, took a sip. Unhurried. "Me? God's got me in the palm of his hand. And that's the gospel truth."

I eased toward the steps. "Good. That's great. I've got to run. I'll pop in later. We'll catch up." I hit the stairs and flew.

"Uh-huh. You do that. Real soon," I heard her say, though by then I was half a flight down.

I was sweating buckets when I hit the backyard. When I glanced up, Mrs. Vincent was still rocking, calm as anything, watching.

I'd been warned away by a rich guy's lawyer, and then caught flat-footed by a cute guy with a dubious connection to a dead man, and something didn't smell right. Someone was lying, and I needed to find a link, a thread that would made everything make sense. Cease and desist. That's what Felton warned. Fat chance. GPS calculated I'd hit Barrington Hills and the Ayers home in less than an hour, give or take a traffic jam or two. I'd figure out my game plan when I got there.

I drove more than thirty miles northwest of the city and knew I'd hit Barrington Hills when the trees got greener, the streets wider, and sleepy horse trails replaced the city's clogged expressways. I circled the white gazebo in the center of the village a few times before GPS finally got it right and pointed me south.

The Ayerses' place came up at me at the end of a country lane, looming large behind a high stone wall covered in English ivy. A black iron gate barred the circular drive, and entry here was strictly monitored by use of a discreetly placed intercom box. Behind me, BMWs, Bentleys, and Range Rovers whizzed past on meandering Woodhaven Lane, the name sounding like something out of a Disney princess movie. I punched the button, marveling at the castle beyond the gate, counting windows, losing interest after reaching twenty, waiting for someone to holler back. There was also a camera on the box, which, of course, made sense. If you live this exclusively, you'd want to see who it is that you've let beyond the velvet rope, or what would be the point of moving all the way out here?

"May I help you?" The voice was stately, deep.

It was probably a butler. A house this huge had to have a butler. "My name is Cass Raines. I'd like to speak with Mrs. Elizabeth Ayers? I'm a private investigator looking into the death of her son Timothy." I held my ID up to the camera, and then smiled nicely.

"Mrs. Ayers is not accepting visitors at this time."

I looked into the camera. "Perhaps I can arrange to come back at a more convenient time?"

"One moment, please." The intercom went cold, and I sat idling at the gate for a good five minutes until a black SUV, with POLICE, BARRINGTON HILLS emblazoned on the side, pulled up behind me, lights flashing, blocking me in at the gate. Two cops got out. I caught on quickly that the answer to my question concerning Mrs. Ayers's availability was a resounding no. I got out of my car slowly, keeping my hands up and out. Out of the corner of my eye, I watched a short, fat man in a pin-striped suit stroll out of the Ayers front door, down the drive, and through the gate where I stood. There was a gold watch fob in his right vest pocket, a pocket watch attached. Watch fob? What was this, 1918? The fat dandy scowled at me as he moved past me to greet the suburban cops, who didn't look all that eager to engage. After a brief discussion, Watch Fob padded over to me. My height, and his lack of it, gave me a bird's-eye view of the growing bald spot on the top of his freckled head.

"I thought you might try and wheedle your way in to see Mrs. Ayers, even after I warned you to stay away." He shot me a self-satisfied smile, behaving as though he'd single-handedly nabbed Bonnie Parker in the middle of a stickup.

I slowly put my hands down, eyeing the cops cautiously. "Robert V. Felton, Esquire. So you decided to camp out here on the off chance that I'd try to swim the moat?"

"I have resources. You have a reputation for being both tenacious and recalcitrant. I thought it best to head you off, which I've successfully done." He pointed to the cops behind him. "These gentlemen will escort you from the premises. If you return, which I strongly advise against, the Ayers family is prepared to press charges for trespassing and harassment." He stepped back, and then snapped his fingers as if summoning his very own pet giant to squash an encroaching villager. "Gentlemen?"

The cops—both white, one tall, one wide, both with buzz cuts—stood staunchly upright, stern faces advertising their unwillingness to take part in a lot of needless chitchat.

"Where were you when Tim fell from his boat, Felton?"

Felton's eyes, ferretlike, bags under them, flashed a warning. "You have no idea who I am, do you?" He smiled, but it was the kind of smile that might send little kids cowering under the covers, screaming for Mommy.

"Actually, I do. You see, I also have resources. Long story

short, you're a bully in a thousand-dollar suit who charges wealthy clients, like the Ayerses, exorbitant amounts to haul their pampered asses out of whatever cracks they manage to fall into. They likely have your number on speed dial, and when they call, like now, apparently, you run right over to make the unpleasantness go away."

Felton's ears turned red first; then his cheeks blossomed. "As I've just done."

I chuckled. "Hardly. Like you said, I'm tenacious."

I moved over and hit the intercom button again. "I don't think Tim slipped from his boat, and I don't think he jumped. I think someone killed him. I don't know why yet, or who, but I'm working on it. I'd like to know why Stephen Ayers lied to the police about his brother's mental state. I'd like to know where he was the night Tim died." I slid a look at the fuming lawyer. "Robert V. Felton, Esquire, can bury me in orders to cease and desist, but I'll keep digging. There's nothing I hate more than someone who likes to play God by taking a life he's not entitled to. If you decide you want to talk, I'm in the book." I let the button go.

"Mr. Ayers died as the result of a tragic boating accident," Felton said, his jaw clenched. "Nothing more."

I smiled, but there wasn't an ounce of good humor in it. "We'll see. Good day, Mr. Felton." I turned to the cops. "Let's go, officers. I want to miss the midday traffic."

The SUV followed me all the way to the feeder ramp of the Eisenhower. I waved at the cops before they peeled off and headed back to Fairyland. They both missed the middle finger that followed it up.

Chapter 17

It was after two when I got back to civilization. The traffic had been horrendous, some pileup somewhere along the line, and my nerves were shot. I scanned the lakefront as I sped down the Drive headed south, looking for a little calming action. The beach at Fifty-seventh was teeming with sweaty city dwellers hoping to cool down in the murky water. Someone was probably getting their beach bag pinched while they were off wading hip deep in the lake, but I breathed in deeply, happy to be home. Even the air smelled different this side of the horse trails and tennis clubs; it was grittier, heavier, like it had attitude, like it was bad enough to slink down your throat and pull your kidneys out through your nostrils.

Felton sure knew how to earn his keep, I thought, but why had the Ayerses felt it necessary to warn me off before I'd even really started? Were they that averse to having their family talked about? Or were they hiding something? I hoped it was Elizabeth Ayers or Stephen on the other end of that intercom. If it had only been the butler, I'd wasted a good, badass speech.

I pulled up in front of Deek's, exhausted from sitting too long in the car, in search of refueling and commiseration. I needed to suck in the smell of griddle grease and Deek's familiar acrimony.

I needed to get back to normal. Quick through the door, I glanced over at my booth and pulled up short. Detective Eli Weber was sitting there, bold as you please. In *my* spot.

Of course, I knew the booth didn't belong exclusively to me, but my preference for it, and the fact that I'd broken in the vinyl seats, in my mind, sort of made it mine. And now there was Weber sitting in it, reading the newspaper, his blazer off, his shirtsleeves rolled up to the forearms. I gave it a moment to see how I felt about that, decided I didn't know, and lightly padded over to the counter, trying not to make noise or draw attention to myself. I slid onto a stool, my back to the booth. I knew he knew I was there. He didn't miss a thing. Muna walked over. I cocked a thumb toward the booth, looked a question.

"What?" she said. "We're supposed to rope it off when you're not here? He came in and was looking for you. I sat him over there, and I don't think he's here to talk business." Her gaze lifted over my shoulder. "Oh, he's straightening his tie. Lovely. What I couldn't do with a man like that. How'd you hook him?"

"I did not 'hook him.' We're not *hooked*. We're . . ." I took a moment to search for the right word, coming up empty. I smiled instead. I was an idiot, a grown-ass woman, too old for the flutter in my belly.

Muna grinned. "Well, if you're not hooked, and want to be, you'd better get on it. Men like that don't stay on the market long."

"I need a cheeseburger," I said.

Muna's eyebrows flicked up. "Nobody *needs* a cheeseburger."

"And fries."

Muna peered over her half-glasses. "Who shot your dog?"

"My day didn't go well, now there's a dangerous man sitting in my spot, and, frankly, I'm not up for it today, all right?"

She looked at me like I was crazy. "And by 'dangerous' you mean?"

I narrowed my eyes. "You know what I mean."

"And you're thinking indigestion's going to fix that?"

I ran my fingers through my hair. Tough day getting tougher. "Ham on rye and a kosher pickle, then."

"That's more like it. What's your beef with Mr. Just My Type?"

"I don't have one." I didn't. There was absolutely nothing wrong with Weber, not that I could see. He was smart and quick and easy to talk to—funny, in a dry sort of way. And he unnerved the hell out of me. "But he has designs."

Muna blinked, waited for more, but there was no more. "And what do you have?"

"I . . . It's . . ."

She smirked. "Yeah, that's what I thought. Get over there and talk to the nice man, before I do."

I could almost feel Weber breathing behind me and he was half a diner away. There was something there, something I wanted, but would I want it when I got it? We could be completely incompatible, oil and water, night and day. I drummed my fingers on the counter, Muna watching.

"Oh, this is ridiculous." I lifted off the stool.

Muna smiled, eyes sly. "I was just thinking that."

I headed over, my shoulders squared. "You're in my booth."

Weber smiled up at me. "I know. And it's bugging the hell out of you."

I slid in across from him, grumpy, but present. "That's what you're trying to do? Bug me?"

"I'll add 'territorial' to the list of things I'm learning about you."

"You have a list?"

"You've got one, too."

I slid a sideways glance at Muna. She was watching from the counter as though this was an Ibsen play and she'd paid good money for front-row seats. He was right, of course. Every woman had a list. I watched as he folded his newspaper and pushed it aside, giving me his full attention. His piercing eyes, the color of almonds, lasered in, and I held the gaze for way longer than I should have. He smelled nice. The graying at his temples, the crinkling around his eyes, were Mother Nature's low blows.

"Look, Weber . . ."

"Eli. Around the district, some of the guys call me Fish, but I don't think I want you calling me that."

I angled my head, smiled, forgetting about the cheeseburger I'd craved when I walked in. "Fish?"

"That's third date information. This is date two." He eyed the plastic tablecloth and Deek's flimsy silverware. "Not exactly four-star, but we're working our way up, considering we started in the hospital."

I leaned back, took all of him in. "You're overestimating my level of interest."

He shrugged. He took nonchalance to championship level. "I don't think so. You're still sitting there."

We sat quietly for a time and the silence didn't feel at all strained or awkward. I couldn't catch a break. I leaned forward again, prepared to rebuff, but lost the will, and leaned back again.

"I ordered lunch," he said finally. "Let's eat."

"I've got a sandwich coming. I planned to eat at my desk." I raised my wrist to show my watch. "Still on the clock."

Muna popped up at the table, silently like a stealth drone, and placed a meat loaf platter in front of Weber and the ham sandwich I'd ordered by default in front of me.

"I gave you *two* pickles," she said, grinning wide. "In case y'all wanted to share."

I watched her move away again, a scowl on my face. With friends like these . . .

Weber unfolded a paper napkin, spreading it across his lap, as though preparing to while away the afternoon. "You're backtracking on the Ayers case, even though it's ours, and by 'ours,' I mean CPD, and more specifically Pena's."

I covered my lap in napkins, too. "Who told you that?"

"You did. With the look you just gave me. Have you found anything we didn't?"

I shook my head. "Not yet, but I think there's something there. I can feel it. You guys, Marta, think Ayers committed suicide."

He forked a morsel of meat loaf into his mouth. "We suspected it, but couldn't say for sure. Ruling accidental, spares the family."

"I think they'd want the truth, whatever it is, don't you?"

He nodded slowly, turning suddenly serious. "Sometimes the truth hurts. Sometimes not having it does more good than harm." He let his words hang there for a moment while he watched me across the table. "You don't agree?"

"Booze and prescription meds," I said. "Why not just stick with that? Why jump into the lake? Why opt for an agonizing end, when a more peaceful one was available?"

Weber didn't answer, just watched.

"What?" I said.

"If Marta could have moved the needle, she would have."

"Maybe." I picked up my sandwich, took a bite. It'd been hours since my morning cereal. "Actually, not maybe, I know she would have. Your nickname's really Fish?"

He raised his glass and took a sip of water, swallowed. "Yep."

"And you're not going to tell me how that came about."

The devilish look he gave me made me smile. "It's called keeping the mystery alive. Did you find that kid, the one on the bike?"

Still chewing, I nodded.

"He wasn't your client before, but he is now?"

"He is."

Weber looked baffled. "And he handed over *real* money?"

"He wrote a check."

"Huh. Go figure. And you think you've got a shot at turning

something up, even though we worked it and found what we found?"

"I might have a shot. There's nothing competing for my time at the moment."

He dug into his mashed potatoes, his eyes locked on mine. "Are there any windmills you won't tilt at?"

I thought about it. "I don't think so. My turn. What are we doing? You keep showing up. I push you away. But you don't stay gone."

He wiped his lips with his napkin, took his time with it. "I noticed that. But there aren't any windmills I won't tilt at, either."

I bit into my pickle. "And I'm the windmill in this scenario?"

He chuckled. What a nice sound it made. "You interest me. I think I interest you. I like the way you handle yourself. You're smart, ballsy. You don't give an inch. Even right now. I have no clue why you keep pushing me away, but that's you, not me. We could talk about it, if you want?"

I shook my head. "That's okay. I got it."

"It takes a lot getting to know somebody," he said. "It's a leap. You have a lot going on."

I went back to my sandwich, listening to him reason it out. "There's something else, too, something I'm drawn to. I saw it the first time we met in your yard. You told me to take a hike, as I recall."

I held up a finger. "I told your *partner* to take a hike."

"Right. Okay . . . I saw that something again in the ER. I see a little of it now."

I bristled, waited, but Weber let the silence hang there. "Is that something extreme irritation?"

He pushed his plate away, folded his napkin neatly on the table beside it. "How's some hippie kid afford a PI?"

"I don't care. Answer the question."

"I'd rather wait until you decide you like me."

I took a sip of water, peering at him over the glass. The smile came slowly. "Neither of us has that kind of time."

Weber laughed full-out this time, the sound of it filling the entire diner. I checked again for Muna, and caught her at the counter, fluttering her eyes, her hands over her heart. She wasn't getting a tip from me today.

"I was separated from my wife for two years before we finally divorced," Weber said. "That's just me letting you know I'm beyond the rebound stage."

"Good to know. Still waiting."

He scanned the diner, turned back to me; the smile was gone now. "I shot a kid, too. He did not survive. We did a search warrant on a crack house on the West Side." He stopped talking for a moment, and I knew he was back in the crack house. "I guess it doesn't matter much where. He was sixteen, same age as my kid now. Jarrod Wigham was his name. He'd be twenty-two next month."

I felt myself close down, but I couldn't make myself turn away or get up and leave. Instead, I stared at him, really looked deep, searching for the something we shared. And there it was, in the eyes, that familiar shadow I'd somehow missed before. I hadn't paid much attention, not going too far below the surface packaging. I'd been too busy closing the door, dead-bolting it, but there it was. In an instant, I knew him; he knew me. He hadn't said "I *killed* a kid." I had a difficult time saying it, too, even now. *I shot a kid . . . he did not survive.*

"I don't talk about it. Neither do you. It's something you hold on to yourself, live with, isn't it? Something you haul around on your back, like a bag of wet sand." He leaned back against the booth. "I've learned not to pick at the scab, to just let it be. The something I saw, I guess, was the trace of what that leaves behind. I'm telling you so you'll know who and what I am. It hasn't broken me. It hasn't broken you. It just is." He nodded, slid me a knowing smile. "You want to run for the door right now, but you won't."

I straightened, stared at him defiantly. "I don't run."

"Except from me." He leaned forward again. "That's it. I've

made my play. Next move's yours. I hope you don't wait too long to make it, though. I'm not getting any younger." The heat off the grin he gave me felt as warm as sunshine. "And make it good. I'm no pushover."

"What if I choose not to?"

"*I'm* choosing not to think about that."

I didn't know what to say, so I said nothing.

"You're not going to finish your sandwich, are you?" Weber said.

I shook my head. The diner disappeared: Muna, the din, the people around us. There was just the booth, and me and Weber. And the next move was mine.

Chapter 18

I stopped Jimmy Pick before he could shoot Ben. He was my partner, my responsibility, and I was his. *Stopped? Killed.* I leaned back in my swivel chair, closed my eyes, tried to keep my breathing steady. It was the only thing I could have done. The only thing I knew to do. Now I had to live with it, carry it around "like a bag of wet sand," like Weber said. Two years and counting, an entire lifetime to go.

I looked around my office as though seeing it for the first time. How compact it was, how utilitarian: the gunmetal file cabinets, the scarred desk, the computer, and the two client chairs. There was an Annie Lee print on the wall, the one titled *Rebirth*. Pop had given it to me, wrapped up nice, the day I was discharged from the hospital I nearly died in. It gave the place some class. The office wouldn't win any awards for interior design, but I didn't need things fussy. I just needed them to work.

I glanced at the coatrack near the door, at the battered, crook-handled umbrella hanging on it. Pop's umbrella. I'd insisted on having it, and I kept it close, here where I spent most of my time. I liked being able to look up and see it; it grounded me, even though it would always be an inadequate substitute, and a sad reminder of what I'd lost. The print, the umbrella, there seemed to be more of Pop in here than there was of me, but I was okay with that, too.

Weber was under my skin now, in my head. It felt like I'd somehow boarded a runaway train with zero chance of getting off it. *I could shut it down,* I thought, *shut him down. Is that what I want?* I wasn't sure. I straightened, shook it off. That was enough. Tim Ayers. That's who I needed to focus on now. That was my job.

I scooted up to the computer, booted it up, and logged into the databases I subscribed to, running Darby's name through, looking for anything I could find on him. I subscribed to several online resources that allowed me to check court records, vital stats, news archives, vehicle data through the State of Illinois. Access cost me dearly every month, but it cut down on the running around.

I needed to know more about Darby. Who was he? Who was he connected to? What was he hiding? After about an hour of fine-tuning the search, I got several hits on the name. I then narrowed my parameters by approximate age and race, and there he was. I slid back from the computer, my eyes glued to the screen. He was an ex-con, just a year and a half out of prison. *Well, if that doesn't just beat all?* I read through what was there: *Vincent Ronald Darby, DOB April 6, 1978.* There was nothing violent, at least not on paper: mainly petty theft, minor offenses, passing bad checks. He served a four-year stint for the checks. Darby had no one listed as next of kin, but the address came back funky. The house he was living in, the Painted Lady, didn't belong to him. The owner was listed as a Peter Langham, deceased.

I leaned in, grabbing a pen and paper to jot down the information. No known associates. So Darby didn't run with a crew, or if he did, he kept it low-key. No employer listed, but then why was he handing out business cards for Sterling Associates? Why was he claiming Tim as a client? The plates on the Mercedes didn't come back to Darby, either. The car was owned by a Nicholas

Spada. Who was he? I was curious about Langham and searched him first. Date of death, January 12, 2019. Just three months ago. He was seventy-eight. No criminal record, no liens, no lawsuits, no family, no nothing.

"Not so much as a parking ticket," I muttered. Was Langham related to Darby? An old uncle who left him the house in his will? I fished around a little more, looking for a boat linked to Darby, but didn't find one. *He doesn't own a boat. He doesn't own the house he's living in.* I then clicked over and searched for Nicholas Spada, surprised when a hit came back almost immediately. Spada owned Sterling Associates. Darby's driving Spada's car, handing out cards to Spada's business? That kind of confirmed his connection. I checked further, but Spada came back clean, just like Latham. He was married. His wife's name was Anne.

I logged out, let the information sink in, then worked it through using the Annie Lee print as a sounding board. "Okay. Darby connects to Sterling, the company Tim worked his settlement deal through, which is owned by Spada, whose car Darby was driving when he busted my tail. Coincidence? Don't think so. In fact, Annie Lee, it creates a tight little circle, doesn't it? Yes, it does."

That left Langham as the odd piece. Who was he and why was Darby, an ex-con with dreamy green eyes, living in the dead man's house? And how'd an ex-con get a job with a legitimate company like Sterling right out of prison? Hadn't Spada bothered to do even a routine background check?

I'd compiled the newspaper clippings from Ayers's case into a file, and went through them again. The news stories simply stated the facts—suspected impairment, an unfortunate fall—nothing on Tim's autopsy results or anything about physical evidence. That's as good as the family wanted, apparently. Short, sweet: "Nothing to see here, folks, move along."

I folded my notes, my mind on Darby's checkered past. It

would certainly account for the roughness under all that hotness. Four years in prison will do that to you. Peter Langham, I mused, deceased.

"You left half your sandwich. Muna packed it up for you." I looked up to see Jung standing in the doorway, rocking back and forth on his motorcycle boot heels, a white deli bag banging against his knees. I hadn't heard him come in. "This is wild, huh? I'm delivering your dinner, but you work for me? It's mind-blowing."

I stood and began straightening up my desk. "I thought Deek fired you?"

"He hired me back. He's got a soft spot."

I eyed him quizzically. The idea of Deek having a soft spot wasn't computing. Jung held the bag up.

"I don't have time for it now. I've got a lead, and though I technically work for you, in every way that really matters to me, I work for *me*."

Jung gave me a long, probing stare.

"What are you looking at?"

"Muna wanted me to see if you were okay, something about a guy in your booth earlier?"

"Tell her I'm fine. And then tell her she owes me a cheeseburger . . . and fries."

"Okay." Jung stood there, rocking. "How's the case going?"

I banged desk drawers shut, locked them. "Jung, seriously, I've got to go."

"But aren't I entitled to a report? The contract says so. I read it. Upon request, it said."

He returned a guileless look, his eyes as big as Bambi's, as innocent as a two-year-old's. I sighed and waved him toward a chair. "Sit. Five minutes." I gave him a quick rundown of my time so far, my conversations with Cantu and Ganz, my ride out to Barrington Hills, my database searches.

"And Vince Darby," I said. "A witness reported hearing him

argue with Tim aboard his boat during a party . . . a party you allegedly attended, by the way. So why didn't I hear about it from you?"

Jung's eyes widened. "I should have mentioned it, right? I didn't think it was important. It was just a party. Tim had them all the time. Darby? Yeah, I remember seeing him, but I don't know anything about any argument. We were all there having a good time, Darby showed, the party was in full swing. I looked up, and he was gone. I remember Tim got pissed about something at one point, but whatever he was pissed about blew over. He asked for a drink, a hit, and he was all good."

"Was Tim depressed that night?"

"Hell no. He was the life of the party till that Darby walked in. After he left, Tim looked like he got buzzkilled, but he bounced back quick. You sure they had it out?"

"No, I'm not sure. Darby says he was there to buy one of Tim's paintings, decided to give it some more thought, then left. He said that's the last he saw of Tim." I ran my fingers over the card. "Darby's handing these out for Sterling Associates. He connects to Sterling's owner, Nicholas Spada. Do you recognize the name?"

"Spada, yeah, he was a friend of Tim's dad and handled some of the family's business. That's why Tim went to him." Jung pointed at the card. "I got one of those, too. That's why I remember the dude. I trashed mine, though. It's like you're tempting fate, or something. And Darby seemed to always hang too close. I never did find out what that was all about."

"Did Tim ever find out why?"

Jung shook his head, held his arms out in a gesture of frustration. "Never did. I don't think the guy would say. But that's hinky, right?"

"It's worth following up on."

"What about Stephen? What'd Tim's mother say?"

"What about Stephen? He won't return my calls. And the

family lawyer met me at their front gate to run interference between me and Tim's mother, after he called the cops."

Jung frowned. "I knew you needed me. They're not used to seeing people like you up there."

"Wrong color?" I asked bitingly.

Jung folded his hands in his lap, shot me a gloomy look. "Wrong color, wrong sex, wrong socioeconomic background, wrong politics . . . I could go on. Life's a lot better outside the bubble than inside it. What'd the police do?"

I held out my hand for the bag with my sandwich in it. As long as I had three and a half minutes left, I might as well start it. "They escorted me out of the neighborhood."

"Sounds about right."

I leaned back in my chair, unwrapped the wax paper. "Do you know Felton?"

Jung nodded. "Back when we were kids, he got Tim out of a few scrapes like it was nothing. One call to him, and *bam*, problem solved. He's a real bulldog." Jung brushed his hands together, universal sign for "done deal."

I grimaced, recalling my encounter with the bulldog. "Does your family have a bulldog?"

Jung smiled slyly. "Michael Greenleaf, Esquire."

I tossed down the pickle. "Peter Langham. Ring any bells?"

Jung shook his head. "Who is he?"

"Who *was* he—he's dead. How could Stephen disinherit Tim? His father would have had a will. Stephen couldn't have held back anything their father left him, unless he was cut off from that completely."

Jung shrugged. "When old man Ayers died, he left Stephen as executor. By then, Tim had gotten a reputation as a screwup and a major disappointment. I guess leaving everything in Stephen's hands made sense to him from a business standpoint. It didn't take long for Stephen to work out his childhood issues by holding up the cash. He held the money over Tim, and enjoyed it. He wanted everything Tim had, freedom, friends, all of it, and the money was his control. That is, until Tim got sick of it and said the hell with it." Jung shook his head woefully. "Maybe Stephen wanted the boat? It was their father's. Maybe he thought he should have gotten that, too? I don't want to believe he'd kill Tim for it."

I nodded. "Ganz said he saw Darby board a boat at the marina. What if he lives there?"

"I never heard Tim talk about any Ganz. Maybe he heard it wrong?" He held the card up, and then stood to pace. "But this Darby. They argued, you said, so maybe he comes back, kills Tim? He thinks he got away with it, but then you show up and he gets nervous. That's why he made that call? Why he rushed out? That's a good theory, right? Or try this on. Maybe this Ganz pulls a fake. Maybe he's the one who has it out with Tim, but he points the finger at Darby instead. One of them, not sure which, could be on the run right now. We need to make a move." Jung turned, saw me still sitting there. "Well?"

"I don't know enough yet," I said calmly. "Neither do you."

"But if Darby was hanging out at the marina, he was right there, right under Tim's nose."

"I've only got one man's word on that so far." I stood. Jung's five minutes were up. "Go back to Deek's. I'll call you if I need you."

"Just like that?"

I padded over to the door, opened it. "Bye, Jung. Thanks for the sandwich."

He stepped out into the hall, turned back. "But the contract says . . ."

I pushed the door closed and locked it. This hadn't been my most productive day. I'd been given the heave-ho, and warned off by Stephen Ayers, albeit it was a warning once removed, coming from his lawyer as it did, but it was a warning just the same. And I was nowhere close to proving anything. I wondered about C.D. Ganz. He seemed forthcoming enough, up to a point, but he was definitely holding something back. Maybe he had concocted that argument to run me around? And, seriously, how *did* he know Tim's case had been closed?

I stood in the middle of my office, not knowing what thread to pull first. It was after seven. I'd have no luck at Sterling until morning. I stood at the window, my mind trying to order disparate bits of detail. I took a deep breath, let it out, then took another, watching as the seven-eighteen Metra local, two minutes behind schedule, rattled by at the corner. When it disappeared from view, my tired eyes shifted to the street to track a tall man with a short dog on a leash making their way up the block. Slow and steady, picking through one lead after another, that's how the work is done. Someone was lying. I had to figure out who and why, but not tonight. I closed the blinds, tossed my notes into a folder, and headed home.

Chapter 19

I parked a block from my building and walked around to the back stairs, up to the third floor, treading lightly so as not to disturb Mrs. Vincent. I didn't want a repeat of this morning's encounter. I'd been doing all I could lately not to lead trouble back to my doorstep, to my family. It was a lesson learned the hard way.

Mrs. Vincent's windows were dark when I crept past them. At seven-thirty PM, she was likely in bed watching television, locked in for the night. Still, I checked to make sure her windows and door were secured before moving on. I avoided looking at the second-floor windows, but thought of little Nate all the same. Up on the third floor, I eased my key into my door, slipped inside, and flicked on the kitchen lights. I was startled to see blue light shining in from the living room, the sound of my television blaring. Not a burglar. No self-respecting thief was going to ransack your place, then sit down to watch *Survivor*, unless he or she was a complete idiot.

Halfway down the hall, I spotted a bedraggled travel sack leaning against the front door, and knew who it belonged to. *Barb*. I relaxed. What was she doing here? She and her jungle pack were supposed to be in Tanzania teaching English to little kids. I turned the corner, expecting to see her sitting on my couch, but found instead Mrs. Vincent, her nimble hands knitting their way through a lap full of lavender yarn.

"I brought you a bowl of red beans and rice," she said, not bothering to look up. "It's in the fridge." She peered up at me through thick bifocals hanging from a chain. I looked around the room; no one else in it. This felt like a setup, an ambush.

"Why's Barb's bag here?"

She balled up the yarn she hadn't yet gotten to and stuffed it into the embroidered bag she kept it in. "She's in the guest room sleeping. It's a long way from Africa."

"Everything okay?" Maybe there'd been a death in the Covey family. Her mom? One of her brothers? No, if that were the case, she'd have called to tell me, and then she'd have gone straight home; she wouldn't be here, asleep in my spare room.

Mrs. Vincent smiled. "She's fine. But you and me need to talk."

I stepped farther in, confident now no one was going to jump out at me. I kicked my shoes off, wiggled my toes. "About?"

"You've been sneaking around here like Mata Hari, using the back door when the front door works just fine." She waggled a finger at me. "Caught you this morning, didn't I?" She folded plump arms across her chest. "I know what you're doing. We're about to talk about that."

No, it wasn't a setup or an ambush, it was an intervention, and I was hemmed in tight, like a jumpy steer squeezed into a rodeo pen. I took a step backward, eyeing the hall, the back door at the end of it. I reasoned I could likely hit that door long before the old lady could mount a decent pursuit.

She huffed. "Don't even think about it. Everybody's worried—Benjamin, Charles, Barbara. They started calling me when they couldn't get you, which might explain why she's here and not there. Follow me into the kitchen. I'll heat up those beans for you. I brought corn bread, too. Hope you're hungry. Even if you aren't, you're going to eat."

She took off on spongy heels, her crepe soles nearly silent on the hardwood floor as she padded down the hall, heading back toward the kitchen. I followed dutifully. There was no getting away.

"I know what I'm doing," I told her.

She scoffed. "Here's what *I* know. You're working yourself into the ground. I can't remember the last time I saw you for more than a quick hello. I decided you needed the time to get things settled—that when you *were* settled, you'd be back same as you were." She turned to face me. "Well, it's been long enough. You think trouble goes where you do, but, child, trouble's out there whether it comes riding in on your coattails or not. I know. I've seen it all and done about half of it." She grabbed the Pyrex dish with her homemade beans in it out of the fridge and slipped it into the microwave. "Sit," she said, pointing to one of the barstools pulled up to the center island. "You need people. You've got people. That's it, plain and simple." Her eyes met mine. "Act like it."

She moved around my kitchen like it was hers, pulling down a bowl, grabbing a spoon.

"You don't know what's at stake here, what could happen. I—"

She cut me off with a mother's glare, part loving, part terrifying. "You were an obstinate child, as I recall, and you're an obstinate woman. Call your friends. Come in through your front door. All this sneaking around is rattling my nerves." She pulled the dish out of the microwave, spooned a good helping of the beans in a bowl in front of me, and topped it off with a generous slice of warm corn bread. "Now, what're you working on that's got you so het-up?" Her warm, dark eyes lasered in. "This is where you do the talking."

I was a bit shell-shocked, but also very hungry. I dug into the bowl. "A drowning case. I'm being given the business at the moment. I have no idea what's going on." I peered up at her, my eyes narrowed. "If you were a killer, would you waste your time killing a dying man?"

Her eyes widened in surprise. "Me? A killer? Lord Jesus."

I waved it off. It was ludicrous. Mrs. Vincent was a churchgoing woman. She sang in the choir, never missed a service. How could she put herself in the mind of a cold-blooded killer? I chuckled. "Never mind. I forgot who I was talking to." I went back to my bowl. The beans were good, spicy, and the corn bread was sweet and melted in my mouth.

"If I was hell-bent on killing a person," Mrs. Vincent mused, a faraway look in her eyes, "there wouldn't be anything that'd turn me from it. I'd have evil in my heart, and my soul would be black as pitch. All I'd be thinking about is how much I wanted the person to crawl and suffer and beg for mercy." I watched her, my mouth hanging open. "Would I care if the person was already dying?" She stopped, gave it some thought. "I don't think so. Whatever they did to make me want to kill them would be all I'd be thinking about. I'd want to be the one to make the light go out of their eyes. It'd be the power and control I was after, wouldn't it?" She shook her head, tidied up the counter, gathering up corn bread crumbs. "Killing is a very selfish act, Cassandra. It's 'me, me, me,' not 'you, you, you.'"

My spoon held suspended between my bowl and my mouth, the beans going cold. The old woman's words sent a shiver down my spine and I watched, a little creeped out, as a mischievous grin spread across her face.

"But you'd know more about that than I would." She wiped her hands on the towel, folded it neatly, and then placed it on the counter. "Two more things, unrelated to me being a killer. One, you're going to rent that apartment downstairs. It's been vacant too long. Two, the letters from your daddy have been piling up in that bowl in the foyer for weeks now. You haven't opened a one. You're going to open those letters and read them, and then you're going to come to some kind of peace with that man."

I sighed. "I've nothing to say to him."

"Your brain's working, isn't it? You're a college graduate? You'll think of something. Now I'm going on home. Tonight's *Dancing with the Stars*." She eyed me closely. "Is there anything else I need to set straight?"

I swallowed hard. "No, ma'am, I think this about covers everything."

She reached out and gave my shoulder a gentle squeeze. "Good, then. Make sure that back door's locked. See? Looking out for folks goes two ways."

She padded out of the kitchen. I listened as she flicked off the television and gathered up her things. When I heard the front door open and close, I breathed easy. I'd just been schooled by a master. I went back to the beans, vowing never to get on Mrs. Vincent's bad side.

Chapter 20

I woke in a dark room, reaching for the ringing phone. It was four in the morning. "H'lo?"

"You have to get down there. The marina. I didn't do it. Whatever they tell you, the cops, it wasn't me."

The words spilled out in a rush, one crashing over the other, and my brain, still foggy from sleep, only deciphered half of them. I made out that it was Jung, though. He sounded frantic, talking a mile a minute. I bolted up in bed, flicked the lamp on. "Jung? What are you talking about? Didn't do what?"

"I was there, but I didn't do it. I'll explain later, but right now you have to get down to Tim's boat. It's swarming with cops. But it wasn't me, just remember that."

I tumbled out of bed. The line went dead. I checked caller ID, but the number he'd called from was scrambled; the ID simply read, UNKNOWN. He was obviously no longer using Bucky's loaner phone. I raced around my room, grabbing up clothes, shoes. My bedroom door slowly opened, Barb peeking her head in, wild red hair mashed from the pillow, green eyes rimmed with red from too much travel, too little sleep.

"What's going on? Who died?"

I blinked, for a second confused. "I don't know. No one, I

hope." I studied her while I shoved my feet into running shoes. This was the second time in a week I'd woken to a disturbing call from Jung. It was getting old. I squinted at Barb. She looked not herself. "You okay?"

She eased in fully dressed, wearing worn jeans and a faded Pope Francis T-shirt, her athletic frame masked by both. She yawned. "I'm still on Tanzanian time. Up when everyone else is asleep, asleep when everyone's awake. I was in the kitchen making a sandwich when the phone rang. Nothing good happens this early. What's up, besides the two of us?"

I didn't bother with shoelaces. They were still tied from the night before, so I jammed my feet in. "That was my client. He's done something stupid. He says he didn't, but I know he has. I'm headed out." I scanned the room, looking for my bag.

"Anything dangerous?"

"Only to my overall health and well-being, I think." I found the bag, headed for the door.

Barb smiled. "Mind if I tag along?"

I stopped, faced her, saying nothing. I was at that place again where I had to choose whether to involve family with the job. Mrs. Vincent had chided me for pushing my friends away, but I had a legitimate reason for doing it. I didn't work in a bank or in a grocery store. I chased criminals for a living, and sometimes they took offense and chased me back. What kind of person would rope a nun into something like that? Even a nun, born and bred on the gritty South Side of Chicago, one raised in a family of battling Irish, one who could likely whip my ass.

"I'll keep you company," Barb said. "Watch you do what you do."

She met my look straight on, unflinching. Barb was always unflinching. I could tell there was something on her mind, though. I'd known her more than half my life—Whip too—and they knew me right back. We were the same in many ways, which is what made it so weird that we'd each gone in such drastically different directions. I became a cop; Barb married God; Whip, until he got pinched and incarcerated, boosted cars for a living. I worried that Whip would revert to his old ways. He said he never would, but the streets, the lure of an easy score, had a strong pull.

Barb gave me half a smile, her green eyes keen. "I saw the letters."

I bristled. The letters from my prodigal father were where I'd left them, unopened on the table in the entryway. The stack by now had to be at least a dozen high. "Is *that* what's on your mind?"

She shook her head. "Just an observation. You're not even a *little* curious?"

I swept past her, my mind on the marina. "If you're coming, come on. You can stay in the car."

I grabbed my keys and checked my bag for aspirin, finding a small bottle tucked in the inside pocket. I had a feeling I was going to need it. Four AM, I thought as Barb and I stepped out into the street. My neighbors were sound asleep in their beds; Jung was somewhere doing Lord knows what; Barb had something she needed to talk about. In my opinion, talking was overrated. People talked too much. Handle your business, keep it to yourself, and keep it moving. Those were words to live by.

Chapter 21

I saw the blue police lights from Lake Shore Drive and pulled into the marina lot, parking far away from the hub of activity. Barb glowered. "If you'd parked any farther away, I'd have to take a bus to see anything remotely interesting."

"That's what I was aiming for."

The talk we were supposed to have on the ride over never happened. She talked about Africa and the kids she missed, her family, her mother, what was new with me—small talk. I didn't press it. You had to give Barb room. When she was ready, whatever it was she needed to talk about, she would. I turned to her. "Please stay in the car." She frowned, nodded. Not good enough. "I need verbal confirmation. Actual words, so I know you heard me."

Barb folded her arms over her chest. "I see Mrs. Vincent's talk is going to take some time sinking in."

I squinted at her, my voice low. "I *knew* that smelled like an ambush. You were in on that?"

Barb grinned. "We'll talk about it later."

I climbed out of the car, holding the driver's door open. "We sure will, along with the other thing we were supposed to talk about on the ride over, but didn't."

I pushed the door closed without further comment and

headed toward the slips, scanning faces, looking for ones I knew. I didn't see the ME's van parked anywhere, which was a good sign. That meant nobody was dead. There was also no ambulance, no red crime-scene tape, just a few squad cars and two unmarked vehicles. I spotted Detective Marta Pena in the middle of a small huddle, which didn't compute. She was a violent-crime detective. Dead bodies were her specialty. Cap was also there and the nosy Eldon Reese, his complaint book gripped tightly in his pale, hateful little hands. The two stood and talked, their heads together. What was that all about? I wondered. Cap said he didn't talk to any of the marina residents, couldn't stand them, in fact, but he and Reese looked downright chummy.

Tim's boat, the *Safe Passage,* looked fine from the outside, but there were uniformed cops trampling all over it. Marta spotted me on the edge of the crowd, grimaced, and charged my way. I waited for her, my hands buried deep in the pockets of my jeans. I had a client up to something and a jet-lagged nun with a secret sitting in my car. An angry Marta gave me the trifecta.

At five six, two hundred–plus pounds, Marta Pena was a force to be reckoned with under normal circumstances. At a hectic crime scene, she was hell on wheels. We'd worked together on the job. I knew her family, her kids. But from the look on her face, I could tell our conversation wasn't going to be convivial. She reached me, pulled her notebook from her pocket, and slid a pen out from between the pages. Her radio crackled, codes being called in between all the static. All business.

"Raines."

That was her greeting, delivered gruff. I'd kind of expected more, given the rudeness of the hour.

"Pena."

"Where were you a couple hours ago?"

I looked out over the lake, which was little more than a large pool of undulating ink in the predawn darkness. The sun wouldn't be up for another hour or so. "What happened over there?"

Marta's dark, almond-shaped eyes went flat, her thin lips pursed. "Answer the question, please."

"Until about twenty minutes ago, I was in bed. Why?"

"Alone?" she pressed.

Our eyes held until I got tired of holding it and let her have it. "Yep. Had I known I'd need an alibi, I'd have cruised by the bars and picked up a fella."

"Cut the crap, Cass. This is official business."

"That I'm getting from the mad cop face. Who died?"

"You're saying you don't know?"

"Marta, I was fast asleep in my own bed, *alone,* in answer to your earlier question, less than a half hour ago. Now I'm here, fast awake, waiting for you to tell me what the hell happened. If you really can't take my word for it, I have a houseguest sleeping in my spare room who's honest as the day is long, though she's acting a little wiggy at the moment. She can vouch for me. She's right over there in the car."

She glanced toward the lot, then let it go. "So you just happened to catch wind of this and headed right down here?"

"Catch wind of *what*?"

She shook her head. "Me first."

"Okay, I got a call."

"From?"

Now it was my turn to shake my head. "Not till I know what we're talking about."

She slammed her notebook closed, stowed the pen away. "Someone reported a male trespasser on Ayers's boat. Normally, this wouldn't be any of my business, seeing as there's no body, but the second I heard it was Ayers's boat, I headed over here. The boat has been tossed. On the uniforms' canvass, they found a witness who reported seeing a guy hanging around, watching the place. He also says he found a lone woman cop, fitting your description, hanging around a couple of days ago, asking questions. Mary Meachum." Marta smirked and shook her head.

"Who will you be next, Lois Lane? Not surprisingly, my witness thinks the two sightings might be related."

I eyed the dock, spying Reese in the center of the action like a little magpie flitting from ear to ear. I looked around for Cap, but he'd gone. "Eldon Reese?"

"Well, that confirms it."

"I took a quick look around, but left everything as I found it. And I never said I was a cop, he just assumed. I can pull out cop face, too, you know."

Marta studied me closely. She was listening to what I was saying, but she was also listening to what I didn't say. She was also analyzing my body language, looking for signs of evasion, untruthfulness, nerves—"Cop 101." And she *knew* me. I could only imagine how much more heat she'd apply to the look if she was dealing with your ordinary off-the-street suspect.

"But that was early *Monday*, not today," I added. "And I haven't been anywhere near here since the day before yesterday. Last night, I had beans and rice for dinner around seven-thirty, got schooled for being a shitty friend, then I went to bed. You have a description on the male trespasser?" I had a sinking feeling this was where Jung came into the picture. "Is anything missing?"

Marta scowled. "Description matches Jung Byson, that weirdo you bugged me about."

"What reason would Jung have to toss his friend's boat?"

"I don't know because I don't know him, but Reese puts him here, 'skulking around,' as he put it. Now I need to know where to put hands on him."

"I don't know where he is or how to contact him."

Marta's eyes dove in again. She took a moment. "If this is you doing your 'shadowy PI stuff,' I swear . . ."

Shadowy PI stuff? It was a dig, and from her defiant expression, it looked as though she'd meant it as such, but no good would come of getting heated over it. I needed to keep the lines of communication open and get Marta working with me, instead of against me.

"I don't know where he is. I did not trash that boat. I don't think Jung did, either."

She tapped the notebook against her thigh. Nervous energy. "He called you. Told you to get down here, right? He's up to his neck in this. You know how I know? Because suddenly he's nowhere he's supposed to be. I sent uniforms to his place. He's not there. He works at a diner, but he isn't there, either. And now, conveniently, you're saying you have no idea where he could be."

"That's what I'm saying." I scanned the slips. "Did you call Tim's family? Did they show up?" All I saw milling around were cops and a few stunned-looking people who appeared to have stumbled off their own boats to take a closer look at the ruckus. "Maybe his concerned brother would have reason to break in and take a look around."

Marta groaned. "You're exasperating, you know that? Get off my crime scene."

"*Your* crime scene? It's a B and E. Or have you branched out from homicide?"

Marta looked like she hadn't slept in days. The bags under her eyes were pronounced. It was the job, I knew. If you did it well, it left you very little in the tank. She heaved out an exhausted breath. "Second case you've horned in on, in as many months. What gives?"

"I didn't go looking for it, it came to me. But something smells fishy here, and I don't mean that literally. Somebody was looking for something tonight. That doesn't get you thinking?" I straightened some, bracing, realizing I was about to step out on ice as thin as fairy glass. "I think you closed too early, based on misinformation."

The cop face was back, and funny thing was, I couldn't blame her. If someone had just questioned my handling of a case, second-guessed the way I'd played it, I'd have taken offense, too.

"The Ayers family is used to getting things their way, so they applied pressure," I said, treading lightly.

"You've got it all figured out, that it?"

"Not by half."

"The boat got broken into because this marina's got piss-poor security my ten-year-old could get around in his sleep," Marta said. "Your pal Byson, for whatever reason, took that as an open invitation to walk off with whatever he wanted when no one was looking. That's what I'm going with."

"*It wasn't Jung* . . . and what's with the 'when no one was looking'? Eldon Reese is *always* looking. The little pissant's looking now. That's his problem. That's the whole marina's problem. Everybody over there's minding somebody else's business."

Marta took a step forward, leaned in. "It's Byson, or at least you think it might be. That's why you're standing here and blowing smoke up my ass until you have a chance to talk to him yourself. It's what you do."

"What do you mean that's what I do? Since when—"

Marta threw her hands up. "It's what you do. You're like a one-woman stray-dog rescue society."

I stared at her, mystified, my temper flaring. "What's *that* supposed to mean?"

Marta sighed. She looked done-in, but after the last crack, I'd lost some of the sympathy I had for her. "Look," she said, "this isn't personal. I know you're solid, a thorn in my side, but solid. Still, I've got a job to do and Byson's on my radar."

"And I'm back to the lack of a dead body on that boat," I said. "Where do you fit in all this? It's a boat trespass, or did I miss a step?"

Marta didn't answer. She just stood there, fuming. And I got it. "Oh, wait. I get it now. It's the Ayerses. That's why you're here. No one's dead, but the boat's got their name on it, so you're hovering over this whole thing so nothing blows back their way, that it?"

"I'm doing my job," Marta growled.

"I know," I said. "And I, for one, appreciate it, but c'mon. Think about this. Things are not adding up—things that have nothing to do with Jung."

Marta stowed her notebook away and fastened her jacket, a signal she wanted to end our conversation. "They add up just fine from where I'm standing."

"Then you know Tim had an argument with a guy named Vince Darby a few days before Tim died, but when I asked Darby about that, he flatly denied it. Also, a witness to that argument says Darby boarded one of those boats over there, one with a blue canopy. If he's living out here, and knew Tim, don't you think he's worth at least talking to?" I gestured toward the slips. Marta turned to look. "Being so close, he'd certainly have no problem getting around security cameras."

"And you've got evidence that puts him on the boat when Ayers fell off it?" she asked.

I paused. She knew I didn't. I knew I didn't.

"See? *Evidence* gets me an arrest. *Evidence* I can build a case on and hand off to the DA. Anything less isn't good enough."

"You had no problem taking Stephen Ayers's word as evidence. He bold-faced lied to your face. None of Tim's meds were for depression, bipolar disorder, or anything like that. No one I've talked to puts him under a psychiatrist's care."

"He took the meds from his own cabinet."

"The meds from his cabinet were in his system. You don't know how they got there. What if Stephen made the whole crazy-brother thing up, knowing Cap would repeat it and that it'd stick? Hell, Cap's probably sneaking around here somewhere right now, telling everybody again what a sick puppy Tim was."

"So I have somebody who told me one thing, you have someone else who tells you different. Again, where's the proof? Because I have a dead guy and no witnesses." She waited. "Go on. Show me and I'll reopen this case so fast, it'll make your head spin." Marta held her hand out, wiggled her fingers. "Well?" She dropped her hand. "Didn't think so. It's done. Walk away now."

"It is *not* done. Did you know Tim offered a friend financing for a club, then didn't come through? People have killed for less, and you and I both know it. Did you know Tim was cut off from his inheritance, by his brother? He had to sell his insurance policy in some weird arrangement just to get by. And where exactly was Stephen the night Tim died? What lie did he tell you? I'd gladly ask him, but he's avoiding me like the plague, hiding behind his creepy lawyer." I eyed the slips again, half expecting to see Felton crouching behind a bush.

We were getting loud, and people were paying attention. I was not only walking on thin ice, I was ice-skating on it, backward and with flourish. The look on Marta's face was enough to freeze a person's intestines, but I had a job to do, too. Granted, it wasn't one I initially wanted, but I had it now.

"No witnesses, no prints, nothing on surveillance, and the victim is half in the bag," she said, ticking off the points on her fingers. "Oh, yeah, and he was dying, which might just screw with your head a tiny little bit. The Ayers case is a slam dunk, and I want you out of my hair. I've got actual homicides stacked on my desk right now with actual killers attached to them. I don't have to go around inventing murders."

I should have stopped, but couldn't. "Nobody wipes their prints off their own stuff before they nose-dive into the lake, they just don't."

Marta opened her mouth to speak. I raised my hand to stop her. "He was not OCD. I got that from someone who'd know. But for the sake of argument, let's say he was. He could have obsessively wiped away his prints from the cabin, but he couldn't have gotten up and over the side without leaving at least one smudge behind."

"It was a monsoon that night," Marta said.

"Not one smudge, Marta? That reeks, and you damn well know it."

Marta flicked a thumb toward Tim's boat. "*This* is the crime we're looking at now, and Byson's on the hook for it." She turned to leave, then turned back, thoroughly pissed. "I do know how to run a case."

"I'm not questioning that."

"Then why are you crawling up my ass?"

"A friend asked for my help, so I'm giving it. I'd do the same for you."

Marta searched my face and grimaced, apparently seeing the truth in it. She stood down, not much, just a fraction of an inch. "You're going to haunt my dreams, aren't you?"

"I believe someone may have had a reason to kill Tim Ayers."

She smoothed down her crop of dark hair, her anger having turned to quiet resignation. I knew she hated murderers as much as I did. That's why she became a cop, and why I did. "Tell Byson I'm looking for him."

"Tim's family had their lawyer shoo me off their property when I went to ask questions," I said. "Who'd they have run interference for them tonight?"

Marta didn't answer. She didn't have to. I knew it was Felton. Where was he the night Tim died? He knew Jung. It wouldn't have taken much for him to hire someone to impersonate him for a break-in.

"They're hiding something," I said. "And you're wasting your time looking for Jung."

Marta turned to leave, saying nothing. I watched as she trudged back toward the slips across damp, dewy grass. I stood for a long time and watched as the cops finished up and slowly moved away from the boat, along with most of the curious onlookers. The department wouldn't have dispatched so many cops or the evidence techs, had this not been Ayers's boat. Wealth had its privileges.

I waited for over an hour, still no sign of Cap. He had to have slipped back inside the office. Ganz could have gotten the part about the boat wrong. Darby's got no boat registered in his name, but if the ex-con hung out here for any length of time, the nosy Cap would have to know who he was and why he was here. As the lot cleared of police, leaving the evidence van lagging behind, I headed for the marina office. The sun was well up now, the Drive just beginning to clog up with morning commuters. I flicked a look toward the lot. Barb was still in the car. It was a miracle.

"Lady PI," Cap said when I walked in. "I thought I saw you talking to that lady cop. She's a tough one, huh?"

I stood at the counter, my hands on it, palms down. He was a little too jovial, a little too friendly. "She's also very good. What can you tell me about Vincent Darby?"

"Who?" Cap grinned, sliding a sideways look toward the tip jar.

"I'm not paying you."

He shrugged, smug. "Your call."

"What'd you and Eldon Reese have to talk about?"

"Reese? That windbag?" Cap chuckled. "He had another complaint, is all."

I pulled my wallet out. "I want to satisfy my curiosity. How much to get a look at your back room?" I laid a hundred on the counter. Cap eyed it like a starving man might ogle a thick steak; he all but smacked his lips, but didn't jump. He was much too wily for that. Not smart, just wily.

"You'd pay a C-note to look at an old storage room?"

Cap looked skittish, dodgy. I laid another hundred down. Slowly sweat began to form in the creases on his forehead, his ruddy face blanched. The jovial mood darkened. He leered at the money as if it were a naked woman with eyes only for him.

"Did I tell you I used to be a cop? Five years. Homicide."

Cap took a step back as if putting air between us would keep me out of his business. "Knew I smelled cop when you came in that first time."

I nodded. "In the absence of irrefutable evidence, the mind is left to think up all kinds of things. I'm thinking you're hiding something back there. I want to know if that something's connected to Tim Ayers. Drugs maybe, or something else. He stumbled onto it, and you and Reese took care of the problem."

He tried to look unimpressed, but he was sweating too much for it. Still, he tried to play it cool. He was going down, but not without a fight. "You been watching too many cop shows, you ask me. It's just a plain old room and it's got nothing to do with you or that boat out there."

I stood silently, watching Cap melt. "If I had to choose which one of you got Tim drunk and pushed him overboard, I'd have to go with you. Reese is a pest, but there's not much 'there' there, if you know what I mean. You appear to be made of sterner stuff."

Cap brushed a calloused hand across his brow to wipe the sweat away, then wiped his hand along the side of his dirty khakis. His chin lifted, and he sneered. "I'm done talking. You got no badge, which means you got no reason to be sniffing around. You just wore out your welcome, so sling your hook."

I didn't move. The money stayed where it was and Cap checked on it occasionally.

"How much would you say you weigh, Cap?"

He shot me a confused look. "What's that got to do with anything?"

"It'd help me figure out how many cops, *with badges,* I'd need to call in to turn you upside down and shake that backdoor key off your belt."

He searched my face, ran his tongue over cracked, dry lips. "You're bluffing. You can't do that."

I leaned forward, my right palm covering the money. "They're going to shake that key off your belt, Cap, and they're going to open that door. If I'm wrong and they don't find anything, you win. If I'm right, well . . ." I let the sentence hang. "You and Reese will go down together, only here's the kicker. Reese can afford a good lawyer, and likely won't spend a day in jail. You?

Depending on what's back there, you won't see the light of day for a long, long time. You're not a young man, Cap, and jail's a dark, lonely place."

"Cops need warrants," Cap barked, but he looked a little unsure.

I chuckled. "Yeah, okay."

Cap thought it through. He tried bluffing. That didn't work. He tried charm. That got him nowhere. Threats would come next, so I waited for them. And, as if on cue, he pounded his fists on the counter, rattling the mini fan sitting on the far end. I didn't flinch.

"You get out of here," Cap barked.

I waited for the rest of it, but apparently that's all he had. I went in again. "You like deals, so here's one. You give me the information I need, and I'll forget about the back room." For now. "I could be wrong. I've been out of the cop game a few years. My instincts could be rusty."

He eyed the money again. He wanted it, but there was no way in Hell I was parting with two hundred dollars. I slid the money off the counter, back into my bag.

Cap sneered. "No money, no deal."

"The deal is information on Vincent Darby in exchange for me walking out of here without dropping a dime on you. Seems like a fair trade to me."

Cap's eyes narrowed to reptilian slits. "You're fishing. You got nothing."

I smiled. "Nothing but the good sense to smell crap when it's lobbed my way."

Cap's bushy brows rammed together, his mouth twisted. He reached under the counter and produced a worn leather sap. I had one just like it in the top drawer of my office desk for troublesome visitors. The look on Cap's face told me that he thought the sap was all he'd need to get me walking. I held my spot.

"You're quick to violence," I said. "Hard to believe you held back with Tim, given the trouble he caused you." I flicked a disdainful look at the sap. "That won't solve anything, though. The offer still stands."

I took a step back from the counter and waited for greedy old Cap to notice the bulge at my right side. I wasn't carrying a sap. I had a Glock 19, fully loaded with a fifteen-round magazine, but I wasn't going to use it unless I absolutely had to; and, unless I'd completely misjudged the old man, I didn't think I'd have to. I stood there, waiting, watching, as Cap slowly realized that he'd brought a sap to a gunfight.

"All right," he groused, jamming the sap into his pocket. "What the hell do you want?"

"Vincent Darby—white guy, dark hair, bedroom eyes—you know him?"

"So what?"

"Which boat does he own out there?"

Cap clamped his lips shut to keep the information inside, obstructive to the last. I stood silently, giving him a chance to think things over. "He doesn't own. He *sits*. A few of them out there hire slugs like him to sit on their boats so they don't get broken into. Darby's on the *Magnifique*. Slip eight."

"Blue canopy?" I asked.

"Yeah, sure."

Tim's boat was in slip eleven. Three slips down from Tim's. "If he doesn't own it, who does?"

Cap took his time, still fighting it. He was boxed in, but that didn't mean he had to like it, that didn't mean he had to make things easy. There had to be something really juicy in that back room he didn't want anybody to see. "His name's Nick Spada. Now get the hell out of here."

Darby was sitting on his boss's boat, which was moored at the same marina where one of their clients, Tim Ayers, was living out his last days. Darby, the ex-con, was also driving his boss's Mercedes and living in a dead man's house. What about that sounded hinky? *Everything*.

"Did you ever see Darby and Ayers together?"

Cap shot daggers at me. "They were friendly till they weren't. None of my business why."

"And you and Reese?"

"He's just another rich cream puff with too much time on his hands, and that's all you get out of me with or without the cops. Now shove off."

I smiled, backed out of the office. No way I wanted a sap to the back of the head. When I stepped through the door, Cap rushed over and locked it behind me. Guess he'd had enough for one day.

Chapter 22

The *Magnifique* was dark, locked up tight. Darby was living high on the hog for somebody just recently out of the stir. I wondered what he was giving in exchange for all the luxury.

I checked the lot. My car was still there, Barb still inside it. I spotted the police evidence van at about the same time I spotted a black SUV with tinted windows idling in a faraway spot. I stopped to watch the car, not liking how close it was to mine. The back window was rolled down partway and a long camera lens stuck through the crack was aimed in my direction. Someone was taking an interest. Was it Felton spying for Stephen Ayers? Was it Ayers doing his own spying? Was it Darby? I flicked a look toward my car again, worried about Barb. The SUV was way too close.

I stood there and stared at the black car, giving whoever was inside a good, long look. Slowly the camera was drawn back, the window raised, and the car sped out of the lot and away. My heart racing, I managed to get just the first three numbers on the plate and a quick flash of a round decal in the rear window. It wasn't much, but it was something. I'd follow up, but for now, I turned and jogged for the evidence van, hoping one of the evidence technicians was one I knew. I got a lucky break when I spotted Cleo Barker loading equipment into the back.

"Cleo, the best ET on the CPD."

She turned, her chestnut hair tucked tightly under a CPD cap, and a digital camera hanging from a strap around her long neck. She smiled when she recognized me, her department windbreaker half-zipped against the morning chill.

"Detective Raines. Oops, I forgot. It's PI Raines now, isn't it? What're you doing out here?"

Cleo also sported a schnauzer pendant dangling from a chain around her neck. She was into dogs, all kinds. She rescued them, found homes for them, and owned at least half a dozen of her own. No kids, no husband, just dogs.

"Working a case. You just processed the *Safe Passage*?"

She grinned, whistled appreciatively. "Is that some sweet setup, or what? Teak decks, all that brass. If I ever hit the lottery, I'm getting one of those, for absolute sure."

"Marta tells me the place was tossed around good."

She rolled her eyes, made a face. "Was it! Stuff was everywhere. Sad, really. It's kind of like taking an axe to the *Mona Lisa*."

I pointed to her camera. It was police property, the photos on it, evidence. I had no right to any of it. In fact, even touching it got me in hot water. Still, I hoped Cleo would be a pal. I smiled sweetly. "Mind if I take a look?"

She drew back, clutched the camera, shielding it as though it was one of her fur babies and I was trying to snatch it from her bosom. "Are you kidding? You know I can't do that."

"Look, Cleo. I've been on that boat. I've searched it. If I could just take a quick look, I may be able to tell if something's missing, which would help you guys out, right?"

Cleo searched the lot wildly as if looking for someone with a star to intervene. She turned back, eyes suspicious, cutting. "It's against procedure. Chain of evidence. I can't let you anywhere near these photos."

"Then don't," I said. "Hold on to your camera. But if you just happened to review the shots while I'm standing behind you, there's no rule against that, is there? That's just you reviewing your work, and me just happening by."

Cleo fingered the schnauzer pendant around her neck, as though it were some kind of talisman, as though it had the power to keep bad juju away.

"Two minutes," I pressed. "One quick scan through, my hands stay in my pockets the whole time, and I'm gone like smoke. I swear." The silence that followed threatened to stretch on forever. "One look," I said. "And I take this to my grave."

Cleo bit down on her lip and caved. "One pass, and only one. No rewinds."

I released the breath I'd been holding. "Deal. Thanks."

From behind the cover of the van door, Cleo queued up the shots of Tim's boat, scrolling through images taken of the tiny kitchen, the gilded bathroom. The main cabin was where the most damage had been done. Everything was overturned, upended, strewn about. Wood paneling was torn from its foundation, the carpet pulled up. This wasn't just a crime of opportunity. It wasn't a burglary. Someone had been looking for something. Cleo flicked through at a steady pace and I stood behind her, my hands nowhere near the camera. She'd taken numerous shots of Tim's paintings, too, the lighthouses. It looked as though someone had punched a fist through the canvases. I counted six. Six.

"Stop." I placed a hand on Cleo's shoulder. "The paintings. Did you find any others outside of the main cabin?"

Cleo frowned. "No. Why?"

I tapped her shoulder again. "Never mind. Keep going."

She ran through the remainder of the photos, but it was just more of the same. Someone had done a complete and thorough job of searching Tim's boat. They'd even sliced the custom cushions and tossed the stuffing about. I'd counted Tim's paintings when I searched the boat, wondering why there were so many, wondering why they were all of lighthouses. There'd been seven, not six. All dated, all signed, all Tim's. I was sure of the number. So what happened to the seventh painting? Had Eldon Reese taken it? Cap? They'd both been here. Would Jung have had any reason to take it?

Cleo came to the end. "That's it." She hastily stowed the camera away, relieved that the ordeal was over. "I have to get going."

I stood there, my mind still on the problem. "Thanks, Cleo. I owe you."

"Yeah, you do, but if anyone asks, I never saw you today."

I smiled absently. "How could you have? I was never here."

She nodded, got into the van, and sped away, leaving me standing in the middle of the lot with wheels turning in my head. I went back to the car, started it, and moved it across the lot behind a stand of bushes, though at this vantage point I still had a full view of the front of the marina office.

"What're we doing?" Barb asked as I peered out of the windshield, barely blinking.

"Shhh. Working. Explain later."

It didn't take long. No more than fifteen minutes later, I watched as Eldon Reese climbed down off his boat and made his way to the office. When Cap met him at the door, the two of them started talking, the conversation becoming quite animated after a time. Something was up. When they disappeared inside, I started the car, dug my phone out of my pocket, and made a call.

"Who'd you call the police on?" Barb asked when I hung up.

"A slippery old coot with a secret room," I said.

Barb turned to me "A what?"

I kept my eyes on the door. *"Shhh."*

When the unmarked car slid into the lot a few minutes later, I had a quick talk with the tact officers, pointed them toward Cap, and then left them to it.

Six, not seven.

Chapter 23

"I know I can count to seven," I said.

The dubious look Barb gave me was a little annoying. "You could have miscounted."

"To seven? I don't think so."

We were sitting in my living room that evening, along with Ben and Whip, and, strangely enough, also Pouch, a semi-reformed pickpocket that Whip was trying to retrain to be a law-abiding citizen. Pouch was a funny-looking little guy, about four eleven, fiftyish, bald, pudgy, white, but with the long, delicate fingers of a classical violinist. Pouch always dressed monochromatically, but also always wore a fanny pack around his round middle, hence the nickname. Today's color was navy blue, and even his suede shoes matched. It was his homage to Elvis.

I'd taken Mrs. Vincent's advice. These were my people and I was letting them in, using them to run through my case, troubleshooting it. I wasn't sure yet about Pouch. It usually took me a while to warm to people. Mrs. Vincent wasn't here. She had a thing at her church, but everybody else was accounted for. It was dinnertime, a little after six. The pizza was on its way.

"But where's Byson?" Ben asked as he lounged on the sofa. "All you got was that one stupid call?"

"Yeah, and I've been looking for him all day. No one's seen him. I even called the hospitals and the morgue, but no one brought in recently matched Jung's description. I don't know which tail to chase first, his or Darby's or Ayers's."

"Hate to say it, but it kinda sounds like he hit that boat, then ran," Whip said. "That's what I'd do. Only a fool hangs around waiting for the cops to show up." He slid a sideways glance at Ben, who narrowed shrewd eyes at him. Ben was a cop. Whip was an ex-felon. Neither was fully comfortable with the other, at least not yet.

"I'm worried about that black car you saw," Barb said. "I wish I'd seen it."

"You would have, if you hadn't fallen asleep in the front seat."

She stuck her tongue out at me. "You travel eight thousand miles and see how long you stay awake."

"I got a partial plate," I said, eyeing Ben. "And a quick look at a decal."

Ben rolled his eyes. "Uh-oh."

"I could ask Marta," I said.

He snorted. "No, you can't. Marta's pissed at you. You know how I know? Because she called me to tell me just how pissed she was at you."

"Are you going to run it?"

He grimaced, sat up. "Suspicious vehicle hanging around an active crime scene?" He rose from the couch, groaning with the effort. "I think I can spin that."

I relayed the numbers from the plate, then watched as he stepped into my dining room to make his call, closing the sliding doors behind him. I stood, paced nervously, waiting. Someone in that car had a vested interest in what I was doing, in what the police were doing. They took my picture. Why? My money was on Stephen Ayers. He was making himself scarce, avoiding me, but that didn't mean he wasn't interested in seeing that his brother's case stayed closed. Maybe Felton had been in the car, gathering evidence to sue me for something. Was there something on that boat Stephen was willing to kill his brother for? And where did Jung fit in? What had he done? Where the hell was he?

"It's good to see you again, Sister Barbara," Pouch said, grinning widely, filling the silence. "And from halfway around the world, too, isn't that amazing? What brings you back?"

I could have sworn I saw Barb draw herself in, which was not like her at all. Normally, she was as open as they come. She said what she thought; she didn't mince words or beat around the bush. Her answer to every experience and every need was always *yes*. She chuckled, put a gentle hand on Pouch's shoulder. "Anyone want something from the kitchen? I'm headed that way."

Everyone declined. I watched Barb go. She was walking too fast. Not so much heading to the kitchen as fleeing from the living room.

Whip chimed in. "Maybe you should go after Spada. He seems to be the guy with all the juice."

"He's clean, at least on paper," I said. "Maybe he has no idea Darby's been squatting on his boat. Darby could be running some kind of side game. He is a con man, after all."

"Or maybe he's just an innocent boat sitter, like the guy said. Like a house sitter, only on water?" Pouch chimed in. "I was thinking of doing something like that, but, well, I got kind of a record."

Whip balked. "Kind of? You were in the joint, same as me. You have a bona fide, black-and-white record, with an ugly mug shot to prove it."

"Point is," Pouch said, "they don't usually give gigs like that to guys like me . . . or him. They're scared we'll make off with the whole shebang."

I turned to Pouch and Whip. "Then how'd Darby get so lucky?"

Pouch and Whip shrugged. Neither had an answer. Ben walked back into the room, sliding his phone back into his pocket. Pouch grimaced, whispered out of the side of his mouth, "Can it about the record, bro, not in front of the H-E-A-T."

"Well?" I asked.

"First things first. Do we have an ETA on that pizza? I'm starving." He drew his phone out again. "I'm calling them."

"Nuh-uh," I said. "Info first, then pizza."

Ben grinned. "Yep, that's the partner I remember."

Barb eased back into the room; I watched her every step. She was empty-handed.

"The car is registered to a company called Fleet Transports, so it could have been anybody inside."

"Not anybody," I said. "Somebody connected to Tim Ayers. Somebody worried about what I'm doing. The name could fit with what I saw of the decal in back. It was white with, like, a winged foot."

Whip suddenly found nonexistent lint on his shirt, which he began to pick at. I watched as he paid it more attention than it needed, then slowly rose and padded into the kitchen. Why was everyone suddenly finding my kitchen the place to be? Like with Barb, I tracked his exit.

"Whip?" I called after him, but he didn't stop.

"Yeah, back in a minute. Need some water."

Ben and I exchanged a look. We recognized evasion and knew squirrelly when we saw it. I followed Whip back, Ben on my heels. We caught up to Whip at the fridge, where he stood with a glass of ice water held to his forehead.

"Start talking," I said.

He looked at me, then Ben, then gulped the water in the glass. "About?"

"I've known you since you were twelve," I said. "The look on your face now is the same one you gave Mrs. Lembeck when she caught you trying to swipe the answers to the algebra test off her desk. What do you know about Fleet?"

He slid Ben a skittish look. "Maybe we can do this in private?"

Ben gave Whip "the face." The face offenders saw right before the cuffs went on and the back door to the squad car opened up to greet them.

"Ben's with me," I said. "We don't keep secrets."

Ben faced me. "Oh? Then where are we with the Weber situation?"

I shot him a dangerous look. "Really? We're doing this now?"

Ben shrugged. "There's a lot I don't know, that's all I'm saying."

Whip tried to quietly ease between us and escape, but I caught him before he hit the door. "Freeze. Sit."

Whip plopped down on a kitchen stool, sulked. "Yep, there's the cop in you. I can't say I like it. Brings back bad memories."

Ben and I sat down, flanking him. "What do you know?" I asked again.

Whip paused before speaking. "What I say isn't for cops. It's only for you, for your case." He held Ben's gaze. "No busting through the door, no anonymous-tip shit."

I knew Ben couldn't promise not to be a cop. It wasn't in him. Yet, to his credit, he sat freakishly still, his face completely blank. Whip was my friend. This was my case. He'd hang back and follow my lead. I also saw the struggle in Whip's eyes and felt for him. He was obviously torn, but a man was dead. That trumped everything else. Whip would have to decide here, now, who he was: one of us, or a con with one foot still in the game.

"Whip, I need to know," I said gently.

He drew out a long breath. "All right. Fleet? It's run by a buddy of mine, and by 'buddy' I mean 'former cellmate.' Maybe his operation's not completely on the square . . . maybe it's a front."

Ben didn't move, not so much as a twitch. I, on the other hand, relaxed some, relieved Whip had made the right choice.

"A front for what?" Ben asked.

Whip shook his head. "We're wandering into snitch territory. Look, I know the place, okay? I know the guy. Maybe I can find out who hired that car. That's all I've got for you." He read the look on my face, held his hands up to fend it off. "Best I can do, Bean."

I stood. "Who's the buddy?"

Whip pressed his lips tight.

"I can find out," Ben said.

Whip shook his head. "Won't be from me, and even if you do, he's not going to talk to anybody with a badge." He slid me a look. "Or anyone who used to have one."

"Are you involved with this front?" I needed to know that Whip wasn't involved. I wasn't about to lose him to the streets again.

"I'm out of the life, like I said. Now I cook. If you want the name, I can get it. You want it?"

"No," I said. Just the one word. I screamed it in my head, but it flew out of my mouth quieter, but firm. I was doing it again. Involving my friends in work they maybe weren't up for. "I'll get it on my own. You stay away from it."

Whip smiled. "You wouldn't get two feet in before they made you, and whether I go or not isn't up to you."

The doorbell rang. The pizza. Whip stood, gave my shoulder a reassuring squeeze. "I got this. Now I'm going back out there and eat some greasy pizza, and if I were you, I'd do the same before Pouch starts in on it. He's a bottomless pit when he gets going."

He walked away. Then Ben walked away. I stood for a moment in the kitchen alone. The scream was back, but no one heard it but me.

Chapter 24

It was well after midnight when things finally wound down. I'd been quiet most of the evening, not in a party mood, worried. I walked my guests to the door, knowing I wouldn't sleep. Whip was going to Fleet Transports to ask his old prison buddy about the black SUV I'd seen at the marina, and it wasn't sitting well. What was I going to do about it? What could I do? I noticed then that Pouch's pack hung heavy on one side. "Pouch?"

He turned, startled. "Yeah?"

"Don't make me frisk you."

Ben took a step forward, towered over the little man. "Or me."

Slowly Pouch reached into his pack and pulled out a crystal doorstop that'd been sitting behind my bathroom door. He sheepishly handed it to me. "I'll get a handle on this eventually."

Whip grabbed him by the back of the collar and lifted him up off his blue suede shoes. "What'd I tell you before we got here, huh? Cass is family. *My* family. You steal from her, I break your little legs." He glanced over at Ben. "He's got to learn."

Ben held his hands up, leaving the discipline to Whip.

Whip set Pouch down. "Now say you're sorry and get out."

Pouch bowed low with all the regalness of a knight in shining armor. "My sincerest apologies, Cassandra. It will likely never happen again."

I watched as he strolled out the door.

"'Likely'?" Whip called after him. "It happens again, and you're a dead Pouch, how about that?" Whip gave me a conspiratorial wink. "I'll be in touch."

"Whip, we need to talk about this," I said.

"We did. I got it. Don't worry."

Then he was gone. I stood at the door and listened as everybody made their way down the stairs and out the front door. I closed the door, locked it.

"He'll be in touch about what?" Barb asked. "What went on in the kitchen?"

"Nothing. I'm beat. Going to bed."

I headed down the hall to my bedroom.

"I know you're hiding something," Barb said.

I stopped, turned to face her, tired of all the tiptoeing around. "What are you hiding? What is it you're not telling me? Are you in some kind of trouble? Do you need help?"

Her eyes widened. "No. NO. It's nothing like that."

That was a relief, one less worry. "Then what is it?"

She didn't answer. She just stood there.

I sighed. "Then I'm going to bed. Good night."

Behind me, I heard the door to the guest room open, then softly close.

Maybe I'd sleep, maybe I wouldn't.

Barb wasn't there when I woke up. She'd taped a note to the guest room door that kept it simple: *Have a thing. Back later. We'll talk.* I had no idea what constituted "a thing" to a nun, and the possibilities for a nonconventional one like Barb could be varied and wide. And again with her wanting to talk? Was I really going to have to worry about all of my friends at the same time? I shoved the note in my pocket, and turned on my phone to find a text from Whip waiting for me.

He was planning on taking an early run at Fleet, the text said, and that he'd call me when it was done, but despite what he'd asked for, that he be allowed to go it alone, I showered, dressed, and headed for the West Side, determined to be there.

I found Fleet on West Armitage sitting between a shuttered auto parts store and an empty lot filled with weeds and garbage. Across the street, a block-long warehouse on the verge of ruin looked out onto the cracked sidewalks. I knew the area. A cab company used to operate out of the garage Fleet now called home. There'd be no foot traffic. You'd have to have a death wish to walk these streets alone without a canister of pepper spray and a weapon in your pocket. It's probably why Fleet was here and Ikea wasn't. I idled at the corner, well away from Fleet's front door, and waited for Whip, checking my rearview every few seconds. He wasn't going to be happy to see me, but I didn't care.

My phone buzzed in my pocket. I answered it.

"Raines, you've still got it." It was Detective Beth Renault, one of the cops I called about Cap's back room. "Guess what we found? Go on. Guess."

"Drugs? Bootleg liquor? Designer puppies?"

"Nope. The bastard's a friggin' Peeping Tom. He's been snapping pics of all the comely ladies on the boats, most of them naked, and posting them online, the sleaze. Eldon Reese helped him scope the women out. Reese was even looking to move a young divorcée he knew into the slip next to his when Ayers's boat moved out. There's tons of stuff, videos, photos. Cap rolled on Reese in record time, but he couldn't beat Reese, who rolled on him first. Both of them must have sweat off ten pounds while we had them cuffed in the car."

"Just women?" Maybe Cap and Reese spied on everyone. Maybe Tim? Maybe Tim confronted them. Maybe they didn't like it.

"Yep," Renault said. "The more naked, the better."

Then nothing to do with Tim. It was disappointing. Cap and Reese were voyeurs, but likely not murderers. I'd have to be keeping looking. "How'd you work out probable cause?"

Renault chuckled. "Don't insult me. How long have I been

doing this? Let me tell you, these fancy people are not going to be happy when this shit hits the fan. Stop by Sal's anytime. I'll buy you a Coke."

I smiled. "You got it. Thanks, Renault."

"No, thank *you*. Nothing's better than busting a couple of old pervs."

I punched END and tossed the phone down. Cap was a Peeping Tom? I had a feeling something was off with him, but hadn't thought that would be it. I'd hoped whatever he'd been hiding had something to do with Tim. It didn't surprise me that Eldon Reese was involved. He was a strange man. That's why he wanted Tim out of his slip so badly. I didn't feel bad for either of them.

I checked the rearview again, still no Whip. Twenty minutes into my idle, I spotted his gray Hyundai turn the corner and head toward me. I flashed my lights to draw his attention, and then watched as recognition dawned on his face and he glowered through his windshield at me. I rolled my window down when he pulled up alongside.

"What are you doing here? I thought we decided I'd take this."

"You decided, not me," I said. "I go in with you, or neither of us goes in. I'll give you a moment to wrap your head around it."

"What am I, a child?"

"No, you're my friend, and I'm going with you."

He softened. "You look like a cop."

I gave myself a quick once-over: jeans, T-shirt, Nikes, sunglasses, baseball hat. Work clothes. Whip caught me looking, and pulled a face.

"It's not your shoes. It's the eyes, the way you walk, talk, move, like you own the place."

"Pull over, give me a minute. I'll leave my car and ride the rest of the way in yours."

Whip threw up his hands. "Am I talking to myself?"

I rolled my window up and put the car into park. That was my answer. I got out, lost the hat, fluffed my hair, rolled up the bottom of my shirt and tied it into a midriff, then slid the top of my jeans down a bit past my hips. "You have any gum on you?"

Whip stood watching, mouth open. Slowly he reached into his pocket and pulled out a pack of Juicy Fruit and handed it to me. I wadded a couple sticks into my mouth, worked it around, then reached into my back pocket and pulled out my earbuds. "Let me see your phone." He handed it over, but my buds weren't compatible. Didn't matter. Who'd check? I stuffed the phone into my back pocket, then stuffed the end of the earbuds in after it. The business end of the buds I stuffed into my ears. "Okay, let's roll."

He shook his head, looked a little frightened. "Who are you?"

I slipped my arm in his. "I'm your girlfriend, Brandi. You're here to see an old pal, ask him a question about a hired car. I could give less than a shit about being here. You promised me breakfast at the White Palace, so I'm going to keep rushing you along. I won't be listening to your conversation. I'm addicted to music. If anything goes hinky in there, stand behind me."

Whip yanked his arm away. "Like hell I will. I'm a grown-ass man. I bench-pressed two-fifty in the joint. And you still look too damn smart. Stop looking all tuned in. These are crooks, not CEOs. This is not going to work."

I smiled, started walking. "It'll work. By the time we hit the door, I'll have lost several IQ points. Let's go."

Chapter 25

The front door was locked. We had to be buzzed in. The wide, brown face peeking through a tiny peephole in the reinforced door did a quick survey before unlocking it. The man who peered out at us from the doorway was massive. He looked as though he weighed three hundred pounds or more. He stood there, wheezing, ratlike eyes taking a slow and thorough survey, like a black Buddha standing at the temple door, waiting for baskets of tribute.

"I'm a friend of Leon's," Whip said, his voice a few octaves lower than his usual tone. "Name's Charlie Mayo." He paused for a moment when Buddha's eyes slid my way. "This here's my girl, Brandi." I let out a deep sigh, checked my nails, the very picture of disinterest. I gave the gum a couple of pops.

Buddha stood there for a time, then turned his head ever so slightly and bellowed. "Leon. Door."

The garage smelled of old rags and even older dust, and there were only two cars parked in the bays, neither of them the SUV I saw at the marina. I kept my cop eyes to myself, to all outward appearances, but I'd already scoped out the garage and everything in it, finding nothing outwardly illegal. I bopped to music that wasn't playing from Whip's phone in my pocket.

"We got to make this quick, Charlie," I said, an annoying whine to my voice. "I'm starving and the White Palace is clear across town. I want my chicken and waffles."

Whip frowned. "Hold your horses, will ya? I got business to take care of. Cop a squat or go play with a tire iron, or something." He pointed to a greasy folding chair sitting in a dark, oily corner. I shot him a look. Like hell I would. These were good jeans.

A fat man in blue overalls waddled out of a back room and walked our way. He recognized Whip halfway to us and began to grin through a row of crooked yellow teeth. "What the hell? Old Charlie Mayo? What the fuck you doing here, man?"

Whip and Leon hugged like they hadn't seen each other in ten to twenty, each backslapping the other like they were long-lost brothers. Nothing bonds men like sharing a communal prison urinal. Leon saw me and the smile disappeared quick. "Who's this?"

Whip grabbed me around the waist, squeezed. "This here's my gal, Brandi. Don't mind her. Had to bring her. She wouldn't fit in the trunk."

I smiled, waved, fluttered all five fingers like an idiot, then sighed again as though I would rather be anyplace but here. I turned to catch Buddha staring at my behind. Seriously, he was three hundred pounds if he weighed an ounce. He couldn't possibly be Leon's idea of muscle. All you'd need to do is whack him in the kneecaps and he'd topple over like a redwood.

Leon kept his eyes on me; they narrowed suspiciously. "Shoulda called first, though. I got business being done." He slid a chubby hand into his pocket. There'd be a gun inside. Buddha had one somewhere, too. "Don't let folks I don't know just walk up in my place like this." He slid an angry glance toward Buddha, who didn't have the good sense to realize he had a chewing out coming later.

"Look, Leon, I said she was cool, all right? She's with me, and you know me. Would I barge up in here bringing you trouble?"

Leon didn't look convinced. I pictured my gun sitting all nice and comfy in my lockbox at home. My decision not to bring it was purposeful. I couldn't have it on me, in case I was searched, and I couldn't leave it in the car, in case someone decided to hotwire it and take a joyride at my expense. So here I was, gun-less, and if Leon didn't lighten up quick, Whip and I were going to have a problem. I struck an impatient pose, foot tapping, arms folded, eyes wandering. Hopefully, Leon would assume I was bored and impatient to go, but I was really looking for a way out of here in case we had to make a run for it. Buddha stood blocking the front door. There didn't appear to be a back exit. *Great.*

Leon still wasn't buying it. He was a career criminal, who didn't trust nobody, no time. I rolled my eyes, turned my back to him to pace around a bit, but I didn't go far. I stayed close.

"So what do you want?" Leon asked.

"Got me a little issue, brah," Whip said, his grammar devolving with each passing exchange. "I picked up a shadow gig, some player's sidepiece. I saw one of your cars hanging on her. I need to know who rolled out of here in it."

Leon's brow furrowed. "One of *my* cars." It was not a question.

Whip scanned the dingy garage, specifically the cars sitting in the bays. "I saw the decal. It said 'Fleet' right on it, plain as day."

I slyly studied the cars, each one with a small decal in the back window on the passenger side. The decal matched the one I'd seen speeding out of the marina lot. Leon had feral little eyes, watchful, like a predatory animal waiting for a gazelle to come up lame. He nodded slowly. "Good eyes."

"Hell yeah, when somebody's paying me. Look, I can't have nobody messing with my money. I need to know who to lean on. This job pays twenty large, and there ain't no way I'm letting whoever it is screw that up."

Leon glared at me. "You never mentioned having no woman when we was inside."

"Why would I? This ain't no love connection. Quit playin', man. Are we solid, or not?"

Leon faced Whip, the look on his face hard as granite. "I ain't seen you since you got out. I don't know what you're into these days, who you're rolling with. You said you had a line on some cooking thing and you were going straight."

Whip frowned. "That didn't pan out like I thought. You know how it goes. But I got this good thing going now and I mean to keep it lucrative. All I want is the asshole in the car. When I find him, I guarantee you he won't be coming back here to complain about a damn thing. Twenty grand ain't no joke, and I got big plans for it. I'm getting Brandi here started in the stripper business."

I stopped pacing, turned, and shot Whip a withering look. I forgot about chewing the gum and about Buddha watching my ass. "Yeah," I said, recovering quickly. "I hear you can live sweet just on the tips."

Whip flicked a thumb my way. "See? She's destined for the pole. C'mon, man. You owe me. Who kept you from getting your ass kicked inside? You'd be dead right now if it wasn't for me, and you damn well know it."

Leon thought it over. Buddha stood there, mouth breathing.

Leon cocked his head. "Buddha, pat his ass down."

I drew in closer. Our eyes met. Whip shook his head almost imperceptibly and I stood down. I watched as Buddha turned Whip's pockets out and felt around his body for anything that shouldn't be there, like a wire or a gun. Whip held his arms up and took it.

"He's clean," Buddha announced.

"Now her," Leon said.

"Hey, back up," Whip barked. "Nobody puts a hand on her."

I took a step back, my eyes on the walking mountain as he headed straight for me, a lecherous gleam in his eye. All I had on me were earbuds and gum. I put my arm out to block him. "No way. He don't touch none of this till he pays up front."

Buddha stopped. Leon froze. The garage got real quiet.

Leon turned to Whip. "Your woman's a pro?"

Whip looked at me, stymied. He hadn't seen the turn coming. He straightened his jacket where Buddha had manhandled it. "She ain't my *only* woman."

Leon laughed. He laughed so hard, he doubled over with it, slapping his hands against his chubby little knees. "You're a pimp, Mayo?"

"And *I'm* his number one." I jabbed an angry finger at Buddha. "So *that* means, he or whoever don't get to touch any of *this*, unless I see some serious money somewhere. Tell 'em, Charlie."

Whip cleared his throat, looking uncomfortable with where the conversation had gone. "Yeah, that's right. She's number one ho."

Buddha slyly dug his hands into his pockets. If he came out with money, I was going to flatten him, Leon or no Leon.

"Hands out your pockets, Buddha," Leon said. "Take a look at her. That's top-notch right there. You ain't got nowhere near enough for that."

"That's right," Whip said, eyeing Buddha. "You can't afford *none* of my girls, so back the hell up."

Buddha abandoned his pockets and took a step back, but shot Whip a look full of malice while he did it.

Leon eyed me, amused. "A pro? I'll be damned. High quality, though. Slim, good lookin', mighty fine." He turned to Whip, standing shell-shocked next to him. "How much?"

I cursed inwardly. I started this. It was my fault. I took the gum out of my mouth, tossed it aside, then stuffed Whip's earbuds into my pocket, ready for a fight. Whip's expression hardened and he turned to Leon, towering over the portly little man. "That one's mine, all day, all night. Nobody in here, not him, not you, touches a hair on her head. We clear about that?"

Leon tried staring Whip down, but backed away after a time,

chuckling lightly. "Just jokin', man. I hear you. Your girl. Got it." Then his smile disappeared. "But this thing we're doing here now? It makes us even. You come back around, looking for more, and Buddha do what he do. You understand?" Whip nodded but didn't speak. "We do this in the office." Leon cocked a thumb at me. "*She* stays here."

I watched as Whip and Leon disappeared out back. My eyes locked on Buddha and stayed there. I kept well beyond his reach, eyeing the office door, unable to get to it for the big man blocking my way. I glowered at him, calculating the risks of taking a run at him. He'd likely knock me out cold, but not before I got a good lick in. We stood and felt each other out, circling; muffled voices came from the office. Buddha's eyes wandered south again, lingered.

"In your dreams," I hissed when his eyes traveled up to mine again.

"Never met a choosy ho," he said.

I sneered. "Till today."

We were still locked in silent combat when Whip finally came back, all smiles, with Leon's arm around his shoulder. I took their camaraderie as a good sign. When we were safely in the car and away, I turned in the passenger seat and socked Whip in the arm, hard.

"That's for 'stripper,'" I said, patting down my hair, fixing my shirt.

"Quit your bellyaching. You got him thinking I'm a pimp. What's worse? Besides, I got you a name." He shot me a satisfied grin. "Want to guess?"

I frowned. "Does it *look* like I want to guess?"

"You know *you're* the one who brought up hookers. I almost had to go up against the Buddha."

"You mean, *I* almost had to."

He grinned. "Lucky for you, he was priced out of the market."

"Whip!"

"All right, all right. It's Darby. Leon says he was sent to pick up a car, no questions asked. I couldn't get the name of the person who ordered it, not without it looking funky, not after me telling him all I wanted was the driver. Leon says he owns the shop, but he likes to play things big. For sure, somebody else owns it and they're pulling his strings."

"Darby works for Nick Spada. If he was sent, he's likely the one who sent him."

"Spada? The insurance guy? You said you didn't find anything on him."

"Nothing popped, but that doesn't mean there isn't something there. I just didn't find it."

"So now what?"

"If Spada sent him, then that means he has Darby looking out. If that's true, then he's got something to worry about, which means there's something he doesn't want me to find."

"But why would Spada want to kill Ayers? He was helping him out of a tough spot, wasn't he?"

I sat back in the seat, thinking. "Was he?"

Chapter 26

I headed back to the marina to find the office not only closed, but shuttered. Cap was likely still locked up, which was probably good for him. I wouldn't want to be him when the women at the marina found out what the old man had been up to. I walked over to Reese's boat and found him on the top deck, sunning himself on a chaise. I'd been right about him. Cap would take the lion's share of what they both had coming. Reese would likely skate. I stood watching him from the promenade as he lay there, seemingly unconcerned with the predicament he was in, along with his cohort in crime. How would he react if someone took secret photos of his naked body and posted them everywhere? After a time, Reese caught me watching and shot up from the lounge.

"It's you. You don't know who you're messing with, girl," he yelled over the distance separating us. "Do you know who I know? And Meachum's not even your real name. I've filed a report. Impersonating a police officer is a crime. You'll go down for that."

I let "girl" go. It was misogynistic and also harkened back to a time of subjugation when black men were always "boy," no matter their age, and full-grown women, no matter their color, were always someone's "girl." Had I been closer, things might have been different, but standing a good distance away from Reese, the slight wasn't worth the shoe leather. There would always be men like Reese. His ignorance wasn't my immediate problem.

I let his vitriol hum along, tuning it out. I'd thought maybe the back room held a secret that might be related to Tim's death, until Renault called to dash my hopes. All Cap and Reese captured were naked women. It was good the two were out of business, but it didn't get me any closer to where I needed to be.

Reese shook his bony fist. "I'll sue you for everything you've got."

I turned my back on him and walked away. He didn't like it. The threats continued at a high decibel. He probably wasn't used to being ignored, which made me like ignoring him all the more. The *Magnifique* was still locked and dark. Darby had been Johnny-on-the-spot while Tim was alive, always around, hovering. Now that Tim was dead, he was gone. What'd that say? Tim hadn't needed a minder or a babysitter, and even if he had, I was sure he wouldn't have picked Vincent Darby, a man it didn't appear he knew that well. What had Darby been watching out for?

I lodged my business card in between the grating on the locked gate as a calling card, then headed back to Peter Langham's place, which Darby now called home. I felt like the tiny ball inside a pinball machine, back and forth, up and down, bouncing off lies and dead ends, slammed doors and stony faces. And I wasn't even sure at this point what I was doing it all for. My client was still MIA, which was beginning to freak me out. Did Jung know more about Tim's death than he was letting on? He'd lied to me before. He'd lied to me a few times now. I only had his word for it that he and Tim were close. And, truthfully, I didn't know a great deal about Jung. Could he have killed Tim? Would he have hired me if he had?

The door opened the second I rang the bell and I stumbled back, startled.

"What do *you* want?" Darby said. It wasn't a friendly greeting, far from it.

"I have a few more questions. About the marina, about Tim Ayers."

"If you're not off my property in five seconds, I'm calling the police."

"You mean Peter Langham's property, don't you? He owns this house, and your boss owns the boat you've been squatting on, and the car you've been driving. And I don't think you'd really call the police. Not given your past experience with them."

Darby drew in closer, his eyes gone stone cold, ugly. He wasn't the least bit attractive now. This was the harder side of him, the side not trying to put on a friendly face; the side that coldheartedly scammed people out of their hard-earned money and then did time for it. This was the criminal, the con, the crook. Maybe he'd figured out how to defraud Tim? Somehow piggyback off his settlement? Skim some off the top? Maybe Tim caught on and that led to their confrontation?

"You lied to me," I said, my eyes steady on his. "You were keeping tabs on Tim. You're still keeping tabs on his boat, on me. What is it you think I'll turn up?"

He stood there, barely breathing, no response, frigid cold emanating from flat, icy eyes.

"What happened between you and Tim Ayers?" Darby gave me nothing, and it was beginning to rankle. "Did you break into Tim's boat? Where's the painting you took away? Why'd you take it?" I searched his face for a reaction, but got nothing. "Where's Jung Byson?" Darby didn't even blink. It was a little chilling. "Who's Peter Langham?" I said, pushing.

There was no way he would answer—I wouldn't have—but I wanted to see whether he'd panic, hold firm, or come apart. Darby's warning gaze was as sharp as knives now. He didn't look like someone you should turn your back on, and so I didn't. I kept a fair distance, watching every twitch. He glanced over my shoulder, his eyes surveying the street, possibly checking for witnesses.

"You're fishing." He managed a slow smile, but I could tell I'd gotten through. What had gotten under his skin? The mention of the missing painting? Langham? He checked the street again. When he turned back, I was still there. "Tim got drunk, hit his head, and went over. That's it."

"How do you know he hit his head?"

Darby's eyes smoldered, and not in a good way.

"It wasn't in the papers. You didn't have access to the police report, as far as I know. So how'd you know?"

The door opened a crack. I took another step back and waited, but Darby didn't step out. He looked like he wanted to—his breathing was quick now, his face a sheet of stone, a tiny vein in the side of his neck pulsed to beat the band—but he eased the door closed again, his hand on the knob. It wouldn't have taken much to put him back behind bars; by his restraint, it was obvious he didn't want to go.

"I think you know what happened to Tim," I said. "I intend on proving it."

Darby made a sound, low, almost like an animal's growl. I moved my hand closer to my holster, took another step back.

"I see you following me or hanging around where I hang around and you're going to regret it." He issued the threat through clenched teeth.

I was mindful of the door's position, gauging his level of irritation. It looked high. I had no way of knowing, however, how impulsive he was, how much of a temper he had. Prodding him might shake something loose that he didn't intend to let go, or it could backfire. Back away or keep going? I stood there for a moment, thinking it over. It didn't take long. I'd never been good at backing away from a fight.

"What'd you do with the photos you took of me? Who'd you show them to?"

I'd stopped breathing a long time ago, but I kept my wits about me, my weight distributed evenly on the balls of my feet in case I had to make a run for it.

"I see you again, I'll break you in two," Darby said.

It looked like he meant it, and the eerie silence that followed the threat was enough to stand the hairs at the back of my neck on end. I had no problem believing that this man, this con, this pretty boy, could kill a man if properly motivated, even a dying one, though that would take a special kind of evil. The corners of Darby's mouth flicked upward, and he cocked his head. "You're still here?" He shrugged, seemingly unconcerned. "Your funeral."

When the door slammed in my face, I let out a long, deep breath, and shook my hands out to get the ice from my fingers. My heart thumped so loudly, I could hear it echoing in my ears. *My funeral? Bah.* If I had a nickel for every time somebody planned my funeral, I'd be up to my ears in Jeffersons. Still, I had to admit, the delivery had been horrifying.

Tim had something Darby wanted or needed. That had to be true. It couldn't have been money. Tim didn't have any to speak of. He'd lived large his last months, throwing parties, traveling, donating to worthy causes. He had his family name, but Darby couldn't get at that in any substantive way. The boat? Surely, even Darby wouldn't kill just for that; besides, he had a sweet deal hanging out on his boss's boat and he looked comfortable living here—however that little arrangement came to be.

I trotted down the stairs, turned back, and studied the colorful Victorian, hoping to see Darby peeping out of a window so I could glare at him one last time. I felt fairly confident that when I found out why Tim Ayers died, I'd find Darby there, wrapped up tightly in the mess, all the way up to his six-pack abs. I headed back to my car in one piece, relieved I could.

On the face of things, Sterling looked legitimate, but after Vincent Darby's threat to break me in two, I had a strong feeling his contribution to the operation wasn't completely on the up and up. I had no problem believing an ex-con could turn it around and lead a productive life—Whip did and he was doing just fine. But there was something about Darby—the way his charming persona shriveled up and died when I'd pressed him, the way he minimized his contact with Tim with what seemed like an obvious lie. Artwork? I don't think so. And now the threat. It told me his time in prison hadn't done much for him. If Spada hired Darby not knowing about his past, that was one thing. If Spada knew full well who Darby was, that said something else. Could the handsome con man be running a con right under his boss's nose? I headed downtown to Spada's office to find out.

Stopped at a long light, I pulled up Spada's company website and found a photo of him. He didn't look like much. He was white, sixtyish, his face well lived in, though it appeared he'd had some cosmetic work done around his eyes, and didn't have even one inch of chin jowl. It was the wide smile, though, that leapt off the screen and grabbed me by the throat and held on. It was just a little too eager, too bright, too much wattage, like a used-car salesman's whose very life depended on unloading a lemon he knew full well had questionable provenance.

Sterling's mission statement pledged to put its clients first and provide the settlement they deserved. *We aren't satisfied until we make your dreams come true*, it read. *Let us take the risk, so you don't have to.* I shrugged. It sounded good. And from what I'd found out about settlements like Tim's, they were fairly common and had been since the AIDS crisis in the late 1980s, when people were dying in great numbers and treatment was costly. The end-of-life business had grown and been refined over the years and it was now quite lucrative. Still, there was some element of risk involved. I wondered if Tim had known that? Even if he had, he'd have had very few options, thanks to Stephen.

On the surface, the whole settlement thing sounded straight-forward. The dying policyholder sold his or her policy for ready cash, and an investor took over the premiums and cashed in when death occurred. Easy-peasy, and all of it meant to be short-term. A win-win for both sides, according to Spada's pitch, but everything had a downside. Nothing was ever truly win-win.

Sterling Associates was in the Aon Center on Randolph, at the foot end of North Michigan Avenue, just shy of the Mag Mile. I rode up to the twenty-fifth floor of the towering skyscraper composing my thoughts, working up a good plan for getting past reception and into Spada's inner office. Maybe I could pass myself off as a dying woman interested in signing up for the same deal Tim had? Maybe a flash of my PI's license would do it? But when the elevator doors opened, Spada was standing right there at the doors. I was coming up; he was heading down. I recognized him from his photo, but when he looked at me his eyes also registered recognition. I'd suspected that it had been Darby in that ominous black SUV in the marina lot, but now I knew for sure. He'd taken my picture and shared it with his boss, Nick Spada. Startled, he stepped back, the color blanching from his overly tanned face. He carried a briefcase and was dressed in a nice suit, and it looked like he was leaving in a hurry. Chances were good his hasty exit had been prompted by a call from Darby warning him that I might be headed his way. That hinted at a close relationship between the two men, didn't it?

I reached over and pushed the button to hold the doors, then smiled. "So, are you getting on, Mr. Spada, or should I get off?" He didn't move.

"You made good time, Ms. Raines."

It didn't look like he'd get on, so I stepped off and let the car go. "It's good Darby called ahead. It saves time. You already know why I'm here."

"Did you actually accuse him of being involved in Tim Ayers's death?"

I smiled. "I wanted to see how he'd take it."

"And what did you learn?"

I stepped closer. "He didn't flinch, or blink, or panic. Most innocent people would do one of the three, perhaps all of the three, when accused of killing a man. So I'm wondering how a man like that came to work for a company like this, and what you know about him."

Spada reached over and pushed the button for the elevator. He pushed it more than once, more than twice, as if that would get the car there faster. "Not going to discuss him or Timothy Ayers with you. Never mind the privacy issues, you're not the police, and you have no authority to question me. Now, if you'll excuse me?"

The elevator arrived. Spada eyed it like a hungry dog might eye a pork chop sitting too close to the edge on the supper table. When he rushed onto the elevator, I followed right behind him. I punched the button for the lobby and we moved to opposite corners while the doors *whooshed* closed and the car began to descend. Spada didn't look happy. He was trapped with the last person on earth he wanted to be trapped with. "Vincent told me you were persistent."

"Did he also tell you that he threatened to break me in two?"

His lips twisted into a crafty smile. "And yet here you are. I'm not sure what that says about you."

Spada watched the floors tick by. It was a slow elevator, despite the size of the building. We were just on floor twenty-one. If the elevator had had a window, the look on Spada's face told me he'd have thought about jumping out of it.

"Do you know where Darby was the night Tim died?"

"How would I? He's an employee. I don't know the intimate details of his comings and goings."

"Do you remember where *you* were?"

He pulled back, stared at me. "You're accusing *me* of murder? Do you have any idea who I am? How many boards I sit on? How much I'm *worth*?"

We were silent for a time.

"I have a theory," I said. "At this point, that's all it is. I think something went wrong with whatever business you and Darby set Tim up with, and that it quickly went from bad to worse."

Spada reached over and punched the lobby button unnecessarily. "I'm not having this conversation. Tim Ayers's death was an accident. In fact, it was a personal blow to me, as I am a good friend of the Ayers family. Of course, I sent my sincerest condolences for their loss. Such a tragic situation, such a nice young man, but his passing had nothing to do with either of us." He slid me a look. "I'd hate to get attorneys involved."

We were closing in on floor eighteen. Did everybody in this town have an attorney on speed-dial? "Who's Peter Langham?"

Spada didn't answer.

"He passed away months ago," I said. "Darby's living in his house. Any idea how that came about?"

Spada shook his head, frowning. "Privacy issues prevent . . ."

The elevator stopped on the fifteenth floor and a white man in his twenties got on. He glanced at the two of us, unimpressed with what he saw, then faced front, his eyes on his iPhone, earbuds in his ears, his fingers moving a mile a minute. The music spilling out of the earbuds sounded like a herd of cats being skinned alive. A bomb could have gone off in the car and he wouldn't have noticed till his hair caught fire. Spada reached into the outside pocket of his briefcase and pulled out a glossy folder with STERLING ASSOCIATES emblazoned on the front. He handed it to me.

"You obviously have no idea what we do here, but we're one of the leading firms in this state for viatical settlements. My company has an excellent reputation, as do I. Top seller three years running." He stood straighter, obviously pleased with himself. "You'll never find one client who isn't completely satisfied with the service we provide. That anyone here would have anything to do with what you're suggesting, well, that's insane." He flicked a look at the oblivious young man.

I leafed through the folder at photos of all the smiling, dying people on the final adventure of their lives: sailing the high seas, standing in front of the Sphinx, drinking wine at an outdoor café in Paris, happy to have the money to go out on a high note. The third wheel, the young man on his phone, barely moved. Tenth floor.

I held the folder up. "You finance dreams."

"We ensure our clients the best arrangement possible. A great amount of work and care goes into it. Each settlement is tailored for maximum success, maximum return. I take personal responsibility. In fact, I handle select clients myself, so your theory that Vincent and Tim had some kind of side arrangement going simply doesn't hold water."

"Who was Tim's investor?"

Spada slid a look toward Mr. iPhone, then eyed the numbers above the door nervously. He wanted out bad. Fifth floor. We stood there, facing off across the elevator car, our eyes holding, the yowling of the skinned cats the only distraction. After a time, the door dinged. We'd finally reached the lobby. I could almost feel Spada's relief as the doors opened. He smiled, checked his fancy watch, then darted out. I followed.

"Did you really expect me to answer that in a crowded elevator?"

"It was a crowd of one," I said. "But we're out now, just you and me. Who was Tim's investor?"

"You're treading on very dangerous ground. Very dangerous. You're going to want to take great care with how you proceed."

"You're the second person from Sterling to threaten me today. What kind of company are you running?" His eyes seemed to cut right through me; then he quietly turned and walked away.

"Good day, Ms. Raines."

"Not yet it isn't," I called after him. He wouldn't discuss Peter Langham, citing privacy issues, which confirmed that Langham had been a Sterling client. Just like Tim. Now both were dead, both connected to an ex-con, and all three connected to Nicholas Spada, self-proclaimed godsend to the terminally ill. How had Langham died? Who stood to gain by Tim dying when he did? Did Stephen Ayers have anything to do with Spada? I gripped the folder in my hands and watched as the wealthy man with the designer tan walked away from me; then I turned and hustled off.

Chapter 27

I ducked into a Starbucks to call Lucy Earles. She was an investment analyst I knew, one I called whenever I had to unravel high-finance issues that made my head hurt and my eyes glaze over. I needed the facts on this whole policy-selling thing, not Spada's high-voltage hard sell, and Lucy was the one to ask. I got a muffin and started in on it at a corner table, Spada's folder of goodies open in front of me. Then I dialed Lucy's number.

"I get the concept," I said. "But how exactly does this thing really work? And what's wrong with it?"

I could feel Lucy's judgment oozing over the line. She had zero sense of humor where money and investing were concerned. She knew money like nobody's business and probably had the first dime she ever made firmly tucked into a vault in her basement, as well as a cadre of little money trolls on call to help her count the stacks.

"Why do you assume there's something wrong with it? These settlements are a legitimate short-term investment option. Are you looking to invest?"

I pictured Lucy sitting in her small office surrounded by calculators and actuary tables, her crisp little banker's suit neatly pressed, her black hair pulled back in a librarian's bun, the *Wall Street Journal* spread out in front of her.

Investing and speculating all seemed a little too nerve-wracking for me. I put my money in the bank, where it grew by pennies a day, but at least I knew where it was and I could get at it if the sky caved in and the zombies showed up. I'd likely die a pauper, but it wouldn't be from stress at watching red arrows rise and fall on the NY Stock Exchange. I popped a piece of muffin in my mouth, swallowed.

"Why are you always trying to get at my money?"

"Because it's not working for you, and it drives me crazy."

"*I* prefer to work for *it*." That was an equation I could understand: *Work. Pay. Deposit. Easy math.* "Let it go, Luce. How short-term are we talking?"

"You do know you're literally leaving money on the table."

I eyed the half-gone muffin and considered another. "Well, now you're just making me feel stupid."

She was quiet on her end.

"Viatical settlements," I prodded gently. "Short-term?"

I took the long sigh on her end as her letting my money buffoonery go. "Short-term. Up to a year, no more than three, I guess, in order to see some kind of return."

"How lucrative is something like this for the investor?"

"It's decent. They're paying the premiums on the policy, of course, as the new holders, but there's no real risk, the person's gonna die. It's only a question of *when*. The market should be such a sure thing."

"I read up on this a little," I said. "A deal like this gets split a lot of different ways, a lot of things could go wrong, but run it down for me. Give me an example."

She hummed for a couple seconds. "Okay, let's say you have a hundred-thousand-dollar life insurance policy. Then you find out you're dying of something and have to finance your care, or you want to live it up while you can. You've got no other assets, so you sell the only thing you have that's worth anything."

"My insurance policy," I said.

"Right. You're probably looking to get about eighty thousand of that to do whatever with. An investor would probably pay a little more than you're getting, eighty-eight thousand maybe, for a guaranteed return of the full death benefit when you go."

I pulled a face. Lucy's explanation smelled an awful lot like death speculating. "Where does the rest of the money go?"

"I was getting to that. The rest goes to a broker who sets up the whole thing. I guess you could look at it like a commission. There's paperwork to file, legal and other expenses to cover. On this hundred-thousand-dollar policy, the broker might pull in seven or eight thousand, easy. Not bad for shuffling paper around. In a year's time, a smart investor could see a return of about thirteen or fourteen percent on his eighty-eight-thousand-dollar pay down. Though, of course, that return percentage decreases the longer they hold the policy."

"You mean the longer the person doesn't die," I said.

"Basically, but like I said, these settlements are meant to be short-term. Your investment returns decrease over time. Your second year in, you might only see a return of six percent. The third year—if things drag on that long—less than that, since you're maintaining the policy the whole time."

"So if I'm an investor and I buy someone's policy, and the person doesn't die when I was promised they would, I basically lose my shirt?"

"The longer they live, the less you get out of it."

"And if the person continues not to die?"

"The less you make on the deal."

"And if I'm really shrewd and buy the policy for less than it's worth, knowing full well the person I'm buying it from is in no position to haggle with me?"

"I'd like to say that could never happen, but reality? People are people. Not everyone's ethical."

I sat quietly, letting the information sink in. I'd forgotten about the second muffin.

"So I might decide to do something about the waiting," I said finally.

"Do something? Like what?"

"Bring about death," I said.

"As in 'kill somebody'?"

"Yes."

Lucy said nothing for a time. "Yeah, I don't like the way your mind works, so I'm hanging up now. I thought we were talking investments, but things have gone way off the rails here."

I had to agree with her, but then I also had to admit that people killed for all kinds of reasons. Spada and the investor, whoever that was, stood to lose a lot if Tim didn't die when his doctors said he would. So, do they just sit there and watch money slip away from them, or do they do something about it? Was that where Darby came in?

"I'd imagine there'd be reputable places where you could set something like this up, but also a few disreputable ones, too," I said.

"Just like anything else, sure. You have to be very careful what you sign off on, that's for sure. But this type of investment is regulated. I mean, there's oversight, laws. This isn't the Wild West."

My eyes tracked an old man as he walked up to the counter and stood stymied by the variety of choices on the menu board. I felt for him. Only Starbucks could complicate a cup of joe. The old man quickly gave up and left. "And reputable or disreputable," I said, "they'd deal in multiple settlements, not just one. So that seven- to eight-thousand-dollar example you gave me could potentially be multiplied by fifty or a hundred, or more."

"Sure."

"Can the broker and the investor be the same person?"

"Hmmm." I could hear tapping from Lucy's end of the line as she considered the question, likely her Number 2 pencil hitting the top of her immaculate desk. "The company could be the purchaser of the policy, thereby becoming the investor. What's going on?"

"Beats me, but I don't think I like it."

"And all those numbers you just quoted me rise if the policy's worth more than a hundred thousand."

"Right. It's basic math. Seriously, what's this all about?"

"Eh, not sure yet. Thanks, Luce."

I ended the call. Tim's policy had to have been worth more than a hundred thousand, a lot more. He was an Ayers, after all. That meant his investor's take would be a considerable amount, but the longer Tim lived, the less he or she got back. What if Sterling Associates had been in line to receive that return? Lucy said it was possible. That would mean Spada had a good motive for wanting Tim to die sooner rather than later. There was no telling how much longer Tim might have lived, were it not for the drowning. Spada, the ultimate businessman, would have been forced to stand by and watch good money fly out the window as Tim held on—and he didn't strike me as the kind of person who'd take that loss, or any other, easily. What had he said in the elevator? He guaranteed his investors maximum results. He staked his reputation on it.

Chapter 28

In my office, I dug some more on Nick Spada. He'd come back without nary a blemish on my earlier run, but that's what worried me now. No one Spada's age who had his wealth and business associations had a closet without a single skeleton rattling around in it. So where was Spada hiding the bones?

I readjusted the search parameters, requested a more detailed report, and left it at that for the time being. About to log off and shut down, I had a thought and searched Fleet Transports, and the building it was housed in. I needed to know who owned the property, because whoever did, the chances were good they also owned Leon. I lucked out. The search came back quick to a single owner: Tavroh Ltd., but there was next to no information on it, except for the name and a P.O. box.

"Well, that bites," I muttered, tapping a pen on my desk blotter.

Frustrated, I shut the computer down and sat at my desk, watching the phone. Still nothing from Jung. I'd swung by the marina after getting the bum's rush from Spada, but Jung was nowhere around, and I'd heard nothing new from him or from Marta, which told me Jung was still out there somewhere eluding the both of us. When the phone rang, I snatched up the receiver, hoping for a break.

"Raines Investigations."

"Robert Felton."

I frowned, and then pantomimed shooting myself in the head, my finger serving as the muzzle of an imaginary gun. "Yeah?"

"I won't waste time with insincere pleasantries. Mrs. Ayers would like to meet. Tomorrow morning. Ten AM. Her home. You obviously know where that is."

I leaned back in my chair, making it squeak, saying nothing for a time. I checked my watch. It was just after three. I'd wasted the entire day riding in elevators and punching computer keys.

"You are still there?" Felton asked, sounding more than a little put-out.

"That sounded an awful lot like a royal summons."

I could almost feel heat radiating from the phone's fiber optics. Felton couldn't stand me, and the feeling was mutual. I didn't think he was used to being challenged, and since the moment we met, that was all I'd been doing. I wondered if Mrs. Ayers ordered him to call, and like the good little family lawyer, he'd been forced to comply.

"It is a request." His words were clipped and tight, as brittle as desiccated twigs.

I swiveled back and forth lazily, enjoying myself. "What's she want to talk about?"

Felton sighed. If he hadn't been under the employ of the Ayers family, he likely would have told me to go to Hell by now, but he was, and he couldn't, and we both knew it. I grinned, tapping out a jaunty tune on the carpet with my happy PI feet.

"If the time is not convenient—"

I cut him off. "Will you be there, or will I be meeting with Mrs. Ayers alone?"

There was another hesitation. "Against legal advice, Mrs. Ayers has chosen to speak with you alone."

I hung on the line, taking a great deal of satisfaction in Felton's discomfort. I let the silence sit there, knowing it was killing him by degrees. I didn't much like being called for, but if this was the only shot I had at talking to Tim's mother, I had to take it. I leaned forward in the chair, my elbows on the desk. I could hear Felton working on his next coronary. He couldn't go back to Elizabeth Ayers without an answer one way or the other. He had been retained to solve problems for the family, not create them.

"Tomorrow. Ten," I said finally, and then I hung up on him before he had a chance to hang up on me. I took my simple pleasures where I could find them.

I punched the intercom button on the Ayers gate at five to ten the next morning, but before I could announce myself, the gate slid quietly open and the same high-brow voice I'd spoken to my first visit instructed me to pull in and follow the winding driveway up to the main house. I expected the trip to be short, but the drive kept going, past leafy trees and manicured bushes, past luscious flowers in full bloom. Suddenly the enchanted forest cleared and I hit a circular drive layered in oyster pebbles, a working fountain in its center, the gravel popping and crunching under my city tires. Before I even had time to come to a full stop under the Ayerses' stark white portico, front doors wide enough to get a Chevy truck through opened. A stiff-looking man stepped out and stood waiting, statuelike, beside a large Grecian column. His hands by his side, his eyes tracking my every move, he registered nothing on his long, gaunt face. He looked old, really old, but he stood straight, his black suit freshly pressed, his hardsoled shoes shined to a fare-thee-well. I'd worn jeans and was likely way underdressed, but I didn't much care. I was here for information, not to impress anybody.

I met the old man at the portico, besting him by a few inches. "Good morning, Ms. Raines. I'm Boykin. Follow me, please?"

He swept a thin arm toward the doors, not bothering to look back to see if I was following along. I was, but not before pressing my key fob to engage the alarm on my car. I was a city girl. I didn't know these people.

I was led along an immaculate marble floor glossy enough to see my reflection in, until Boykin stopped at another set of double doors. "Mrs. Ayers will join you in the library. Please make yourself comfortable."

No smile. No eye twinkle. I assumed he was human and not a robot, but I had no outward evidence of that fact. I stepped inside, then turned and watched Boykin back himself out, taking the doors with him. The ceiling was high and molded, the room long and Versailles-like. For want of anything better to do, I strolled around, reading the titles on the bookshelves, scanning the gilded tchotchkes on the end tables. There was a fireplace big enough to roast an elephant, if one were inclined to do such a thing, and on the mantel stood family photos in sterling-silver frames. I drew closer to study them, hoping to learn something of the Ayers family dynamic. I easily recognized Tim from his photo in the papers. He stood with his family: the disagreeable Stephen, I assumed; a woman who must have been Mrs. Ayers; a stern-looking old man, who had to be the late patriarch of the clan. Everyone looked unhappy and resigned, hard to say which was worse. I picked one of the photos up to look at it more closely, paying special attention to Tim. Resignation was worse, I decided.

The doors opened and I turned to see Mrs. Ayers standing in the doorway. I put the photograph back on the mantel and stood waiting for her to enter. She wore pearls and heels, and her golden hair streaked with wisps of gray looked like swirls of vanilla ice cream on top of a very pale cone. Maybe she was in her early fifties, but it was hard to tell when it appeared every cosmetic effort had been made in an attempt to turn back time.

Icy blue eyes took a full and thorough assessment. I stood there, letting her get a good look.

"Ms. Raines."

She glided over to a chair covered in fine gold linen with lion's paws at the arms and legs, her dress swishing as she went. "Please sit."

I took a seat on the expensive couch across from her, the two of us separated by a glass table with nothing on it, not even a finger smudge.

"Coffee? Tea?"

"No. Thank you."

But the doors opened, anyway, and Boykin entered carrying a silver tray with a teapot and china cups on it. He set the tray on the table and proceeded to pour Mrs. Ayers a cup of tea, setting it neatly beside her on a dainty saucer. She ignored the cup. She ignored Boykin. She appeared to be waiting for something. I politely declined Boykin's offer of tea and he quietly slipped out of the room again, closing the doors. Ayers reached for the cup, took a sip, ignoring me, then set the cup down and folded steady hands in her lap.

"How much?" she asked.

I was sure I'd heard her right, but I asked, anyway. "Excuse me?"

"How much to stop this ridiculous intrusion into my son's death? I assume money is what this is about?" She searched my face, no expression on hers. "I've shocked you, it appears. I'm a forthright woman. We're both adults. Let's not be coy. It's always about money, so give me your figure."

I watched her. I could tell she was used to getting what she wanted, when she wanted it, and cost was obviously no consideration. How many people did her bidding? I wondered. Felton, obviously. Boykin, assuredly. Stephen? Tim? Money could buy a lot of things—fealty, silence, protection, love, or its facsimile— but not me.

I stood. "I guess that would depend on how much you'd pay to see your son's killer go free."

She looked up at me. "My son was weak. He killed himself, bringing shame on our family. Those are the facts. Now, name a figure or I will terminate this meeting and let things take their natural course. But before you speak again, know this. I'm very rarely denied satisfaction. I've grown quite accustomed to getting what I want."

I nodded, holding her gaze. "Not today. Not with me."

She drew back as though I'd cuffed her on the chin.

"Where were you the night Tim died?" I asked. "When you heard your son, your boy, was dead?"

She didn't answer, didn't so much as blink.

"All right, then, I'll just talk. I believe Tim might have been killed because he lived too long. Even as I'm saying it, it sounds bizarre, completely sick." I drew closer to her, and she moved farther back in the chair. It was as far away from me as she could get. "I've found a con man who was keeping pretty close tabs on Tim. I think it had something to do with his insurance policy. I believe Tim trusted someone who took advantage of him at his lowest point, and then betrayed him. I don't have evidence yet to prove that theory, but if there is any, I'll find it."

Her porcelain face held no expression as those cold eyes lasered in. I stood there, waiting for a sense of caring to assert itself. She was a mother. Certainly, somewhere, there was some spark of anguish, some flicker of wreckage for the child she'd brought into the world. So I stood there and waited for it, towering over the frozen woman who couldn't bring herself to break. She was used to making deals, money for service, money for patronage, money for love, but her money wouldn't work this time. Here, she was going to have to be human and it didn't look like she was cut out for it. There were no tears. Her ramrod posture didn't falter. Elizabeth Ayers had gone her entire life like this, I thought. It left little room for affection, for compassion, for Tim. I moved back to the couch and eased into it so that we could begin again.

"Nicholas Spada brokered a deal by which Tim sold his insurance policy for cash—cash he needed after Stephen cut him off. It was to be a short-term deal, seeing as Tim was ill and wouldn't get better. Only Tim kept going. He kept going well beyond all expectations. I think that's where the trouble started. Spada claims he's an old family friend. What can you tell me about his connection to your family?"

"Who hired you to do this?"

I sighed. I hadn't gotten through at all. "Someone who cared about Tim."

Her thin lips curled into a snarl. "One of his unsuitable lovers?"

"Does it matter?"

She didn't move—not a muscle, not an eyelid, not even air it seemed. "Nicholas Spada?" I was holding up well under her withering stare. "You're going to need more than Felton."

Her chin rose. "He was an acquaintance of my late husband's, who filled the occasional foursome. We did not socialize."

"He led me to believe you traveled in the same circles. He said that's why Tim likely came to him."

I hadn't thought it possible, but the hardness in her gaze got even harder. "He wouldn't be the first to claim such a thing. We're an old, established family. Nicholas Spada owned gas stations or storage facilities—nothing professional, nothing of consequence." She twisted her lips distastefully, signifying Spada's humble beginnings were an affront to her refined sensibilities. "Although he's apparently managed to elevate himself well above his station."

My eyes wandered around the well-appointed room. "So money alone doesn't buy entry into all this?"

"There's breeding, lineage. You wouldn't understand."

"Oh, I understand perfectly. Spada lacks pedigree. He's good enough to fill out a foursome, not good enough to hang with the cool kids." Ayers gave me no reaction at all. I'd gotten used to it.

"He's a businessman," I said. "He strikes me as being very ambitious, very hungry for recognition, status. He'd want to get Tim's deal done as promised. You know him better than I do. Is he the kind of man, the ambitious kind, who'd kill to better his bottom line?"

Mrs. Ayers rose in one seamless motion, like a queen from her throne. "You have a most active imagination. You've invented this entire theory out of magic thread and fun-house mirrors. Timothy was much too smart to be taken in by someone like Nicholas Spada."

"Your husband did business with him. How smart was he?"

"The man insured our horses, some of our lower staff. He never handled any of our important business."

"But your son had no other choice."

She shot me a warning look, but I'd swear I saw a slight break in the ice. "Nicholas Spada wouldn't dare touch a hair on my son's head."

"Maybe, besides the money he stood to lose, that's why he did it. Maybe he didn't care much what happened to Tim. Tim was a member of an old, established family. A family that shunned him socially, one that thought so little of him that they'd only let him insure their horses."

Her eyes shifted, but she held herself straight as an arrow. I could tell, though, that she followed the logic, that she could imagine the upwardly mobile Spada doing such a thing, and not giving it a second thought. Killing Tim, dragging the Ayers family name through the papers, would be the ultimate payback for being frozen out of the Ayerses' inner circle.

"Money and hate," I said. "Those are things people kill over."

She moved behind the chair, held on to the top of it, her fingers digging into the upholstery. There was a spark of something in the ice. "I don't believe a word you're saying."

"I'm wondering if maybe Stephen was somehow involved, too. The brothers weren't close, I've learned. And, strangely, Stephen made a rather interesting visit to the marina before Tim died. He told everyone there that Tim suffered from depression, though I could find no evidence of that. He told the police the same thing. Did you know?

"You don't have to believe me. The investigating detective on Tim's case can corroborate. Detective Marta Pena. Look her up. The lies, and they were lies, sound like Stephen was laying the groundwork for murder, diverting attention from the actual motive for Tim's death by painting him as a prime candidate for suicide. Maybe he did that to help Spada. Maybe he did it to help himself. Even people from fine families have resorted to fratricide."

Not one single muscle seemed to move in Elizabeth Ayers's entire body. I'd have thought her made of marble, were it not for the slight rise and fall of her chest as she breathed in and out. Slowly she began to grin. She squared her shoulders, and again lifted her patrician chin defiantly. "It's been a while since I've been involved in a good fight. Felton will be very happy." She moved back around to the front of the chair, sat again. "I'll ruin you if you even think about repeating such a thing."

"Do you know where Stephen was the night Tim died?" She stared at me, her face blank. It was as if she'd already checked out. "And, again, where were you?"

Elizabeth Ayers pushed a small button on the side of her chair, then stood, clasping her hands in front of her. Boykin appeared at the door. He was my confirmation that the visit was over.

"My son and I were in New York on business. Felton handled the details in our stead."

" 'The details'? Tim, you mean?"

She rose. "You do realize that I can make things very uncomfortable for you?"

I stood, buttoned my jacket. "More uncomfortable than this?"

She glided out of the room, disappeared down the hall. Boykin saw me out, ushering me through the doors and back out to the portico. My car was where I left it, and seeing it again was like reuniting with an old friend. The sun felt warm, welcoming. I was thrilled to be out of the icehouse.

Chapter 29

The stink of smoke and the wail of fire engines pulled me off my painter's ladder at two AM Sunday morning. The trucks sounded close. I padded to the front windows in the second-floor apartment to see red lights flashing, black smoke billowing up, and my car on fire. Two hook and ladders had blocked the street, onlookers watching from the curb, as hoses shot water through the car's busted-out windows. I blinked, stared, not believing what I was seeing. *My car. My car.* I ran for the stairs, bounded out of the front door right into a huddle of gawkers, seemingly mesmerized by the angry flames. I fought my way through to the curb, my eyes on the smoke, my nose burning with the stench of toxic rubber and plastic.

"Stand back, lady, this thing is still blazin'," a cop yelled when I got too close.

"That's my car," I shouted, fighting to be heard over the murmurs of the crowd and the force of the water hoses, the rumble of the trucks.

The cop looked me up and down, then consulted his notebook. "What's your name?"

I stared, transfixed, at my melting Maxima. "Cassandra Raines."

"You got ID?"

I held my arms out. No wallet. "Not on me. Is there some-body else out here claiming the burning car?"

He glared at me, not pleased with the snark. "All right. Settle down."

"What happened? Did anybody see anything?"

"What happened was somebody tossed a cocktail through your side window there. No witnesses."

I blinked. "What'd you just say?"

"Molotov. Cocktail. We found shards of the exploded bottle inside and the whole thing reeks of gasoline. Basic, but, hey, sometimes basic gets it, right? So, what are we looking at? Angry boyfriend, crazy ex-husband, what?"

I ignored the question. "Was anyone hurt?" I scanned the front windows of my building, glad Mrs. Vincent was missing all of this. She didn't hear well. She likely hadn't heard the sirens.

The cop pointed toward the crowd. "Some of your neighbors tell us hacking people off is what you do for a living. You're a private cop, right?"

I stared at the crowd, danger in my gaze. Turncoats. Backstabbers. "Which ones?"

The cop flipped pages in his notebook. "Lady, I can't count that high."

"Whatever. Did anybody see anything *useful*, or are they all just out here swapping stories about my personal business?"

"All they saw was your car going up like a Fourth of July rocket," the cop said. He tore a sheet from his notebook. "Here's the report number for the insurance. You're going to need a tow. Have a nice day."

"Hey." Ben squeezed into the booth across from me. It was early, just after six AM. Deek's was deserted. I was hungry, and it was the only place I could get to without a car. I'd need to rent one, until my insurance company did what it did, but it was all too much to think about in the moment. Right now, all I wanted was pancakes. I'd left Mrs. Vincent safely at home, sweeping charred debris off the front stoop, though I politely told her I'd handle it myself. She'd looked at me as though I'd lost my mind. Some battles weren't worth fighting.

Ben eyed the table. "What's that?"

I took a sip of tea, savored it for a second. "You know what it is."

"That's the pipe from your trunk."

I sighed. "It's the only thing that didn't burn."

"So you're going to just carry it around with you like that?"

I sat my cup down, held his gaze. "Until I get another trunk to put it in."

Ben watched me, his mouth agape. He shook his head. "Okay, give it to me straight. Whose shoes did you step on?"

I looked around for Muna, but she was in the back somewhere. I needed more hot water, a fresh tea bag. Truthfully, I could tick off a list of names, but didn't. "I'm just glad whoever it was chose my car and not my house." I took another sip of tea. I smelled like a melted tire. "My money's on Darby. He did threaten to break me. What if he killed Tim for his boss's bottom line? Maybe Stephen Ayers was in on the whole thing. I haven't met him yet, but if he's anything like his mother . . ." I shivered, remembering the coldness. "I can't link the mother or Stephen to Darby, but they link to Nick Spada, and *he* links to Darby. Who says Stephen and Spada didn't team up?"

Ben's eyes narrowed.

"The cocktail," I said. "I heard you. I'll be ready next time."

"You're thinking there's going to be a next time?"

"I'm chasing a killer, or maybe killers. Of course there's going to be a next time."

Ben checked his watch. "Look, we need to talk."

"Sure. Go ahead."

His phone rang. He slid it out of his pocket, answered it.

"Uh-huh. Uh-huh." Ben's face turned serious. "Dammit. Okay. I'm rolling." He ended the call, put the phone away. "Gotta go." He scooted out of the booth. "I'll call you."

I stared up at him as he loomed over me, getting a hint of something in the tone of his voice. "What's going on?"

"It'll keep. But, FYI, Weber's been asking about you again. Now he wants to know where you buy your ammo. Anything you want to tell me?"

"Nope."

"Sure?"

"Yep."

Ben adjusted his blazer to cover his holster, smiled. "Okay then. Watch yourself. This shit is starting to get serious."

I blew out a breath and eyed my trusty pipe, which was now homeless. "Tell me about it."

Monday morning, I got showered, dressed, and headed downtown on the train to Stephen Ayers's office. The *train*. It wasn't a pleasant ride. The car I was in reeked of funk and fuel and piss and I wasn't in the best of moods to begin with because someone had *torched my car*. My money was on Vincent Darby. He might have been pretty to look at, but he had a mean streak a mile wide.

The Ayers family owned manufacturing and industrial service companies, apparently, and had their pampered little hands in banks and boards and conglomerates and such, which meant next to nothing to me, since my money didn't travel in those circles. I pushed through the glass doors to Ayers, Thurston, and Morgan to find a prim-looking, middle-aged woman sitting at the receptionist's desk. She was smartly dressed in a lavender suit with gold buttons, her auburn hair coiffed just so, her nail polish matching the suit. The nameplate on the big wooden desk read H. GARDNER.

"Good morning," H. Gardner said. "May I help you?" Her

smile was effusive. Here was a woman who enjoyed her work, or at least appeared to enjoy it.

I returned the greeting, and the sparkle. "Cassandra Raines to see Mr. Ayers."

"Certainly," she said, reaching for a leather-bound appointment book.

"You won't find me there. I don't have an appointment. But Mr. Ayers will know why I'm here. I only need a moment of his time."

H. Gardner closed down on me. She pinched her face, her shoulders bunched up, even her hands laced into tight little balls. "I'm afraid if you don't have an appointment—"

"Perhaps if you let Mr. Ayers know I'm here, he'll choose to see me *without* an appointment." I kept the smile up. "It really won't take long."

I could tell she doubted me, but she picked up the phone and punched 4-6-6-3, which I duly noted, even though from my vantage point I was seeing the numbers upside down. I hoped she was dialing Ayers's extension and not building security.

"Mr. Ayers, there's a Ms. Cassandra Raines here. She . . . Yes, sir. Of course, sir."

Gardner listened for a few seconds, making affirmative noises, letting the big guy know that she was listening and that she understood. All the "yes, sir" utterances were a bit too deferential for me, but different strokes, I guess. After a time, Gardner put the phone down and stood. "Please have a seat."

She quickly headed off toward the back, and I watched her go. The moment she disappeared from view, I quickly scanned reception for security cameras, but didn't see any. Didn't mean much; they could be hidden anywhere—behind a potted plant, at the edge of a picture frame—still, I decided to go for it. I leaned over the desk and twisted the appointment book around, flipping through the pages, reading the names, looking for one I might recognize, like Vincent Darby or Nicholas Spada. Neither name was there. I heard Gardner returning and hastily flipped the book back around and moved away from it, the very picture of innocence.

"Mr. Ayers is unable to see you at this time," Gardner offered condescendingly—as though I ever had a chance of getting past her desk. "He refers you to his attorney, Mr. . . . ."

"Robert V. Felton, Esquire," I said, finishing her sentence. "I've had the displeasure."

Gardner scowled. Apparently, she preferred to work alone.

"Tell Mr. Ayers I'll wait," I said, copping a squat on one of the fancy couches. "As long as it takes."

"But . . . ," Gardner began to sputter. She looked as though she'd never seen such a thing. "He's very busy."

"As am I," I said, crossing my arms over my chest. "I'm trying to find out who killed his brother. So I'll wait." I eyed the end tables with magazines fanned out over them: *Smithsonian, National Geographic, Barron's.* Gawd, even Ayers's reading material was pretentious. I grabbed *Smithsonian.* "Oh, and if Mr. Ayers is thinking about sneaking out the back, you might want to tell him I'll come back tomorrow, and the next day, and the day after that, until I speak with him personally." I smiled sweetly, then settled in for a long, unproductive wait.

Gardner disappeared again, flustered this time, and stayed gone for at least ten minutes. She and Ayers were probably back there trying to decide whether or not to call the police and have me escorted out. They could do it, sure, but how much of a ruckus would I make? That was the unknown variable. Rich people didn't like ruckuses. I'd moved on to *National Geographic,* and an in-depth piece on the Amahuaca Indians of Brazil, when Gardner returned.

"Mr. Ayers will speak to you, but not here. He has a meeting at City Hall. He'll meet you in Daley Plaza. Eleven-thirty."

What rube truck did they think I fell off of? I checked my watch. It was eleven. I stood and tossed the magazine down on the table. The Amahuaca Indians would have to remain a mystery. This was obviously a ploy to get me out of the office without causing a scene, but, frankly, I was tired of waiting, anyway. I strode up to Gardner's desk, smiled, and went all in.

"Fine. I'll play along. Daley Plaza. Eleven-thirty." I headed for the door, turned. "Or back here shortly afterward to wait until the dawn of the apocalypse. Oh, next time you see Mr. Felton, let him know I was here, would you? We had a bet, and I just won it."

Chapter 30

I stood by the Picasso in Daley Plaza and watched busy people hustle by, heading someplace else, scattering the dirty pigeons pecking at dropped bits of bread and bedraggled French fries from the McDonald's across the street. I glanced up at the towering cubist monstrosity above me and wondered what illegal substance good old Pablo had been on when he came up with the idea for the thing. I didn't know a lot about art, only what I liked, and this wasn't it. This looked like something conjured up out of a sick man's fever dream. City Hall stared at me from across the street. I let it.

I dialed Bucky T.'s cell phone, still looking for a line on Jung, but no one answered. The flashing light told me I had a voice mail waiting, and I dialed in for it, hoping it was Jung, only it wasn't. The message was from someone inquiring about my apartment for rent. *Already.* I slid the phone into my pocket, my stomach suddenly queasy. "Nope. Not today."

I swept my eyes over the plaza just in time to see a determined-looking man in a Burberry trench heading straight for me. It was Ayers. I recognized him from his depressing family portrait. I watched as he powered forward on angry heels, his back straight, his defiant chin set. He looked like a man used to running things, making things happen. He looked an awful lot like his mother. He wouldn't meet in his office, likely because I had initiated it. This meet was his, and by the sureness of his stride and the iron in his spine, it looked like he meant to shut it down quick. I glanced at my watch. It was eleven-thirty, straight up. I braced for the confrontation.

"I'll ruin you," he said when he reached me. "I should have you arrested for harassment. You come to our *home*? My business? Who do you think you are? If I see you again after today, you'll regret it."

I watched as his pale, narrow face began to color over. He couldn't have been more than five or six years older than Tim, yet his hairline was receding, his hair was starting to turn gray, and he looked like he ate stress and anxiety for breakfast and drank his lunch, the remnants of highballs or martinis or whatever showing in the mottled sag beneath glacial blue eyes. It couldn't have been easy following in your father's footsteps when your father was a business titan and family legacy was all. And then there was Elizabeth Ayers and her inability to forgive Tim's bold grasp for a life of his own, and Tim himself, who despite the shunning, lived life on his own terms, leaving his brother shackled to the family name.

"Well?" Ayers barked. "Did you hear me?"

I nodded. "I think the entire plaza heard you." A ratty pigeon, his head bobbing, walked around in circles close by, pecking at dreck. I eyed him warily. "If you're done barking, maybe we can discuss the issue at hand like civilized adults? You've spoken to your mother, to Felton, so you know what this is about. I have only a few questions and then I'll be on my way. Or we can continue this little pissing match, wasting my time and yours, for as long as you think it's necessary . . . which would you prefer?"

His eyes, stunningly cold, a carbon copy of his mother's, went hard, vengeful, his thin lips tightened. This was not a man who skipped lightly through fields of tulips or snuggled kittens. "My family's affairs are none of your concern."

"I agree. I'm not interested in your family's affairs. I want to know what you know about Tim's connection to Nicholas Spada. I may have discovered a reason why he might have wanted your brother dead. *That's* my concern, my one and only. I'd like your help, if you're willing to give it. I know you and your brother weren't on the best of terms, but he *was* an Ayers. I'm hoping that means something to you."

"Why the hell would anyone want to kill Tim? He didn't have anything. He wasn't important. Now you think Spada is somehow involved with him falling off that damned boat? Father should never have left it to him in the first place." He chuckled meanly. "As for Spada, he's a wannabe, a lightweight. He might have used Tim to get to us, but he wouldn't dare kill him. Our family is—"

I cut him off. "An old, established family, yes, I know. Your mother told me." I exhaled deeply, tired of the exchange. I checked over my shoulder, feeling more than a little exposed. I turned back to Ayers. "Do you know a man named Vincent Darby?"

"I don't, and I don't know Spada, except by dubious reputation. He's *nuevo riche*." Ayers sniffed the air as though he smelled something foul and distasteful. I understood then why Tim had been so adamant about getting away from him and his mother. There was a smugness to their wealth and position, a flintiness of spirit. "So if whatever agreement Tim had with him went sour, it's his own fault. If he'd done what was expected of him, he'd be alive today."

"Is that why you threw him under the bus by telling the police he was a prime candidate for suicide? Is that why you cut him off?"

The corners of his mouth turned upward, his eyes narrowed. "Who in their right mind would give up what he did? And I cut him off so he couldn't piss away another nickel of Father's money."

"So that's why you couldn't be bothered to even identify his body. You sent Felton."

"Mother told you we were in New York on business the night Tim killed himself. And now I'm walking away. I don't want to see you ever again."

"If not Spada," I said, "who else might want to hurt Tim?"

He chuckled, but there was no lightness in it. It was a mean, spiteful, unforgiving chuckle. "You don't give up, do you? Do you know how many lawyers I have?"

"Do they all wear watch fobs like Felton?"

Ayers glared at me. "Felton said you were a smartass. You want to pin Tim's death on somebody, fine, go hound some of his predatory friends. That should give you a long list of suspects."

"I'd be glad to. Give me their names."

Ayers turned to leave. "I don't think I will. Goodbye. Get lost."

"Do you know where Felton was the night your brother died? He was at the marina mighty quick to ID Tim's body."

He turned back, appearing far more irritated than he had been already. "How would I know where he was? What does it matter anyway? Tim's dead and buried, his problems right along with him. It's over, done, finally." He cocked his head. "I think I'll enjoy yanking your license."

"If you want it, you can have it now." We stood and faced each other, neither of us happy to be in the situation. Stephen Ayers stared at me; I stared back. The Picasso sculpture stayed out of it; the people passing paid us no mind; neither did the rangy pigeons. "I'll keep coming back. I'll keep asking. You'll need a million Feltons to turn me away."

"You haven't the resources to fight me in court."

"I'll hold a garage sale."

Neither of us spoke for a time. Ayers appeared to wrestle with something internal. All I could do was wait and watch him do it. He looked uncomfortable, stretched past his limits, but I hoped he could see the resolve on my face. "I'd already cut him off at the knees," he said. "He was no threat to me. Even if I *wanted* to kill him, why would I bother? All I had to do was wait a few more weeks, days maybe, and he'd be gone, anyway." He grinned. "Don't look so shocked. Our relationship was always adversarial." He looked around the plaza, inhaled deeply. "I'm done having to insulate the family from Tim's screwups. You want to know who wanted him dead? It wasn't Nick Spada. . . . I'll tell you, but only because I really hope he did it and has to spend the rest of his pathetic life in a prison cell. It'll be better than he deserves."

"Who're we talking about?"

"My brother's blackmailer. I see you had no idea. It cost me two hundred thousand to keep him from dragging our name through the mud, but it doesn't matter now. Tim's dead. Now I want him to pay, just like I had to. I could ruin him financially, of course, but I think seeing him in prison would be much more satisfying. I might even come to visit him, just to see him squirm behind bars."

"You never told the police about any blackmailer."

"It was family business, not police business. Just another of Tim's mistakes. This *friend* found out Tim had money, and went after it. Why not? He threatened to make things unpleasant, so I authorized the payment to make him go away. You'd think Tim would have been appreciative. He wasn't. He said I did it for us, not for him. He was right, of course, but he was also an ungrateful bastard right to the end."

That sounded like Teo Cantu, the Slinky artist, the ex Tim dumped unceremoniously, but I kept quiet, waiting to see what else Ayers would share. Just a moment ago he was in a hurry to be free of me, but now it seemed he had all the time in the world.

"In the end, the amount was negligible. Getting Father's boat back more than makes up for it."

Thank God I wasn't an Ayers. Money couldn't buy happiness, and it couldn't buy heart, compassion, or empathy. Stephen Ayers was an empty suit, a hollow man, a dead man walking amongst the living. I'd asked for the blackmailer's name, but Ayers looked as though he enjoyed stringing me along. Could it be Cantu? If so, was it the blackmail and not the settlement that led to Tim's death? Did Cantu somehow connect to Spada and Darby? Could Spada actually be legit? If so, where did that leave Darby? And Leon?

"Tell me who the blackmailer is," I said.

Ayers watched me, appraising. "Why not, right? Why not sic you on him, and see if he can wiggle out of it. He can use my money to try and keep himself out of prison, if he hasn't squandered it all."

"Who?" I repeated, finding myself getting more desperate for the information with each passing moment. "Give me the name."

Ayers paused, smiling, enjoying the power he held over me, the control. This is what Tim Ayers had come up against his entire life, this level of manipulation, cunning, and cruelty. Ayers casually glanced at his watch. "C.D. Ganz. That's the son of a bitch. Now go make his life a living hell, and leave me and my family alone."

My heart skipped a beat; my mind reeled, recalculated. "Ganz?"

Ayers walked away from me, and I stood stunned, silent on the busy plaza, pigeons circling my feet.

C.D. Ganz.

The sandwich board outside of Sophie's Place announced that a female impersonator named Crystal was performing inside. I'd spent the better part of the afternoon doing a background check on C.D. Ganz while I waited for the club to open. That was PI work—half tech work, half legwork, waiting for something to pop. Ganz had no criminal record, and didn't cross with either Darby or Spada, but he was up to his eyeballs in serious debt. Had he resorted to blackmail when Tim backed out of his promise to finance the bar? He'd said he had found financing elsewhere. Had he meant Stephen? Is that why he pointed the finger at Darby, maybe even fabricating the argument on the boat, to hide the fact that he'd extorted money from Tim's family?

It was just past five, Happy Hour, and the lively street was jammed with evening revelers out for a good time. I walked inside and checked the bar, but Mutt wasn't there. On stage, the flame-haired Crystal vamped it up in a sequined gown and killer stilettoes. He was a real stunner. I slid onto a barstool, ordered a Coke, and watched the show and the crowd, hoping to spot Ganz milling around beneath the baby blue gel lights. The place was packed, and the lights and the close quarters made the room hot.

"Crystal's a real barn burner," I said.

The bartender, a thin black guy with a bushy moustache, worked his damp rag along the surface of the slippery bar, sopping up wet spots. "He brings them in, that's for sure."

"I'm looking for C.D.," I said. "He around?"

He grinned. "Depends."

"On what?"

He angled his head toward the stage. "On how you want him."

Crystal had put her finishing flourish on Whitney Houston's "How Will I Know?" and was starting on Nancy Sinatra's "These Boots Were Made for Walkin'." I turned toward the stage, really looking this time.

"*That's* C.D.?"

The bartender grabbed a promo card out of a dispenser on the bar and handed it to me. "By day. By night . . . sparkle, sparkle."

Crystal, aka C.D. Ganz, stared up at me from the glossy card. His makeup was flawless and he wore a feathered gown Cher would have strangled Bob Mackie for, but it was the red hair that registered most. Good old Cap recalled seeing a good-looking redhead visiting Tim's boat days before he died. A professional woman, he said, with a briefcase and a cute little wiggle. Dressed as Crystal, C.D. could also have passed for a hooker to a nosy perv minding someone else's business and peeking through keyholes at naked women.

"Holy moly," I muttered.

The bartender squinted. "You say something?"

"He does this every night?"

"Couple times a week. Why?"

"Does he ever dress like a woman outside of the club?"

The guy blinked, shrugged. "No idea. I just pour the happy juice. I don't follow him home."

Ganz dipped and swished and worked the room, throwing his boa around the necks of delighted patrons. He bore absolutely no resemblance to the man I'd spoken to a few days earlier: the one with the box cutter and the attitude; the one who refused to tell me how he'd found out about the status of Tim's case. I turned back to the bar. "You wouldn't happen to know a guy named Vincent Darby, would you?"

The bartender looked confused. "The name doesn't register."

"Have you seen a three-hundred-pound bruiser in here who looks like a walking tree? Or a short, fat guy with eyes like Satan's?"

He took his rag and moved farther down the bar. "This some kind of put-on?"

I waved him off, turned back to Ganz and the vamping.

"You gonna wait for C.D.? He's got, like, three sets and two breaks tonight." The bartender asked, though something in his voice told me he hoped I wouldn't.

I smiled, sensing a breakthrough coming. "Wild horses couldn't drag me out of here now."

Chapter 31

It was almost nine PM and I was waiting at the bar for Ganz to change out of his dazzle clothes and meet me there. I wasn't afraid he'd duck out the back and leave me hanging. We'd made eye contact midway through his second set. He knew the jig was up. He also knew running would only postpone the inevitable. It was late; it'd been a long day; I was in no mood to monkey around with him. I'd gotten little from Spada's double-talk or Ayers's high-handed attempt at intimidation. I had a theory, but I had a feeling my luck was about to change big-time.

If I believed Stephen Ayers, and I didn't much, C.D. Ganz was a blackmailer. I had a feeling there was more to it than that. Ganz didn't strike me as being the dodgy sort. After a time, C.D. emerged from the back, dressed in men's clothes, a sheepish look on his freshly scubbed face. Those sitting at the tables paid him no mind at all. Ganz held on to a sparkling leash with a jumpy little ratlike dog on the business end of it. I watched the dog.

"I knew you'd be back," he said when he reached me, "but you've got the wrong idea." He eyed the bartender, who was wiping down the bar and didn't appear to give a fig about what else was going on. "Look, I've got to take care of Vivian. Do you mind taking a walk?" Vivian, a fluff of hairy orange, looked up at me with black marble eyes, her pink tongue hanging out of her mouth like it was too long to fit. The dog's blue collar matched the blue bedazzling on the leash. It was way too much.

I stood, gestured toward the door. "After you."

The doggy park was empty when we got there. Maybe folks didn't exercise their dogs this late? The small enclosure was cordoned off by wrought iron, and the second Ganz unhooked ratdog from the leash, Vivian lit out, tearing around like a bat out of Hades. Ganz and I sat down on the nearest bench, watching as she rolled around in wood chips.

"She's a Pomeranian," Ganz said, though I hadn't asked. "I didn't kill Tim."

"You were seen at the marina days before he died, dressed as a woman. You're deep in debt, and you blackmailed his family. Is that what paid for all the boxes I saw stacked up in the bar the other day?"

Vivian was back, flapping her nub of a tail. Ganz tossed her a treat from a plastic bag with the dog's name spelled out on it in fake rhinestones. Seriously, way too much. The dog caught the snack midair, chewed a couple times, swallowed, and then pranced off. I scanned the street.

"Yes. But I didn't think of it as blackmail. What's it going to take for you to believe me?"

"Start talking. I'll stop you when I've heard enough."

Ganz took a deep breath, tossed another treat. "Okay, it wasn't just business between us. Promises were made. Things ended badly. You have to understand, I had the club hanging over my head, bills. I needed that money. Maybe I panicked. Maybe I made the wrong choice. I did. I *did* make the wrong choice.

"The night of the party, afterward, I thought that if I couldn't get the money from Tim, I might be able to get it from his family. They weren't concerned about him being gay. I mean, it *is* the twenty-first century. It was the bar, his friends, our social unacceptability they didn't want to deal with. I threatened to play it up, make things sticky. I knew they'd pay to keep me quiet. Their lawyer, Felton, is a horrible person, but I couldn't give in to his threats. The club was literally dying right in front of me. I'll admit it wasn't my finest hour."

"How'd you get the money?"

"I picked it up from his boat. The brother delivered it to Tim. I came to get it . . . in a briefcase . . . as Crystal."

"The same day," I said, recalling Cap's account.

Ganz nodded. "I apologized to Tim. I really was sorry. Surprisingly, he accepted it. He was dying, he said. He didn't have time to hold on to grudges or hate me. He said he should have given me the money outright, since he'd promised it. It was just one of those things." Ganz turned to face me, bewildered. "That's what he said, 'one of those things.' In hindsight, I don't think him reneging was about meanness or spite. I think he was just . . . cavalier . . . obtuse, wrapped up in himself. I had no reason to kill him. I'd gotten what I needed, though I'm not at all proud about how I got it."

I leaned back on the bench, tracking the dog as she raced around the borders of the fence like she was running laps at the Olympics and had her eye on the gold medal. "Blackmail," I muttered.

Ganz hung his head, turned away from me. "I tried convincing myself it wasn't, but, yeah, blackmail. It was dirty and it was low. He was dying and I shook him down for cash. God, I hate myself."

"Who told you Tim's case was closed?"

Ganz slid me a look. "Robert Felton, the only guy I hate more than myself right now. He called after I'd gotten the money, after Tim . . . died. He said, and I believed him, that if the family heard from me again, he'd make sure I lost everything. He gave me gooseflesh."

I stared at him. "I've only your word that the transaction went smoothly. Tim's not here to corroborate."

"And my word is no good, for obvious reasons."

"I don't fly on faith."

Ganz fiddled with the bag of doggy treats. "I have proof. I was in St. Michael's Hospital having a cyst removed from a most undignified place the night Tim died. I have my discharge papers, if you need to see them."

"I do."

"I told you about the argument at Tim's party, with Darby. That's the truth. But there was someone else. I saw him hanging around the marina after Tim died. I don't really know why I felt I needed to be there, but I was, post-op pain and all. Unfinished business, I guess. One night, I saw him there, watching, so I watched him for a while, trying to figure out what he was up to. He climbed aboard Tim's boat and stayed a while. When he came out, he had something with him, something big. I couldn't tell what. He could be the one you're looking for."

"You didn't call the police?"

Ganz shrugged. "My hands weren't exactly clean. I didn't want to draw attention. Besides, the police are never my first call for anything."

"Describe who you saw."

"It was the weird guy I told you about, Tim's friend, the one from the party."

I swallowed hard. Jung.

"I stopped watching when I saw someone else taking an interest," Ganz added. "No one I recognized. At that point, I gave it up. Tim was dead. I'd done what I'd done. I had to make peace with it. I didn't see the second guy's face, just his outline. He was tall, not fat. It could have been anybody. He got into a black SUV."

I stood. The black SUV. Was Vince Darby following Jung? Why? And now I couldn't find Jung anywhere? That wasn't good.

Ganz watched me closely. "Are you all right?"

I shook my head, thinking. "Don't think so."

"But at least you don't think I'm a murderer?"

I ignored the question. What was Jung up to? How had he gotten himself on Darby's radar, and what was Darby willing to do about it? "I'll need to see those discharge papers."

Chapter 32

The next morning I went to rent reliable wheels and ended up with a white Chevy Cruze that had a strange vibe and smelled like other people, but I had no choice but to push on with it. I tossed my pipe in the trunk, along with a few other PI essentials—a camera, binoculars, a clipboard, emergency rations—and headed out again to look for Jung. He took something from Tim's boat, and Vince Darby watched him do it. Now Jung was in the wind. I had a bad feeling that wasn't a coincidence, but first I had a stop to make.

I was leaning on the Cruze, my arms folded, when Weber strolled out of the area, saw me, and grinned. He was dressed in a jacket and tie, and his trench billowed behind him as he strolled over, cool as anything. He made quite the picture, and I was beginning to take a proprietary interest.

"Tiller's Gun Shop," I said when he reached me.

He shot me a confused look, cocked his head.

"You wanted to know where I buy my ammo? Tiller's." I searched his face, saw amusement creep into it, and realized instantly that I'd been played. I smiled, shook my head. "And you don't care where."

He got closer, stood facing me, hands in his pockets. "I knew me asking about you would tick you off, and that you'd come around to tell me just how much."

"Smart," I said. "Sneaky, but smart."

"How'd you know where I'd be?" he asked.

I shot him a sly smile. I'd asked around. Cops talk. "You forget what I do for a living?"

We stood there for a time, staring at each other, pretty much there and then deciding without uttering a word between us that we'd passed GO. Weber broke off first, eyeing the rental.

"Where's your car?"

I pulled myself off the Cruze. "Out of commission."

"For how long?"

"I'm thinking indefinitely. Fatal flaw. I'll need to replace it."

"Not so fast. What's wrong with it? I know a great mechanic. He'll give you the policeman's discount and everything. Is it the transmission?"

Yes, it was the transmission. It was also the tires, the engine, the seats, the mats, the steering wheel. There was no reason to lie to the man. "Cocktail."

Weber's brows knit together. " 'Cocktail'?"

"Molotov. My car went up like a Roman candle."

His eyes widened. "Say what?"

I walked around to the driver's side, slipped the bulky rental key into the lock. "It's water under the bridge now . . . easily handled. And in case you're thinking this was me making my move, it wasn't. It was also not a date." I smiled, my eyes narrowed. "But we're making good progress."

I drove away and left Weber standing there.

I buzzed Jung's bell, but got no answer, so I jimmied the vestibule door, headed up to his apartment, and jimmied that lock, too. If I found Jung asleep in his bed, I was going to kill him. If I found Jung dead in his bed, I was going to kill him again.

I stepped gingerly into his apartment into a sea of disorder, nearly bowled over by the stink of dirty socks and hippie dude. For a moment, I thought the room had been tossed, but on closer inspection, it became clear that Jung was just a piggish man-baby who needed to settle down and get his life together. There were dirty plates and glasses stacked everywhere, clothes flung over every piece of prefab furniture, shoes, sandals, empty pizza boxes strewn around the floor. But no Jung. I padded back to the bedroom, peeked inside. No bed. It figured. Jung had anchored a hemplike hammock to the wall, and it hung diagonally across the small room. No furniture, just books stacked high everywhere, and more clothes on the floor. I looked up to find strings of Christmas lights crisscrossing the ceiling. Curious, I flicked the light switch and the bulbs came to life. Some of the bulbs were multicolored; the others were white and blinked on and off. *What the hell?*

I backed out of the room and shut the door behind me. When I turned back for the front room, out of the corner of my eye, I caught sight of something. I turned to find a painting propped up against a wall in a niche right off the kitchen. I padded back, picked it up. *A lighthouse. It's Tim's.* Was this the missing seventh painting? Is this what Jung was seen taking from the *Safe Passage*? If so, what was he doing with it? Was Marta right? Had Jung trashed Tim's boat for this?

I left everything as I'd found it and walked out, a sinking feeling in my gut. What if my client was a murderer? What better cover than to hire someone to look into a murder you yourself had committed? Him sending me off headed in the wrong direction to beat the wrong bushes would have given him plenty of time to get out of town, or out of the country, before I or anyone else even thought to look for him.

I sat in the car and thought it through, getting angrier by the minute. My phone signaled. I had an e-mail, a summary of the deep-dive report I'd requested on Spada. He'd come back just as clean as he had on my first run-through. He was, apparently, a man without blemish. After spending more than enough time with him in a close elevator, I knew that had to be a crock. Who the hell was he?

My phone rang in my hand. It was Turk, the janitor in my office building. Turk, a tatted-up biker partial to white T's and motorcycle boots, had somehow landed a job in building maintenance. On the surface, it didn't seem like a natural fit, but he proved to have an almost encyclopedic brain for fixing everything from a busted toilet to a wonky carburetor. He held the broken-in building together with little more than a pipe wrench, duct tape, and a confounding unflappability.

"Yeah, Cass, I thought I'd better call. You got a delivery here. I didn't see who dropped it off, but they set it right outside your door. You want me to do something with it?"

I frowned. I wasn't expecting any deliveries. "What is it?"

"Big box. Heavy. If it's a piece of furniture, I can go ahead and put it together for you, if you want?"

"Is there a return address?"

"Hold on." I could hear rustling on his end. I guessed he was checking the box. I waited, my breath holding, watching a couple of U of C students meander down the block toward the campus. My birthday was nine months away; Christmas six months away. There was no reason anything should be sitting outside my office door.

"Tell you the truth," Turk said slowly, "it must have taken more than one fella to get this in here. It's got to be a good hundred pounds or more. Nope. No address, just your name scrawled on the side. Want me to open her up?"

I started the car, peeled away from the curb, headed his way. "No. Get away from it, and keep everybody else away, too."

"It's early yet. Nobody here but me." I could hear the confusion in his voice.

I took a red light, then two others, weaving around slow traffic. "Leave it. I'm on my way. Three minutes."

Turk was changing a lightbulb down in the lobby when I rushed through the front door.

"It's still there," he said calmly as he climbed off his ladder. "I blocked off the hall so no one could get at it. What's going on?"

"I'll let you know in a minute. Stay here."

I brushed past him and raced up the stairs to the third floor. I couldn't miss the box. It was a big cardboard sucker, the kind refrigerators or stoves come in, and I was absolutely certain I hadn't ordered either appliance. I approached slowly, studying it. Like Turk said, no address tag, no stamps, no UPS bar codes, just my name in black marker scrawled on the side. Standing over the box, I was relieved to discover that it wasn't ticking, but that meant very little, really. Bombs didn't have to tick. And who'd send me a bomb, anyway? Scratch that. I could come up with a few names. The box was taped along the top and sides with heavy packing tape. No nicks, no scrapes. It looked brand-new.

"See? Just a regular old box."

I jumped, startled by the voice. So engrossed in the box, I hadn't heard Turk walk up behind me.

"I told you to stay put."

Turk nodded, staring at the mystery box. "I heard you."

"Then why are you *here*?"

"This is my building. I run it—it don't run me."

"This thing was here when you got here?"

"Nah. I got here at six, the hall was empty. I spent the morning upstairs waxing the floors. When I got down here to do this one, the box was sitting here. I asked Gupta and some of the third-floorers if they saw who hauled it in, nobody did."

"What time was that?"

He shrugged. "Just before I called you. I needed to get to the floors. The box is in the way."

We both peered down at the box as though our combined concentration would unlock its secrets. Turk suddenly hauled off and kicked the side of it, the loud thud caused by the steel toe of his heavy boot echoing off the walls. I reeled. "What are you doing?"

"I'd say it's not a bomb, but whatever's in there's got some weight to it."

I glowered at him, then started in on my pockets, feeling around for my keys to use to make a dent on the tape.

Turk watched, caught on, and then reached behind to his waistband and pulled out a knife big enough to gut a whale. He handed it to me, hilt-side first, the hilt covered by what looked like crocodile hide. I shook it at him. "This? Right here? Illegal."

Turk looked unimpressed. "Better to be judged by twelve than carried by six."

"Step back," I ordered. Reluctantly he took a tiny step back. I motioned with the mega-knife. "Three more. *Big* ones."

Turk hesitated before complying. Only then did I take his knife, slit the tape away from the top of the box, reach over, and pull the flap back.

"Well, what is it?" Turk asked.

I began pulling plastic away. "Don't know yet, so far it's just a lot of . . ."

I heard myself scream; then I recoiled. Staring up at me from the box were glassy green eyes the color of Chinese jade attached to a face, a dead human face. The recoil was so strong, I lost my footing and landed on my backside. Like a crab, I skittered backward, fast, until my back hit the opposite wall. I squeezed my eyes shut, tried breathing, but I could still see the eyes. The stench of death was now shooting out of the box like the decomposing rot of a mummy's tomb.

"Holy crap!" Turk yelled, holding his nose. He'd crept forward to take a look. "Is that a real head in there?"

I took a moment, then two more. It's not like this was my first dead body. It's just that you do not expect to see a dead person's head in a box with your name on it, a box delivered to you, like a gift. I stood, shaking off the heebie-jeebies, my skin crawling.

Turk shook his head, frowned. "Man, that is not cool."

I approached the box again, pulled back the flaps for a better look. The head was still there, the eyes, the rot. I covered my nose, held my breath. The head was detached from its body. I found the rest—legs, torso, arms—stacked up beside it like a cord of wood, bloodied, its cut edges jagged. I turned my attention back to the eyes. They weren't quite so dreamy now. This was Vincent Darby, the man who'd threatened to break me in two.

I was in the women's room, washing my hands for the fifteenth time, when the police arrived to take possession of what was left of Darby. I'd been in there a while, washing and washing again, trying to rinse away the shock and revulsion, with little luck. I checked myself out in the mirror. The light wasn't good in here, but even in dimness, I looked like a woman who'd just found a dead body in a box. You couldn't mistake my shell-shocked expression. After a few more breaths, duly braced, I headed for the door, then thought better of it. I turned and went back to wash my hands again. The door squeaked open behind me and Detective Marta Pena walked in. I turned to face her. She nodded. I nodded back.

Her star hung from a silver chain around her neck. From the bags under her dark eyes, it looked like she'd been up for days. "You okay?"

"Sure. Why? Don't I look it?"

The look she gave me told me no, but she was polite enough not to say anything. Instead, she eased her notebook out of her pocket and flicked the top of the ballpoint nestled between the pages. "Tell me about the dead guy in the box."

"His name's Vincent Darby, and up until about twenty minutes ago, he was high on my list of suspects in the death of Tim Ayers."

At the mention of Tim's name, Marta's eyes locked on mine and her face went deadpan, like a rock, like one of those presidential visages carved into the stone of Mt. Rushmore. As far as she was concerned, Ayers's case was closed. She was wrong, of course, and I'd argued as much, but it was obvious she didn't appreciate having it brought up again.

"Darby worked for a guy named Nick Spada, who specializes in life settlements."

She sneered. "Not exactly a high-risk line of work."

"Nick Spada and Darby held Ayers's end-of-life policy."

I waited to see if the connection sank in. I could tell by the narrowing of her eyes that it was beginning to.

"I've been digging into Darby hard. He refused to tell me he was living on a boat just three slips down from Tim's, or that he argued with him before he died. I believe that argument was about Tim's run of good luck, the fact that he was still alive when his doctors told him he shouldn't be. If that's true, that ropes Spada in." I leaned against the sink, arms crossed. "I think Nick Spada killed two people, maybe more. Maybe even Peter Langham, whose house Darby was living in. I need to check on that next."

"So Darby being here?" she asked.

"Is a warning. We're dealing with a psychopath."

Marta sighed. "I'll need a list of everybody you talked to in regard to Darby."

I shook my head. "I can give you what I know of him, but the rest is my client's business, until that point when it becomes police business."

Marta's three-mile stare would have withered the gonads of any ordinary criminal, but I'd seen it before. She didn't scare me.

"A man's dead body is lying not ten feet from us. That's homicide. *That's* police business."

"Yes, I saw. It's serious and someone's going to pay. Maybe Darby was into something he shouldn't have been, but no one deserves to end up the way he did. It's cruel. It's sick. When I prove Tim was murdered, and I will, I believe I'll know who killed Darby."

"This is not a time for you to go lone wolf," Marta said. "This is what *we* do."

"It's also what *I* do."

"I should take you in for obstruction."

"That'd be a bonehead move, and you know it."

We stood in silence for a time, my mind reeling. I had nothing. I'd been running around chasing threads for days, finding nothing that led to anything else. Darby's death elevated things, sped the clock up. Someone out there, someone I'd approached, felt threatened enough to start cutting ties with loose ends. Was that his boss, Spada? Was it Ganz? Leon? Someone else?

"I'll give you a head start," I said. "Darby likely had enemies, unrelated to his association with Ayers. He's an ex-con with an extensive record, fraud, mostly. He was a scam artist not above bilking the vulnerable. Maybe that's why he latched onto Ayers, I don't know. Who's more vulnerable than a dying man hoping to get the last bit of happiness out of the time he's got left?" I blew out a long breath. "Or maybe I've pegged Darby wrong and he'd gone completely straight. Maybe he lied to me because he's spent his entire life lying to cops and he hadn't found a way to break the habit. I've got bits of information, a handful of people with stories to tell, but no proof, no straight line. The work's not done."

Marta stared back, her eyes intense. "You didn't get any of that from us, did you?"

"I've got resources outside of the department, thank you. Are you going to take the information I have about Darby, or not? Maybe his troubles stemmed from his job. I talked to Spada. He seemed harmless enough, though he's a bit narcissistic, but when there's money involved, people get greedy. I looked him up. He came back clean, but I'm getting a feeling. You might want to check him out on your end. Maybe you'll get something on him I didn't."

"No, I think you'd like to send me off chasing my tail with this Spada to throw me off your client's scent. I've got him for the break-in. Maybe Darby saw him, too? Maybe Byson's not only a thief but a killer, which is why he's on the run." I thought about Tim's painting in Jung's apartment, and my own suspicions that he might be a killer. However, until I knew for sure what was going on, I had no other choice but to stick with him.

"You're being ridiculous. You've met Jung. Would he have the sense to run?" It was a good question, one I'd asked myself a million times since leaving his apartment. "He could be hiding. The question is, why's he hiding from *me*?"

"Because he knows he's been had," Marta said. "Now let's go. You're going to run through this whole thing again, step-by-step, telling me everything you know."

"Oh, come on. I don't have time for that. You heard me. My client may have dug himself deep into a hidey-hole."

"You're a witness in a homicide."

I shook my head. "I'm the innocent recipient of the worst gift *ever,* that's all. And if you'd taken me seriously when I told you Tim's death wasn't accidental, we wouldn't even be here right now."

"This got anything to do with your car getting torched?"

I wasn't surprised she'd heard about it. Marta was good, thorough. "Darby couldn't have done that from the box. He looks, and smells, like he's been dead for some time."

Marta reached for the doorknob, frowned. "I'm done with this buggy bathroom. Your office. *Now.* And if you even think about getting cute and leaving out one tiny detail of this twisted sister of a story, I'll lock the cuffs on you myself."

My car burned to a molten lump. Jung missing. Darby dead in a box. Someone was sending me a message, and I didn't like it. Doesn't anybody send Western Union anymore?

Chapter 33

My small office was packed with cops, some uniformed, most plainclothes. Everybody wanted to know what I knew. I slid an aggrieved look toward Marta. This was a circus, and she was enjoying dragging me around the center ring. Suddenly a solitary trip to the police station didn't seem all that bad. I looked for Turk and found him across the hall in a huddle of detectives. He looked angry. Someone had disrespected his building, and he wasn't okay with it.

Marta clapped her hands to get everyone's attention. "All right, everybody, clear out. We need the space. Reingold with me. DeLancie, you're on the ME, and let me know the minute you get something from the techs."

Slowly the room emptied. When it did, Marta closed the door and the room fell quiet. Through the frosted glass in the door, I could see the silhouettes of cops milling around in the hall, walking back and forth. Their voices were muted; the noise of their activity reduced to a low murmur. I sat behind my desk, relieved at last to be off my feet.

There were two client chairs facing my desk. Marta took one, her partner the other. Reingold, she'd said. I didn't know him. He was white, slightly balding, a strawberry birthmark on his right cheek. There was no wedding ring on his finger, and he exhibited no outward signs of having a welcoming personality. His beady eyes stayed pinned to mine. No smile.

I leaned forward. "Are we really doing this?"

Reingold and Marta exchanged a look, but the almost imperceptible communication from partner to partner was lost to me. Each team had their own language, their own shortcuts. All I could do was wait until they hashed it out and got back to me. I leaned back in my chair, closed my eyes for a second.

"We're going to go over it again," Marta finally said. "We'll stop you when we've heard enough." Her notebook was at the ready, so was Reingold's.

I opened my top drawer and took out a bottle of aspirin, held it up. "Anybody else need one of these?"

Neither cop responded.

I slid two tablets from the bottle, swallowed them dry, and then set the bottle front and center. "Well, if you change your mind, here they are."

"You got security cameras in this dump? Do we have any shot of getting a look at who dropped that box off?"

"No, and no, and I take exception to the 'dump' crack." It *was* a dump, but I could say so, they couldn't.

Reingold cocked a thumb toward the hall. "How about Easy Rider out there? Looks like he could be into something."

I stared at him, unamused. "Dead end. Turk's solid. You'll have to try harder than that."

Marta let out a low, frustrated growl. "Slide me that aspirin, dammit."

For more than two hours, I answered the same questions at least five times. No, I didn't know who might have wanted Darby dead. Yes, I did know the deceased. No, not intimately. Yes, of course, I had access to a box. Who couldn't get their hands on a box, if they needed one?

Marta and Reingold tried angling for more information and even tried slyly steering me toward revealing details of my investigation—with no success. It was a soul-draining, relentless back-and-forth that quickly began to take on the rhythm of a go-for-broke tennis match, neither side willing or able to give up a single point. The aspirin had a tough time keeping up.

"Look," I said finally. "This has turned out to be a real sinkhole of a day. I'm tired, you're tired. We've gone over this a hundred times." I stood, hoping the gesture signaled the end. "What I know about Vincent Darby, you now know, so either take me in or cut me loose."

Marta and Reingold stood. There was a knock at the door. Reingold opened it and a cop stuck her head in. She and Reingold spoke in whispered tones. I could make out nothing, but the looks on their faces didn't look promising for me. The cop ducked back out; Reingold walked back.

"Besides the slice and dice," he said, "GSW to the chest on the victim."

Marta stepped forward, held her hand out. "I'm going to need your gun." She read my look. "Don't make it ugly."

I turned to Reingold. "What caliber round? What kind of gun?"

He didn't answer. That meant the ME didn't know yet, which meant Reingold didn't know.

I turned back to Marta. "Go fish. Unless I'm under arrest, or until you know what kind of weapon you're even looking for, my gun stays with me."

She drew her hand back, nodded, a slight smile on her face. She knew I knew she'd just tried to pull a fast one. "I'll be in touch."

"I'll count the minutes."

It took a while for the building to empty, but when it did, I sat quietly at my desk, my door open, staring out into the hall, my eyes on the spot where the box had been. Turk had been Johnny-on-the-spot with a clean mop and floor wax, once what was left of Darby got bagged, tagged, and carted away. He'd scrubbed the hall twice, no doubt hoping to rid the place of the dead man's juju. His building, he reminded me, his prerogative. I knew Marta would be back to me quickly when the ME determined what kind of gun Darby had been shot with, but she'd only be wasting time. For some reason, she seemed determined to show me up or prove me wrong about Ayers. I couldn't understand the competitiveness, but it didn't worry me, either. I had a job to do, same as her.

I really had told Marta everything I knew about Darby; everything else I'd learned about Jung and Ganz, I held back, at least for now. She'd have her leads to pursue, and I had mine. There had been an e-mail from C.D. waiting for me on my phone, showing a copy of his discharge papers. He actually had been admitted the night Tim died. The blackmail—well, there were extenuating circumstances involved with that. The elder Ayers paid up, Tim accepted C.D.'s apology, and Ganz got what Tim promised him in the first place. I considered the whole thing done and done. It was Nick Spada who deserved a closer look. He hadn't struck me as odd when I met him, just obstructive, but our encounter had been rather brief. Even psychopaths can hold it together the length of an elevator ride. Had he killed Darby, or had Darby's past finally caught up with him? Mobsters make creative presentations of their victims: They fit them with cement shoes and toss them into the river; they cut out their tongues and shove them down their throats; they cut them up into little pieces and stuff them into a box. But nothing I'd uncovered so far hinted at Darby having any ties to these types of monsters, Mob connected or otherwise.

I glanced out the window at the rain. It was coming down

hard, not in gentle droplets meant to caress flower petals, but in torrential sheets of angry projectiles heavy enough to dent dirt. Biblical rain—rain a person could drown in. I swiveled in my chair, staring at all the wet. A car horn sounded from the street below; my view of the apartment building across the street was muddied by a blanket of rolling fog as dense as chimney smoke. I needed to move. I needed to turn over rocks, push my way in a door, knock something loose, but Marta had warned me away from anything having to do with Darby. That wasn't what was holding me back, though. She likely knew even as the words were coming out of her mouth that I had no intention of backing off. I had a case I hadn't yet solved, a client I couldn't find, and a sinking feeling that both were now closely connected to two dead men. What Marta didn't know wouldn't hurt her.

I grabbed my keys, my bag, and locked up. I needed air, even if rain came with it. I took the stairs at a fast clip, two at a time, toward the ground floor, but stopped when my cell phone rang. For a moment, I considered not answering it, but I did. It was Barb.

"What are you doing?"

"Heading out. Why?"

"Important?"

"It could be."

"Then never mind. It can wait."

There was something in her voice. "What can wait?"

"I thought maybe if you had time to meet, but that's okay, it'll keep."

This was it, I thought. She was finally ready to tell me why she was suddenly back from Africa. I checked my watch. I really needed to keep going. The longer Jung wasn't where I could see him, the greater the chance he was doing something dumb. "Where?"

"The church." She didn't have to say which one. I knew. "I

know," she said in answer to my silence. "But it's this place I want to talk about. If you want to meet somewhere else, we can."

"It's raining like crazy."

She paused. "The sun's already peeking through over here. I'm taking it as a good sign."

I descended the last few stairs, flicked up the hood on my jacket, and pushed through the lobby door out onto the sidewalk. "I'm on my way."

Sure enough, the sun was out by the time I pulled to the curb in front of St. Brendan's. I parked and sat there for a moment, peering through the window, watching Barb pace the small courtyard, the top of her wild red hair moving left, then right, and back again over the top of the shrubs. I eyed the rectory, the gray stone church, an overwhelming ache of absence echoing through me. It was like coming home and not finding a single thing there you loved anymore; and though every brick and window sparked a fond recollection, the place felt hollow, foreign, no longer mine. I got out of the car, headed over, flexing my hands to warm them. It was June, but my hands were like ice.

"Told ya. No rain. You made good time."

I shrugged, my eyes on hers, not on the church, not on the rectory. "It sounded important."

Barb tilted her face skyward, saw the sun, unzipped her yellow slicker. We might have talked about the weather, but Barb had as little patience for small talk and circuitous conversation as I did. If we had something to say, we said it . . . usually, which was why her secretive behavior over the last couple days was so out of character. I gave her the room, though it wasn't easy. Obviously, now she no longer needed it.

"I owe you an explanation," she said.

"Okay."

She rocked on the soles of her feet, watching, stalling. "How's your case?"

"Someone sent me a dead man."

She started to laugh, then realized I wasn't joking and went ghostly pale. "What?"

I shrugged. "I'm over the shock of it."

Her mouth twisted into a pained grimace. I waited some more, by all outward appearances patiently, though my insides would tell a different story. I could tell Barb was thinking about the dead guy, but I needed to move things along. Jung was out there somewhere stuck on stupid.

"You had something to tell me," I prodded gently.

She breathed in, let the breath out slowly. "I'm not going back to Tanzania. I'm going to be teaching here."

The news surprised me. I'd been expecting something awful, something dire. But it was just like Barb to gush it out like that, no toying around with it. "How'd that happen?"

She eased down onto the stone bench behind us. The very spot where I'd met Pop. "After, well, you know, I couldn't get this place out of my head. Father Ray put a lot of years into this parish, into us—you, me, Whip, hundreds of others. He left a lot undone. I know I can help." She looked up at me. "I called Father Pascoe."

I frowned, but made no comment. Pascoe and I had gotten off to a rocky start. He'd tried to stop me from investigating Pop's death, and then slipped seamlessly into his job, his office. Too soon, I guess.

Barb registered my reaction. "He's a nice man, a little stiff, but it takes a variety of flowers to make a garden. Anyway, he was short a teacher and I jumped at it. I figured if I could teach halfway around the world, why not teach right here in my old neighborhood?" Barb stood, dusted off the seat of her jeans. "It'll be like reclaiming this place for good after so much bad. What do you think? You're not saying anything."

"The neighborhood has changed a lot since we were here. Gangs, guns. You won't have an easy time of it."

"I've run up against African warlords."

"You're also very white. You'd be like a radish amongst a sea of onions."

Barb surveyed her arms as though her complexion was a new thing she hadn't yet noticed. "Only on the outside."

"Then there's the other thing."

She was getting testy. "What *other* thing?"

"You're as obstinate as a mule, and you've never met a rule you didn't try to break." I thought for a moment, then smiled. I'd just described Pop to a tee. He was a constant thorn in the archdiocese's side, and in Father Pascoe's, a man who always colored inside the lines. "Pascoe has no idea what he's done."

She nodded, her eyes dancing, her grin wide. "No, he doesn't."

The church bell sounded overhead, as if on cue. I glanced up at it, back at Barb. I wondered if she took the ringing of the bell as a good sign, too, a nod from Pop. "When do you start?"

"I taught my first class yesterday. Summer school. I'll teach sixth-grade English when regular classes start up again after Labor Day. Till then, I'll spend some time with the family . . . work up my lesson plans . . . unless you need another investigator? I think I'd be good at it."

"Thank you. No," I said, smiling.

She shrugged. "Your loss."

Barb glanced around the tiny courtyard, the look on her face lovingly proprietary, as though she were the keeper of everything she laid her eyes on. "It looks a lot smaller than I remember it, but I'm feeling good about my decision. This is where it all started. This is my spiritual home."

"Spiritual home" sparked a recollection. "Of course. Swami Rain." I could have kicked myself for forgetting it. "I think I know where Jung is."

"Back up," Barb said. "I'm still on Swami Rain."

"Jung's yogi. I was afraid maybe Darby had taken Jung, but Darby's dead. He's got to be hiding at the yogi's."

"You don't look too happy about it."

"Oh, I'm happy. I'm *very* happy, but if Jung *is* there, he won't be for long."

Chapter 34

I leaned hard on the bell at the sad-looking yoga center tucked into a converted brownstone a block from the U of C. The door was locked, the blinds drawn, but I could see light shining through between the slats. When the bell didn't bring anyone to the door, I started pounding on it, which sent the wind chimes dangling from the top of the door frame into hyperdrive. When a brown eye finally peeked warily through the blinds, I smacked my PI's license against the glass and waited for the door to open. When it did, a short white man, who looked an awful lot like Bill Maher, stood facing me. He was dressed in cotton yoga pajamas, and his long sandy hair, flecked with gray, was neatly pulled back from a receding hairline into a paltry ponytail.

"Swami Rain?"

He smiled serenely. "When I'm working." He held out a hand for me to shake. "Jeff Wilbourne, otherwise, and you are Jung's detective. He's been expecting you."

He slowly stepped aside and led me into a large airy room with yoga mats on the floor and posters of waterfalls and rain forests on the walls. The room was empty except for little Bill Maher and me. I should have felt relieved, but despite all the tranquility and smiles, all I could think about was the time I'd wasted looking for Jung. I'd begun to think he might be dead, that somebody might mail me his head. Then I'd begun to think he was a cold-blooded murderer playing me for a fool. I couldn't kill him, could I? No, of course not, but what if I did? What jury would convict me after I'd explained what I'd had to deal with?

Swami Rain led me past the yoga mats to a back room with a closed door. He opened it, stepped aside, and I walked in to find Jung Byson, my client, in the middle of downward dog, his scrawny behind pointed toward nirvana. He was safe. He was alive. He wasn't on the lam. I took a moment to let all that sink in, then walked up to the mat and snatched it out from under him, sending him toppling over in a surprised heap.

"What? Hey."

I slung the mat against a wall and pushed the door closed, stranding Swami Rain in the hall. Jung took one look at my face and scrambled to his feet, backing away, fast. He was dressed in yoga pants and a black Coldplay T-shirt, his hair plastered to his head with sweat. Despite that, he looked well rested and well fed, which was more than I could say for myself.

I advanced. "Do you have any idea what I've been doing to find you?"

There was an old couch shoved aside. Jung jumped up and over it, using it as a buffer.

"One frantic phone call, and then nothing," I said. Jung skittered farther away, taking the couch with him. "Stop moving."

He froze, his eyes wide, scanning the room, as if looking for an escape route. He was out of luck. I stood between him and the door.

"Have you been here 'downward dogging it' this whole time?"

"I figured no one would think to look for me here, except you. Though you kind of took a long time with it, didn't you? Swami's running out of provisions. I'm literally down to his last bag of kale chips." He pulled himself up to his full height. "And just as a side note, not cool, your harshing my mellow like this."

I caught myself before I took another step. "Sit!"

Jung hopped over the couch and sat, his lips pressed tightly together, a petulant child caught playing hooky. Swami Rain rapped lightly on the door.

"Hello? Is everything okay in there?"

I jabbed an angry finger at Jung. "Move and I use my keys to scoop out your liver."

I opened the door for Swami Rain. He looked around, saw Jung sitting there, then turned to me. "I can see you're in distress."

Out of the corner of my eye, I saw Jung twitch and I reeled to face him. He stopped cold.

"Maybe I can help?" Swami asked.

He had already, I thought, more than he knew. I'd come close to smothering Jung with a yoga mat.

Swami Rain offered green tea in an earthen mug, which I took him up on. The aspirin from earlier in my office had long since worn off, and I couldn't get Darby's dead eyes out of my head or the queasy thought that I may have pushed too hard in the wrong place, resulting in his murder. The tea was supposed to fill me with calming energy. Frankly, it would have to be a magical brew to accomplish that, but I sipped it, anyway, while seated at a small round table beside Jung's moveable couch barricade, glaring at him. Jung and Swami Rain sat across from me, a united front. I was at the table to find out what Jung thought he was playing at; Swami Rain was there in case the tea didn't work.

I set the mug down, folded my hands in my lap, right reason restored. The chase was over. I'd found Jung. Even the desire to tighten my hands around his scrawny neck was dissipating. "Okay, let's have it."

Jung leaned forward, crossing his arms on the table, the picture of conviviality, like this was a routine social call and we were here to chew the fat. I glowered at him and he slowly eased himself back again.

"I'm feeling a little under pressure here," he said.

I managed a weak smile. "I'll start you off. You called me in the middle of the night, for the second time, making no sense, babbling something about the police, the marina, and your innocence, and then you hung up on me, leaving no forwarding number. Days went by. *Days.* And nothing. I checked your apartment, I badgered your friends. I called hospitals, I checked the morgue. *The morgue.*" I stopped, took another sip of tea, waited for it to settle in my stomach. "A witness saw you on Tim's boat. The police now think you burgled it. And, were they inclined to believe Tim was murdered, you would likely be their prime suspect for that, too."

Jung's eyes got as big as dinner plates and he lost what was left of his coloring. Swami Rain gasped, turned to him. "Dude, major karma kill."

"Suspect? *Me?*" Jung screeched. "Are you serious? Why would I hire you to find out what happened to Tim if I'm the one who killed him? That's crazy. Okay, I didn't exactly have a key to the boat, but it was totally innocent. It had nothing to do with anything. The place was wrecked when I got there. Honest. I could hardly find anything in that mess." His words tumbled out, one over the other; it was difficult to keep up. "I've never killed a thing in my life—okay, maybe a bug, but that's it—nothing with feet, nothing human. I'm a peaceful guy."

"What were you looking for?"

Jung turned to me, a blank look on his face, a deer caught in headlights. "What?"

"You said you could hardly find anything in that mess. What were you looking for?"

He tugged on the collar of his sweaty shirt. "Nothing, but if I had been looking, I'd have had a hard time finding anything. That's what I'm saying."

I sat watching him, the tea coating my gut, keeping me calm.

Jung was lying, badly. I glanced at Swami Rain, a potential witness to Jung's homicide.

"We'll come back to that," I said. "Tell me about Vincent Darby."

For a second, it didn't look like he recognized the name. "Wait. That guy from the party? What's he got to do with anything?"

"He turned up dead. Shot and cut to pieces. We may both be on the hook for that one."

Jung blanched. "Me? Why would I kill *him*?" He ran his fingers through his hair, then grabbed tufts of it in his fingers and pulled. It was an act of utter frustration. He was over his head, out of his element. "I'm living a nightmare."

Swami Rain raised a timid hand. "Excuse me, could we get back to the part about him being a murderer?"

Jung reeled on him, anger flaring. "What's wrong with you, dude? I'm no killer."

Rain pointed to me. "She said you're a suspect in two murders and that the police are looking for you right now."

"And *I* said I'm almost completely innocent."

Swami Rain's hands flew up. "What does that even mean?"

I took another sip of tea. It was amazing how quickly transcendental gobbledygook fell away when you were accused of murder. I cleared my throat, silencing the back-and-forth.

"We're going to start at the beginning, with the break-in, and then work our way all the way through to the moment I walked in here and found you exercising in your pajamas. Understood?"

Jung gulped. He nodded. Swami Rain nodded.

"Okay. Good. Why were you on Tim's boat? And why did you steal one of his paintings?"

Jung shook his hands out, as though trying to work the circulation back into them. "I guess I have to tell you. I guess he'd give me permission, considering the circumstances." He began to wring his hands. "It was my solemn duty as his best bud. We made a pact. His number came up first is all."

"What are you talking about?"

"I need to stand up first." Jung didn't move.

"Then stand up," Swami Rain barked. "What the hell, man?"

"Dude, you heard her. She told me not to move."

I didn't say anything, just gestured for Jung to stand, which he did, slowly. He then lifted his shirt to reveal layers of plastic wrap wound around his hairless middle. There was a white envelope under the wrap. I stared at it, at Jung, watching as he unwound the plastic. When he got down to the last layer, the one plastered against his skin, the pain of the extraction showed on his face. When he was done, he handed the soggy envelope to me.

"There. This is what I went to get. It was taped to the back of his Fender. He paid serious money for it at some silent auction years ago. It's actually signed by Jimi Hendrix. Tim was into retro stuff, me too. Retro's way cool."

I stared at the envelope. It was creased and damp from Jung's yoga sweat. "What is this?"

"Don't know. Didn't open it. Bro code. There was some other stuff, too. We made a deal, if anything happened to either one of us, the other would go in and get, you know, stuff. Personal stuff you don't want another living soul to see?"

I blinked up at him, so did Swami.

"You know . . . things, maybe, or . . . like . . . your stash . . . or . . . porn?" Jung looked at me, then Swami Rain. "Am I really the only one who knows what I'm talking about here?"

It looked like Swami Rain wanted to clasp his fingers around Jung's neck. His eyes blazed, and his lips twisted into an angry snarl. I stared at the envelope. "You broke into Tim's boat for this envelope and porn?"

"I was obligated."

"And you didn't toss his place looking for it?"

"Why would I have to? That's what I'm saying. That was in back of the Fender, where he told me to look. Even in all that mess, I went right to it."

"What about the painting? I counted seven when I was aboard

the *Safe Passage*, now there are six. I found one in your apartment."
Jung moved away from me; his eyes danced around the room; he
began to pace. "I told you Tim left me a painting. I only took
what he wanted me to have, and what he told me to take."

"Where's the rest of the stuff, then? The porn?"

"I burned it."

Swami Rain bolted up. "You burned it? What do you mean,
you 'burned it'?"

"Dude! I mean I *burned it*. Lighter fluid, match, burned it,
okay?"

I held up the envelope. "But you didn't burn this, why?"

Jung turned back to me. "I thought it might be important."
He turned back to Swami. "I knew for sure the porn wasn't.
Look, I didn't break in. The door was open." Jung searched my
face. "I had to get his personals . . . and the painting. I had to do
it on the sneak before Stephen stepped in and moved the boat
and got rid of all his stuff."

I opened the envelope and shook out a folded newspaper clipping with a business card attached to it. The card was Nicholas
Spada's.

"Shit. That's all that was in there?" Jung asked, leaning over to
see. "That's what I had taped to my bod this whole time?"

"Appears so," I said.

Jung hovered over me. "I thought there'd be something a lot
more interesting, like the number to a Swiss bank account.
Why'd he want me to grab this?"

I stared at Spada's name, and then separated the card from the
clipping. I looked up. "Why'd you run here? Why didn't you go
home?"

Jung backed up a little, but didn't go far. "I started to, but then
I got creeped out with all the skulking around. I started to think,
what if Tim had something really important in there and somebody killed him for it? If they saw me, maybe they'd figure I had
it. I couldn't take the chance of going back to my place. That's

when I called you. To tell you to go to the marina and find out what happened. If I'd known this was all I had, I *would've* gone home. But I got skeeved out, okay? We could be dealing with some real spy stuff. They can track you by satellite these days. I had to cue you in and then find a place to lay low."

Swami Rain glowered at Jung. "So you came *here*?"

"Dude, what *is* your problem? Where else was I supposed to go? You *are* my spiritual adviser, aren't you? I came looking for sanctuary."

"This isn't a church, doofus," Rain shot back. "It's a yoga studio. I've got a wife and kids, for Christ's sake." He folded his arms across his chest, seething. "Unbelievable."

There was a brief, awkward silence, which I gently broke. "Maybe more tea, Swami?"

Swami bit into his lower lip, sneering at Jung, then shot up from his chair, gave me a nod. "Yeah, sure."

I smiled. "And maybe take the long way back?"

Swami stormed out of the room, slamming the door behind him. Jung stared after him, totally clueless. He'd been willing to jeopardize the man's well-being for his own safety, but didn't understand why Swami Rain might not be okay with that. It only proved what I already knew: Jung was book smart, but people dumb.

"What's with him, huh? *I'm* the one who could be in danger here, right? I've had potential dynamite strapped to me this whole time."

I shook my head, unfolded the clipping, read it. Below the newspaper story in bold block letters Tim had written a name and put a question mark behind it. Jung leaned in, reading over my shoulder.

"Peter Langham? Who's that?"

Langham. Spada's deceased client. The owner of the house Vincent Darby was living in. The article was a short piece on a freak carbon monoxide accident that claimed the life of one elderly man, Langham. The story was made all the more tragic, the reporter noted, because Mr. Langham, the father of four and grandfather to twelve, had been in the late stages of pancreatic cancer and had been given just weeks to live. A faulty furnace had been cited as the cause of the carbon monoxide release. The grainy photo at the top of the piece captured firefighters standing around outside the house, while in the background a crowd of curious onlookers stood and watched. Why would Tim keep this? Hide it? Carbon monoxide. Faulty furnace. I stood up, slipped the clipping and the card into my pocket. "Get your things."

"What is it? What'd you see?"

"Not sure yet. Let's go."

Jung picked up his shoes, grabbed his messenger bag. "Where?"

"I'm turning you over to the police."

He stopped, dropped the bag. "What? You can't do that."

"They're looking for you. I'll drop you off. You'll go in, they'll see that you're completely clueless, and they'll let you go and move on. Simple. If you continue to hide from them, they'll make your life a living hell. Now get your stuff and let's go."

"Why can't I stay here? All I need is a few snacks, some beer."

I eyed the door. "Yeah, about that. You might want to start looking for another spiritual home. I'm afraid you've burned your bridges with Swami Rain."

Chapter 35

Tim, Spada, Darby, Langham—of the four, only Spada was still alive; that either made him the luckiest so-and-so on God's green earth, or somebody who knew a lot more than he was letting on. I rode the elevator up to his office to find out which was which.

Langham was in his seventies when he died, Tim more than fifty years his junior, hardly running buddies. But they were both Spada clients. That had to be important. I mean, it could be coincidental, but the odds would be extremely high. What couldn't have been a coincidence was Vince Darby living in Langham's house. I could see a circle forming. I could feel that I was getting close to something. I stared at the changing numbers above the elevator door, willing the slow car to climb faster, my mind busy.

Langham was terminal, but died from carbon monoxide poisoning, ruled accidental. Tim was terminal, but died by drowning, also ruled accidental, though suicide was suspected. And there was Nicholas Spada and Vince Darby, who stood to make more money the quicker Langham and Ayers died. Had the two figured out a way to make sure their clients passed away sooner rather than later?

Maybe Tim stumbled across something that made him suspicious of the scheme. Why else save the clipping of Langham's death and attach it to Spada's card? Why hide it and leave special instructions for Jung to get it? Is that why Tim's boat was broken into? Had someone been looking for the clipping? If so, that would mean whoever tossed it knew Tim was holding something of value and knew, if found, it'd lead back to them. They'd missed the guitar, obviously, and Jung was able to retrieve it, as he'd promised Tim he would. Had Tim counted on Jung to make the necessary connection?

Would Spada, desperate to make a name for himself, really resort to murder to make his business successful? He was ambitious, hungry, determined. He needed the numbers. He needed the prestige. He was the top seller, after all. A real social climber, that's how Elizabeth Ayers portrayed him, but without the necessary pedigree. Maybe Spada thought the money was all he needed; he'd underestimated the importance of lineage and good breeding. Had he taken out his frustrations on Tim?

Or had that been Darby's job? He was the ex-con, the scammer, murder wasn't that far a leap, was it? But if the two men were in it together, then why was Darby dead? And why was his body sent to me? I was a nuisance, sure, and I was digging for anything I could find, but I didn't have anything concrete. Was Darby's body meant to scare me off?

The elevator opened on Spada's floor and I walked into his office to find a young woman at the reception desk packing up for the day. She smiled, a bit harried, seemingly anxious to get gone. "May I help you?" She appeared amenable, but I could tell she probably hoped she could be of no assistance and I would soon be on my way. Maybe she had a train to catch or a hot date to get to.

"Is Mr. Spada in?"

The girl gave me a sad little pout, insincere, but she went for it, anyway. "Sorry. He's gone for the day. Would you like to set up an appointment?" She reached for her computer.

"Will he be in tomorrow?"

She eyed me warily, then pecked around on the keyboard. "He's got tomorrow blocked off." She ran a manicured finger down the screen. "The whole week, actually. Is there someone else who might be able to help you? Is this about a policy?"

"I'm looking to purchase a policy, yes."

"Oh, well, in that case, I can get you in tomorrow at two with Mr. Gilland."

As I stood there, staffers filed out quickly, briefcases and tote bags swinging. It was quitting time. No time for dawdling. The girl eyed the fleeing staffers longingly.

"You know what? Let me think about that. I don't have my schedule with me." I slipped a card from the holder on her desk, tucked it away, smiled. "I'll call back in the morning. You have a good night."

I eased out into the hall, bypassed the elevator, and tucked into a corner at the far end, my eyes on Spada's door. More staffers streamed out, caught the elevator, and disappeared. They probably had no idea what kind of side business their boss was up to. It'd only work if Spada kept the circle small, just him and Darby. Too many deaths, too many accidents all at once, would raise suspicion, but a mishap here, one there, who would catch on?

I perked up when the receptionist trotted out and headed toward the ladies' room, one last pit stop before hitting the street. When she disappeared, I padded up to the door and slipped inside, moving swiftly past her desk, headed back toward Spada's personal suite. Where was he? I wondered. He wasn't planning to be in the office all week. I had no way of knowing if that was normal for him. He could be off on a planned vacation; he could be at a conference or seminar; he could be running for his life. I was halfway down the long hall, my sights on wide double doors at the end with Spada's name stenciled on them, when the front doors opened behind me, signaling the receptionist's return.

I ducked into an alcove, squeezing in behind two massive

copiers, listening for the sound of approaching footsteps, but she didn't appear to be coming my way. I waited, crouched low, inhaling toxic toner. I checked my watch. Almost five-thirty. I drummed my fingers against my thighs, itching to get moving. What was the woman doing? Suddenly the lights went out. I rose up a bit, cautiously optimistic.

I heard the front door open, then close, and then I heard the scraping of a key in the lock, followed by eerie silence. I gave it a good thirty seconds more before stepping tentatively out from behind the machines. I looked right, then left. I was alone. I took a moment, breathed deep. I was in, but how was I going to get out? Did the door unlock just as easily from the inside as it locked from the outside? If it didn't, I'd be found here in the morning without a plausible explanation, and nothing about that ended well for me. I rushed for Spada's double doors. I'd worry about getting out later.

The corner office had "executive" written all over it, from the gold-plated knickknacks on Spada's banker's desk to the rich leather chairs and glass tables. Everything all but screamed, *"This is a man who made it!"* Had he sat at this very desk and promised the dying and desperate that he would take care of everything, put their minds at ease? Had he then callously gone about having them all dispatched?

I stared at the gold-framed family photos sitting on Spada's desk. There were four of them and he'd positioned each so that whoever sat across from him in his client chair couldn't fail to see them. Nick Spada, family man. In one, Spada posed with a woman I assumed was his wife, a striking blonde who looked to be at least twenty years his junior. *Second wife?* In another photograph, the children, a couple of gangly preteens and two smaller kids, smiled for the camera in their Sunday best, a basket of yellow Lab puppies at their feet. Unfortunately, they would all share in what Spada had coming. I wondered if that would even matter to him when this was all done.

His desk drawers were locked. I tried the file cabinets, too. Locked. I took another glance at my watch. Ten minutes. From my copier crouch to now, ten minutes. I had to move fast and get out of here before security made their rounds. I dug latex gloves out of my back pocket, along with my set of picklocks. The file cabinet was first. This wasn't legal, but, truthfully, I careened off the legal path the second I cruised past the reception desk and ducked behind the copiers. And as far as illegalities stacked up, mine versus the ones I had a strong suspicion Spada may have committed, murder trumped criminal trespass all the livelong day.

The lock wasn't complicated. It took seconds. I quickly scanned the hanging files inside, looking for anything with Tim's or Langham's name on it or anything having to do with accidental deaths. I moved swiftly, but thoroughly, through every file, every drawer, but after I got through them all, there didn't appear to be anything out of the ordinary. There was just standard insurance paperwork—claims, policies—nothing relating to death and dying. I slid behind Spada's desk, sinking into the butter-smooth leather, luxuriating in the feel for a second, noting my time on Spada's expensive-looking colonial desk clock. Twenty-two minutes. It felt like twenty-two years. My hands were sweating inside the latex gloves.

I stared at the desk. It was one of those heavy antique jobs built to impress, but built well. If I forced the lock, I'd likely splinter the wood; if I jimmied the lock, I'd probably nick it. Either option would tip Spada off that someone had been here. He'd assume that someone was me, thereby adding "criminal damage to property" to my long list of offenses.

I settled on the picklocks and went to work—jockeying the tumblers, feeling for the give, moving slow—careful where I placed the picks. When the lock snicked free, I slid open the top drawer, expecting paper but found instead a 9mm Glock. It was black, matte finish, unholstered, sitting next to Post-it notes, paper clips, and a tin of Altoids. What was an insurance guy doing with a gun in his desk? Who'd he plan to use it on? I wasn't about to touch it, even with the gloves. If I left even a partial print on it, a single ridge or swirl, there was no telling what kind of trouble I'd set myself up for. Instead, I grabbed my phone out of my pocket and snapped a picture of the gun, then quietly slid the drawer closed again.

I found what I was after behind a hidden panel in the bottom drawer. The thick accordion file had been pushed far back in the recess, bound tightly by thin brown string. This was Spada's secret cache. I counted a dozen files. The forms inside were not at all like the others I'd seen. I flipped through them, quickly moving through, noting names, vital stats, anything that would connect to Tim. It didn't take long to determine that these papers pertained to viatical settlements and that, on closer inspection, every form belonged to someone with a catastrophic illness who didn't have long to live. Quickly on the heels of that revelation came the sick fact that for cause of death, in each case, accidental death had been the determination. In the last slot of the folder, I found a stack of hundred-dollar bills in a ten-thousand-dollar bundle. *Darby's unclaimed pay? Spada's cut?* Acid roiled in my stomach as I read my way through.

Omarr Weaver, sixty-five, colon cancer, stage four. Cause of death: accident. Weaver had fallen down a flight of stairs at home and had broken his neck. Agnes Tynan, thirty-nine, breast cancer, stage four. Cause of death: smoke inhalation suffered in a house fire. Accidents. Just like Tim. All long after they were supposed to have died from their diseases. I read on, my eyes widening when I finally came across the names I'd expected to find: Tim's and Langham's. In addition, it appeared that Langham, with no family, had left his worldly possessions—his house, his things—to Spada. That's why Darby was in Langham's house. The house belonged to his boss, though obviously he hadn't yet gotten around to switching things completely over. I tossed the folder on the desk, no longer wanting to touch it. I stood, stepping away from the desk, the folder. It was sickening, all of it.

Why keep these files, even if they were well hidden? Arrogance, I decided, documentation of his cleverness. Or maybe they were Spada's leverage against Darby double-crossing him? I reluctantly went back to them.

Margaret Gardner, thirty-two, Hodgkin's lymphoma. She'd been given only a few weeks to live, but held on for more than a year and a half. She died of a barbiturate overdose on her thirty-second birthday. There were at least a handful more. Then the word "homicide" leapt out at me, and I focused on it. Bertrand Tillis, forty-two, prostate cancer. He'd lived eight months past his projected death date. Cause of death: homicide. Tillis had been mugged and beaten to death steps from his back door . . . on Christmas Eve. His killer had never been found.

I upended the file, shook it to make sure I hadn't missed anything inside; I had. Next to the money, wedged on the bottom, folded, was one more form, this one with a red dot at the top of it. It was the same as the others, except for the dot, and except for the fact that there was no death date filled in. Stella Symonds. End-stage Lou Gehrig's disease. She'd been given three months, conservatively. That was six months ago. Was she still alive? With Darby dead, maybe Spada didn't have anyone to arrange for her "accident"?

I photographed everything before putting it all back the way I'd found it, except for Symonds's file. Since there was no death date filled in, it was possible she was still alive, I thought, feeling the urgency bubble up from my gut like a toxic brew. Was she safe now that Darby was dead, or would Spada arrange for someone else to solve the Symonds problem? I couldn't take the chance. I slid her paperwork into my bag. I'd have to warn her.

Who was Spada to decide when people died? And for what? Money? I glanced at Spada's expensive toys, the framed photographs of his perfect family, those documenting his rich-man's pastimes: boating, golf, fly-fishing. Nick Spada had discovered a way to make dying his business, and I was going to make sure he didn't get away with it. Unfortunately, the files only proved that the deaths were to Spada's benefit. They weren't evidence that either he or Darby had committed murder.

I pulled the newspaper article on Langham's death out of my pocket. I unfolded it and laid it flat on the desk. Why had Tim kept it? It didn't appear to have any connection to Spada. The short article offered nothing new. I'd stared at it a million times, all but memorized it. The photo was just as grainy as before. There were the firemen standing around, the crowd looking on. The crowd. Looking on. Something there. Something I'd missed.

I got real still, afraid to move or even blink, for fear that what I thought I saw would evaporate like mist. I searched Spada's desk for a pair of eyeglasses, a magnifying glass, anything to get a closer look, finally finding the latter tucked inside his mahogany in-box. I lasered in on the photo, studied it, every dot, every murky shadow, every face. Not the firemen. Not the house. The tall man standing in the back, partially hidden by the crowd: dark, curly hair, handsome. "Darby," I muttered, my heart pounding. It was Vincent Darby.

I rose slowly. That was it. Why Tim kept the clipping. He'd somehow stumbled upon what Spada and Darby were up to. He knew why Langham and the others were dying. When he saw Darby in the picture, had he put two and two together? Had he accused Darby that night on the boat of rigging Langham's furnace, flooding the old man's place with carbon monoxide? Was *this* the big picture Tim Ayers missed? That was it. I was sure of it. I grabbed up the clipping, put the magnifier back where I'd found it.

Just then, a vacuum cleaner started up down the hall and I nearly lost my lunch. The loud roar of the industrial machine was underscored by the rapid-fire exchange of a foreign language. Polish? Russian? I pedaled over to the door and eased it open a crack, in time to see the night cleaning crew. There were three older women in light blue smocks, grabbing rags and bottles of cleaning solution off a big rolling cart and slipping into one of the front offices. A fourth woman, the one with the vacuum, had headed toward reception, cutting off my exit. I closed the door, pressed my back against it, envisioning the next two to five years inside Logan Correctional. This, the moment you realized the jig is up, was why crime did not pay. This was the point where consequences for bad behavior clocked you on the chin like a big angry fist.

I stared longingly at the window; I was twenty-five floors up. Not an option. I took a moment to settle myself, then pulled it together and lifted off the door. Another peek confirmed the women were still there, though the hall was temporarily clear. The vacuum still roared up front. I counted to three, swung the door open, and bolted, racing down the hall, my eyes on the office with the women in it. My plan was to streak right past them, one fast blur of humanity they wouldn't be able to identify. However, halfway there, I saw the vacuum cleaner heading back and I skidded through an open door and hid behind it.

This office was a lot smaller than Spada's and hadn't a single knickknack in it, but it offered the same trap. I could not get past the cleaners. I pressed my head against the door and thought it through, my brain picking away at the problem. I suddenly got an idea.

I lunged over and flicked on the lights, then ran for the desk, pulling papers out of the in-box, grabbing a pen. When I heard the women approach, I slid into the chair behind the desk, snatched up the receiver and held it to my ear, like I was listening to someone on the other end, remembering almost too late that I still had on the latex gloves. I cradled the receiver between neck and shoulder blade, scrambled out of the gloves and shoved them into my pocket, just as the women appeared in the doorway.

The women jumped and gasped when they saw me, surprised, it appeared, to find they were not alone. I hoped none of them recognized Spada's staff by sight. If they did, I was busted. I calmly held up one finger to signal that I'd only be a minute. My eyes landed on a framed photo on the desk of a white family: husband, wife, and two towheaded toddlers. I flipped the photo facedown. There was no way I could pass any of them off as relatives.

"Fine," I said to the imaginary person on the other end of the line. "I'll send you the contract tomorrow by FedEx. It's nice doing business with you, Andrew." I put the receiver down, stood, straightened my clothes, then heaved out a sigh. "*Whew.* Long day, huh, ladies? I didn't realize it was so late. Time flies."

"Late," the taller of the three women said, her gray eyes narrowed suspiciously. "No one here works so late." Her accent was thick and definitely Slavic, definitely Polish, not Russian. "That's why we clean first here." She held up a list attached to a clipboard. "See? First."

"Then I'll get out of your way," I said.

Her eyes stayed narrowed. "The door was locked. Yes?"

"Yes, it was locked. *I* locked it."

"You have key?"

I reached into my pocket and pulled out the keys to my apartment, flashed them. "Right here. You didn't expect me to work in here, a woman alone, with the door wide open, did you? That's not safe. I could get assaulted, mugged, God forbid, murdered. But if you're still concerned about it, I'll just call Mr. Spada and he can explain to you why I had to work late when I told him almost a month ago that I had theater tickets for tonight." I shrugged dejectedly. "Good money down the drain."

I moved for the phone, hoping I wasn't going to have to make another fake call.

"Everything good," she said, the others concurring with smiles and nods. "We come back."

I smiled, slipped politely past them. "No need. I'm finished. Good night, ladies." I turned back, remembering the phone and my prints on it. "Oh, I forgot. There's a cold going around the office. Would you ladies mind wiping the desk and phone down really well for me? I'd hate for anyone to get sick."

They nodded, smiled, then went to work. I stood for a moment and watched as one of the ladies began wiping down the desk with disinfectant, running the rag across the blotter, picking up the receiver, wiping it clean. Not foolproof, but good enough. I'd be long gone by the time they got around to the family photo.

Moving quickly, I headed for the door, hoping it was now unlocked, holding my breath until the very moment I pushed through the glass and stepped out into the hall. I rode down to the lobby like a woman who'd just narrowly missed getting creamed by a garbage truck. I felt a little rattled, yet euphoric, as though I'd teetered on the edge of a cliff and lived to tell about it. It was then that I glanced up and saw the security camera staring back at me. Neither of us blinked. I assumed it was operational and not there simply for show, which meant I was being recorded. Funny, I hadn't bothered to look for it on my way up.

Building security would have the date and time of my arrival and departure duly time-stamped. Resigned, I offered the camera a weak smile. The kind a naughty four-year-old might give her mother after tracking mud all over the living room carpet. What else could I do? Spada would know he'd had an after-hours visitor. He'd call building security, they'd pull the tape, and there I'd be. When the elevator hit the lobby, I strolled through it and out into the night. I'd just have to wait to see which one of us made it to prison first.

Chapter 36

"It's him," I said, sliding the clipping across my desk to Ben.

He eyed it and frowned. "Maybe, but we'll get back to that. What did you just tell me?"

I'd just relayed the evening's events: Spada's Glock, the files, the Polish women, and, of course, the security camera. It might have been that final detail that made him blanch. I swiveled my chair around to my computer and began transferring the photos I'd taken at Spada's so I could print them out. "I'll admit, it wasn't an ideal situation, but I left the place exactly as I found it . . . more or less."

His brows raised. " 'More or less'?"

"Maybe a few picklock scratches . . . and the file, but before you start carping about it, Stella Symonds is a potential murder victim. Now that Darby's gone, Spada could very well hire somebody else to take her out. And ID'ing Darby at Langham's place lays that so-called accident right at Spada's feet." I smiled. "I've closed the loop."

He looked as though someone had Tased him, his eyes glassy, blank, with a faraway look in them. "That's unlawful entry and destruction of private property."

I frowned. "You're *still* on that? Haven't you heard a word I just said? Technically, *maybe*, but I don't think Spada's going to push back on it, do you? He's got bigger worries than that. I'm thinking about the greater good here, and I'm going to see Marta right now to discuss the whole thing."

I loaded up the copies, stuffed them into my bag. I glanced at Ben, who just sat there in a stupor. "Why'd you stop by, anyway?"

He shook his head, dazed. "I honestly cannot remember."

"Okay, then get out." I held up my bag. "I've got work to do."

Ben stood, headed for the door. "Don't worry. I'm leaving before you make me lose my job."

"I'll call you later," I said.

He waved me off. "If it's from jail, don't."

I heard Ben trot down the stairs as I finished packing up. I made extra copies of Symonds's file; I put one in my bag to show Marta, one in the safe under my desk, and a third I tucked into a stamped envelope addressed to a PO box I used for situations like this. I tossed the envelope into my out-box, like ordinary mail, then flicked the lights off, locked up, and raced down the stairs. I had car keys in my hand, my bag slung over my shoulder, eyes and ears on alert, scanning the street. Now that I knew for sure Spada was not above ending a life, I didn't want mine to be the next one he took.

I heard a CTA bus in need of a brake job pick up steam two blocks over as I headed to the car. I kept my pace steady and took a deep breath, smelling rain, grease from Deek's griddle . . . and cigarette smoke. I tensed, got a weird feeling, and eased my hand down into my bag for my gun, but that's as far as I got.

Two men in dark colors shot out of nowhere. One man—wide, tall, built like a Mack truck—seized me by the front of my denim jacket, twisting me almost off my feet. He wore driving gloves. Leather. His hands looked as wide as catcher's mitts. My bag tumbled off my shoulder, taking my gun with it. The force of the grab strangled the expletive in my throat. His accomplice angled himself somewhere behind me. I couldn't see him.

I braced, fists raised, forearms out. I tried to break the viselike hold with short chops to the man's forearms, but it was like chipping away at tempered steel. I tried to twist around to see the man behind me, but couldn't. Cold sweat trickled down my back. This wasn't good, not good at all.

Man Number 2 stepped around front. I craned to get a look at him. My feet barely touched the ground. He was at least six three, two hundred pounds. No gloves. He was black. He wore a gold signet ring on the right hand. I couldn't make out the letter. He disappeared behind me again.

Dammit.

I stomped down on my attacker's instep; he yowled and grabbed me tighter. Then I got snatched from behind. One large hand tugged at the back of my jacket. A blanket of dread spread over me. *I was a PI sandwich.*

There was a lot of heavy breathing, mine and theirs, and the sound of three pairs of frenzied feet scuffling across uneven asphalt. If there was anything else taking place on the street, I did not notice it. Nothing but hands, bulk, and menace made it through the surreal bubble of assault in progress. My fight for position and escape ended in a sudden explosion of pain as I kneed Mr. Gloves in the kneecap and was conked from behind by something incompatible with the fragility of human bone and flesh.

Starbursts exploded behind my eyes and for a couple seconds they were all I could see. I slumped like a rag doll as strange hands grabbed me up, keeping me upright, twisting me around. Through the haze of near unconsciousness, I knew I was being moved, shoved. Backward or forward I couldn't tell, until I slammed hard against brick and got my bearings. I was pinned against the building. A throbbing white heat radiated from the back of my head and down the length of my spine.

"You've been sticking your nose where it don't belong," the man who hit me whispered into my left ear, his rancid breath warm on my neck. Despite his closeness, his voice sounded as if it were coming from Cleveland. I had to strain to hear it.

"Yeah, and *we* don't like it," Mr. Gloves added, his voice even farther away. *Pittsburgh? Rochester?*

Everything started to go dark. *Who turned the lights out?* I couldn't feel my arms or legs. My head felt like Dumbo was sitting on it.

"Hey, hold her up. She's passing out," one of the voices said. "Hurry up. Make it quick."

"Where is it?" Gloves hissed. "Yo, check the bag."

A pair of hands let me loose, and my knees buckled. A hand slapped my right cheek twice, rousing me enough to get a second wind. Unfortunately, I acquired no common sense with the wind. I began to fight back.

"Get off me, you pieces of shit!" I shrieked. I punched and kicked, aiming for noses, eye sockets, Adam's apples, sternums, kidneys, kneecaps, but it was like boxing a granite wall. I got nothing for my effort but a head shove to the bricks. I groaned and squeezed my eyes shut to steady the dancing lights. Another goose egg on top of the one already forming. *Wunnerful.*

"You got to give it to her," one of the men said. "She's got guts, but that's just what the man don't want. I found it. Let's go."

More furious than prudent, I rammed the heel of my right hand into the nose nearest to me and shoved up. I heard a growl. It was mine. Mr. Gloves screamed and clutched his nose, which started to bleed through the nose holes in his mask. His gloves were getting messy. "Aaaah, godammid. I dink she broke by dose. *Fuck it all doo hell.*" He lunged for me, grabbing me by the neck with bloodied fingers, rearing back to smack me with the other hand. His partner stopped him midswing.

"Back off. We got it. Let's go." He then grabbed the bottom of my face in his monster grip, a thumb to one cheek, index finger to the other. "You're done with this, if you know what's good."

Gloves cradled his nose, glaring at me through the holes in his messy mask. "Dext dime."

"Hey, what's going on down there? Hey!"

Another man's voice had been added to the mix, and he sounded pissed off. All hands flew off me. The human cluster I'd been in the middle of melted away and I could feel night air on my face. My shirt and jacket front were bloody and bunched up around my chin. I felt along my chest, taking inventory. I'd lost only a couple buttons, thankfully. Buttons I could replace. Teeth? Now, that was a whole other story.

"Oh, good Lord!" a woman screamed from a distance. Or at least I thought it was from a distance.

It was Muna. *Muna?*

I teetered against the side of the building alone, fresh air flooding over me like a wave of good fortune and newfound redemption. Angry voices being raised in defense, and then the sound of running feet, gave way to the start of a car engine and the squealing of angry tires.

"You all right?" Muna asked.

I gave focusing a try. Two Deeks. Two Munas. Both staring at me. The apartment building across the street undulated lazily like the psychedelic ooze inside a lava lamp.

"Far-out," I heard myself say.

And then the lights went out . . . and stayed out.

When I came to, I was lying on my back on something cushy. And I was moving. Streetlights in a box flickered past. Out of the corner of my eye, a felt-covered puppy dog nodded lazily at me. Everything smelled of fake pine. *Streetlights in a box?* Not a box. A window. Streetlights whizzing past a window. Of a car. I was in the backseat of a speeding car. I slowly opened my eyes wider, focused. The something cushy was Muna. My throbbing head was in her lap.

I bolted up, or tried to, but the force of the action sent my brain swishing around in my skull. I eased back down, gritting my teeth. "Owww." Cass Raines, mistress of the understatement.

"Don't you worry," Muna said. "We're two blocks from the

emergency room. Step on it, Deek." Stunned, I looked a question. "Yep, Deek's driving. We didn't want to wait for the ambulance, us being so close like we were. You lay back now. Don't worry about a thing."

"My bag."

"I got that right here."

I struggled up, my head throbbing. "Let me see."

Muna handed it to me, and I searched it feverishly. My gun was still there, though it hadn't done me a bit of good. The copies I'd made from Spada's files were gone. The thugs had taken them. "My phone?"

"I have that, too. It must have fallen out. I found it by the curb."

I eased back down, smiling. Then I began to laugh. The thugs would go back to Spada, their job accomplished, but I still had a duplicate set of the copies.

"She's laughing," Muna said. "Why are you laughing? Step on it, Deek. She's delirious. Good thing I called your emergency numbers."

I stopped laughing. "Whoa, whoa. What?"

"I found them in your phone. I called the numbers with stars next to them, Detective Mickerson, Mrs. Vincent. I figured they were your go-to people. They're meeting us at the hospital, so just relax till we get there. Good old Muna Steele's got everything all worked out."

I groaned and buried my face in my hands. I was never going to hear the end of this. Deek suddenly took a corner on two wheels, and it took another half block before my brain swung back to its central position. Muna patted my head to soothe me.

"Truthfully, I nearly had a heart attack when I saw that gun in your purse. I don't care for guns myself. I don't hold to violence of any kind."

I opened one eye, looked up at her incredulously. "You keep a bat behind Deek's counter."

"Sure do. People are crazy. But a bat's civilized."

I closed my eyes again, tired now of talking. "Would you mind letting me out at the bus stop? I'll walk home."

"Shush. We're here. Open up, Deek."

The car jolted to a stop and the car's overhead light went on when Deek got out on the driver's side. The light felt like the sun and nearly burned my corneas, filling my eyes with dancing spots, which were now the least of my worries. When the back door swung open, Deek, still in his greasy apron, reached in and lifted me out like a sack of potatoes.

"I'm fine. I don't need to be carried. I can walk in on my own."

"Keep quiet." His face held its usual scowl. "How do you think you got in the car in the first place?"

I nearly choked on surprise. *"You?"*

"Well, it sure as hell wasn't Muna."

Chapter 37

"You've got a concussion," Barb said as she unlocked my apartment door and stepped aside. She then held the door open for me while I toddled through on leaden legs, a half-melted ice pack pressed to the back of my head, compliments of the U of C Hospital's ER. My head felt like a Macy's Thanksgiving-parade balloon, only bigger, and I was still seeing two of everything.

"The doctor said *mild* concussion, and so what? There's a guy out there killing dying people. I don't have time to be coddled right now."

"I've never seen anybody so pigheaded," Mrs. Vincent said.

"Huh," Ben sneered, "don't *I* know it. I partnered with her for five years. See what you're signing up for?" Ben was speaking to Weber, who brought up the rear. He'd shown up at the hospital, too, after Ben called to tell him I was there. And we'd definitely talk about that when my head stopped spinning. Weber said nothing, though he was likely adding "pigheadedness" to his mental list.

"I can beat that," Barb said, but then caught the look on my face. "But I won't."

Everybody had completely ignored both my countless declarations that I was fine and my bazillionth request that they all go home and leave me the hell alone. It was well after one AM, and I had work to do, connections to make. I tossed the ice pack on the table and headed for the phone to call Marta.

"Drop it," Ben ordered when I picked up the receiver. "There's nothing more you can do with this tonight."

"What part of 'murderer' and 'out there' don't you people get?"

If I thought I could have pulled off an end run, I'd have made a play for the door.

"You should rest," Mrs. Vincent said.

Barb handed me back the ice pack. "At least a few hours."

Ben padded over and took the phone out of my hand. "*I'll* call Marta. I'll tell her you made dupes of the files those idiots took. She's going to want to know how you got them, though, and let's face it, you're not on the side of the righteous here."

"Tell her I got them from a source." That would hold her off, I thought. At least until the footage from Spada's security camera surfaced. By then, though, I hoped Spada would be in custody and in no position to get all high-handed.

"She's stubborn," Ben said. "She ain't stupid."

"I don't care what you tell her, then. There's a woman out there with a target on her back. That's priority one. If Marta wants to come after me for the rest of it, she knows where I live."

Ben scowled. "Forget it. I'll handle it. Go to bed." I didn't move. "I'm not saying you can't." He knew me. "This is me saying I got this."

I stared at him, at them all, uneasy with the thought of leaving things in someone else's hands, but, deep down, I knew they were right. I was dead on my feet, my brain scrambled, the room a little off-kilter. I was done in and outnumbered. Without another word, I turned and headed for my bedroom. I groused some, but the bite had gone out of it. Still, I fought for the last word.

"This doesn't count as number three," I called back to Weber. "I'm still waiting on that move," he replied.

I could hear Ben asking him what the number meant as I closed my door and flicked the lights off. I climbed into bed fully clothed, asleep the moment my head hit the pillow.

I woke with a start in the dark, every bone and muscle I owned throbbing like a decaying tooth. The bedside clock read 7:00, which meant I'd gotten about five hours of dead man's sleep. It hurt to breathe, but I had little choice in the matter. I swung my legs over the side of the bed and stood holding on to one spot, waiting for everything to settle. When it did, more or less, I padded to the bathroom. Peeling gingerly out of my clothes, I stood at the mirror and marveled at all the bruises quickly forming up and down my neck and across my back, chest, and shoulder blades, gifts from the giant goons who grabbed me and slammed me into a very hard wall.

I stood in the shower till the water went cold, then got out and headed back, dressing in a quiet, painful hurry, so as not to wake my keepers. I wasn't sure who was still here to guard me—Ben, Barb, Mrs. Vincent, or Weber—but I was sure they hadn't left me completely alone. I grabbed a bottle of aspirin from the dresser, shoved it into a pocket of my jeans, then tiptoed out of my room and down the hall past the guest room, where Barb was sleeping soundly. She was a committed nun, a fantastic teacher, but a lousy prison guard.

Slowly lifting my keys out of the ceramic bowl by the front door, I grabbed my bag and eased out, mindful of the door's squeaky hinges, backing out of the quiet apartment as stealthily as a sobered-up one-night stand trying to get out before things got weird. Down the three flights of stairs, out the door, I raced for the curb where the rental sat. I jumped in, started it up, and peeled off. Home free.

Spada had to know I was onto him, that's why he'd sent his goons. They'd taken a copy of the photographed files, but I'd built in redundancies. Let them think they'd gotten what he sent them for; let Spada think he'd won. But that still left Stella Symonds, the last name on his death-and-dying hit list. Was Spada cocky enough to make one final play for her now, or would he cut his losses and slip away? I guessed the former. He struck me as being too arrogant a man to leave a job undone, even if that job was murder. He'd go for Symonds.

I could call Marta, but I didn't know how much time I had before Spada made his move. Besides, Marta would be of little use. Her hands were bound by department bureaucracy, which ran deep, and the law, which ran even deeper. Ben's call to her last night couldn't have been met by an open mind and a willingness to cooperate, or else she'd be all over me now, and she wasn't. Spada was a prominent citizen and likely had a cadre of lawyers at his disposal, which meant he'd be given the royal treatment. No, Marta would need a lot more than a few photocopies and my word to stick her neck out. My traipsing through Spada's private files and the names I'd gotten were fruit of the poisonous tree. No good in court. Spada would walk. I would go to jail. For the time being, I was on my own.

The Symondses lived on the southwest side in a small bungalow at the corner of a quiet block. Some of the backyards would have prefab pools sagging in the center; each house would have a grill. This was a neighborhood of Saturday-morning Little League games and potluck dinners, Blackhawk banners and American Legion halls. And change. Old stalwarts, such as the Poles, the Irish, and the Italians, were slowly being replaced by Hispanics, blacks, and Middle Easterners—and the changeover wasn't going down easy. Those who'd been here for years now locked their doors, shuttered their windows, and kept to themselves out of fear and ignorance. The new ones coming in ignored the shutters and the locks, expecting as much, and the fraying at the edges, the tension, crackled like fresh tinder on a campfire.

Overhead, Southwest planes, red and yellow tail fins gleaming in the sun, streamed by, heading toward and away from Midway Airport. Announcing their presence with roaring engines, which rattled the windows of the matchbox houses, they left behind a trail of chemical particles that rained down on the rooftops like droplets of summer rain, tingeing the air with the stench of aviation fuel. I sat in the car for a moment, studying the two fake geese sitting on the Symonds porch; they were dressed in yellow rain slickers and matching Gloucester fishermen hats. Cute, I supposed, if your sensibilities ran that way. Weird, if they didn't.

Stella Symonds was just fifty-six and in the late stages of Lou Gehrig's disease. Her husband's name was Ron. I knew my presence, no matter the reason, would be an intrusion on private time. I eyed the house, not wanting to go in, but I was sure that Spada wanted Stella Symonds dead. Someone had to tell them what was headed their way.

As I gathered my things, a silver compact Ford pulled in behind me at the curb and a blond woman got out. I stared at her through the rearview, watching as she powered up the Symondses' walk, all business, dressed in a blue smock and carrying a nurse's bag. Neither were good signs. At the door, she exchanged a few words with the man who opened it, and then the two disappeared inside. I flicked a look at the dashboard clock. It was a little before eight, way too early to ruin a person's day, but I got out of the car and walked toward the door, glancing back at the Ford. On its side, a sign read TEMPLETON HOSPICE CARE. Would even Nick Spada stoop so low as to kill a woman in hospice care?

I rang the bell. The same man returned. "Yes? Can I help you?"

"Mr. Symonds?"

Tired brown eyes rimmed with red stared back at me. It looked like he'd been crying. According to the file, he was fifty-eight, though he looked decades older now. His hair, more gray than brown, was shaggy and uneven, as though he hadn't had a haircut in months, and his shirt and jeans, seriously rumpled, hung loose, both at least a size too big. I'd have gladly taken a long drive in the desert with thugs than add to this man's sorrow.

He opened the screen door. "Yes?" He addressed me, but his eyes checked out the street and the sidewalk behind me, as though he hadn't seen either in years. "Are you with Templeton, too?"

"No, my name is Cass Raines. I wonder if I might talk to you about Nicholas Spada?"

The beginnings of worry showed in the deep furrows on his forehead. "Spada?"

"More specifically about the settlement your wife received through his company."

His eyebrows rose. The Symondses were not wealthy people. The settlement would have enabled them to keep their creditors at bay and to stay in their home as expenses mounted. There would be meds to purchase, doctors to see, final arrangements to make. Dying was expensive.

"We signed all the papers. He said everything was taken care of. Is there a problem?"

I did not want to tell him, while standing on his front porch, that his dying wife was targeted for murder. I just didn't. "Maybe we could talk inside, Mr. Symonds?"

The look on his face said, *Not so fast*. He would be worried about the money, sure, but not so worried that he'd open his home to a stranger. "Do you work for Spada?"

I reached into my bag for my ID and presented it to him. "I don't, no."

He looked from the card to me, bewildered. "Private investigator? And this is about *our* settlement?"

"I can explain how, if you'll give me a moment of your time."

He eyed me for a moment longer, his suspicious gaze taking me all in. I didn't think I looked dangerous, but I sure felt it. I wanted to put a stop to Nick Spada in the worst possible way, and I had the feeling he was someplace gloating, thinking there was no way in Hell I could. Finally Ron Symonds stepped back and let me in. I'd cleared the first hurdle, I thought, as I stepped into his living room. There were more to come.

I was led into a neat, unfussy living room decorated for comfort, rather than show. Two broken-in recliners, a small fireplace between them, faced a big-screen television set with a thin film of dust on the screen. It looked as though no one had dusted it or even turned it on in weeks. Pale green drapes matched a pale green carpet, the couch and lamp shades were the color of warm oatmeal, subtle accents placed around the room pulled it all together. Stella Symonds had made her house a home, though she probably hadn't been able to attend to it in quite some time.

The house smelled of antiseptic and sickness, and I might have shuddered, were it not for the fact that I'd lived it all before. Symonds's pain, his living in unrelenting stasis, waiting for the inevitability of his wife's death, was something I understood. My mother, diagnosed with cancer in March of my twelfth year, was gone by the Fourth of July. There'd been the hospital bed and the nurses and the hushed tones of adults searching for a way to tell me what I already knew—that death was near.

I stood in one spot next to the Symondses' couch. Its cushions were wrinkled, creased, as though he'd been sleeping on it. He fussed around me, gathering up old newspapers and clearing away coffee mugs and odd bits of clothing—a sock here, a sweater there.

"Sorry for the mess. They moved the hospital bed in a few weeks ago, so I've been camping out down here. We don't get a lot of visitors anymore."

"Please don't go to any trouble."

He tossed a stack of papers onto an end table, smiled weakly. "I should get our copies of the settlement papers, right? Like I said, everything's supposed to be squared away. We even had a lawyer look them over before we signed off." He moved to snake past me. I stopped him.

"You don't have to. I have copies from Spada's files. They're what I'd like to talk to you about."

He gestured for me to sit, and then eased down into the chair facing me. "I can't imagine what any of this has to do with a PI. I don't think I've ever even met one before. *Why* do you have our files?"

I cleared my throat, then started. "I'm working a case, an accidental death. This person signed on for the same kind of settlement as your wife... through Spada's company, Sterling." I stopped, took a breath, pushed on. "This person was ill, like your wife, and like your wife, he lived beyond his doctors' projections."

He nodded. I could tell he was keeping up, that he was following me so far, but I hadn't yet relayed the worst of it. I took a moment, more for me than for him. He spoke before I was ready to go on.

"Holding on is a curse and a blessing, I guess." He ran his nervous hands up and down his thighs, as if warming them. "I'm glad I still have Stella, of course, but her quality of life, well, it's not so good. I look at every day as a bonus, a gift, though it feels like we're both kind of living on borrowed time."

I smiled. "Yes, I understand." I scooted closer to the edge of the couch, closer to Symonds. "While investigating that one accidental death, I discovered that there had been others. Each victim had a viatical settlement, and each lived longer than they were expected to, and each person was a client of Nick Spada's."

I could see the confusion in Symonds's eyes, but I kept going, wanting to get it all out and done with. I fanned Spada's paperwork on the coffee table and turned them so Symonds could read them. He pulled a pair of battered readers out of the pocket of his button-down shirt, slipped them on.

"You can see the dates. None of these people died from illness. These appear to indicate that Spada, or someone working closely with him, arranged accidents in order to maximize profits. The deaths were caused by house fires, tragic falls, a mugging, and, in the case of my client, a suspicious drowning." I picked up his wife's file, handed it to him. "This is your wife's. There's a red dot along the top. As far as I can tell, she's the only one on Spada's books still living."

Symonds looked from the file, to me, and back again. This is where I lost him. He couldn't make the jump on his own. He couldn't grasp the horror of it. "What are you saying?"

"I believe Nick Spada killed these people. I believe your wife could be his next victim."

Symonds sat in stunned silence, his eyes on mine. He didn't say a word for a long time. I could almost feel his skin go cold. I sat on the edge of the couch, waiting. The floorboards upstairs creaked as someone, presumably the nurse I'd seen, moved about and cared for Stella Symonds. But downstairs, here in the small living room decorated for comfort, there was little of it, only shocked silence and dread. Then Ron Symonds's pain found its voice.

"This is some kind of cruel joke." He rose slowly. "A scam. What sick person put you up to this?"

I stood. "This is not a scam. It's a warning. Spada is a dangerous man, and he has to be stopped."

He nearly chuckled. "You're nuts, you know it? That nice man? A killer?" He glared at me. "How dare you come into my house and tell me this crap. Have you no decency?" He bent down, gathered up the papers, and shoved them at me. "I want you out of my house, *now*, or I'll call the police and have you dragged out."

"Did you know Vincent Darby?"

"I said I want you *out*."

"Please, answer the question. Vincent Darby, did you know him?"

It was the cop in my voice that got his attention and held it. It startled him, pulled him up short. "He came with Spada when we finalized our arrangement. He didn't say much, after that we dealt directly with Nick. And none of *that* has anything to do with *you*."

"Darby's been murdered." Symonds froze. "And I know that firsthand, because someone—I think Nick Spada—delivered his body to me as a warning to mind my business. I don't know how many so-called accidents there have been. I don't know how long he's been doing this."

Symonds shook his head, unwilling to accept what he was hearing. "You don't know who or *what* you're talking about."

"He checks in with you, doesn't he, for updates on your wife's condition?" Spada would want to keep tabs, I thought. He'd want to know if he needed to proceed with his plan, or if he could afford to let nature take its course.

"He's taken a personal interest, so what? He said Stella reminded him of his own daughter. He brings her flowers, for Christ's sake, sits with her, talks to her." He shook his head, beating back even the thought of something so heinous. "There's no way he'd kill her. Just leave us alone. Get out, or I'm calling the cops."

I stood my ground. "Go ahead. Call them. I'll wait."

The nurse descended the stairs and tentatively walked into the living room. She was carrying a plastic yellow pitcher, and her eyes, the color of robin's eggs, were steady, sharp, assessing. Hers were eyes that didn't miss much, but there was something else in them, too.

She smiled, bowed her head apologetically. "So sorry to interrupt." She held the pitcher up, revealing long, manicured nails painted a scarlet red. "I need ice chips from the kitchen."

She slipped quietly through the room while Symonds and I stood there, neither of us speaking. He made no effort to reach for the phone, which was encouraging. I listened to the nurse fill the pitcher with ice from the fridge, her hard-soled shoes click-ing back and forth along the linoleum tiles. We were still stand-ing, still silent, when she headed back through and climbed back up the stairs. I watched her go, her three-inch heels making no sound on the carpeted steps. My head hurt.

"The police will come," I said gently. "But they won't stay, because they'll have no grounds to. Nothing's happened yet. There won't be an offer of around-the-clock protection because there's not enough to arrest Spada on, not yet. There's hardly enough to call him in for questioning."

"You've got the wrong end of the stick here," Symonds said, nearly pleading. "This just can't be."

"He'll get every break, every advantage. The law works differ-ently for those with money. That leaves you and your wife ex-posed. And if I'm right, and I believe I am . . ." I stopped. *A hospice nurse? Manicured nails. Three-inch heels.* I slid a side-ways glance toward the stairs, listened for the creak of the floor-boards.

Symonds grimaced. "I don't believe you. What you're say-ing's not possible." His panicked voice carried, the fear in it seeping into the walls, the furniture.

I held up Stella's file. "Her doctors gave her three months at the time you signed this. She's lived twice that long as of today. They die on time, Spada wins. They linger, he loses. He makes damned sure they don't linger."

Symonds's eyes narrowed, his mouth twisted into a horrific scowl. "You're a *monster.*"

I felt like one. I wanted to stop, but couldn't. "The longer she lives, the less he pockets. He's a businessman at the apex of his profession, the top seller, and he's proud to say it."

I was repeating the words Spada had spoken to me when we met. I searched Symonds's face, hoping to see a flicker of recognition. He had to have heard him say much the same thing. Spada was nothing if not consistent.

"He's a master of the game," I added, "who never leaves a single piece on the board."

When it looked like he couldn't take any more, that Ron Symonds might just break into a million pieces, I stepped back and gave him space. "I'm here to protect your wife, whether you believe that or not. But you call the police, if you want. Like I said, I'll wait."

I could tell he didn't know what to make of me or the situation. He had to know that if I were a con artist, I'd be long gone by now. But who comes to your door and tells you someone wants to kill your dying wife? His eyes darted wildly around the room. He was trapped in Hell and there was no place he could hide. *The nurse,* I thought, *the eyes.*

He ran his hands through his hair, his hands shaking. "I can't deal with this anymore. First that new nurse, now you with this shit story about killers and accidents and dead people."

I took a step toward him. "*New* nurse?"

He didn't hear me. He was someplace else in his head.

"Mr. Symonds, *what* new nurse?"

"Templeton's. Stella likes Beverly, responds to her. But this one today says Beverly called in sick. She never has before. What if Stella goes today and Bev's not here? She should have Bev when the end comes."

I could hear the echo of my own heartbeat pounding in my ears. "Where's your wife now?"

He looked past me, toward the stairs. "Our room. Top of the stairs. Why?"

I raced for the stairs, taking them two at a time, my legs protesting, my brain jockeying around in my head like marbles rolling inside a spinning bowl. No nurse worth her salt has long manicured nails or works in three-inch heels.

"Hey, where do you think you're going?" Symonds yelled. "You can't go up there."

"Call the police. *Now!*"

I reached the top, Symonds racing up behind me. A door across the hall stood ajar and I ran for it, pushing it open, rushing in. The nurse was standing at the side of a hospital bed, leaning over a frail woman, Stella Symonds. One hand in a surgical glove was pressed over Stella's mouth and nose, suffocating her. Ron Symonds ran for the bed; I ran for the nurse. Bodychecking her, grabbing her by the shirtfront, I shoved her back.

"*Stella?*" Ron Symonds yelled.

I shoved the nurse away from the bed, pinning her against the wall, holding on to her as she fought to break my grip.

"Get your hands off me! She's my patient."

"I saw you!" Symonds yelled. "You were killing her."

I gripped the nurse tighter, my face just inches from hers. "Spada sent you, didn't he?"

The woman jerked and flailed, desperate now to be free. "Let go of me." Her teeth clenched, her eyes spit fire. *There it is*, I thought, the something I saw downstairs. *Evil.* I pressed my forearm against her windpipe, wishing I could press harder.

Symonds tried desperately to rouse his wife, who lay unresponsive on the bed. I slid him a sideways glance, waiting for his report on her condition, watching nervously as he slapped her cheeks gently, trying to bring her around. The nurse kicked out at me and I slammed her back against the wall, hard enough to give her something to think about. Suddenly Stella's eyes fluttered. She was alive.

"She's breathing," Ron Symonds said. "Thank God."

"Call an ambulance," I ordered. "Then the police." I stared at the nurse, smiled, our eyes holding. "It would have looked like she suffocated on her own, was that the idea? You didn't count on anyone being here to stop you."

Symonds reached for the phone on the table next to the bed and called for help. The nurse gave me a calm, patient grin that sent shivers down my spine. "I give you nothing."

I applied more pressure to her windpipe, but didn't challenge her on it. It made no difference, anyway. The cops would find out who she was in due time. Realizing her time was short, the woman began to fight again, kicking desperately in hopes of knocking me off my feet. I yanked her off the wall, twisted her around, and took her down, pinning her to the floor. My knees dug into her back to keep her there. My hand automatically went to my side for cuffs, before I remembered I no longer carried them; meanwhile, the woman bucked and twisted under me like a rodeo steer. I palmed the back of her head and drove it into the floorboards, the sound her head made against the hardwood unmistakably brutal. She yelped, quieted, and the bucking stopped, but I knew I only had seconds before her head cleared and she came back at me again. It was times like these that I missed having a partner. This was definitely a two-person job. I frantically searched the room for a substitute for the cuffs, my eyes finally locking on an unused length of IV tubing. It would have to do. I leaned over, grabbed it.

"You almost got away with it," I said as the woman began to slowly stir. "She's dying. It wouldn't have taken much. It would have looked like she just passed away on her own, right? Spada's going to be very disappointed in you."

As the woman groaned beneath me, I wound the tubing around her wrists, prepared to tighten it, when Stella began to gag and wheeze from the bed. It was a horrible, desperate sound. I turned to see, and realized instantly that I shouldn't have. I turned back, but it was too late. My one moment of inattention gave the nurse the chance to jerk her arm free and twist around onto her back. Before I could make the adjustment and flip her back, she hauled off and clocked me in the side of the head hard enough that I saw stars. I fell back, taking the tubing with me, watching helplessly as she scrambled to her feet and took off. I stumbled to my feet, the room spinning, and took off after her.

Down the stairs we went, the evil nurse well ahead. If she got away, I'd never find her. She hit the bottom step, raced through the front room, and then bolted out the door, bursting out onto the porch. She ran like a frigging cheetah. In heels. I wasn't going to catch her. I burst out onto the porch just in time to see her trip on the last couple steps. I managed to gain a few strides on her, but she quickly recovered and sprinted for the Ford.

I had my gun, but couldn't use it. She was running away from me. I couldn't very well shoot her in the back. I had nothing else on me, except for the IV tubing, and I had to actually catch her to use that. Bolting down the porch steps, I stopped, went back, and grabbed one of the decorative geese. I got a good grip on its neck, then Frisbeed it across the lawn at the fleeing woman, the ultimate Hail Mary pass. I was aiming for her back, but the goose in the rain jacket clipped her right behind the kneecaps and she went down. She was halfway up when I tackled her. We went down in a heap and the flailing began again. Angry beyond measure now, I pinned her to the lawn and ground her face into the grass.

"Get off. You bitch." With every word, she spit out blades of grass, which pleased me immensely.

"Sure thing," I said, fumbling with the plastic tubing. "You wait right there." I got her wrists tied off, then pulled hard to tighten the knots. The woman let out a bloodcurdling scream of frustration, almost as loud as the noise from the airplanes.

"I'll *kill* you."

I leaned over, patted her on the head. "Not today, you won't."

I was still sitting on her when the first squad car pulled up. When the cops rushed over, I rolled off and stretched out on the grass, gulping in air. I slid my PI's license out of my pocket and placed it on my chest for identification purposes. I was breathing too hard to tell the cops who I was. I lay there, on my back, my head spinning, watching the planes fly by, wondering where everybody was going.

"She tried to kill my wife!" I heard Symonds yell. I hoped he wasn't pointing at me, but I was too spent to lift up to check.

"The nurse," he said. At that moment, I figured I wasn't going to jail, at least not for this, so I closed my eyes and let out a sigh of relief, fighting back the urge to throw up all over the Symondses' lawn. And it wasn't even noon yet.

Chapter 38

There were twenty-six messages on my phone, and when I scrolled through the log, I was not surprised to see who they were from. I sent back a group text, letting Barb, Whip, Ben, and Mrs. Vincent know that I was alive, and, though not technically well, still moving under my own steam. Then I turned the phone off to head off any angry replies.

Sitting at the Symondses' kitchen table, out of the way, while the paramedics checked Stella, Marta's face slowly came into focus. "You look like *you* need the paramedics."

I pressed a Ziploc ™ bag of ice cubes to my head, courtesy of Ron Symonds. "Who called *you*?"

She straightened. "Does it matter? What happened?"

"Ask Ron Symonds. I doubt you'd take my word for anything."

"Getting pissy, are we?"

I shot up from the chair, and then slowly eased back down again when my head began to pound. "Yeah, I thought I might. I've gotten little to no cooperation from you for days, now suddenly you turn up everywhere I go, wanting information. Oh, and let's not forget another man's dead and there's a woman upstairs who's well on her way, thanks to the lunatic sitting in the back of a squad car outside. A lunatic, by the way, who has vowed to kill me."

Dark, even eyes searched mine. "She says you flew in and took her down for no reason."

I repositioned the ice pack, fuming. I'd had just about enough of goons, dead-eyed killers, and Marta Pena. "I'm done talking to you, Marta. If I'm under arrest, take me in. Otherwise, shove it. I've still got a job to do. Yours *and* mine, apparently."

"You own a nine-millimeter Glock," she said. It was not a question.

"So?"

"That's what killed Darby."

"You know who else owns a nine-millimeter Glock? Half of Chicago . . . oh, and Nicholas Spada."

"And you know that how?"

I shook my head, instantly regretting it. "I'm not saying another word without my lawyer. Till then, you're just going to have to take my word for it, or not. At this point, I couldn't care less."

"I'll concede the fact that you've managed to get yourself in the middle of something more complicated than a drowning," Marta said.

I stared at her, let a beat pass. "Wow, that actually looked like it hurt."

The corners of her mouth curled up. It was almost a smile, but not quite. "The paperwork's not enough, but you know that already. I can reach out to Spada, ask him to come in for a chat."

"Really? He'll just come on down for a chat? What about Stella Symonds?"

"We have the nurse outside. She's not going anywhere."

"But you don't have the one who hired her."

"I have no proof yet that someone did hire her, neither do you. She's not talking, at least not yet. The best we can do is take her in and see what we come up with."

I stood again, slower this time. "You do that." I stuffed the bag of ice into my pocket. I might need it later.

Marta looked like she was about to come back with something snarky, but then a uniformed cop popped his head in. "Detective? You're gonna want to see this."

She flicked a look at me. "Stay here."

She followed the cop out. I followed her out. Aggravated by my disobedience, she turned and glared, but didn't say anything. Outside, the trunk on the nurse's car sat open, a couple of detectives standing over it. I looked inside, and Marta did, too. Lying on her side in a fetal position was a petite Asian woman, forty-ish, with a bullet hole between her eyes.

"Beverly Ocampo, RN," one of the cops told Marta. "The hospice nurse. ID's in her purse."

"Jesus H. Christ," Marta muttered. "Then who's that in the back of the squad?"

"Good question," he said.

Marta turned to me, all business now. This wasn't some random slip off a boat. There was Darby's body in a box, now an innocent woman shot to death and stuffed into the trunk of a car. "What the hell's going on?"

The paramedics came out of the house without Stella. We watched as Ron Symonds walked toward us. He searched our faces and stopped before he got close to the car. "What is it now? What's happened?"

We stood there, the cops, Marta, me. No one said anything; nobody wanted to. The Symondses had grown close to Ocampo. She was their nurse, the one Stella wanted when the end came, and now she was gone. I unstuck myself from the spot, headed for him. He didn't need to see inside the trunk.

"Let's go back inside." I walked him toward the house. "How's Stella?"

"Alive. They wanted to take her in, to check her out, but there wouldn't be much point to that. What's going on with that car? Who was that woman?"

Inside again, I asked for more ice, anything to keep him busy, his mind off the Ford.

"We don't know yet. She isn't talking."

He searched my face. "This was Spada, like you said."

Before I could answer, Marta walked in, all pistons firing. Her eyes were hard; her face was hard. The body in the trunk had done it; the fake nurse had knocked the brakes off the wagon, and Marta was now all in. We exchanged a look. There would be a time for Symonds to hear the news of Beverly's death, but now wasn't it.

Marta drew closer. "Mr. Symonds, when was the last time you saw Nick Spada?"

He looked at Marta, then me, before answering. "About a week ago. He brought roses. So you're saying he definitely did this?"

"Can your wife communicate?" Marta asked.

Symonds eyed her cautiously. "Why?"

"I'd like to ask her a few questions."

"She's dying, for God's sake. What is wrong with you people?"

Marta said nothing. What could she say?

"If she dies without telling the police what they need to know," I said gently, "then Spada walks."

Symonds backed away from us, giving himself some space. "She can't speak; she blinks. One for yes, two for no. It works, if we keep it simple."

"Then that's what I'll do," Marta said. "May I go up?"

His fierce expression told us he'd protect Stella at all costs. "Not without me and not without *her*," he said, pointing to me. "Stella would be dead if she hadn't been here."

Marta shot me a look. She didn't like to share. I shot her one back. At this point, I didn't much care what she didn't like.

"Then let's go," Marta said, following Symonds out.

We headed up to Stella's room, no one speaking on the stairs; but with every step, I had the greedy feeling that Nick Spada was closer to being mine.

Chapter 39

Stella's eyes opened and quickly landed on me.

"You wanted to thank her," Ron prompted. Stella blinked once.

I stepped closer to the bed. "It isn't necessary."

Ron turned to Marta. "Just five minutes."

Marta stepped closer to the bed, held her star up so Stella could see it. "I'm Detective Marta Pena. I'd like to ask you about Nick Spada. Is that all right?"

Stella's eyes locked on Marta's. She blinked once. Stella's body had turned on her, locking her inside a vessel that no longer served her. However, her mind was there, you could see it. She was still in the world. I watched as Marta took a moment to structure her questions in the limited time she had so that they could be answered by a blink of an eye. A strand of Marta's black hair had come loose from her ponytail, and she took a moment to smooth it back before she started. "Do you remember Nick Spada coming to see you?"

One blink.

Marta appeared to struggle. I felt for her. This wasn't normally how cops did things. I gripped the bed's side rails. "Did he threaten you?"

One blink.

My heart nearly leapt out of my chest. A single tear slid down Stella's cheek, her eyes imploring me to go on, to ask another question she could answer, the *right* question.

"Did he tell you he'd killed others? That he planned to kill you, too?"

One blink, then another. There was iron in her look, resolve. She couldn't move her arms or legs, but she could think and she could hold out against Nick Spada, refuse to die. Marta and I exchanged a look. She hadn't believed me before, but she believed Stella Symonds now.

"What about the nurse?" Marta asked. "Did she tell you Spada sent her?"

There was no response from the bed. Instead, Stella's eyes scanned the room, looking for her husband, finding him sitting quietly in a chair near the window, his eyes fixed far away. This had to be his worst day ever. Maybe she wanted to spare him the truth, but we were well beyond that point now. When she turned back, she blinked once.

My fingers squeezed the side rail so tightly, I thought I might snap it in two. "And if you could, you'd tell him where to get off, right?"

Her eyes seemed to twinkle. She blinked once. Ron Symonds stood, signaling the end of our time. When Stella's eyes closed, and stayed closed, he led us out of the room, the three of us huddling at the top of the stairs.

"We'll book the fake nurse for attempted murder and assault," Marta said. "And we'll have a talk with Spada, though we may not be able to hold him unless the nurse gives him up."

Symonds's eyes widened. "What about Stella? What if he sends somebody else?"

Marta descended the stairs, her mind likely already on the next thing. "I'll implement a special attention, send a car out. If you can, get someone, a relative, a friend, to stay close till I end this."

Symonds turned to me, frightened. "What does that mean? We don't have anybody. It's just Stella and me. We're on our own."

I thought for a moment, then dug my phone out of my pocket. "No, you're not." I dialed the number, waited for the pickup.

"Whip? I need you."

I was sitting on the Symondses' front porch, nursing a headache, when a black GMC Yukon pulled up in front of the house and stopped. I eased my hand into my pocket, gripped it around my gun, my eyes on the truck's windows. Ron Symonds was inside with Stella. It was just me standing watch until the squad car showed up, the one Marta promised. Even still, I knew the squad wouldn't be there for nearly long enough, not if Spada chose to play the long game. I braced myself when the doors opened, then relaxed when Whip eased out of the driver's seat. I'd been watching out for his old beater. I hadn't expected the Yukon. I drew my hand out of my pocket, then stood and watched as three guys nearly as tall and as broad as tackling dummies got out of the car next and sidled over, Whip taking the lead. I'd requested muscle, but this was something else entirely. Whip smiled, but the other three looked as sober as hangmen, as humorless as Tolkien's Orcs, their arms covered in faded tats, each dressed in jeans, a white T-shirt, and Timberland boots. Ex-cons, apparently—the success of their rehabilitation, at the moment, suspect.

"Hey," Whip said, gathering me up in a big bear hug, which hurt like hell. "You okay?"

I stared up at the three giants, eyes slanted, my gaze one of suspicion. "Yeah, I'm good."

The three mountains didn't smile, blink, move, or even appear to breathe. They just stood there, blocking out the sun.

"You asked for muscle, I brought muscle," Whip said. He looked absolutely elated that he was finally able to provide something I needed. "Let me do the introductions. This is, uh . . ." He stopped, suddenly embarrassed. "I'll stick to Christian names, how's that?"

He pointed to the first guy, about six five, dark, bald, a gold hoop ring pierced through his nostrils like a bull. "This is Phil." He moved to the second muscle—Hispanic, dark, heavy eyelids, jowly, a thin surgical bandage under his right eye. I knew instantly why. He was having the teardrop tats removed from his face, in stages. "That's Antonio." And the third—one brown eye, one blue, white-blond hair cut short, eyelashes to match. "And this is Seamus." He turned back to me, his arms akimbo. "Good enough?"

"You understand I only want a deterrent," I said. "A safety wall? No one comes near the house who shouldn't be here." I made it a point to make eye contact with each guy. "No one gets hurt. No one dies." I got no reaction at all.

"Yeah, I explained all that coming over," Whip said. "We blanket the house and stick here till we hear from you." He frowned. "You look worried. What's up with that?"

I stepped away from the group, waving for Whip to join me. "You said you knew guys who specialized in security. You brought me ex-cons?"

Whip looked at me like he didn't see the problem. "Yeah? So? *I'm* an ex-con. Who'd you think I was going to bring? Harry Potter and the rest of those baby wizards? This is the best security I know. All totally straightened out, by the way. Phil works construction, Antonio's an ace mechanic, and Seamus is a personal trainer. Besides, who knows better than a bad guy how to *stop* a bad guy? And they don't even half mind that you used to be a cop."

I took one last assessing look, then got my head around it. I needed the house covered and I didn't have time to do it myself. I had to get to Marta to see if she had Spada on ice.

Whip draped his arm over my shoulder. "Don't worry, Bean. We got this. Not even Santa Claus could get into that house while we're sitting on it."

Chapter 40

I dunked the tea bag into a Styrofoam cup of tepid water, pulled it out, dunked it in again. I'd done it now more than twenty times. Marta was in with Spada and his lawyers, and I wasn't allowed anywhere near them. Instead, I'd been relegated to a grungy interview room at the district to wait it out, sitting across the table from Jung, his eyes closed, snoring lightly, his mouth slightly open so that he emitted a low whistle every time air flowed in and out. He'd been here since I dropped him off after Swami Rain's. It'd probably taken this long for Marta to get anything not weird out of him. I'd given him a full report before he nodded off, per our contract, and had had to endure a string of *"No way, dude"* and *"Holy crap."* Yet, finding out that everything had culminated in my barely preventing a dying woman from being killed hadn't been enough to keep him awake. Now I sat glaring at him, having overcome, at around the tenth dunk, an overwhelming impulse to stuff the tea bag down his throat. I faced quite the moral challenge.

Marta had the fake nurse in custody and Spada was in the building. But here I sat, watching my dippy client sleep as though he hadn't a care in the world. I supposed that was what he was paying me for, to sweat the big stuff and the small stuff, to worry so he wouldn't have to. Still . . .

The files meant nothing without a witness or a confession or some other irrefutable evidence. It was obvious to me, though I couldn't prove it, that Spada hadn't done any of the heavy lifting himself. I needed something or someone to tie Spada to the nurse and to Darby's death. I stopped dunking, and thought of the guys who'd accosted me and stolen back Spada's files. They were too big and too dumb not to have records. Maybe if the fake nurse wouldn't roll over, they would? I could ID them. Who could forget faces that ugly? If I could tie them to Spada, that, along with the attempted murder of Stella and her voiceless testimony, might force Spada to try and make a deal. I didn't care how Spada got put into a cell, only that he got there.

I stood, scraping the legs of the metal chair along the floor, but even that didn't wake Jung. Granted, Marta had been grilling him for hours straight about the boat break-in before I got here, but still, who sleeps that soundly in an interview room? I walked out onto the floor filled with cops, all moving around, but there was no sign of Marta, Ben, or Weber. I wasn't under arrest, I was free to go, but I wasn't going anywhere until I found out what was going on.

I finally spotted a detective I knew and made a beeline for him. Detective Londell Scott was a pudgy black guy, midfifties, jovial. When he turned and saw me, he started to chuckle, his wide neck straining his collar, his three chins hanging over it. He waved for another cop. "Yo, Baumgartner, she's out. Where's my fifty?"

"No way."

I turned to watch a woman approach, her auburn hair cut short, her eyes a steady sapphire blue. "Detective Baumgartner. Shana." She offered a hand to shake, a smile. "I've heard a lot about you. Mythic. You're a PI now, Scottie says."

I turned back to Scott. "Fifty?"

"We took bets to see how long you'd stay in interview. Shana here gave you the benefit of the doubt and bet me a cool fifty.

Dumb on her part." He checked his watch, grinned. "Twenty-four minutes."

I shook my head. He was the same old Scott, a regular Minnesota Fats. "You still shorting the snack fund, Scottie?"

The communal kitty, fed by cops, paid for the chips, cookies, and snack food that kept the uniforms, detectives, and even the arrestees and witnesses going. For Londell Scott, though, the cookies and chips and sodas went down his throat, but nary a nickle ever left his wallet, though that was never the way he told it.

"Hey, what? Don't start, Raines. I always pay my fair share, you know that. I put twenty in just last week, or was it fifty?"

Baumgartner rolled her eyes, but kept her mouth shut. She knew Scottie shorted the snack fund. Every cop in the building knew Scottie shorted the snack fund. Every cop who'd ever worked with Scottie, wherever Scottie worked, knew Scottie shorted the snack fund.

"Same old Scottie," I said.

He wagged a thick finger at me. "And same old Raines."

I looked around the floor. "Where's Marta?"

They both stood there, mouths pinched closed.

"Really?" I asked.

Scott shrugged. "She's following a lead."

"A lead *I* gave her."

"Well, now she's on it, and she's got her hands full by the looks of it."

Baumgartner bounced on her heels, hands in her pockets. "Rich guy showed up with five lizard-faced lawyers. I heard they're burying her in paper as we speak." She glanced over my shoulder. "Speak of the Devil."

I reeled. Marta trudged in, looking like she'd just been batted around by a jungle cat. She flicked her head toward the interview room and then headed that way. I followed.

"Hey, Shana," I heard Scott say. "I say only one comes out standing. Put you down for twenty?"

I headed for Marta. "If you've got twenty burning a hole in your pocket, Scottie, put it in the damn money jar!"

A round of applause went up from around the room, cops cat-calling Scott. I left them to it. Marta was standing by the table, watching Jung sleep, when I walked back into the room. She slammed the files she carried down on the table hard, the reverb finally startling Jung awake. He looked at Marta, then me. "Get out," Marta told him.

Jung blinked. "I can go?"

"You could've gone hours ago. Why the hell are you still sitting here?"

He glanced over at me, staring as though he'd never seen me before. "Wait for me in the hall," I said.

Jung got up and hurried out, and I closed the door behind him. Marta turned to face me. "Spada's got times, dates, and witnesses that put him nowhere near Darby or Symonds. We've got no physical evidence linking him to anything. The nurse hasn't opened her mouth since she got here. He came in when we asked him to, so that's on his side, but he arrived with an entire law firm trailing behind him. Each one of the little stiffs was dressed in a five-hundred-dollar suit, each one ready to tap-dance all over my spleen and foul up my pension." She lifted the folder. "See this? Legal mumbo jumbo that basically says we, meaning the Chicago Police Department—and, by extension, me—cannot talk to, contact, or even think about Nick Spada in regard to Ayers, Symonds, or Darby. If we do, we get our asses chewed up and handed back to us."

"There wouldn't be any physical evidence leading back to him. He hired the work out—Darby, the psycho nurse."

"We may think it, but we can't prove it."

"Then get the nurse to flip."

"What do you think I've been trying to do? We've got Florence Nightingale solid for aggravated battery against you and Stella, and we're investigating her for the dead nurse in the trunk. But, like I said, she hasn't said a word about that or about Spada, and until she does, we've got nothing else. And, let's get real here, though we've got Stella Symonds's nonverbal account that Spada threatened her, she's a dying woman. All he has to do is wait her out. Long story short, we took a bite of the apple and got nothing. We go back for a second bite with nothing more than we have now and we get bulldozed."

"Where's Spada now?"

"He's probably waltzing out the front door like he owns the place."

I raced out of the room, through the office, heading for the ground floor. I pushed through the doors just in time to see Spada open the door on a black Cadillac. He stood there for a time, conversing with a gaunt little man in a blue power suit holding an expensive-looking briefcase.

"Spada!"

The startled look on his face quickly melted into a self-satisfied grin. When I reached the Caddy, the lawyer moved to act as a buffer between us. His mouth opened to protest, but Spada placed a hand on his shoulder to quiet him. "Ms. Raines, I suppose I have you to thank for this inconvenience?"

"That's all it is to you?"

"I'm not quite sure what you think I've done, but I promise you I'm just an ordinary businessman. Besides, this is police business, isn't it? Nothing to do with you?"

"It became my business when you had Darby's body delivered to me."

He shot me a woeful look that didn't come close to looking sincere. "I was absolutely horrified to hear what happened to Vincent, but I had nothing to do with his death. He was a man with a colorful past. It's ludicrous to think I had anything to do with that."

"And slanderous," the lawyer added.

"My lawyers seem to think the police don't have a leg to stand on, and neither do you. Isn't that right, Jerome?" He flicked a look at the lawyer, who reached into his case and came out with a legal document, which he shoved into my hands. A cursory glance told me it was a cease-and-desist order that put me in the same boat as Marta and the CPD. I was not to contact, harass, or approach Nick Spada from this point onward. I sneered at the order and thought of Big Percy Prescott and Earlene Skipper. What goes around comes around, I guessed.

I waved the paper. "You think this is going to do it?"

"I'm certain of it."

Something over my shoulder caught Spada's attention, and I turned to see what he was looking at. Jung was standing in the doorway, watching us.

"I assume that's the young man who started all of this? Ayers's friend?"

I turned to face him. "How do you know that?"

"You'd be surprised at all the things I know." He leaned in, his cloying breath a mixture of stale coffee and mint. "The next time you stop by my office, I'd appreciate your making an appointment first."

I glared at him, watching as he eased into the backseat of the big car. "Jerome?"

Jerome moved to push me back. "One finger touches me, Jerome, and you'll eat that briefcase."

Jerome moved away quickly, positioning the case over his vital organs as though it were a shield. He got into Spada's car on the street side and the car sped off. *He knows a lot of things? But he couldn't know about Jung unless Darby told him.* Darby had been watching the marina, living on his boss's boat. He had to have seen Jung hanging around. It wouldn't have been difficult to put a name to the face, not with Spada's means and access. I stared at the order, then stuffed it into a pocket, heading back inside.

"That's the guy?" Jung asked when I reached him. "The guy who killed Tim?"

"Yeah."

"Then why aren't you going after him?"

"I am. But first I need to ID a couple of thugs."

Chapter 41

It's easy to underestimate the number of criminals trolling city streets every day, until you're forced to pick through hundreds of their mug shots. They go on forever, one hardened face after another; some with tats, some without; some not so bad looking, others with a face only a mother could love. They came in all shapes, sizes, colors, and levels of depravity, running the gamut from petty thieves, who pinched toothpaste and gum from their local CVS, to stone-cold killers, who'd gut their own mothers for a pack of cigarettes and a scratch-off Lotto.

It took me more than two hours to find the thugs; by then, my eyes were shot, my head throbbed, and I was in a dark and dangerous place. Rayvon and Draymond Williams were their names. It turned out they were brothers, and they were just as ugly on the page as they had been in person. By the time I ID'd them, of course, I'd acquired an audience: Jung, Ben, and Weber. Scott hadn't gone far, either. He'd wagered I'd find the right faces in record time, or die trying. He won another fifty. Marta was still working on the fake nurse and I knew she'd work her till she got something. Marta didn't like being bullied any more than I did, and Spada's priggish lawyers had punched every last one of her hot buttons.

"That's them," I said, pointing at the photos.

The group leaned in over my shoulders to take a better look.

"Couple of real winners," Ben groused. "Twins?"

"Draymond's two years younger," I said. "His nose is the one I broke."

"They're on probation," Weber said. "That should make things easy."

"We'll haul them in, get them in a lineup for a formal ID. By the book," Ben said. "You'll need to finger them again."

I noted the Williamses' last known address, then stood, my knees and back stiff from sitting too long in the chair. I knew their neighborhood. I knew people who lived there. I might just have a string or two to pull. "I'll be glad to. Let's go, Jung."

Jung had been peeking over Ben's shoulder at the mug book. He looked at me, eyes wide. "Where're we going?"

Ben eyed me, suspicious. "Yeah, where *are* you going?"

I looked from Ben to Weber. "I've just picked out a couple of dangerous criminals. I would think that gives you both plenty to do without sweating over where *I'm* going."

Ben shook his head, his mouth twisted into a distrustful smirk. "Uh-uh, don't worry about what we've got to do. I want to know what you think *you've* got to do."

"I'm taking Jung home. Unless, of course, I can sit in while Marta works the fake nurse?" Both stood still, eyes averted. Of course I couldn't. "That's what I thought." I motioned to Jung. "Let's roll."

"Stay out of this," Ben called after us.

I waved good-bye, keeping it moving. "I'm taking my client home, if that's all right with you, Grandpa."

"'Grandpa,' my ass. Go home. Keep close to your phone. I'll call when we grab these idiots up."

"On my way."

I shoved out into the office, Jung walking beside me. "You're not going home, are you?"

"Nope."

"You're going after those guys?"

"Yep."

We headed for the elevator, weaving through busy cops. They didn't appear to take notice of either of us, but I knew they saw us, all the same. In fact, if pressed, every single one of them would likely be able to give a detailed description of Jung and me, right down to the color of our socks. It came with the training. Cop eyes missed very little.

"They work for Spada?"

I slid him a sidelong look, smiled. "Yeah, looks that way."

Jung stopped walking. I stopped to see why he stopped. "So that old man killed Tim for money?"

He stared at me, hurt in his eyes. I'd forgotten for a moment that at the bottom of this case was Jung's grief for his friend, that it was more than just a battle now between Spada and me. "Mostly for money, but I think he got off on the control, the power, choosing who lives or dies, seeing it done. Like this whole thing is some kind of game."

Jung nodded, his jaw clenched. I was looking at a different face than the one I was used to. This wasn't the easygoing sandwich guy prone to existential jabberwocky anymore; I was looking at a less innocent Jung.

"Money and control," he muttered, looking as though he couldn't get the concept into his brain, let alone have it live there. It appeared inconceivable to him that sacrificing a human life for money alone was an acceptable swap. It was a testament to Jung's moral center, but naïve nonetheless. He balled his fists, then unballed them, scanning the room in frustration, as though he were looking for something he could hit or punch or tear apart with his bare hands.

"We'll get him," I offered gently. "And he'll pay for what he's done."

"But Tim and the others will still be dead." Jung walked away, his head down. I followed. "Money and control," he muttered mournfully.

As I drove away, it became clear to me that I couldn't just take Jung back to his apartment and leave him there. Spada was nuts and, despite the temporary insulation his lawyers provided him, he had to know the walls were closing in around him. He knew who Jung was, and likely knew exactly where to find him. If he had no qualms about killing people at their most vulnerable, he'd certainly lose no sleep coming after Jung, even if killing him netted him nothing in the end.

I watched Jung as he sat forlornly in my passenger seat, staring off into the night, the light from passing streetlamps casting shadows across his face. He was angry and frustrated and didn't appear to know what to do with either emotion. He hadn't said more than two words the whole way.

I approached the turnoff to Jung's place, but kept going. He didn't notice. Leaving him to fend for himself now would be like throwing a puppy headfirst into a wood chipper. He needed to be where I could keep an eye on him. It wasn't until the car stopped in front of my building that Jung snapped out of his trance.

"Hey, this isn't my place."

"No, it's mine. You're staying here for a while."

"What for?"

"You'll be safer here."

His anger, suppressed by grief up until this point, flared hot. "This is because I hid out at Swami Rain's, isn't it? Now you think I can't handle myself? That I'm some chickenshit? I'm not afraid of that guy."

I gripped my hands on the steering wheel, took a breath. "You should be. He's dangerous, and he's out there right now, free as a bird, and he knows who you are. He made a point of telling me."

"He won't make money killing me."

"Not a dime, you're right. He doesn't *need* to kill you, but he sure wants to—that's the part you're missing."

"Let him try then," Jung said, girding himself for a fight even he, deep down, knew he wasn't fit for. "I'm ready."

"You're not, and you won't be fighting him, you'll be fighting whoever he sends in his place. You won't see it coming. It could be anyone—someone posing as a UPS driver, a student sitting next to you in class, someone panhandling for change on the street. You'll have to look over your shoulder every second of every day, not knowing if the person you just passed is the one aiming to punch your ticket. Is that what you're ready for?"

"Yeah." Jung answered defiantly, but the uncertainty, the fear in his eyes, told a different story.

"Get out of the car, Jung."

I got out and shut the door behind me. Jung got out on the other side. "I don't need a babysitter."

"Good, because you're not getting one. I'm offering you a safe place to be, that's it."

He slammed his fists on the roof of the rental car, the reverb cutting through the night like a single beat of a deep drum. "I've got to make him pay for what he did to Tim."

"Hey. Back up." I jabbed an angry finger at Jung. *"Now."* He moved back, watching nervously as I checked the car for dents and scratches. On top of everything else, I did not want to have to battle the rental car company over damage to the Cruze. Relieved the car was fine, I took a moment, counted to ten, keeping my breathing steady, remembering Jung was in way over his head and more afraid than he'd probably been in his entire life. I watched him, seeing, beyond the fear, the person he was before all this started. "How? How do you plan on making him pay?"

Slowly Jung seemed to deflate. It was clear he hadn't a clue. He was a student on the lifetime plan, a yoga-loving, vegan-eating sandwich tosser. "I'll track him down. At the marina. His boat. I'll do to him what he did to Tim."

We stood quietly. He was talking nonsense, and I think he knew it. Finally I headed for my front door, hoping Jung would follow. He did, eventually.

"I can't make you stay," I said, my key in the lock. "If you want to take off, go on, I won't chase you. But stay or go, tell me now."

Jung's chin fell to his chest. "They had him and they let him go."

"There was nothing solid yet to hold him on."

"And there never will be. I've been around people like him my whole life. They believe their money protects them, and they're right. There are always lawyers and more lawyers to cover things up and do the dirty work. Now you want to hide me here while he has the run of the city."

I pushed inside. "That's right, I do. The apartment below me is vacant. You'll stay there. You don't tell anyone where you are, and you do not leave until I tell you it's okay." We trudged up to the second floor and I unlocked the Kallishes' door and led him inside. The place smelled of drying paint. "Lights work, bathroom's back there. No furniture, but I've got a fairly comfortable air mattress you can use. I don't think you'll need to be here more than a day or two."

"So I'm just supposed to hang around here, cowering in a corner like a rat?"

I padded to the front windows, checked the street, then pulled the blinds down. "How you hang around is up to you."

"What about food? People? My *life*?"

"You won't starve. No people. Your life will resume when this is over." I padded down the hall toward the back of the apartment, Jung behind me. "You have the run of the apartment. Just don't do anything weird in here. This is my home, respect it."

I flicked on the light switch in the master bedroom. "I'll get you that mattress, and bring blankets and stuff to make you comfortable. Maybe a radio or something."

Jung didn't look overly impressed. "What'll you be doing while I'm locked up here?"

I stared at him, giving him all kinds of slack. "I'll be doing the work you paid me for."

I headed back up the hall, toward the front door.

"I sleep in the nude. Is that going to be a problem?"

He was trying to needle me. He was a petulant child denied a privilege and trying to get a rise. "If I see you nude, yes, that's going to be a problem for you."

He let out an aggrieved breath. "I'm a prisoner then. What happened to my civil liberties?"

I opened the door, my hand on the knob. "You lost them when you stepped inside my house. You'll get them back when you leave."

Chapter 42

I pulled the baseball cap down low, flipped my jacket collar up, and slid into the backseat of a dark Chrysler with a missing tailpipe, easing into the seat as it pulled away from the curb. At the corner two blocks up, the car turned left and ducked into a dark alley and stopped. The driver switched off the ignition, turned to face me.

"Whassup?"

"Hey, Dobie."

He shot me a toothy grin, his leather Kangol cap topping a dark, thin face and a graying soul patch. "Look at me driving and you sitting back there. You live long enough you see everything, huh?"

I smiled. I was used to hauling Dobie Tavares into the district in cuffs, me driving the squad car, him cooling his heels in back, trying to explain how I had him all wrong. Now here we were, no cuffs, no hauling, just me looking for information from a trusted confidential informant.

Dobie was a car thief—fast, thorough, nonselective—which made me wonder about the car I was sitting in. He didn't much care about make or model. If it had wheels and he felt like taking it, he took it. He could watch you walk away from your car and have it hot-wired and halfway to the choppers almost before you got where you were headed. Despite his nimble fingers and long arrest record, good old Dobie, the Caribbean Cruiser, was the pride of his large Dominican family. It figured, since most of them were car thieves, too.

"I'm not going to lie. It's a little strange." I looked over the backseat, more than a little curious about the car's history.

Dobie read my mind. "No worries, Officer Raines, this one's cold as ice."

I handed him a pair of fifty-dollar bills. "I'm looking for a couple of guys who hire themselves out for muscle work. They're from your neighborhood." I held up my phone and showed him the photos of the Williams brothers, which I'd snapped from the mug shots. "I need to know where they hang out, who they hang out with."

Dobie focused, snorted, then looked at me as if he thought I was joking. "You're serious?" He searched my face and saw that I was. "They're small fries," he said incredulously. "Little fish. Dum-dums? Hell, I got shoes with more sense than them two."

I put the phone away. "Tell me about them."

"I just did." Dobie handed one of the fifties back. "They ain't worth a hundred. Besides, I still owe you for keeping my sister's kid out of the soup that one time. Dobie Tavares always pays his debts."

"Okay, fill me in." I was getting a little impatient. We'd already been in the alley too long. This was Chicago, not Shangri-La. Sitting in dirty alleys in a darkened car in the middle of the night was not a thing you did if you had long-term life plans.

"Never met them, but I've seen them around. They hang out at the laundromat picking up odd jobs, breaking legs, roughing up. They're hard hitters who'll work for just about anybody." He pointed an index finger at the side of his head and drew a circle a couple of times. "And neither one of them is wrapped too tight, if you feel me."

"Laundromat?"

Dobie chuckled. "You've been off the beat too long. It's a shell. In the front, you fluff and fold your tighty whities. In the back, it's a whole different story."

"Guns, drugs, girls, what?"

"Yep. Those two float in and out of the action because they spend most of their time in the can. You got to be smart to work the streets. These two I know because I used to, *allegedly,* run cars through their cousin's shop." Dobie grinned mischievously. "Why don't they work for the cousin on the regular, you're probably asking yourself. Well, I'll tell you, because even though they're *familia,* these two Einsteins aren't smart enough to pour piss out of a boot. Hiring on morons leaves you open for all kinds of bad shit."

"How would they come in contact with a rich white guy?"

Dobie's eyes slanted. "Is he a public defender?"

"Insurance."

"Then I got no clue. I don't think those two know what that is."

I leaned back in the seat, out of ideas. If there was a connection between the morons and Spada, I couldn't see it, but a lot had gone on in a relatively short amount of time. I'd been thwarted, manhandled, thrown out, and had doors slammed in my face. I'd had a dead body delivered to my doorstep and even had my own client running from me as though he were trying to give the Devil the slip. There was a connection, but I just couldn't see it. Why else would the goons grab me, rifle through my bag, leave my gun and wallet, and take only the copies I'd made of Spada's files? Spada had to have sent them. Our encounter wasn't some random shakedown. And how dumb did you have to be to be banished from a chop shop? A shiver ran up the back of my neck.

"The cousin's shop. Where is it?"

"Aw, c'mon now, you know I can't tell you that."

"Dobie, this is important. Where?"

He shook his head. "The thugs you get, the shop you don't get. You mess in these people's business and you guarantee you don't breathe so good, and your fifty don't come close to paying for a decent funeral."

I leaned forward, gripping the back of the driver's seat, my heart racing. "Fleet Transports. On Armitage. Is that the shop?"

Sweat began to bead on Dobie's forehead. He glanced out of the window, not wanting to look at me. I was right; he didn't have to say it. Fleet Transports where Vince Darby got the SUV he drove to the marina, the place Whip and I talked our way into under false pretenses. The goons were related to Leon, who was connected to Darby, and Darby to Spada.

"He owned gas stations or storage facilities, she said." I was muttering to myself, recalling my conversation with Elizabeth Ayers, working it through. Or an old garage used as a front for a chop shop? Surely Elizabeth Ayers wouldn't have taken the time to make the distinction. I grasped Dobie's shoulder. "Spada owns the chop shop. *That's* how he connects to Leon. *That's* why Darby went there for the car, and Leon supplied them with muscle." I smiled, nearly giddy inside. So light was my spirit, it almost felt as though I could fly.

"I need the name of that laundromat."

Dobie shook his head. "I ain't no snitch."

"It stays with me. C'mon, Dobie. Don't stop now."

Dobie turned it over in his head for a moment, obviously unhappy with the position I was putting him in. I was asking him to go against the code of the streets, to put his safety at risk. It would come down to whether or not he trusted me, whether he knew or not that I'd have his back. It took a moment for him to work it through. "You're killing me here." I waited while he took his cap off, fanned his face with it, and then put it back on. It was nervous movement, stalling action. "The Dudz and Sudz, all right? There, I gave it to you. And for the record, this? Us two right here? Never happened, understood?"

I handed Dobie back the fifty. He'd earned it. "Thanks, Dobie. I owe you one."

Chapter 43

The Dudz and Sudz was a depressing little hole-in-the-wall on South Homan; it was wedged between a greasy hoagies shop and a nursery school advertising curbside drop-off. The grimy front window plastered with colorful community flyers looked in on three short rows of coin-operated machines that, from across the street, looked like they dated back to Milton Berle's heyday. For a time, I idled at the curb a few doors down, watching the door as feral-eyed street folk slipped in and out, a few carrying dirty laundry to wash, most with only the clothes they had on. I assumed these were the people who had business dealings in the back. No sign of the Williams brothers, and I wasn't going to be able to sit in the car long before someone took notice and came to make something out of it. After about ten minutes, I took one last look and drove away.

The night was quiet, hot, sticky—the kind of summer night that propelled the criminally minded out into the street to see what kind of trouble they could kick up. It was nearly eleven, but the Dudz and Sudz kept up a steady flow. I ducked the car into the alley and got out to peek around the corner; the smell of sour milk, rotten garbage, and small dead things wafted up my nose, turning my stomach. I stuck to the shadows, but this wasn't a good vantage point. I could barely see the door from where I stood. I needed to get closer. I needed to find a spot that I could hunker down in for a while without anyone seeing me.

My eyes swept up and down the street. I checked the dingy alley. There was no good spot to burrow into to watch the door. Slowly my eyes drifted upward toward the rooftop, and my hands began to sweat. I'd nearly died on a rooftop. I'd taken a life on a rooftop. My police career ended on a rooftop. I squeezed my eyes shut, giving it a minute for the memories to settle. When I opened them again, I was fine, or at least fine-ish. I squared my shoulders, centered myself, and then jogged back to the car. I pulled a pair of binoculars and a camera out of the trunk before heading around back, looking for a way up. *It's fine,* I told myself. *The rooftop is fine.* I ran it through my head like a mantra. *It's fine.*

I rattled the lowest rung on the unsteady fire escape ladder, eyeing it dubiously, taking a moment to mentally confirm that my health insurance premiums were paid and up to date. The ladder didn't look sturdy enough to hold the weight of a gerbil, let alone my 130 pounds, but the six-story building to which it was attached was directly across the street from the Dudz and Sudz. Therefore, it was the one I needed to make work. It would be a real shame, I thought, if I fell, broke my back, and had to lay in sour, dead garbage while being nibbled on by yellow-eyed rats. The thought sent a shiver through me, but I tucked the camera and binoculars inside my light jacket, jumped up to pull the ladder down, and started up. *No guts, no glory.*

Halfway up, I had another horrifying thought. What if my climb up was all the ladder could take? How would I get down? I glanced back at the alley floor, making sure the car was still there, and noticed just how far down the ground was from here. *This is stupid. I am an idiot. Ben is right; I have a serious problem.* I planted my foot one rung up, added my weight, and let out the mother of all yelps when the rung crumbled underneath me, the broken pieces crashing to the asphalt below with an ear-splitting rattle. I clung to the ladder, my heart slamming against my rib cage. I was going to kill Nick Spada. I was going to yank his wicked heart right out of his chest and stomp it into a bloody pancake. I started climbing again.

Every rung cleared was a gift from Heaven. When I finally slid my body onto the rooftop's tar covering, I lay there, hugging it, my cheek to the sticky surface, sweat streaming off me like a waterfall. I'd made it. I didn't die. I'd live to eat breakfast in the morning, work myself out of debt, grow old in Key West. When my legs and arms stopped shaking, I rose up on all fours and crawled over to the rim to peer over it. There it was, the Dudz and Sudz, just where I left it. I lay on my stomach, flat against the roof, and got out the binoculars, training them at the door. I'd be here when the goons showed up, and if I didn't figure out a better way to get down, I'd be here for a lot longer than that.

The Williams brothers walked into the Dudz and Sudz three hours into my ill-advised rooftop sit-in. They drove up in a white Dodge Charger with tinted windows, no front or back plates. The car was likely hot. Maybe the two were trying it out before they drove it into their cousin's chop shop. I quickly switched from binoculars to camera and snapped away at the ugly twosome. They were standing out in front of the Dudz and Sudz, chewing the fat with a squirrely-looking guy in a tank top and basketball shorts. I snapped him, too.

I was still snapping when a maroon Bonneville eased up to the curb and a familiar face got out. It was Leon the chop shop guy—Whip's ex-con friend, the one who owed him a favor. What was up? Some kind of sleazy crook board meeting? The three greeted each other with warm hugs and happy back slaps. This was some kind of meeting, but which one of them called it? Had Spada made contact and given them all instructions? If he had, I had a good idea who'd be on the receiving end of their last-ditch push to clean up the mess, and I wanted no part of that. I snapped photos feverishly until the men disappeared inside, then slid my phone out of my pocket and called Ben.

"I've got the Williams brothers," I said when he came on the line. "It's another nail in Spada's coffin."

"Where are you?"

I looked around the roof, ignored the question. "Did you hear what I said? I found the twits that roughed me up. They're meeting with Leon, the owner of the chop shop. They just walked into the Dudz and Sudz on Homan. Check the white Charger, no plates, and the maroon Bonneville, both parked out front. You need to get over here and, for Pete's sake, ditch the lights and sirens. If they spook, we'll never see any of them again."

I heard muffled talking on Ben's end of the line, and then he was quickly back. *"Where. Are. You?"*

There was no answer to that question that was going to get me anywhere I wanted to be. However, considering the state of the dilapidated ladder, I was either going to need a Chicago Fire Department hook and ladder or an ambulance, so I decided to just come out with it. "I'm on the roof across the street. If you don't see me out front when you get here, check the alley. I'll be laying spread-eagled on a mound of Hefty bags."

I ended the call, put the phone away, and waited. I'd get to the ladder when I got to it. Right now, I kept my eyes on the door.

I soon spotted squad cars rolling in, one benefit to my bird's-eye view. At least a half dozen of them cut cleanly, quietly, dark, through the side streets, like a herd of killer sharks honing in on an unsuspecting seal. Three cars approached the front; three turned off to speed down the alley one street over to cut off any rear escapes. Leon and his cousins were caught in a vise and didn't know it. I smiled, watching as the cops roared in, tires squealing. Authoritative shouts came next as the cops bounded out of their squads and stormed inside. The Dudz and Sudz emptied quickly, everybody frantically tumbling out of the front door clutching armloads of laundry meant for the machines—one woman pulling a crude wagon with a sleeping baby in it, another hastily buttoning her blouse. I didn't even want to guess what *that* was about. A few minutes later, a team came out with the Williams brothers in cuffs, but no Leon.

I snapped a photo. "Leon made it to the back room. Dammit." The cops wouldn't have had a warrant for that, not yet, but at least they got the thugs. I stuck my tongue out in their direction. "Take *that*, you ugly creeps."

I was so busy watching the brothers getting put into the back of the squad car that I missed the unmarked car when it rolled up. By the time I caught sight of Ben and Weber standing in the middle of the street, looking up at me, it was too late. I ducked back from the edge, and then quickly crawled back to the top of the ladder. I eyed it unenthusiastically before forcing myself over the side, heading down. I'd die or I wouldn't, but I wasn't going to wait up here like a dim-witted damsel in need of rescue. I'd take my chances with the "death ladder." I took the rungs hard, double-time, no slow and easy climb this time. I figured the faster I went, the farther down I'd be when the whole thing came crashing down on my head.

Nearly there, the ladder began to creak and sway and it felt loose in my hands. I glanced up toward the roof and saw the supports practically dangling from corroded mounts. My mouth went dry. I glanced down. Not close enough. If I fell from here, it was going to hurt like hell. A loud snap followed. I glanced up again to find one end of the ladder completely unhinged from the building. Maybe I had a good ten seconds. I scanned the ground—nothing but concrete and a Dumpster a few feet to my left. A Dumpster. There were bound to be rats in there. A whine of distressed metal broke into my panicked thoughts. Five seconds. I dove from the ladder into the Dumpster, landing on my back on a mound of slippery garbage bags. The ladder crashed to the alley, a cacophony of skittering bolts, rusted rungs, and worn metal. Dogs began to bark somewhere. The stench was horrendous. I clambered to my knees, clamped my hands onto the side, and hoisted myself over and out as fast as I could.

"*Ack! Yuck. Blech.*" I danced in one spot, beating my clothes to loosen vermin, thinking of rats and crawly things. The sense of relief to have my feet on solid ground was secondary. I fanned at my hair, shook my head, stomped my feet. I snorted hard to get the stench of rot out of my nose, then turned to see Ben and Weber walking toward me. I composed myself and moved away from the Dumpster. I eyed the pieces of ladder littering the alley, lucky to be alive.

"We got them. They'll roll on Spada. They're too stupid not to." These were the first words out of my mouth. I'd survived a Dumpster jump. I felt invincible.

Ben and Weber eyed the ladder, then me; neither spoke. Ben looked at the rusted ladder lying on the ground, shook his head. Weber just stared at me, bewildered.

"I got a tip," I said. "I followed it through. It panned out."

Ben opened his mouth, closed it, then opened it again to speak. "I don't know where to start."

"The back room is where all the action happens," I said. "But I wouldn't waste time getting a warrant to search the place. They're probably in there now shredding and burning everything worth looking at. Another thing, can you check to see if Spada comes back as the owner of Leon's chop shop? I'm still looking for a connector. The shop might be it."

Ben took in the broken ladder lying at our feet. "So we're not going to talk about these rusted pieces of—"

Weber cut him off. "I don't really think you want to, do you?"

I turned and headed for the rental.

"Hey, where are you going now?" Ben asked. "We need you to pick these jokers out of a lineup."

"I will, but I've got one stop to make first."

"Uh-uh, you go with us. We'll get your car picked up later."

"Are you nuts? Look where we're standing! If I leave that rental here, it'll be up on blocks and stripped clean by the time you send your guys back to get it. I'll meet you at the district."

Both of them looked skeptical, and, frankly, I couldn't blame them. Even I knew I was a flight risk.

Ben pointed a warning finger at me. "Cass, no fooling around. You'd better be there."

"I will." I purposefully left out the word "eventually." I would definitely make it in to ID the brothers, but first I had something to do. As I walked to the car, I kept smelling tar and rotten food and tracked the smell to the sleeves of my jacket. I quickly stripped out of it and tossed it into the trunk, lamenting the cleaning bill. Ben and Weber were still standing there when I drove away.

Chapter 44

Fleet Transports, the front for Leon's chop shop, was locked up tight when I got there around four AM. One bare lightbulb sputtered over Fleet's front door, but it didn't offer much in the way of light. It didn't help that half the streetlights weren't working. Somewhere a dog was barking itself hoarse. The metal door had a mail slot cut into it, but that wasn't going to work for me, so I dug out my picklocks and got busy while Whip stood and watched my back. Stella Symonds had died just hours ago. She wouldn't be able to bear witness to Spada's depravity. It was one more thing to hate Nicholas Spada for.

"Far as I know, chop shops are a twenty-four-hour business," Whip whispered. "Somebody called and cleared the place out."

I fiddled with the short hook, raking it over the lock's pins. It was slow going, and I had to work by feel alone. "Somebody from the laundromat got to a phone."

Whip sighed. "You know I can pick that lock faster, right?"

"Not without going back to prison, you can't." The last pin slid up and I stood, shoving the picks into my back pocket. "There. We're in."

The place was dark and, despite the sultry night, dank, a scent of fuel in the air. I found the light switch, but when I flicked it, nothing happened. I pulled the compact flashlight out of my pocket, Whip did the same, and we slowly swept cone-shaped beams over the deserted space and along the craggy walls caked with decades of motor oil, exhaust grunge, and city muck. The place reeked of man sweat and gasoline, the floor felt slick with it, like they'd had some kind of spill. No sign of Buddha, or anyone else, thankfully. Whip might have been able to take him after a couple rounds, but I didn't want him to have to. In and out—that's what I wanted, hopefully after finding something here that confirmed the links I thought I'd made, something that would put Leon back in a cell.

The cars were gone, except for one left behind. It was hidden under a canvas tarp, up on blocks. There'd be no VIN, no plates, no easy way of finding its owner. It was now an orphaned auto ready for the scrap. Nothing about Fleet Transports was legit. Besides the chop shop component, it was also a place you could come to get an untraceable car with few questions asked, for a price. That's how Darby ended up in one of Leon's dodgy vehicles.

"If Spada owns this, then that's how he knows Leon," I said.

Whip swept his flashlight around the garage. "He'd have the scratch, that's for sure, but so would the kid's brother. Like I said, gut feeling."

I grinned, but didn't say anything. Whip was a better con than he was a cop. He'd overlooked motive, opportunity.

"But, for sure, Leon would need a boss," Whip said. "He's cutthroat and mean as a junkyard dog, but he's no entrepreneur."

We picked our way in, careful where we put our feet. "I ran the building. Spada's name wasn't on it. It came back to a company called Tavroh. He could own that, though. I asked Ben to check it out."

Whip ran the beam of his flash along the ceiling. "Rich folk got all kinds of ways of hiding dirt. If he owns it, he sure wouldn't want to advertise. Chop shop and insurance don't really go together."

I ran my flash briefly over the tarp, then turned away from it.

"The office," I whispered as I headed straight there, Whip following.

"You aren't going to find anything. I was in there, remember? This is a chop shop, not a Honda dealership. No paper trail. They drive the hot cars in, they dice them up, and the parts go adios."

I slid him a sideways glance, smiled. "I know how a chop shop works."

"You *cop* know, you don't *con* know." He swept his flash right to left and back again, paying close attention to the shadows. "They zero in on the wheels, the air bags, the catalytic converters, high-value stuff." He spoke as though he were teaching a class in chop shop—slow, step-by-step. He turned back to eye the tarp. "They must have been moving too fast to get that one off its blocks. Good money tossed down the can, you ask me."

I glanced over at him. "We're looking for anything that definitively connects Darby and Spada to the Williams brothers and your friend Leon."

"I know, but first, get it straight. You and me are friends. That's why I'm creeping around in here and not home watching *American Ninja Warrior.* Me and Leon? We were in the joint together and I saved him from getting shanked in the back. That doesn't mean he wouldn't shank me if he felt like it."

I stopped, held the flashlight up so I could see his face. "No honor among thieves?"

Whip snorted. "Depends on the thief . . . and what you consider honorable."

"Darby's a con, Leon's a con. Spada could be a con," I said.

"And maybe he did his stint with either Darby or Leon?"

"Or both."

Whip chuckled. "You do meet a lot of interesting people living on the state's dime."

"So they get out and now everybody's just itching to do Spada's bidding?"

Whip nodded. "If the price is right, only you can't say for sure because Darby got himself chunked up and the cops don't have Leon yet."

We eased into the office, which was even darker than the garage had been. No windows, just an old table and a few scarred chairs, the table littered with used paper cups smelling of old coffee, some girlie mags, a deck of cards. I turned to Whip, looked a question.

"Told you. You don't need a lot to get the chopping done."

"So let's say Spada is a con, and let's say he's got his hands in a lot of different pies. He somehow gets this place and sets Leon up to work the chop shop, but he's also got Sterling, which is semilegitimate, with this secret-death part built in. That's where Darby and that fake nurse would have to come in, right? Spada would know how to get his hands on killers. Maybe Spada's an alias. That'd explain my not turning up anything on him." I looked at Whip. "It's so easy for cons to get hooked back into this crap. It's a revolving door of crime and incarceration."

Whip picked up the card deck, shuffled it a bit. "You're thinking like a cop. This is the life, for Leon, for Darby, maybe for Spada. They probably all got out of the can and fell right back in with the same crowd they ran with before." Whip tossed the cards down on the table, eyed the girlie mags, but left them where they were. "Take Leon, because he's the one I know. He probably got out, got himself a good meal, a woman, two maybe, then he starts looking around for his next move.

"He spreads it around that he's out and ready to get back into things, so a guy he knows sets him up with a guy *he* knows, maybe this Spada, and suddenly Leon's back in the game. This time, it's cars. Next time, it could be high-end whiskey that falls off the back of a truck, maybe even hookers. It doesn't matter to Leon. When the profits get split, he's there to take his cut and the 'circle of life' continues." Whip grinned. "Just like in *The Lion King*."

I watched Whip, listening to him explain it, saddened knowing that he'd lived the life he'd just described. That he had once been in Leon's spot, in and out of prison, heading fast in the wrong direction, that it could just as easily be him headed back to prison now, instead of Leon. "What turned you around?"

Whip sighed, fiddled with the flashlight in his hand. "I got tired of screwing up." I stood quietly, not sure what to say. "Uh-uh, stop with the sad eyes. Get on with what you're doing, so we can get the hell out of here." He turned for the garage. "I'll check out there and see what I see. My car needs a muffler. I might get lucky and find one lying around." He looked back, smiled. "See? That look you're giving me right now? Proves there's no way you could be a decent crook, you're too upstanding. Besides, there's no way I find a Hyundai muffler out there. Leon can't turn a profit on low-end crap like that."

I watched him go, thinking about the turns lives take, hoping it was true in Whip's case that his criminal past was dead and gone, knowing I'd fight to make it true, even if it wasn't. I turned back to the office, but I didn't hold out much hope I'd find anything useful. Gangs, I thought, or organized crime. Maybe Spada was connected? Maybe Darby had been? The place didn't look like it did a high-volume business. There'd been little activity my first visit here, only Leon and Buddha, just a few cars. That wouldn't have been enough to interest any decent Mob outfit.

I could compare Leon's prison time with Darby's and check for overlap, I thought. I could do the same for Spada, once I found out his real name. Had Darby crossed Spada somehow? Had Darby crossed Leon? No honor among thieves.

I looked under the table and chairs, but found nothing but a few wadded-up nubbles of chewing gum. The office was a bust. The shop was a bust. Whatever was going on here wasn't going on here now, and there was little chance anybody would be back. I swept my flash along the ceiling, my beam landing on a dusty skylight.

"Who puts a skylight in a garage?" I said loud enough for Whip to hear me.

"What?"

"There's a skylight."

"*And?*"

I stared up at it. "There is no 'and.' I just don't see the point, do you? It's a chop shop. Who's going to sit in here and gaze up at the stars on a clear night?"

"*What?*"

"Nothing. Never mind."

"It's a Benz. A two-door coupe. Stripped clean. Nice job, too. Leon's guys are good."

I walked out of the office to find Whip standing at the car, admiring Leon's handiwork. The car was black, or had been before being liberated of most of its exterior panels. Darby drove a black Mercedes two-door coupe. I'd tailed it the first time I met him. I drew closer.

"Tell me they missed the VIN plate," I said, checking the car.

Whip chuckled. "No self-respecting chop artist misses the VIN plate. What's it to you?"

I swept my light over the car. "I think I tailed this car. Last time I saw Darby, he was driving a Mercedes just like this. It belonged to his boss, which I can't prove without the VIN."

"Well, if he drove it in here, he sure as hell wasn't in any condition to drive it out." Whip padded over to the passenger side, checked inside. "Nothing in here says Darby or Spada. It could be any black Benz."

"Could be, but what if it's *the* black Benz? Why leave it?"

"You're forgetting the time factor."

"No, if they were worried about covering things up, they'd make damned sure they took *this* car first." I moved to the trunk, opened it, and found a knotted rope, like the kind sailors use to batten things down. I immediately thought of Tim's boat. *Is it Tim's?* I picked the rope up and found beneath it a single sheet of paper, which I picked up and read: *I WIN.* Just the two words. Written in big block letters. I held the note up for Whip to see.

"Doesn't say it's for you," he said.

I turned it over. Spada's letterhead was at the top. I eyed the rope, shone the light on it. There was blood seeped into the fibers. *Darby's blood?* He'd have had to be restrained before he was killed. "This is Spada, which means it *is* for me. He's gloating."

The two simple words weren't a confession, they were a taunt, but why even that when we were scrambling around, looking for evidence to put him away? I looked at the car again. Its presence here bothered me. The bloodstained rope, the blood possibly Darby's, might also have trace evidence of his murderer on it. The note, too, might hold fingerprints, mine now, too. Why was Spada being so cavalier, so reckless? I sniffed, froze. "Do you smell smoke?"

Whip sniffed, too. "Yeah."

We wheeled around, sniffing harder, trying to get a bead on the source of the smell. "There." I pointed at the front door, at the black smoke beginning to billow in underneath.

"Well, that ain't good," Whip said.

Suddenly the floor, which had given off the faint smell of gasoline when we came in, began to smolder. We exchanged a panicked look and ran for the door, but when we reached it, the knob was already scorching hot and we couldn't touch it. The smoke flooded in, the stench of gas grew stronger. Whip wrapped his hands in the hem of his T-shirt and tried turning the hot knob, his boxer's muscles straining. No go.

"Locked from outside. Your picklocks?"

I eyed the dead bolt. The smoke was forcing its way in now, thick and fast. It now covered the tops of our shoes. There was no way I could get anywhere near that door. I shook my head, pointed to the overhead door. "Try this."

We raced over and together tried raising the metal door, but it wouldn't give, not an inch. Black, acrid smoke now slithered its way along the oily floor, undulating, crawling like a devilish snake, spreading outward, staking its claim. We gave up on the overhead, beginning to cough, wheeze, both of us desperate now for an out.

"That's it for doors," Whip said.

The smoke pushed us back toward the center of the room. My eyes began to water, my throat burn. I flicked a look at Whip. He was in the same boat. Flames suddenly shot up from the smoke and latched onto the front wall, the fire's tentacles clawing its way toward the ceiling, one horrifying inch at a time.

"Cell phone?" Whip croaked.

"Yep . . . in the car . . . yours?"

"In my jacket."

I glanced over at him. He wasn't wearing a jacket.

"In the car." He coughed. "Next to your phone."

The office was the only place the smoke hadn't yet gotten to; we pedaled backward, then turned and ran for it. Halfway there, I peeled off and headed for the Mercedes. I needed that rope and the note. I knew now why Spada left it behind. He intended to burn the car, the note, the rope, and me in this dilapidated garage. He knew I wouldn't let things go. He had to know that once the laundromat got cleared out, this would be my next stop. He planned the fire, knowing it would obliterate everything, including me.

"Cass, c'mon. Leave it."

"Go." I reached the trunk, dove in. "I'm coming." I stuffed

the note into my back pocket, the rope under my belt, then turned and sprinted for the office, meeting Whip at the door.

"That was stupid. Nothing's worth your life."

"There could be evidence on it. DNA. He wants it all to go up in the fire."

My eyes burning, I searched for a landline, but didn't find one. And why would there be? I thought. This was a chop shop. Who were they going to call? Who'd be calling them? I could hear the fire roaring now and see the dance of reds, blues, and yellows reflecting off the glass in the office door. The fire *crackled, hissed, whooshed,* the dangerous sounds enough to make a person's blood run cold.

Whip faced me, the neck of his shirt pulled up over his nose and mouth. It was a temporary solution. The fire was hungry, eating up the oxygen we needed in big, fat gulps. Soon it would take it all. I shut the door, but that wouldn't give us more than a few more seconds of living. We were in trouble. Big trouble.

Smoke slowly rose from the oily floor. The ravenous flames would follow. They'd quickly hit the Mercedes, and if there was gasoline left in the tank, the two of us were going to go up like bottle rockets. I thought of my car and the Molotov cocktail. What was it with Spada and fire?

I tugged on Whip's sleeve, pointed up. "The skylight."

He followed where I pointed and gave me a thumbs-up. The small window in the ceiling was the only shot we had.

"We need a ladder," Whip said. "Stay here. I'll go look for one."

I pulled him back. "We both go. Stay low and stay together." I took the lead as we pushed out through the door, back out into the garage, keeping low, watching the flames, scouting for anything that would get us up and out. Half crawling at one point, our lungs quickly filled with smoke and our vision blurred. We didn't have long. The doors were now completely engulfed and the front wall was a sheet of fire. Maybe someone passing along on the outside would notice and call the fire department. Maybe they wouldn't. It seemed like forever before I spotted an old painter's ladder propped against the back wall, but my elation was short-lived. The ladder was sitting next to several cans of house paint, the sight of which caused my heart to seize, and then nearly stop. Flammable, toxic paint and Darby's discarded Mercedes, likely filled with gas. This was not going to be pleasant.

"Here." I called out to Whip, who was right behind me, his hand on the small of my back for guidance. We lifted the ladder, Whip on one end, me on the other. We ran it back to the office, the sound of the fire taunting us and ringing in our ears.

We extended the ladder, set it up. "You first," Whip said, his hands on the bottom rung to steady it.

"Like hell. *You* first."

"This is no time to get coppy. Go."

"Stop arguing," I croaked. "Move. I'm right behind you."

Whip coughed, sputtered, and started up reluctantly.

"Wait." I handed him my gun. "You might have to break the glass. Hurry."

He headed up, fast, looking back every rung or two to make sure I was keeping my word to follow him up. I eyed the ladder. It didn't look as though it could hold both of us. I would have to wait for him to get off before I got on. It was not lost on me that this was now the second time tonight that I'd trusted my life to a rickety ladder.

I checked the progress of the fire, turned back to Whip. He'd made it to the top, but he was struggling to unlatch the window. The fire grew, getting meaner, closer, louder. Whip put his shoulder to the glass and pushed, but it still wouldn't give. When he turned my gun over in his hand and smacked the butt of it against the glass, it didn't break. The glass in the office door shattered. I turned to see tendrils of red flame forcing their way in, thick black smoke rushing in behind them. We had seconds, if that. I looked up again, willing Whip to move faster. He struck the glass again and again and again . . . until it finally shattered. I sidestepped the falling shards as best I could, then hustled up, the fire now practically nipping at my heels. I could barely see. I climbed by feel alone, then missed a rung, and tumbled back down, just catching hold of the ladder before I hit the smoldering floor. I started up again, faster, more desperately. When I reached the top, Whip grabbed me by the arms and pulled me through the jagged hole.

"Move!"

I felt my back pockets, my side, and my heart sank. The rope and note weren't there. "Wait. Stop. They're gone."

They must have fallen out when I slipped off the ladder. I scrambled back to the skylight and peered back through the opening. The floor was covered in smoke now, the flames just moments from flashing over. Even still, I grabbed the ladder, preparing to go back in. I could make it down and back, I thought. I had to.

Whip pulled me back by the scruff of my shirt. "Are you out of your mind?"

I tried twisting out of his hold. "I can get it. I only need a few seconds. Let me go."

He spun me around, grabbed me by the shirt, and shook me hard, his eyes intense on mine. "You're not going anywhere but over the side, got it? It's gone. You'll get him some other way. Now I said *move!*"

I pushed him off, screaming out in frustration, but knew he was right. I felt the crushing weight of defeat overpower me. It was dark, bottomless. I'd just lost my best chance at getting Spada. I'd let solid evidence literally slip through my fingers. I was angry at myself, angry at Whip, angry at the world. Spada had won. He'd beaten me. He was going to get away with all of it. Whip headed for the edge of the roof, but wouldn't go another step without me. "C'mon."

"No, we need the ladder." I was thinking clearly now. "Grab it."

Struggling, we managed to haul the smoking ladder up and out through the skylight, holding on to it for dear life, as we lay, for a moment, gulping in air, our backs to the flat roof. When we got our second wind, we eased the ladder over the rim and leaned it against the burning building. This time, I went first, but only because we didn't have time to argue about it. Another ladder climb, another opportunity to end up dead. Whip and I hit the street, coughing, bleary-eyed, and took off running as far away from the chop shop as we could get. We'd just made it across the street, a safe distance away, when the flames went nuclear. Something inside—the car, the paint cans—exploded and the roof of the building blew off and rained down onto the street. Whip and I watched in horror as the fire ate the chop shop alive.

Whip doubled over, gasping for air. "That almost sucked."

I turned to face him, wheezing, both our faces covered in soot and grime. "Almost? What part of that *didn't* suck?"

Despite his distress, he began to chuckle, then laugh. It had to be nerves. No sane person could find humor in what we'd just gone through. I eyed him curiously. We'd come uncomfortably close to burning alive, which had to be the worst way to go out, and I was in no laughing mood. Whip collapsed onto the curb, watching the fire, rivulets of sweat and tears streaming down his face. I squinted toward where I thought I'd parked the car and headed that way. I needed my cell phone to call 911. Halfway, I flinched and ducked as, presumably, another paint can went up.

Somewhere close, a car engine turned over and I reeled to see a black SUV screech away from the curb up the street and disappear around the corner. I didn't have to guess who'd just tried to bake us like an Easter ham. Nick Spada was getting desperate, which made him ten times as dangerous as before. The taunting was beginning to get under my skin, though. He was playing me, and I didn't like it. He left those things behind for me to find, knowing I wouldn't live long enough to tell anyone about them. He'd underestimated me.

I retrieved my phone, staring at the angry flames, kicking myself over the loss of the rope and note. Spada was wrong. He hadn't won, not yet, not ever. I was alive and I was coming for him.

Chapter 45

My head lay nestled in the soft center of a giant marshmallow as I drifted along on a cloud. Time meant nothing, space either. I had nowhere to be. I closed my eyes, breathed, and took it all in, falling off to a contented slumber fit for baby angels ... until someone dropped a hammer.

I jerked awake and looked up into the scowling faces of Detectives Pena, Mickerson, and Weber. I stared at them, and they stared back. No one spoke for a time. I searched my memory bank, trying to place where the hell I was. Fire at the chop shop, I remembered, then the mad dash down the ladder. I took a tumble, and lost the rope and note, tangible evidence Nick Spada was a craven killer. Then Whip went Rambo and stretched out the back of my shirt. I remembered fighting off the paramedics, who tried taking me to the hospital, and recalled identifying the Williams brothers in a lineup. I straightened in the chair. Police district. I was at the police district. I looked around, frowned. I was in an interview room ... again, and I'd somehow fallen asleep. How long had it been since I'd slept in my own bed? I sniffed, grimaced. I smelled like burned rubber and spoiled cabbage.

I blinked up at the cops, my eyes feeling like someone had

poured a gallon of sand in them. "How long have I been in here?"

Ben smirked, but didn't answer. Weber just stood there, half smiling. I couldn't quite peg what the other half was. Maybe he was rethinking his desire to date me. I stood to even things up. "Look, I almost died today, tonight, yesterday . . . what the hell time is it?"

Marta glanced at her watch. "It's seven AM. Friday. And you've been in here forty-two, no, forty-*three* minutes."

I glanced over at Weber, and felt just a pang of self-consciousness. I wasn't exactly looking my best. I'd come close to being eaten by fire and I was smoky, tousled, and singed at the edges. "Where's Whip?"

"He's in the other room," Weber said. "We just talked to him, now we're here to talk to you."

Ben glared at me. He wasn't happy. *"So sit."*

"I'm good standing."

"You look like you're about to keel over, and you smell like you've been working the pit at the Indy. You call that good?"

My eyes narrowed. *What is his deal?* "I'm fine. Okay?"

"Dammit, Cass." Ben's face turned a splotchy red.

I picked up the chair I'd been sitting in, walked it to the door, and set it outside in the hall. When I got back to the table, it looked as though Ben might explode. I dusted my hands off, then plunged them deep into smoky pockets. "No chair. No sit. Can we move this along now?"

Marta shook her head. "Unbelievable." She leaned back against the table. "I take that back. Since I know you, it's all too believable."

I ignored them and relayed the night's events. Halfway through, I was kind of sorry I'd banished the chair to the hall. I really could have used a good sitting down, but Ben was acting snippy and strange, and I didn't want to give him the satisfaction of being right.

"There was blood on the rope. It might have been Darby's. And the note was written on Spada's own letterhead. They weren't meant to make it out of the chop shop. There was no plate on the SUV. If Spada wasn't driving it, whoever was has reported back to him by now that his little 'fire trap' failed. What about the Williams brothers? Did they say anything?"

Marta scrubbed her face with her hands. She'd been on this thing nonstop since the Symonds place and it looked like it. "They're the dumbest tools I've ever seen. It didn't take long for them to roll over on Leon."

"Not Spada?"

"They say they never met him. It was Leon who asked them to rough you up. They had no idea what the copies were all about, they didn't ask. It was just a job, though they did have the impression that Leon was taking directions from somebody higher up the food chain."

"And Leon?"

"He asked for a lawyer the minute we cuffed him," Weber said.

"Legal aid?"

"Private."

I looked at each of them. "Anybody want to guess who's paying for that?"

Nobody did.

"Well, did you find anything else on Spada? What about an alias? Any connection to Tavroh?"

"We're working on it," Marta said.

Ben began to pace the floor, glancing over at me occasionally to give me the stink eye. I watched him out of the corner of my eye, but said nothing. I knew him. He wasn't happy about the fire, the fact that I almost died in it.

I ran my fingers through my hair. "And the woman from the Symonds place?"

"No ID on her and nothing came back on her prints."

"She could be a pro," I said.

Marta consulted the file in her hands. "Well, if so, she must be really good at it. She's a ghost. I hate ghosts. Whoever she is, though, she hates the ground you walk on. I think she anticipated a much easier time with Symonds. She'll talk, eventually. She'll want to make a deal."

Meanwhile, Spada skates. "I had that note. I *had* it."

Ben stopped pacing. "But it's gone now, isn't it? It burned up in a fire, a fire *you* were right in the middle of. And even if it hadn't burned, it'd be inadmissible, seeing as you picked your way into that shop. Taking your childhood buddy, the ex-con turned hash slinger, along with you for the ride." He resumed pacing, too agitated to stand still. "You're out of control, you know that? You're trying to get yourself killed, that's what you're doing. You've got no backup, no nothing. I ought to lock you up."

Marta and Weber stepped back, melting into the background. I stepped back, caught off guard by the heat. That's what he was worried about? Not being there to back me up? I watched as he put distance between us, livid, unable to even look at me. I realized then that I hadn't seen Ben with his partner, Paul Grimes, for a while. Grimes was green, but a fast learner. I thought they made a great team. "Where's Paul? Why is Weber always with you?"

Weber cleared his throat, stepped forward tentatively. "Grimes transferred out. We're partnered up on a temporary basis. Seeing how it goes."

"What happened to Farraday?" Even saying his name tensed me up.

"Yeah, that was a nonstarter, for obvious reasons."

I stared at them, first one, then the other. My ex-partner and Weber were now partners. I let that sink in, and then took a moment to panic about it. A lot of confidences had flowed back and forth between Ben and me in that unmarked car. Suddenly it felt like the walls were closing in. "When did all this happen?"

Ben turned to face me. "I tried telling you. If you hadn't been climbing on and off buildings like Spider-Man, I might have found a chance to try again, or you might have noticed long before now."

I stared at Weber, waiting for an explanation. He'd had plenty of time to tell me. We'd been circling each other for days. He commandeered my booth at Deek's. I waited for an explanation.

"I thought it should come from him," Weber said.

Ben paced a couple steps more, then rushed out of the room without saying anything more, banging the door back as he tore through it. I worried him. It was a little weird still for the both of us not being there when the other hit the streets. Ben had a new partner, another *new* partner. I was doing it alone. At that moment, it dawned on me that he'd had three partners since I turned in my star. He hadn't been able to stick with any of them. I squeezed my eyes shut, feeling all of two inches tall.

Neither Marta nor Weber said a word as I walked out of the room.

When I got home, I tried calling Ben, but he didn't pick up. I needed to apologize, to clean up the mess. I found Jung in my apartment with Barb. She was in the kitchen making pancakes and bacon, a Santa Claus apron over her shorts and T-shirt. She smiled when she saw me, but the smile quickly died when she really took me in.

"What happened to you? Why do I smell tires?"

Jung popped up from a stool, an anxious look on his face. Thankfully, he was not naked. "What happened? Did you get him?" He sniffed. "It's smoke. You smell like smoke."

I snagged a couple slices of bacon from a plate, turned around, and headed for the shower. "Long story. Shower first."

"I'll make you a stack," Barb said.

I gave her a thumbs-up. I was out of sorts, done in and running against odds. I'd lost my only witness, though Stella Symonds likely wouldn't have made it to Spada's trial, anyway.

And he was out there. Somewhere. What was his next move going to be? I was confident he couldn't get to Jung, at least not easily, and there was no way he'd try and kill anyone else, not with the police looking closely at him now. What other option did he have other than to run? I tried calling Ben again from my bedroom, still no picking up. What was I going to do to fix this?

I stood in the shower, water raining down, washing away the soot and dirt and smoke. How selfish of me to think I'd been the only one affected by the shooting. I'd taken a bullet, taken a life, but Ben had been there right beside me. He saw me go down and there wasn't a thing he could have done about it. Did he think what happened was his fault, his miss? We'd never really talked about it. I didn't, so he didn't. I figured we both had shoved it down, moved on. Maybe he hadn't? Hell, maybe I hadn't. Was that why he couldn't stick with a new partner? Is that why I charged ahead thinking, without him, I was the only one I could rely on? I lathered up and rinsed a half-dozen times before I could no longer smell the chop shop. What a couple of messed-up people we were, Ben and me. Fear crawled around in the bottom of my stomach, not for Spada, but for what the future held for the two of us. Dressed, I stood in the center of my bedroom until I found my equilibrium, then padded to the kitchen for pancakes.

I gave Jung his report. I minimized the fire, though the look on Barb's face told me I wasn't fooling her. I also omitted my Dumpster dive. And the mess I'd made with Ben. I barely tasted the pancakes. I needed them for fuel, nothing more. I was too worried, too antsy, to enjoy them.

"You look exhausted," Barb said. "Maybe you should rest."

"I'm good," I lied. I felt groggy and sore from the ladder climbs and I could still smell smoke on my skin. "I need to keep moving."

"Why can't I help?" Jung pleaded. "I could go with you."

Elbow on the table, I rested my head in my hand. We'd gone

around and around on this already. "No."

Jung stood. "I could walk out of here right now. You can't stop me."

Barb brandished the spatula. "*I* can."

"What are you going to do, flip me to death?"

Barb grinned. It was a sneaky, conniving grin, the Covey grin. Jung had no idea. "Do you know what I could do with a spatula?"

Jung backed up, gulped. "You're a nun, right?"

Barb's eyes narrowed. "*Am* I?"

I shoved the plate away, stood. "I have to go. Stay put. Both of you."

"For how long?" Jung whined. "This is nuts. Not only am I being forced to hide here, but you've left me with a very scary nun with a spatula."

"You're not hiding, you're waiting."

"I'm waiting for you to do what *I* should do. He was my friend, not yours."

"No calls, no contact with your friends, understood?"

"Yeah, yeah. I got it."

I turned to Barb. "He doesn't step foot out of this building. If you need help keeping him here, ask Mrs. Vincent." I glanced at Jung. "She won't need a spatula."

Barb scoffed. "And *I* won't need Mrs. Vincent."

The two were arguing when I slipped out of the apartment. That was good. At least I knew Jung was being kept occupied. I was done playing mouse to Spada's cat. Marta said I couldn't approach him, but she didn't say a thing about approaching his wife. Did she know she was sleeping with a psychopath?

in there, I was in for a world of trouble. *Stay away from Nick Spada*. That's what Marta had said, and I couldn't pretend now that I hadn't heard her or that I misunderstood the warning. *Still . . .*

So, should I go, or not go? Not going would be the smarter choice. I'd pointed the police in the right direction. They now had a case they believed in, as well as two thugs, and possibly Leon, willing to tell all they knew. They'd get Spada. There was no dishonor in stepping out and letting them take it the rest of the way. Yet, here I was, skulking under a tree next to baby swings, unable to give in and let go. I knew why: Tim, Stella Symonds, all the others. They deserved to have justice done, and I was going to make sure they got it. It was Spada who had made it personal, who'd made it a game. Whip and I nearly died in that chop shop. And Jung wouldn't be completely safe until Spada was in a cage.

A little after lunchtime, a moving van crept up the narrow street, lumbered up to the Spada house, then stopped. I straightened, focused, and watched as a woman about my age flung open the door to the brownstone and stood in the doorway to meet the movers, her rail-thin arms clasped around herself. It was Spada's wife. I recognized her from the photos in his office.

She was dressed stylishly in a pale pink top and tan capri pants, her gym-fit body revealing not an ounce of excess body fat. Her blond hair offset a perfect tan that looked like she'd spent good money on it. Unfortunately, the Botox had robbed her angular face of all expression. While she waited for the movers to climb out of the truck, she nervously clocked the time on a silver bracelet watch that sparkled in the sun. Diamonds probably, and, frankly, why wouldn't they be? She was certainly not dressed for moving day, but I had a feeling she had absolutely no intention of touching a single box. That's what the movers were for. The fact that they were moving at all was the problem. Nick Spada was folding up his tent and getting the heck out of Dodge.

Chapter 46

I took up a position across the street from Spada's brownstone on West Webster in an empty play lot under a full, leafy shade tree. I wondered if he was inside, lounging in an easy chair, sniffing brandy, contented, while his victims lay cold in their graves. He'd fronted his place with top-of-the-line fencing, and the wide red door at the top of the stairs sported a door knocker in the shape of a lion's head. I could practically smell the pretension from where I stood. Spada thought a great deal of himself, and not nearly enough of anyone else, but his confidence was wholly misplaced, given that he killed people for profit.

The house was likely worth millions, more than Stella Symonds would have ever hoped to see in her lifetime. The whole thing rubbed me raw, and I could admit to a certain amount of petty resentment on her behalf. A luxury brownstone in the right part of town, a boat tied up at the marina—how many "accidents" had paid for it all? Did his well-heeled neighbors know he was a whacked-out nut job? Doubted it. I took a deep breath. Even the air on this side of town smelled different, like wet dollar bills left to dry in the sun.

Nick Spada had Darby, an ex-con, and a hit woman. Maybe he'd hired more than one? I watched Spada's windows. If he was

Six burly guys in tan short-sleeved shirts and jeans climbed out of the truck; after a moment of introduction at the door, they disappeared inside, ready to get stuff moving out. No sign of Nick Spada. I'd have considered that a good thing a moment ago; now it worried the hell out of me. Where was he? Was he already long gone? Had I lost my chance to bring him in? To go or not was no longer a choice. I ran across the street, climbed the stairs, and sidestepped the movers, who were making trips in and out of the house, weighed down by high-end stuff.

"Everything's been packed," I heard Mrs. Spada explain, her back to the door and to me. "Except the drapes, they're not coming with us. It all has to be on the truck and on its way quickly, please."

She turned and gasped when she saw me. My reputation, apparently, had preceded me.

I stepped squarely into her living room, the furniture gone, boxes everywhere. "Mrs. Spada?"

Her head jerked in frantic disagreement. "You can't be here. Get out. Get out *now.*"

I looked around. "Where's your husband?"

Her blank face lost all its color. "You're supposed to leave us alone. You were *ordered* to leave us alone. Do you have any idea who we are?"

The movers slowed, then stopped what they were doing, to pay attention to our exchange. Mrs. Spada noticed and tried goosing them along. "Keep going. I'm not paying you to gawk." She turned back to me. "I'm calling my husband, *then* I'm calling our lawyers. You have no idea how much trouble you're in."

"Is your husband here, or not?" I could feel time running out on me, and could kick myself for the time I'd wasted standing under the tree. Nick Spada had means. If he wasn't here, he could be halfway to Bora-Bora by now, thumbing his nose at me the whole way.

She looked to the movers. "She's a stalker. *That's* a crime."

Her helpless look implored them to come to her defense. I watched them consider it, exchanging wary looks between them, coming to a nonverbal consensus. Finally they inched a bit closer to me, ready to make a play.

"Uh-uh." I slid my PI license out of my bag, holding it up for them to see. "Back it up, and stand down. This doesn't have to get any more unpleasant than it already is."

They backed away. Anne Spada was on her own. She had a curious audience, nothing more, and the boxes weren't going anywhere fast for a while.

"That's it. I'm having you arrested." She plucked a slim cell phone from her pocket, dialed, then held on the line. I figured she was calling her husband, but I had a feeling she wasn't going to get anywhere with that. Nick Spada didn't strike me as being the chivalrous sort. He was running for his life and he'd left his wife behind to fret about it, only she didn't know that yet. She still thought she mattered to him.

He didn't answer, so she left a pleading message. "Nick, she's here. What should I do? Call me, please. It's urgent." She hung up, her hands gripping the phone tightly as though it might jump out of her hands and race out the front door. Maybe a part of her knew.

"He's not answering your calls. He's left you behind. Where would he go? Who would help him?"

Her back stiffened. "You have no idea what you're talking about. He's at the office. He has meetings there all day." She dialed again, turned to face me, defiant, but appearing less sure of it as the moments ticked on. She held on the line, biting her lower lip nervously, anxious for someone to pick up.

"Your husband's a murderer. He can't get away."

Her frightened eyes fired. "How *dare* you. He's no such thing. You're crazy. Nick said so."

The movers didn't make even the pretense of working now. "Maybe there's someplace private we could talk?"

"*Absolutely not.* You shouldn't even *be* here. I . . ." She stopped when someone picked up on the other end. "Constance, this is Anne. I know Nick's in meetings, but . . ." Her eyes widened, she gulped hard. "He isn't?" As she listened, her face fell and her flat expression hinted at somberness. Defiance was gone now, too, replaced by sheer panic as the reality of her situation slowly set in. She turned her back to me, to the movers, and lowered her voice to a quavering whisper. "He hasn't been in at all? I *called* his cell. . . . He doesn't answer. I need to speak with him right away . . . Yes, try, and call me when you've reached him, will you? It's urgent." She ended the call.

"He's looking out for himself. He's left you to face the shame of what he's done."

Without a word, undaunted, she raised the phone and dialed again. She'd call the lawyers next. It was all she likely knew to do. But they were Nick's lawyers, not hers. I stood listening as the receptionist on the other end blocked her call and took her message. She was getting it. She knew what kind of man she'd married; deep down, she knew.

"This move. Whose idea was it?"

"None of your business. How dare you! You don't know me. You don't know my husband. You don't know *anything.*"

The movers lifted boxes and moved them out, silently. There'd be a story to tell their wives and girlfriends when they got home at the end of the day, but for right now, there was only lurid curiosity and a tinge of pity for the left-behind rich woman in the pink top. You could see it in their eyes.

"Where'd he say you were going?"

Tears welled in her eyes, but there was still a little fire left. She pressed her lips together, holding on to Nick Spada's last secret, as though there was a chance left for her. "Will I have to call the police for you to leave?"

I watched her, wondering what she'd do when the world found out what her husband had done, and her little bubble of wealth and privilege burst wide open and dropped her like a stone. "Would he run to the boat?"

Anne Spada brushed past me, heading toward the back of the house. I followed. We ended up in the massive kitchen. Many of the boxes were gone already, hauled out by the movers, but a few remained. She didn't seem interested in the boxes at this point, in where she or they were supposed to be going. She turned to find me there.

"This is harassment. You have no right. Go away!"

I pulled the hit woman's picture out of my bag and showed it to her. "Do you recognize her?"

She gasped. "Where'd you get that?"

"I took it while she was sitting in police custody. She tried to commit murder for your husband. Who is she?"

"You're insane."

"You know I'm not. Who is she?"

"You're bent on ruining us, aren't you?"

"Not you, him. He's the one I want to stop." I held the photo higher. "Her name?"

Anne Spada stood silently for a time, her world destroyed, her options dwindling. "She's our housekeeper. Nada. She cleans, she cooks, she picks up my dry cleaning—all of it badly. Nick hired her."

"Do you know anything about her? Where she's from?"

She shook her head, said nothing.

"Her last name? *Anything?*"

Anne Spada buried her head in her hands, pulled at her hair. "I don't know. I *don't.* I told you Nick hired her. Nick hires *every-one.* She's just a *housekeeper.* Now go away."

She took off, heading back toward the front room. I didn't have time for this. The movers double-timed it when they saw us heading back. Their morbid interest gone now, they wanted no part of this train wreck and fled for the door. Some were carrying boxes, some running empty-handed. Anne Spada paced around the room, wringing her hands. She had no one else to call. She looked to be close to emotional collapse.

"Would he run to his boat?" I asked again.

She continued to pace, and didn't answer. Which one of us did she hate and distrust more at this point, me or her husband? I waited, wanting to grab her and shake the information out of her. The movers snuck in, slid boxes out, and disappeared again. Anne glared at me, no doubt considering which side to come down on.

"He hates that boat. He won't even set foot on it." The words shot out of her mouth like nails out of a nail gun. "He won it in the divorce, not that he wanted it. He just didn't want *her* to have it. She was a horrible woman, a bitch, that's what Nick said."

"Is that why he let Vince Darby stay on it? Because he didn't care what happened to it?"

Her eyebrows shot up. "Vince? Why would he let his driver stay there?"

"Darby was his *driver*?"

"He's whatever Nick tells him to be. Why did you say 'was'?"

"He's dead. Murdered. Horribly."

She lost it. "That's a lie. You're lying."

"Where are your children?" She shot me a confused look. "I saw photos in his office of a family—you, kids."

"Another lie. The photos are fake, studio shots he got from somewhere. Men with families are thought to be more trustworthy, he said, but he *never* wanted us to have children of our own." The shock was gone now; now she was angry, hurt. "He wouldn't even consider it. We don't even have a dog." Tears trickled down her flushed cheeks. "I want you to leave. Haven't you done enough?" She turned to the movers, who were hustling like heck to get every box on the truck so they could get the hell out of there. "You too, all of you. Get the hell out of my house."

"Darby was an ex-con. Maybe your husband is, too. And I

don't think Spada's his real name." She went ghostly white, deathly pale. "If your husband is an ex-con," I added slowly, "and if he's got another name . . ."

That's as far as I got. She took off running toward the back of the house. I followed. At the end of the long, empty hall, she burst into a room filled with stacked boxes the movers hadn't yet touched. She began tearing into them, searching for Lord knew what. I stood and watched her go at it all, frenzied, half-crazed.

"'Never come in here.' That's what he said," she screeched, eyes wild. "*His* office. *His* things. I knew. Deep down, I knew he was lying to me." Paper fluttered to the floor, the boxes gutted, but Anne kept at it.

"What are you looking for? What was he lying about?" If I had to guess, I'd say everything, but I needed to hear it from her.

"The papers. Where are the papers?" She dropped to her knees, closer to the boxes.

I picked a few of the sheets up from the floor, but they didn't look like much. "*What* papers?"

She stopped, and then burst into tears—mean, angry, duped tears. "That son of a bitch! They're gone!"

"Will you get a grip on yourself? What the hell are you looking for?"

She looked up at me, her face streaked with dumped-wife tears. "Last week, I found papers on his desk that didn't make sense." She stood, wearily, as though even that was too much. She glanced around the near-empty room, maybe seeing it as it had been back when she was happy and oblivious and important. She leaned against a wall, and hung there for a time, staring at nothing.

"They were for an Edward Horvat, but Nick's photograph was attached to them. He said Horvat was a client . . . he was so damned convincing. He's always so damned convincing, but his photo, and the look on his face. I'd never seen that look before."

I looked around the floor at all the wasted paper. Was Spada's real name Edward Horvat, or was it the name of another victim?

"None of it's here now," Anne said. "He's taken it. He's taken everything."

"You've heard about Timothy Ayers's death. He had to have mentioned it. Where was your husband the night Tim died?"

She looked over at me, no expression. "If asked, I was to say that he was at home, here with me."

"But he wasn't."

"No," she said. "He wasn't."

Anne Spada looked like she was in some kind of trance. There was nothing I could do to lessen her shock. Her entire world had just come crashing down on her. I dug my phone out of my pocket, stepped out into the hall, and called Marta. The good news was I now had the hit woman's name, which might give her some leverage. I also had another name for Spada, which she needed to check out. The bad news was that whatever his name was, he had a huge head start.

Chapter 47

I raced down the stairs of the Spada home more than an hour later, and only after I'd made sure there was nothing else in the boxes that could put Spada/Horvat behind bars for good. I was glad to be free of Anne's misery. She'd finally gotten it together enough to call a friend to come over and comfort her. When the friend had walked in, she seemed surprised to see an unfamiliar black woman holding Anne's hand, trying to soothe her. Suspicion followed, and I got the distinct impression that she thought I was the help, but I left her to it. I didn't have time to run it all down for her. I had a murdering psychopath to catch.

I slid into my car, called Marta again, my brain worrying at the edges of a recollection. "Anything?" I asked when she picked up.

"Leave me alone. I'm up to my ass in lawyers." She hung up on me. I glowered at the phone, then startled when it rang in my hand. It was Barb.

"Jung's gone." She sounded hacked off. "After lunch, he went downstairs to take a nap, and when I went down later to see if he needed anything, the apartment was empty."

I plastered my forehead to the steering wheel, considered banging it, but didn't. Nick Spada, now Jung. I couldn't catch a freaking break.

"What time did you last have eyes on him?"

"About three-thirty?"

"Are you down in the apartment right now?"

"I'm standing in the middle of it, next to the air mattress."

"Look for a note. He's strange, but he's not a complete moron. He wouldn't go off without telling us where." *Except for the last time he did exactly that.* "Check everywhere."

"I've checked. No note."

"Considering this is Jung we're talking about, try looking someplace dumb."

Barb told me to hold on and I listened to the muffled sounds of her searching the empty apartment. I was going to kill Jung. I was going to skewer him and roast him over a roaring fire pit. I was going to shave him bald, slather him in honey, and deposit him in the middle of a swarm of angry bees.

"Found it. Guess where?"

"I don't care. Read it."

"It was in the kitchen, taped to a box of Pop-Tarts."

"Barb!"

"I'm reading. I'm reading. It says, 'I'm no coward. I don't need anyone to fight my battles. Killers always go back to where it all started. I'll be waiting. And thanks for the air mattress. It rocked. Where'd you buy it? Never mind, I'll find one.'" Barb started to chuckle. "I'm sorry. This isn't funny." She cleared her throat, started again. "He signed it, 'Jung Byson.'"

I started the car, squealed away from the curb. Back to where it all started. That meant the marina. "Barb, call Ben. Tell him I'm going to the marina. Jung's there." And I hoped to God he was alone.

I slid into the marina lot, but didn't see Jung anywhere. There was no one in the small lot, on the footpaths, or on the boats moored in the slips. I looked around for a shock of blond hair attached to a lanky, clueless body, but came up empty. Cap's office was dark, the blinds drawn. There was a storm coming and the sky was darkening fast, but that did little to cool things off. It was sticky and buggy and there wasn't a single breeze anywhere. The rank smell of fish and algae spread like a miasma along the water's edge. I was alone, and, apparently, the only one misguided enough to skulk around a marina in weather like this.

Was Spada here? Not if he was smart, and he'd been smart up until now. He had to know he'd have no hope of getting away by boat. CPD had a marine unit, and if by some chance he managed to get beyond their jurisdiction, there was the US Coast Guard to contend with. Unless he wasn't planning on getting away; unless he intended to end things right here in the slips . . . and take Jung with him? I headed toward the boats on high alert. Jung had promised he'd stay put and he'd broken that promise. I understood why. I'd have likely done the same. But that didn't mean we weren't going to discuss it.

Traffic on Lake Shore Drive whizzed past, oblivious to Jung's predicament . . . or mine. The constant procession of taillights and headlights was a taunting reminder that the world didn't stop, no matter what went on in it. No sign of police lights yet. I held my watch up toward the streetlamp. Just twenty minutes since I'd left Spada's house; enough time for this place to be swarming with cop cars. Hadn't Barb been able to get through to Ben?

I hung back behind a tree and watched Tim's boat. Nothing moved on deck, and all the lights were off. Was Jung hiding on board, waiting for Spada? What if he didn't come? Was Jung prepared to lie in wait indefinitely? I headed that way, but stopped when I heard scuffling behind me. I reeled to see two dark figures on a boat moored some feet away from Tim's—three slips down, to be precise. It was Spada's boat, the *Magnifique;* the one Darby was living on in order to keep tabs on Tim; the one Spada's wife said he refused to step foot on.

I pedaled backward, out of the dim glow of the lights, my eyes glued to the top deck of Spada's boat. The figures walked slowly topside, both keeping low, the figure in front moving unsteadily. They moved like men, not women, I thought. The figure in front was tall, thin, like Jung, but I couldn't be sure it was him.

Suddenly the figure in front fell and the one behind reached down and dragged him along; then someone yelled out, "Dude!"

My breath caught. It was Jung. Who else could it be? Spada had him and he was going to kill him. I marked the distance from the tree where I stood to the boat. There was no way I could make it without being seen, and the only chance I had was the element of surprise. If Spada saw me coming, he'd kill Jung on the spot. I searched the Drive for cop lights, sirens. Nothing.

Spada disappeared around the side of the boat, taking Jung with him. When I saw him again, he was alone and standing at the boat's controls, his back to me. Was he taking the boat out into open water? Finally there was the sound of sirens; I turned, hoping to see the blue flash of police lights, only there weren't any yet. The cops were coming, but they weren't nearly close enough to be much help. I turned back to the *Magnifique* just as Spada started her up, the loud rhythmic rumble of the engine as loud as rolling thunder. He'd apparently heard the sirens, too, and he was taking off. I raced for the slip, the sirens louder. Now I could see the blue pulse of police lights as at least a half-dozen squad cars streamed up the Drive from Balbo and raced over from Michigan Avenue, heading my way. But the *Magnifique* was heading out now. They weren't going to make it in time. I dug in, desperate to hit the slip before the boat tore away from the dock.

My lungs on fire, my heart in my throat, I hit the pathway, the boat almost clear of the slip. I was too late. I slammed into the marina gate. It was locked. I shook it, kicked it, then grabbed hold and clambered up and over, landing hard on the other side. The boat was going. Jung was going. I raced down the dock, watching the boat's towline drag along the surface of the water, trailing behind the escaping vessel like a tiger's tail. In Spada's haste to get away, he'd failed to retract and secure it. I shot a quick look toward the lot. It was now lit up by flashing lights. The cops were here.

I watched the towline as it slowly disappeared below the water, the boat's powerful engine churning up waves. The *Magnifique*, seconds from escape, steamed ahead toward the breakwater. There was no use yelling for the police. They wouldn't hear me. I watched dejectedly as they headed for the marina office. The wrong way. Out of time. I couldn't wait.

I raced to the end of the dock and dove in, landing squarely in the boat's wake, my hands fumbling for the end of the sinking towline. It took a few terrifying moments before I managed to grab hold of it underwater and clutch it tight, bobbing and twisting in the midst of the muddy chop, winding the thick rope around my forearms so I wouldn't lose it in the dark. The shock to my system that the cold water gave me nearly blasted my hands from the line more than once, but I held on.

Where was Spada headed? How long would I be able to hold on to the line? As I rolled in the gunky water, gulping it in, spitting it out, holding my death grip on the line, the marina and the cop lights got smaller and the jagged tops of the city's skyline melted into the night sky. The boat gunned it past the breakwater, then past the Shedd Aquarium. The skyline was now just one big blob of white light. We had to be miles out now. If I let go of the line now, I was as good as dead.

My legs and arms were going numb and I felt as if I'd already swallowed half the lake. I needed to get out of the water fast. Then, through walls of rushing waves, I caught sight of something shiny along the side of the boat. It looked like some kind of handle, or grab bar. If I could get to it, I'd have something sturdier to cling to than the line.

Just then, the boat hit a rough patch and I went under and rolled, sputtering back to the surface seconds later, not quite sure if I was upside down or right side up. Chastened, but not deterred by the cruel dunking, I pulled myself up a little higher on the line. My arms were weakening, the lights from shore now the size of dancing fairies. It took everything I had to focus on the shiny thing. I squeezed my eyes shut, opened them again, blinking through the wake. It wasn't a handle; it was the rung of a ladder. A swim ladder.

Another *ladder? What the hell?*

I'd have to let go of the line first. I couldn't grab for it without my hands. And if I missed the grab, I'd lose the line, too. I took a moment to visualize the intricate release-grab move I'd have to make. Risky didn't begin to cover it, and I'd only get one shot at it. If I missed, I'd have to drink the lake dry to come out even. I tried banking a lungful of air, but drew in a mouthful of water instead. I coughed, sputtered. When I could see straight again, I went for it, swinging myself along the side of the boat, letting go of the line. My hands, nearly frozen now from the cold, clawed through air, clutching for metal before finally smashing hard against the bottom rung. I snatched at it, got it, and held tight, wrapping my arms around so completely that it would have taken the Jaws of Life to pry me loose.

I hung there for a time, trying to catch my breath, my legs dragging along the top of the water as the boat sped along. The thought of having to do more nearly brought me to tears. My arms were spent; my legs weren't that much better. I trembled all over as fatigued muscles revolted, but I started my climb, stopping for air and rest every rung or two. Both hands were covered in bleeding blisters, my forearms in welts. Grabbing for the ladder, I'd scraped the skin from my knuckles and they were bleeding, too. My jeans, shirt, and sock clung to me like a second skin and felt as though they weighed a thousand pounds. Every rung was both triumph and suffering as the wind batted at my face. Spada wasn't fooling around. He meant to get as far away from the cops as he could get on one tank of boat gas.

At the top, I swung my legs up and over and slid spread-eagled onto the slippery deck of the *Magnifique*—all in, but lucky to be alive. I squinted up, but couldn't see the captain's chair from where I lay, but if I couldn't see it, Spada couldn't see me, either, and that was a good thing. I took a moment to breathe, rest, center. *Jung. Right.* He was probably below deck. I needed to get there.

I counted to twenty, giving myself just a little more time, and then stood, my legs trembling, my body compensating for the sway of the boat. Suddenly the boat's engine stopped and the boat went whisper quiet. Why? I bolted for cover, crouching low, and slammed chest first into a dark niche under the boat's overhang, my wet Nikes squeaking. It wasn't much cover, the niche. If Spada passed by, he'd surely find me, but I had nowhere else to go.

Had I been spotted? Is that why the boat stopped? I made a move, and my shoes squeaked again. I had to ditch them. I kicked them off, along with my socks, but I couldn't leave them here; I underhanded the shoes and socks into the lake. Good money gone to waste. I checked my gun, tucked into the holster at my back. The Glock was soaked, just as I was. I held the muzzle downward to drain the water out of it, and then waited for another chance to move.

Above me, I heard Spada leave the wheel and head toward the cabin door. I tracked the sound of his footsteps overhead all the way to the narrow stairs, listening as the cabin door opened and then shut behind him. I needed to get Jung and me off this boat alive. I didn't much care how Nick Spada left it.

Chapter 48

The sound of angry voices rose from below, Jung's and Spada's. I couldn't make out much, but I had a good idea what was going on. The knob on the door turned freely in my hand. Still, I drew my hand away and stepped back. It was narrow below deck, confined, too easy to get cornered with no way out, certainly not a place for a confrontation. I needed Spada to come out here instead, preferably without Jung.

I eyed the pilot's chair. I didn't know how to drive a yacht, but how hard could it be? There was nothing out here to run into, except fish. I zipped up the ladder and ran for the controls. I would drive the boat back to the slips and deliver Spada into the arms of the police. When the engine fired, Spada would, of course, try to stop me, but I'd deal with that when it happened.

The big silver steering wheel looked easy enough. The gauges and dials meant nothing to me, but how much did I need to understand in order to make a big loop in the water and head back? To the right of the wheel was a slot where a key would go, just like a car. Got it. But there was no key. I checked the chair. No key. No key on the massive dashboard. I hauled off and whacked the wheel, cursing it, and then scanned the water. No police boats. No helicopter. Seriously? What were they waiting for? An invitation?

The door below me burst open and I flinched, ducked, and ran for the shadows, sliding across the overhang, my body flat against the wet fiberglass. Jung appeared, and Spada right behind him, one hand gripping him by the back of his T-shirt, prodding him along roughly, the other holding an empty Scotch bottle. I rose up on hands and knees, readying myself to move. Spada stopped for a moment, reared back, and tossed the bottle into the lake, then pulled a gun from his waistband and jabbed it into Jung's back. I recognized the gun. I'd seen it in Spada's desk drawer.

Dammit. The gun raised the stakes. I eased down again; pouncing was no longer an option.

"March," Spada ordered. "Hurry up."

Jung tried pulling himself free. "Let go of me, you lousy murderer. I know you killed him . . . I know it. You . . . I . . ."

What did Jung think he was doing? He needed to comply, buy time. He needed to shut the hell up. And what was wrong with him, anyway?

"I said *march.*"

Spada steered Jung toward the front of the boat. I followed, sliding along the top of the overhang, looking for a way down that wouldn't snap my ankles. Thankfully, Jung kept his mouth shut while Spada goosed him along, the gun poking into his spine. What was Spada's endgame? What good would it do to kill Jung now? And why stop the boat here when he had to know the police were on his trail?

Jung was younger and stronger than Spada, but it didn't look like he could capitalize on either advantage. He appeared sluggish, unsteady on his feet. Had he been forced to down that bottle of Scotch? Had Spada mixed it with some of the meds from Tim's cabinet? This had to be how he and Darby dispatched Tim Ayers.

Jung fought against Spada's hold, but got nowhere with it. "Get . . . off."

The two reached the front of the boat and Spada shoved Jung hard into the railing. He looked determined to see Jung dead. "You're going in, just like your buddy Tim. It's too bad I won't make a dime off you." He wiped his brow, scanned the lake nervously. He knew his time was growing short. "But you're no Ayers. I doubt they'll send anyone to even look for you at the bottom of the lake."

I scrambled to my knees, looking for a good jumping-off point. Spada turned, his back to me, and Jung glanced up and saw me there. His eyes widened, then narrowed, focused in. He opened his mouth to speak, but I drew a finger to my lips to quiet him. He chuckled softly instead. That's when Spada yanked him to his feet and rammed him up against the railing again. "Nobody laughs at me."

"He killed Tim," Jung shouted, his back pressed to the metal, half out, but fighting to stay lucid. "Darby helped . . . he admitted it. They boarded his boat, got him drunk, drove him out, and then shoved him over . . . marina shifts . . . no, *skiffs*. That's how they got away."

I cringed, stopped breathing; he was talking to me. I watched Spada, afraid he'd catch on, look up, and find me hiding, but he didn't. Instead, he stuffed his gun into his waistband, ready to get done what he needed to get done.

"And I'm going to kill you, too, so you can take all that with you when you drown."

Jung teetered for a moment, and it looked like he might collapse, a marionette with cut strings, but he hung on the rail, fighting it. I had to give it to him. He shook his head as if to clear it. "Can't . . . undrownabubble . . . *undrownable.*"

Spada laughed. "It's too bad Darby's not here to test that." He leaned in close to Jung. "But, well, he ran into a little trouble, didn't he? Chop, chop, chop. Nobody crosses me. It's you first, and then Raines. I'm going to enjoy seeing her in pieces."

I shivered, remembering Darby in the box. Spada grabbed

Jung up again, but this time Jung grabbed back. He literally threw his entire body at the man with the gun, the two struggling as the boat swayed. I knew Jung would come out on the losing end. There was no way he wouldn't.

Not good. Not good. I bolted for the rim of the overhang, flung my legs over the side, and jumped, landing hard, jamming my knees. I took off, running the length of the boat, my bare feet, as cold as ice, slipping along the deck. Jung was fighting for his life. I had to get there. He wouldn't last long in the water. He wouldn't last at all with a bullet in his head.

I skidded to a stop a few feet from the two of them, gun drawn, watching as Spada's arm tightened around Jung's throat. His other hand had a gun in it.

He reeled, shocked to see me, his wild eyes confused by my presence. He checked the lake again, but there was nothing there, not yet. "Raines. How? When?" He pulled Jung closer to him, using him as a human shield. Jung slumped back, his eyes half-closed, no more fight left in him.

"Drop the gun. Let him go."

Spada laughed and the sound of it sent shafts of icy fear shooting down my spine. "Or?"

My hands, the blood drained from my fingers, the blisters throbbing and tender, tightened on the grip of my gun. I didn't want to consider the "or." I didn't respond, but I watched him, closely, every muscle tic, every inhale of breath.

He laughed. "Thought so. You've got nothing. *He's* got nothing. A few files? *Stolen* files, and the word of a few low-life scum? I have money. Money talks, remember that." Spada checked the water, still nothing. "He's going over, and then you're going over after him. That's how this ends." He raised the gun, waved it in Jung's direction, but I didn't have a shot. Jung still stood between Spada and me. "Or it ends like this. Your choice."

I needed to stall for time. The cops were coming. "I could be wearing a wire."

Frankly, he'd just dragged me halfway to Union Pier by his towline. If I had had a wire, it would have conked out ten miles back, but, again, stalling.

Spada looked me over, saw that I was soaked to the skin, then grinned maliciously. "Nice try." He tightened his hold around Jung's neck. "No one saw anything, not even that idiot in the boat next to Tim's. No witnesses, no proof."

Eldon Reese heard what sounded like a buoy hitting the side of Tim's boat. That had to have been Spada and Darby boarding the *Safe Passage*. That fixed the time. Reese would have it all written in his little book.

"Edward! That *is* your name, isn't it? Edward Horvat?"

The name pulled him up short, surprised him. He lowered the gun a bit and his taunting smile disappeared. The boat rocked and angry waves slapped against the sides, the smell of the lake mixing with the sweat of fear—mine. I flicked a look at Jung. Nothing.

"You were in my home."

"And I met your wife. Lovely woman. Too bad about the fake kids, though."

He appeared lost in thought for a moment. Was he trying to figure out a way to cover up my discovery? He'd have to kill me, of course, which he already planned on doing, but then he'd also have to kill his wife, and even then he couldn't be sure I or she hadn't mentioned his true identity to anyone else, in my case the police. How many more would he have to kill? He had to know he was sinking further and further into the hole he'd dug for himself.

Horvat. It came to me then, after niggling at the edges of my brain since the Spada house. I knew now why it seemed so familiar. It was "Tavroh" spelled backward. Tavroh, the company that owned the building Leon's chop shop ran out of. Spada owned the building. He owned Leon. Leon owned the goons. Funny how the brain worked, not so much when you wanted it to, but almost always when you needed it. "You're an ex-con, aren't you? You, Darby, and Leon. Did you serve time together? Is that how this whole thing got hatched?" I thought of Tim, Peter Langham, Stella, and all the others. All of them denied the chance to die in peace. That's what Tim argued with Darby about.

Spada said nothing.

"This boat's going nowhere," I said. "All I have to do is hold you till the cops come." I could hear a helicopter approaching, the roar of boat motors. *Finally.* But Spada heard it, too. He backed up along the railing, dragging Jung with him.

"Don't do it," I warned. "Don't make me."

He wet his lips, sweat beading on his brow. "Without Darby, you can't pin anything on me."

"Is that why you killed him?"

"That was your fault. You spooked him. He didn't want to go back to prison and demanded a bigger cut so he could pull up stakes. But we had a deal, just like with Tim and all the others, and I never renegotiate. . . . All they had to do was die when they were supposed to. I only held them to what they agreed to. It was business. . . . Don't look so pleased with yourself. None of this will do you any good. You two will be dead and gone before the police get here." His back was to the railing now, Jung just inches from going over. Jung slumped and Spada flicked a desperate look at him, then glared at me.

He raised his gun slowly. My fingers tightened on mine. His hand twitched some, as the gun drew closer to Jung's head. I calmed, inhaled, held my breath.

"You're a two-bit PI way out of your league," Spada said, "and I'm going to blow his . . ."

I fired. The round caught Spada right below his right shoulder, and he flew back against the railing, sending Jung tumbling out of his grip. He'd left me no choice, but, honestly, I didn't regret it all that much. The man tried to fry me and Whip alive in an oily chop shop. By rights, I should have shot him twice.

Spada's gun fell from his hand as he went down, and I quickly closed in and kicked it away, beyond his reach. Writhing around on the deck, he groaned pitifully, his eyes fastened on the night sky, a stunned expression on his face. He mumbled something, but I ignored it. I went to check on Jung, keeping my distance. Jung was out, but breathing. I could see the lights of police boats now, and the helicopter, its searchlight breaking through the clouds, the *whump, whump* of its rotors music to my soggy ears.

"Self-defense." Spada winced, pulled himself up to a sitting position, and cradled his shoulder. "You two lured me here to kill me, some twisted vendetta, you can't prove otherwise."

"You're a killer ten times over. I have your files. It won't take much to match them to all those cases of accidental deaths. The Williams brothers and Nada are all in custody and they're talking a blue streak." I didn't know for a fact that Nada was talking, in fact, last time I checked in, only the ugly siblings were unburdening themselves, but Spada didn't know that. "And then there's the fire, the assault on my person." I ticked it all off on my fingers. "The second you left the dock with Jung, that was kidnapping, so there's that. Oh, and then there's your very salty wife who, by now, will likely swear on five stacks of Gideon bibles that you were nowhere near her the night Tim died. And there's Jung, whom you just spilled your guts to. I'll have to check on the marina skiff. In short, you're up shit creek without a paddle, a canoe, or a snowball's chance in Hell."

Jung began to stir, his eyes opened. He was coming around.

"Darby killed Tim, not me." Blood seeped through Spada's fingers, but he managed a smile. "He killed them all."

"And you killed Darby. Why send his body to me?"

Spada shook his head, pressed his lips together. He wasn't going to say anything more, which was fine. The cops would get it from Nada, or one of the others. In addition to his files, I had a witness to Spada's confession and a witness to Darby's stalking of Tim Ayers. It wouldn't take Marta and the others long to connect the dots. They'd track Spada through every alias he'd ever had. They'd find his prison record. One piece of paper, one forgotten piece, and he'd be sunk.

He omitted a low, mean chuckle. "Why not?"

The horn blew on one of the approaching boats, and I watched as the first one closed in, just a minute or so out now. Even through the fog he was in, Jung heard it, too, and stumbled to his feet. He turned to scan the lake, only to suddenly lose his footing, pitch backward, and, in an instant, seamlessly, slip beneath the railing and fall overboard.

"Jung!" I ran for him, but it was too late. I turned back to Spada and found him crawling fast for the gun I'd kicked away. I fired again, missed, thanks to the rocking boat, but the round was enough to beat Spada back. He recoiled, and then curled on the deck in the fetal position, his ducked head shielded by bloody, trembling hands.

I raced for his gun, but stopped halfway there, a decision to make. Jung was drowning. I locked eyes on the gun lying on the deck, then on the lake, and on the approaching boat. *Go for the gun, or go for Jung?* That moment of hesitation, just that one moment, was enough. Spada sprang for the gun again and got it. I turned and bolted for the side of the boat.

I didn't need to check behind me to know he had the gun pointed at my back. I didn't have time to turn and fire again, only enough to haul ass. I hit the railing, grabbed it with both hands, squeezed my eyes shut, bracing for the bullet, and swung myself up and over into the water.

Spada fired and missed, but the shots kept coming, the rounds torpedoing into the water all around me. I dove deep, waiting to be hit, wondering about the police boats, and knowing Jung was out here somewhere, taking on water. One, two, three, four, five shots; Spada emptied his clip, firing wildly. When the bullets finally stopped, I surfaced slowly to see him weaving toward the controls of the *Magnifique* just as the marine unit roared in.

The water was dark; the night was dark. My exhausted arms

trembled. I couldn't see anything beyond the reach of my own fingertips. No use calling out. Jung wouldn't hear me. I dove again, feeling around below the surface, hoping I got lucky and happened upon him, popping up empty-handed, only to try again. The water suddenly lit up like daylight and I turned to see the CPD boat idling a few feet away, its engine rumbling, searchlights trained on the patch of lake I was bobbing around in.

"Out of the water," a gruff voice announced over the bullhorn. "Swim toward the boat."

The life ring tossed from the boat missed my head by inches, but I grabbed it, ducked inside it, and held on.

"There's someone else in the water!" I yelled up to the boat. "He needs help."

The searchlight moved along the surface in a wide arc, but no one jumped in to help in the search. All I could see from my vantage point were the tops of the waves.

"Out of the water," the voice repeated.

I groaned, pounded a fist on the surface, and then turned my back to the boat. I slipped out of the ring and took another sightless dive. I came up empty again, but thanks to the lights, I spotted a dark mass floating as flat as a board in the chop a few feet away. It was Jung. I swam over and grabbed him from behind, hoisting him up under his rib cage. I checked for a pulse, two blistered fingers to the side of his neck. There it was. He was still breathing. He was alive.

"Hold on. I've got you." Jung sputtered, coughed, and I slowly steered us both toward the nearest boat.

"Somebody pushed me out of bed," he croaked. "Now my feet are cold."

"That's the least of your worries." The cops had extended a long pole that I was apparently supposed to grab hold of to maneuver our way in. Fat chance. Jung was deadweight and I was running on empty. My legs, treading beneath me, felt strangely detached, numb, like they belonged to someone else.

Jung's eyes popped open. "What's that knocking?"

"That's my heart beating. Stop . . . talking . . . to me." A cop from the boat steadied the pole, pointed it in our direction.

" 'I hear you knocking,' " Jung muttered, " 'but you can't come in'. . . . That's Fats."

I kicked, my legs about to give out. "Shut it!"

I grabbed the pole and held on. The cops pulled Jung up, and then it was my turn. I'd never been so happy to be out of the water in my entire life. I watched as the cops boarded the *Magnifique* and put Spada in handcuffs. I could see him talking a mile a minute, trying to explain himself. *Self-defense, my ass.* Jung was beside me, loopy as all get-out. "We got him," I said. "And thank God he's a lousy shot."

Jung shot me a drunken grin. "Told you I could help."

I turned to face him. He looked like a drowned cat. I likely didn't look that much better, but I got Nick Spada, so I was okay with it. "Pop-Tarts?"

Jung smiled, his eyes glassy. "Strawberry frosted. The. Best."

I shook my head. "I don't know how you get by in the world, I really don't."

Chapter 49

I was seated in the backseat of an unmarked car, the back door open wide, sipping a weak hot chocolate from a thermos top. It took all I had not to stretch out across the seat and go to sleep. Holding the cup was tricky. The paramedics had applied some kind of ointment to the angry welts on my palms and forearms and then wrapped several inches of gauze around them, and I was cloaked in an itchy wool blanket that smelled like someone had died in it. There were shoes on my feet that I'd acquired from somewhere, but I was too exhausted to check them out. They'd taken Jung off to the hospital, but it looked like he'd be okay. I'd refused to go, which was why I was in the back of the police car.

"You look like you went over Niagara Falls in a busted barrel."

I looked up to find Ben standing there, Weber beside him. "I feel like I did. Where's Spada?"

Weber cocked a thumb toward the other side of the lot, where an ambulance was idling, the vehicle surrounded by squad cars and cops. "He's a fast talker, that one." My eyes followed where he pointed. I couldn't see him, but I could feel his ominous presence. "He says you shot him, tried to kill him."

"Yep." I took another sip from the thermos, and then shivered inside the dead man's blanket. "Where's Marta?"

Weber grinned. "Back at the district. Guess who talked?"

I glanced up, hopeful. "Nada?"

"Pena cracked her like an egg," Ben said. "Apparently, she's got more to answer for besides this, most of it over in Europe, where prison living isn't so good. She decided to cut a deal and take her chances here. She's got names, dates, contacts, everything. She'll go down for the nurse, but she's all right taking Spada or Horvat, or whatever the hell his name is, with her."

"Who is she, really?" I asked, my teeth chattering.

"Her real name's still up in the air. She's got a ton of aliases. We tracked her as far as Croatia, if you can believe it. She says our guy's Croatian, too. Guess they lost their accents somewhere between there and here, wherever *there* is. Looks like they're a couple of heavy hitters from the old country, real badass criminal types. Spada sets up this business angle, using the fake name, figures he's gonna need some hard-core help getting it done and he tags Nada. He hid her out as his housekeeper until he needed her. She was also sleeping with the guy right under the wife's nose."

Weber shook his head. "Real winners. After Symonds, she was gunning for you . . . and the kid. They needed to clean things up."

Ben stared at me, with meaning in the look. "Guess you got lucky and nailed them first."

He was still a little angry, I could tell. I peered up at him, thinking about how much damage I'd done. "We should talk," I said. "Really talk."

He slid his hands into his pockets, looked away. "Yeah, sure. Dry out first."

I glanced toward the ambulance. "Tim somehow figured out what they were doing. He came across that clipping and recognized Darby. I don't know how he stumbled onto the fact that there were others, like Langham, but somehow he did, and Darby got wind of it. It would have been over for him after that."

"He should have let us sort it out," Ben said.

I frowned. "He had one grainy photograph. He wouldn't have gotten far, and you know it." I stood, handed the hot chocolate to Weber. "I need paper and a pen."

The two stared at me. "What for?" Weber asked, reaching into his pocket, handing over both.

"One last thing." I scribbled clumsily, the bandages slowed my progress, but I managed it, then I headed for the ambulance. As I walked there, I could see and hear Spada still trying to bluster his way out of the jam he was in. I stood at the ambulance's back doors. His uninjured arm cuffed to the gurney, an IV going, and a cop standing by, but the arrogant look on his face was still there. He turned to face me with such a look of contempt in his eyes. I held the sheet of paper up so he could read it, and then watched as he did it. The note read simply: *Tim wins.*

Spada wanted me dead, I could tell, but he'd lost his best chance out on the water. Nada was talking, Leon and the Williams brothers wouldn't go down without fingering someone else first, and Spada had certainly lost the loyalty of the wife he'd tried to stick holding the bag. I was looking at a dead man, and both of us knew it. He'd considered it all a game, a game he'd lost in the end. Spada opened his mouth to say something, but I didn't wait for it. I turned and walked back to the car.

I looked from Ben to Weber and back. "The three of us? We're going to have to set some ground rules, or else it's gonna get stupid."

Ben grinned playfully. "Not for me. I got the best seat in the house."

Weber shot me a look. "I got this. *You* got this?"

I studied him. "Oh, I got this."

Ben grumbled. "Ground rule number one? Can *that* shit. I'm standing right here. And, seriously, what were you thinking?"

I fanned my shirt, trying to dry myself. "Just now?" I glanced over at Weber, grinned. I was sure Ben didn't want to know what was running through my mind at that moment.

Ben pulled a face, his hands fisted on his hips. "When you jumped into that lake."

"I remember thinking, 'OMG, this water is friggin' cold.'"

Ben's eyes narrowed. "I'm done talking to you. Get in. I'll drive you home."

"No, drive me to the hospital. I need to check on Jung. The rental should be okay here till morning, right? I can't afford to lose two cars on this job." I shot a dangerous look at the ambulance as it sped away. "Shoot, I forgot to ask him which one of his hired numskulls torched my car."

Ben stared at me in disbelief. "What difference does it make who torched it? *It's torched.* And you'll go to the hospital for Yoga Boy, but not for yourself?"

I tossed off the smelly blanket, held it out for him to take. "I don't need to go for myself. And I guess you're right about the car." I slid into the backseat of Ben's unmarked vehicle. "It's gone. Maybe I should trade up next time. Get something flashy, like a Benz or a Bimmer. Give my pipe something real dope to ride around in."

Ben and Weber slid into the front, Ben behind the wheel. He started up, pulled away slowly. I stretched out on the backseat, halfway toward a complete crash; for the first time, I got a good look at the shoes Ben had given me to wear.

"What the hell's on my feet?"

Ben flicked a look back at me. "Golf shoes. They were all I had in the trunk."

"Why do you keep golf shoes in the trunk of a department vehicle?"

He flicked a look at me through the rearview. "Drop it."

I made a face. The shoes were tan and blue and clunky . . . with weird tassels. *Ick.* They were too small to be his and at least a half size too big for me. "Whose?"

"Geena's. Three girlfriends back. We played a few rounds. What's the problem?"

I remembered Geena. Big boobs, not too bright. "They're butt ugly's the problem. And what was she, part Sasquatch?"

"Well, pardon me if I didn't have designer pumps in your size, Princess Grace. Watch yourself, Weber. This is your last chance to look before you leap."

"Don't need it," Weber offered simply.

There was a moment's silence.

"In case you were wondering," I said, "this is also *not* a date. A date is me in a little black dress, *not on pain meds,* and you in a nice suit jacket, maybe even a tie. A date's dinner reservations at a nice place, a quiet spot after, then we see how things go."

Weber turned in the front seat to face me, smiled. "Oh, I know what a date is."

I smiled. "We'll see."

"Seriously, I'll stop this car and put you both out. Shut up!"

I slid Weber a sly look, smiled, and then closed my eyes to sleep until we got to the hospital.